The Fabulous Emily Briggs

The Fabulous Emily Briggs

Jacqueline deMontravel

Strapless

KENSINGTON PUBLISHING CORP.
http://www.kensingtonbooks.com

STRAPLESS BOOKS are published by

Kensington Publishing Corp.
850 Third Avenue
New York, NY 10022

All Kensington titles, imprints and distributed lines are available at special quantity discounts for bulk purchases for sales promotion, premiums, fund raising, educational or institutional use.

Special book excerpts or customized printings can also be created to fit specific needs. For details, write or phone the office of the Kensington Special Sales Manager: Kensington Publishing Corp., 850 Third Avenue, New York, NY, 10022. Attn. Special Sales Department. Phone: 1-800-221-2647.

ISBN 0-7582-0628-3

First Kensington Trade Paperback Printing: February 2004
10   9   8   7   6   5   4   3   2   1

Printed in the United States of America

The Fabulous
Emily Briggs

1

An asthmatic wheezing sound pounded in my head. I was unable to breathe, as if suffocated by various slabs of flesh—an arm, a stomach. I was under attack by these globs of gummy skin. This was a sex dream, but not the good kind.

I made myself wake up.

I looked to the colored pencils and sketch pad next to my bed—in case I needed to put an inspiring reverie to paper. Nothing came to me, but I took a moment to admire my wall of drawings, framed in vanilla-colored wood.

"It was all just a bad dream," I said, mothering myself. The morning sunlight felt good, but it could have been more penetrating. The old heater rattled, coughing up misty heat. First time it had been on this season; fall had arrived. Still, I was a bit cold. Why was I so cold? I peeked under the covers. I was nude.

I don't sleep in the nude—too drafty. And what was that on the floor next to my panties? No. A pair of boxer shorts, next to my Pucci panties? Not a cool pair of boxers. Not even Gap boxers. No, this was a pair of poly/cotton blend boxers, the three-in-a-pack kind.

"Oh. My. God. Could it be?" My vision panned to a piece of footsy panty hose, which I don't wear. No, it was a cellophane-y piece of something. Oh. God. It was. It was a condom!

It wasn't a dream. I had had sex with Stewie Berkowitz.

* * *

"I haven't been with someone for ten months." I said it defensively, not thrilled with having to explain myself to Dash. "Before I accepted abstinence as part of my life, I did what I had to do to stay in practice."

"In other words, you were a total slut." Dash swiveled his drink in the air and the ice chimed against the glass.

In an attempt to collect myself, I took a large swig from my gimlet, more appropriate to a pint of Guinness at a World Cup soccer game. The sharp, sour taste had no effect on me.

I was unable to collect myself.

"You're calling a girl who hasn't had sex for ten months—despite many opportunities may I add—a slut?" My voice was a notch too loud for a public place.

This was my classic behavior: debating a point even though there was no argument to be won. Rationally, I knew Dash's attacks were in jest. He knows that I am not a slut. Dash continually questions my feeble sex life, always bringing to my attention the delusional standards I have for men and dating. He was probably even relieved that I had broken this dry spell—yet his power to taunt always got the better of me. Truthfully I was not particularly proud of the fact that I had had sex with Stewie Berkowitz. The boy just had the luck of my pathetic timing.

Dash was just getting started on me. Luckily the bartender came by to refill our drinks.

"Do you want another?" Dash asked tenderly, pointing to our empty glasses.

This bartender knew when to intercept a doomed conversation. He also had looks that could get him a job convincing girls like me that they need to add to another already owned pair of strappy sandals at Gucci. I gladly broke my two-gimlet Tuesday-night limit.

Dash started a polite conversation about the Yankees with the bartender, while I started ogling him. I loathed baseball. Such a bore. Why are those games so damn long? And the players aren't cute enough to sustain my stares.

Dash smiled knowingly, aware of my thoughts. We've exhausted and stopped discussing our views on men and sports.

One of the reasons why I adored Dash was that he could come off intelligently to his fellow sex by playing the "guy's guy" role—talking sports, scores, teams—yet he found no value in altering his life just to watch the big game. As he laughed with the bartender, I found that my gaze was now focusing on Dash. He was much better looking when acting civil.

I have always been drawn to Dashiel Hatch. He is my best friend. We both began jobs together in MTV's marketing department. Newly plucked from our New England schools, campuses that will keep the LL Bean Norwegian sweater and bloocher moccasin in perpetuity. We assumed that we had scored the best possible postgraduate job, while our friends worked at investment firms or took unpaid internships at companies that weren't nearly as cool as MTV.

We started on the same day, October 5, 1991. We dressed alike. Dash wore khakis and a Brooks Brothers purple gingham shirt, and I wore a purple plaid miniskirt with calf-hugging boots. Well, this was essentially dressing alike, when you considered the tattoos, shaved heads, and pro-anarchy T-shirts of the other assistants. MTV was where Dashiel became Dash, to give a little edge to his congenital preppy demeanor, although he wouldn't admit to that.

Dash and I were the most qualified MTV assistants, which is not saying much considering that the latest Microsoft software has made our old jobs obsolete. Occasionally writing an internal press release or assembling a focus group were the perks that kept us sated in an otherwise watch-the-clock position. The routine of making a surreptitious sprint for the elevator minutes before 7:00 P.M. would usually elicit the "what, half day?" remark from someone who needed to be getting out of the office more, having a more interesting life.

While every overly qualified administrative assistant must endure the painfully humiliating tasks of the office peon, Dash and I did not employ the "pay your dues, build the resume" career strategy. And as cool as fish tanks and graffiti-painted halls were, the MTV offices didn't motivate us. My job lasted a month, but resulted in the longest postgraduate adult relationship of my life.

Dash segued his MTV experience into a job as a production assistant at one of the local news stations. He was now one of the youngest executive producers at a network newsmagazine show. I have become an illustrator. You may have seen my name, Emily Briggs, inscribed on the latest Sin Spa campaign.

I used to work as an art director for a home decor magazine, for an editor who played politics by day and maintained her sinewy editrix image, courtesy of the David Barton Gym, by night. She looked at commissioned art with the exacting standards of an auction house appraiser, yet waited to share her opinions until the last rational moment before production. In need of a drawing of a Louis XIV chair, unbeknownst to my editor, I resorted to sketching one myself. To my relief, and surprise, it met with her approval. So I composed a portfolio—with my chair drawing and images taken from my doodle scrapbooks—and began looking for freelance work. Now a campaign I have for a city department store pays more than my annual salary at that estrogen-ridden magazine.

The bartender left the table so I stopped staring at Dash. Tonight he was wearing khakis and a pale purple gingham shirt with Tod driving moccasins. Not much had changed in ten years. He still had his sandy blond hair that doesn't seem to get blonder even after a summer at the beach, his ski-slope nose and his sliced eyes. Just think Tom Brokaw in his prime. I supposed Dash was cute. I think I even had the hots for him that first day we were introduced at MTV, but due to my being in a relationship and his search-and-destroy period with women, a romantic interlude was not about to happen. We became such quick best friends, and, well you know how it is with best friends, you just don't see them in *that* way.

I was wearing a corduroy skirt where the floral print was adorned with beads. It was a fall purchase, worn for the first time. I looked good. Clothes always look their best the first time you wear them. Not because they come with those perfectly manufactured creases (which soon lose their definition after a day in a closet the size of a gym locker), but because you purchase them with a complete outfit in mind. The magazine-ready perfection of your outfit doesn't last long, as your new purchase inevitably becomes one of many functional pieces thrown on in a preworkday frenzy.

The red and black flowers perfectly complemented my Chanel dual-tone ballet flats and my all-dependable red Birkin bag. I am not one of those girls who have a bag for every occasion. After closing my savings account to make the purchase, I rationalized that choosing the bag instead of the New School art program was justified because I would use it every day.

Now Dash was staring at me—a stare laced with judgment and smugness as he reveled watching me squirm over his knowledge of the Stewie Berkowitz incident. It was almost cruel, I thought, how well he knew me, knew how to torment me. He was finding immense pleasure in my agitated state, until I began to argue my case.

"Oh, stop positioning me as this desperate, open-my-legs-for-any-guy-with-a-presentable-face type of girl." I repositioned myself on the bar stool. "You should know better. And Stewie isn't all that bad, even if he is a little gummy bear."

"Gummy bears are cute, Emily," he said, again with that dry smugness.

I reviewed my mental picture of Stewie—his moon-shaped face, bagel rolls and dark eyes that popped out like a marsupial. Once his hair begins to thin he will resemble a corrupted hobbit in good clothes but bad boxers.

Reminded of the morning incident, which I had been trying to block out, I suddenly remembered hearing the flush of the toilet. He had used my toilet. And he hadn't put the seat back down. I remembered hearing the bathroom door close, the floorboards creaking as he approached. Each step thumping to the beat of my heart. Now I knew how a victim felt in the path of a slasher-style murderer. Oh. My. God. Stewie Berkowitz had walked into my bedroom with no pretense. He was fat. He was naked. And I couldn't help but see his penis. What had I been thinking?

Dash interrupted my post-traumatic stress. "Well, to put the therapist hat on, I have noticed a pattern with you."

"Pattern?" This should be a good one. I blinked my eyes to shake off the morning flashback.

"You grew up with Stewie. He's another one of those city kids. Correct?"

"Dash, how many times must I tell you that Westchester is *not* part of the five boroughs that comprise Manhattan? And yes, as a matter of fact, I do know Stewie from Rye."

"This isn't the first time you've reconnected with someone from your childhood. There's something safe in the familiar."

I suppressed an Emily pout. "Not to put a hole in your theory, Dr. Phil, but what I like about people from Rye is that I don't have to put up with the 'Where are you from?', 'What was your childhood like?', blah, blah, blah, crap. I can just cut to the real things. It's a great time saver, actually." I turned to my fresh gimlet and pounded it. The sweet taste made me feel pleasantly loopy.

"It also helps that he found you an office space."

Sometimes Dash's intuitive analysis is disturbing. I do things, calculated things, which I can rationalize as acceptable but not let on to others because it may be perceived as shallow.

"Right. I chose Stewie out of convenience. Since he found me a studio, I figured I might as well take him up on the date that he'd been halfheartedly proposing to me."

At the suggestion of a friend I contacted Stewie, solely for the purpose of finding a work studio. My constant impulse to inspect the refrigerator or clean the apartment is not conducive to being in business for myself. And then there was the 2:00 P.M. diversion of napping during reruns of *Northern Exposure*. I figured that the money I'd save in productivity could be spent toward an office. Even though Stewie specifically brokers corporate spaces, he still agreed to help me—finding me the most adorable town house space, above a flower shop on Irving Place. There were skylights, a fireplace and honey-dipped hardwood floors—all steps away from my apartment in Gramercy. I suppose this was a bit prostitute of me?

Dash was now staring into his drink as if he were considering diving in. He was two sips away from needing a refill and I had finished mine in what seemed hours ago. Dash motioned to the bartender by pointing to the two drinks. The bartender nodded in approval.

I continued, "Better a smart guy who makes me laugh than some loser whose career highlight was starring in a Saab commercial. And now I'm back. Back in the mindset where it's okay to flirt with the Saab commercial guy. It's all about getting out there, which you wouldn't know considering you're a boy and all."

Dash suddenly changed from banter to gravity. "So, are you going to see Stewie again?"

"He's basically useless now. Broke the spell."

"Heartless," said Dash.

"Realistic," I shot back.

"Emily, I also noticed that you have a thing for guys in banking or real estate."

"Hmmm. That's a tough one," I said, then raised my voice. "Is that really surprising, *considering that this is Manhattan?* Anyway, there've been a few lawyers in there."

"Lawyers representing banks and real estate."

"You should talk. What is it with you and chicks in television, fashion, or PR?"

"I believe that the problem of limited Manhattan professions applies to me as well. So do you think . . ." Dash paused for a moment. "Will you end up with . . ." He again hesitated.

"With what? Get to it, Dash."

"A real estate–Stewie Berkowitz type?"

"God, I hope not." I caught myself and tried again. "I guess the real issue is whether I can be big enough to not be so judgmental. Evaluate the person for who he really is and all of that seventies VW decaled bus BS. So who really knows; I suppose I have no idea."

"So if you were allowed to choose the ideal, the one, who would he be?"

Now this was an easy question as it's been the subject of many after 2:00 P.M. fantasies—between 2:00 and 3:00 P.M. is, biologically, my most inactive period of the day. Preschool children and freelancers get to take naps.

"Remember *Sixteen Candles?*"

"Emily, look who you are talking to—'girl's underwear!' " Dash said, parroting lines from the movie.

"The Michael Schoeffling character, Jake Ryan. They just don't come like that anymore. His Italian-sculpted physique, the way his hair spiked up in the front, his brooding eyes, the Levi's cuffed at the bottom, the olive shirt and coordinated Fair Isle vest. Take me now!

"I can understand Anthony Michael Hall's disappearing act, but Michael Shoeffling? I've got to see if he has a Web site or something. He is The One."

I again saw that agitated-with-Emily look on Dash's face. "Okay. Okay. Fine. I get it. Let's say Michael Schoeffling isn't an option. Now who would it be?"

"I am so tired of this who's-the-one search. I just won't know until it happens and, until then, I will indulge myself with fantasies of meeting a grown-up Jake Ryan."

Dash swiveled around his bar stool and, I believed, intentionally looked away from me. His voice grew softer as he took the last sip of his Seven and Seven as the bartender delivered our new drinks.

"You don't ever get anxious?" he asked without meeting my eye, looking to the cute bartender guy with a thank-you smile for the new drinks.

"Not really. Do you?" I smiled a thank-you flirt to the bartender. He winked back!

"Well, I didn't. Until the World Trade Center attack. Emily, who was the first person you called?"

"Considering that my mother, father and brother all called me before I was even aware of what was happening, I guess it was you."

"You were the first person I spoke to after my mom," he said in earnest.

"What are you getting at?"

"If we were in relationships we would have been trying to connect with our significant others. There is a key person missing in both our lives."

"You're not getting all traditional American-valued on me now?"

"Seriously, Em, I've been feeling a little lonely, incomplete almost. And I think it's time that we—that I—made some changes."

My fourth drink. Considering that I can get sloshed from an extra shot of Nyquil, I was in no shape to understand what it was that Dash was trying to say.

2

"Please don't make me go to that dumb benefit!" I moaned to Dash. Ever since his single status rant, Dash had been on a committed pursuit to find The One. An effort that entailed attending ridiculous black-tie events padded with the phonies—the socialites—a breed that used words like "delish" and "yummy" to describe things other than food.

It was Monday night. A sacred night devoted to Sushi Samba takeout and bad television. No phone calls. No working into the late hours. No effort allowed, except perhaps a two-step facial. Dash, apparently comfortable enough to arrive unannounced, was wearing a tux and held two $1,000 tickets for a museum dinner benefit celebrating the opening of some exhibit.

"Oh, Dash," I whined. "No way. Besides, I have nothing to wear."

Dash shot me an are-you-completely-mad gaze and strode over to my closet. "And what's the point of going to all of those Badgley and Mischka sample sales if you're not actually going to wear the little evening numbers you get such a rush from buying?"

Okay, I could see Dash's point here. Spending hundreds of dollars on dresses that are worth thousands isn't truly a bargain if I am never to wear them. But I couldn't let him win that easily.

"Can't you find another partner in your wife-hunting expedition?"

"God, no. If I ask some random girl she'll have all of these expectations: assume that I'm interested, make phone calls and write E-mails that I'll have to dodge. It will be a real setback to my life, not to mention that it would be difficult to trawl for women with someone else glued to my side."

Not the response I was looking for, and Dash could read it in my face.

"Look, I know how you women work. The guy with the most beautiful escort on his arm becomes the object of attraction to all of the other beauties. You are the ultimate chick magnet."

Okay, that response worked for me. I sorted through my closet, stumbling upon two dresses. Dash selected the silvery Calvin Klein slip dress and then went into the kitchen to make us some drinks while I quickly got ready.

In the car, we went over the terms. After a quick walk-through, if it was a truly pathetic crowd, we'd have one drink and call it a night. If it was fun, we'd hang around and go with it. But we must leave together as it is cheesy to hook up on a school night. (That last one was my rule, which I would naturally abandon if a Michael Schoeffling replica pursued me.)

The car arrived after a particularly bumpy ride. It always seems bumpy driving on city streets. I usually take private cars, but not because I am a total princess—I choose walking over cabs. I suddenly wanted to remain in the comfort of the heated Lincoln rather than face the sudden chill of early autumn. I was beginning to question my eschewing an overcoat—Dash had suggested a more flattering wrap. *It's just from the car to the entrance,* I repeated to myself; my mantra for all black-tie events during the colder seasons.

The lobby was buzzing with the usual players on the benefit circuit. The overly botoxed plastic surgeon you always see late nights on public access—how he gets clients with the cheeks of cherries I'll never know. The swarm of girls stuck in the *Preppy Handbook* phase, with names like Breezy, Misty and Stormy— they're either trying to be weather girls or auditioning for one of Snow White's dwarves. In a city where everyone is sized up by what they do for a living, these benefits attract those profession- als who never had a formal interview. The socialites with their day jobs working for the family business—essentially a customer service position with a lofty title. However, they do add glimmer to musty collections and a buzz of evening chatter to an otherwise vacant museum corridor.

I immediately targeted the bar while Dash loyally followed.

"Hey, you!" A guy who works out at my gym, whom I can always depend on seeing at every *Avenue*-advertised function, spotted me. A boring banker type who's as desperate to find a society wife as Andrew McCarthy was to snag a part after *St. Elmo's Fire.* The responsibilities of this wife, which she will be richly compensated for, will be to attend to the upkeep of their home, social activities, vacations, wardrobe and the one annual project that begins in late summer—the Christmas card list.

His intrusion was actually welcome, since I was getting bored with slugging gimlets like soda water and screaming at Dash over the loud music, rehashing the days that we'd already gone over.

Christmas-card boy asked me to dance and Dash gave me the go-ahead nod of approval.

"So is he your boyfriend?" asked Christmas-card boy as he took my hand, leading me to the only vacant space on the dance floor.

"Who?" I asked primly, knowing exactly whom he was referring to.

"That guy you're always with, who always eyes you protectively. The one who belongs in a Whit Stillman film?"

I always found it interesting how others perceived Dash.

"No, we just have sex during those lull periods."

Christmas-card boy shot me a look of terror and I soon realized that chugging gimlets can bring on heightened, druglike effects.

"Sorry, he's just an old friend."

As the effects of the alcohol were beginning to wear off, Christmas-card boy no longer held my interest. I politely excused myself but stumbled over his name. I have no idea what his name was. After the 1,800 times we'd introduced ourselves to each other, I couldn't possibly own up to the fact that I didn't remember his name. He'd think I was either completely shallow or had taken one too many hits of acid during my summer with the Grateful Dead boy. Not that I really cared what Christmas-card boy thought; I just can't have anyone thinking that I fell for the Dead thing.

"I am Emily, by the way," I reminded, hoping to prompt his returning the name exchange favor.

"Emily Briggs!" he countered, a bit overenthusiastically. "The Gramercy Park illustrator. I am a secret fan of yours."

He didn't mention his name.

Just then my cousin Anne sashayed over to us. I can't stand Anne. Can't really say that I was surprised to see her, she's always at these ridiculous things. Now I would have to play all nice and initiate some phony topic. In my entire lifetime I've had nothing more substantive to discuss with my cousin than outfits and holiday destinations.

"Hello, Emily," she hummed, with a feline stroke to my arm. Wearing a dress that's not worth what she paid, shifting from stiletto to stiletto, her contrived movements resembled Vanna White twirling another letter. Anne is one of those pretty girls who become prettier with all of the makeup, clothes and come-hither feminine gestures—which include flirting with girls even though they're *not* lesbians. I always feel awkward around such extreme displays of femininity, as I am *not* one of those girlie-girl types.

Anne looked over at Christmas-card boy and returning her stare he looked like a social climber being introduced to a gossip columnist. I was expected to introduce them. Okay, this was awkward—still had no clue what his name was. So I dropped my clutch, bargaining for some time, hoping that they would assume the responsibility in making the introductions. Returning to eye level, Anne looked to me impatiently as I rewarded her back with the Emily stare.

"Hello, I'm Anne Briggs," she said coolly, obviously annoyed.

"Oh, a cousin of Emily's!" he said with fervor. "I am Jason Whitten." Jason Whitten. I would never have remembered. Perhaps I *had* taken too many hits of acid that Grateful Dead summer.

"You have quite a tan for the month of October," continued Jason in what appeared to be a flirtatious voice.

"Yes, I was in St. Barths for the weekend. At Susan Meeker's wedding," she added, a bit inorganically. I wondered how much it cost her to be able to say that.

"You knew about Susan's wedding, Emily?" She redirected the conversation to me because (1) It showed that I hadn't been in-

vited to Susan's wedding, and (2) It would give her the upper
hand with Jason, since he was a phony and Susan was the phony
of all phonies.

"It must have been great fun," I said simply.

Anne gave me the Anne gaze, which was my anticipated cue to
exit. Thank God, at least I was able to get his name after all of
that. Jason Whitten, Jason Whitten, I began to repeat twelve
times to get it in my memory.

I looked back over my shoulder. A party photographer was
snapping them—Anne was having a productive night.

Homing in on the bar with stealthy precision, I was committed
to reaching it without interruption. My mission was to drink
heavily. But I would need to make one major diversion—Dash
was sidled with Katrina von Friedrich, another phony whom I'd
met a dozen times but knew better from her photos in magazine
party pages and mentions in "Page Six." Her father is the head of
something or other. I believe he's some German shopping mall
Leslie Wexler type, giving Katrina easy entrée into the socialite
sector. She was quite pretty, the way that Anne was, with a million-
dollar dye job, expensive maintenance and limited-edition runway pieces padding her wardrobe.

What I found distracting were Katrina's cat lips, which twirled
up like the bottom of an anchor. Guys may be into that, leading
me to not quite figure out what lascivious sexual fantasies they're
into, and I'd rather not know.

Katrina was all about being feline, skilled in those frisky ma-
neuvers and, apparently, having great success with my innocent
Dash. Could his eyes have been bulging any more? It was as if the
Park Avenue plastics guy injected his eyeballs with botox. Dash
noticed me staring at the two of them. How was I always caught
at the most inopportune moment?

"Emily, over here." He waved eagerly. I obeyed, sauntering
over to them and making extra sure that my back was catwalk sultry. Then I felt that my boobs were sticking out and suddenly felt
a bit self-conscious.

"There's someone I want you to meet," he said, waving up his
hand as I came closer.

She was wearing a red slip dress with a breadcrumb rim. Her

nails were so polished she could flag down a commuter plane during a snowstorm.

"Yes, we know one another," Katrina said in her pseudo-German accent. Please, the girl's lived in New York all her life, spare me the accessorized accent. And since when did we know one another? I'd spoken to her maybe ten times. But *knew* her? I knew Katrina as well as I *knew* my dentist. Oh, gosh, I really needed to make a dentist appointment. I was afraid to think how many years it'd been.

"Katrina works at the U.N. She speaks seven languages," waxed Dash, seemingly speaking to me even though his eyes were focused on Katrina. Suddenly my job as an illustrator seemed tremendously uncool.

"Five languages," she was quick to correct.

Oh, please.

She spoke again with her sultry pseudo-accent. "And I loved your drawings for the Heidi Ingersoll excerpt in this month's *Vogue*."

I knew what she was up to. Pretty calculated. Katrina was diverting the attention from herself to me, to gain my affection so that I would leave Dash alone with her, and to show Dash that she was not some self-absorbed socialite. Well, I wouldn't let her win this game. Did I mention that I hated her?

"What a memory you have, Katrina," said Dash with an entertainment-television-host obsequiousness.

"I haven't read the book yet. What's it about?" I was lying. It's a true story about a British heiress's experimentation as a dominatrix—very *Belle du Jour*—that has been on the UK best-seller list for over a year and has now caught on in the U.S., if you're among the trash readers, that is. This would be sure to turn Dash off, as he was too much of an intellectual for some tawdry tell-all tale. He was never the type to be aroused by lesbianism—I don't think he's even seen *Basic Instinct*.

Dash was riveted. Completely entranced as Katrina summarized the plot, going into deft detail, withholding key sexual parts to play up to her prudish frailty—it was like watching a Hitchcock heroine cast her spell on James Stewart's boyish naiveté just before she intended to ice him. This wasn't happening. Some socialite was manipulating my Dash. I was suffocating. Air was going into my lungs, but I had forgotten how to exhale. The gimlets, the crowded room—I was about to have a fainting spell, Edith Wharton–style. Dash looked over to me in concern.

"Are you okay, Emily?"

Finally, his attention diverted from Katrina.

"Fine," I said happily, beginning to breathe normally. I then gave him a stare that said it was time to leave—enact our original plan. Dash, deciding that I was not going to have some weird attack, returned his focus to Katrina. She was babbling some literary bullshit commentary, probably hoping to prove how educated and worldly she was. Now my inclination to go home was a priority, so I drove my stiletto into Dash's shoe like a cigarette stubbed into an ashtray. He looked to me as if I were the devil. I started to feel like the devil.

So I just stood there and listened to Katrina's erudite blab. Waiting. Bored. I soon stared around the room. Suddenly Christmas-card boy seemed like an appealing diversion. Dash added to Katrina's spiel, an opportunity for him to slip in a private meeting he'd had with some random Pulitzer Prize–winning guy who was on Dash's show. Was Dash trying to impress her? Please.

They were conversing but not conversing, as if the words coming out of their mouths were the lyrics of a song—it was really all about the beat. I felt like I didn't exist. Hello? Hello? *Hello!* I screamed to myself. I was standing next to them but they had no intention of including me in their discussion. I was superfluous.

They then entered into a topic—something about futures and how it affected the economy. I heard the word "Greenspan" announced. Now they looked to include me. Now! Great. Katrina planned this. Deceitful, cunning, blonde, cat-lipped. Oh!

I had no idea what to say. Why couldn't this be about fashion? Hunter green had quite a run in the early nineties.

"Yes, futures," I say hurriedly yet assured. "Buying. It might be better to wait—not in the *near* future."

What the hell did I just say?

"Right," said Dash. He looked to me like I was spitting drool from my mouth, which was sort of true.

God, I hope they're as buzzed as I am and no one knows what

anyone is really saying. Isn't that the agenda behind these tiresome events anyway?

Dash showed no signs in leaving Katrina's side. My terms for playing escort to this disastrous affair—which he had bamboozled me into, I reminded myself—were not being met. I felt awkward and impatient. I figured I had two options: (1) Scurry away and let the two of them have one another, which would probably meet with Dash and Katrina's mutual delight, or (2) Insist that Dash fulfill his end of the evening's terms and get me out of there.

I went for option one. I was a loser.

"Hey, um," I feebly broke into their conversation. They both turned to me all blushed and smiley. The smiles dissipated as they realized that I was still there and needed to be tended to.

"Late. Better be off," I mumbled.

"Okay, then, Emily," said Dash, leaning over with a kiss. "We'll catch up tomorrow."

Katrina walked in closer to Dash in her spiked Gucci's. Their height had a degree of difficulty that rivaled a skateboarder jump. As if she really needed to add the extra six inches to her endless height.

I hated that Katrina could walk in those things with the effort of cross-trainers.

"Right, then." I twirled around sadly.

"Bye, Emily," I heard Katrina hiss like a vexing vixen. She got her way on this one. I believed Katrina was the kind of girl who gets her way a lot.

Escaping the museum to catch a cab, I felt as if I were Cinderella trying to get to her carriage before it turned into a winter squash. I nearly lost my shoe before saving myself from an unseemly splatter on the museum steps. Running with stilettos was a skill I had yet to master. My cab moved away while another one slid into its position like an automated ticket, but that cab was quickly taken by an overly smiley couple before I had a chance to regain my balance. Transfixed by the departed taxi, I soon became chilled and saddened. I was standing outside in the cold, misty night—like London in the late winter—without proper attire and with no apparent means of getting myself home, away

from this tormented place. My watch said it was just past midnight. Figured. It seemed that another ten minutes had passed
and I was still stuck in this horrendous evening. The couple who
stole my cab were probably in the throes of a heated backseat
hookup by now, windows steamed and a cabbie whose attention
was not on the vacant city streets. A limo rolled to my side as if its
driver had just let go of the break. The hum of a tinted electronic window revealed a man in a dark suit.

"Do you want a ride?" he asked. The most welcomed question
I'd received all evening. I didn't nod or give any gesture of ac-
knowledgment, simply became a bundle of georgette silk spilling
into the backseat. During the ride I fell into a hazy sleep. As my
head hit the seat I awoke, stunned, briefly forgetting where I was.
Circling into Gramercy Park, it was as if I was returning home
after a late-night arrival into JFK from a long trip abroad.

"How much?" I asked when the driver stopped outside my
building.

"My treat," said the driver. I did have a fairy godmother. I
reached inside my bag for my reserve twenty and slipped it over
the plush seat. My dress was completely rumpled above my knees
and there must have been a nice view in between my legs. I
guessed the ride was free in exchange for the show I'd given
him.

Heading straight for my stairs, thinking about opening my
freezer, I was almost knocked down by a couple linked arm
through arm, wobbly and giggly. "Sorry," they said in unison.
They huddled closer together sharing *hee, hee, hees,* a secret language that I could only interpret as a dig on my pathetic appearance—a lonesome girl with a tattered hem and a face drawn out
from too many drinks. And no prize to show for her inebriated
effort.

Making it to the fridge after my long journey I found, lo and
behold, a full pint of Ben and Jerry's low-fat Chocolate Fudge
Brownie, hidden behind some frozen edamame that I had
forgotten about. Someone might have been looking over me
after all.

3

My Tuesday morning was not beginning well. The receptionist from the office of my dentist, Dr. Gustato (more like Gestapo), was lecturing me on why I hadn't scheduled a checkup in almost a year. (And it had really been two years, but I wasn't about to remind her. And wasn't it her job to schedule these things?)

I hated Tuesdays. Even for a freelancer they were a completely nothing day. I usually tried to employ my Aunt Sophie's (cousin Anne's mom) method in pegging days to certain themes. When I was eight my parents abandoned me for a trip to Europe (that I was unable to accompany them on due to my obligations as a matriculating third grader) and under Aunt Sophie's care it actually turned out to be a fun-filled fortnight.

She had a special treat for me every Monday through Thursday. Tuesday was especially noteworthy, entailing a visit to the neighborhood card shop for presents, usually the latest Hello Kitty character made into puffy stickers. Tuesday was also junk food day. This became a tradition, unbeknownst to my Aunt Sophie, which I still employed. I always indulge in some form of junk food, usually a bag of sugar-free chocolate chewies and frozen yogurt from the nut shop around the corner. Though I no longer collect puffy stickers, I do make certain that I add something to the collection *du jour*—often a treat such from the shoe floors from Bergdorf's or Barneys.

We also spent Saturdays seeing the sights through tourists' eyes. My favorite place was The Museum of the City of New York. I loved, and still love, the glass-enclosed displays of dolls that depicted typical Victorian-era New York scenes. But my favorite was the room with antique toys, notably the Stettheimer House—a dollhouse modeled after the artistic and affluent Stettheimer family that recreates a Christmas party.

I have what's called a selective-memory—probably why I'm so happy and a bit, only slightly, delusional. Anne was very much a factor in my life during this period but—how should I say this? The girl was about as annoying as those self-promoting hosts on the TV Guide Channel so I prefer not to remember the Anne parts of my childhood.

And there's very little to remember—playing with Anne an impossibility. Take Barbies for instance. Firstly, I was more the athletic type and, as much as I appreciated those little plastic stilettos that didn't quite fit on their tippy-toed feet and the retro and now very in Malibu Barbie beach house, I never quite caught on to the concept of actually playing with dolls. Dressing up these molted Pamela Andersons with unrealistic body proportions while Mother routinely mentioned she'd rather have me run around the house with scissors than play with such toy things that objectified woman.

Anne on the other hand was an excellent Barbie player. She knew what to dress them in and had a gift for creating storylines that would have interested Aaron Spelling. When it came time to reenact her scenes (always involving an evil twin—as she had many duplicate dolls—and some sort of scrupulous plot to kill the malevolent sister), she would never allow me to play with any of her Barbies, which seemed to be in the range of 1,800.

The only one she would give up was this rather sad brunette whose hair Anne chopped off (remember, this was before Olivia Newton John's "Physical" made short hair quite the trend that went perfectly with sweatbands and leg warmers). Yet you still knew the bald brunette was a girl because of that enormous rack balancing on a concave stomach.

Anne wore Tinkerbell perfume and actually knew what to do with our moms' foaming mousse. Her snacks of choice were

Scarsdale Diet fare, notably cottage cheese with cubes of pine-apple and melba toast, while I went for peanut butter with marshmallow fluff and weaned myself on Hershey's chocolate syrup straight from the bottle. It should be emphasized that we were six.

When my parents returned from Europe, it was only to collect me along with a few packable belongings before relocating to London. My father ran his family's money management firm, and part of the reason my parents didn't give me a little brother or sister was that more kids would have restricted them from living in various parts of the world. We spent three years in London and a year in Hong Kong. Returning to New York my parents decided to take a break from urban life and settled in Rye. I gather that suburban life didn't suit them, because right after I entered my freshman year at Dartmouth they moved back to the city.

The year I decided to work freelance, Mom became pregnant. My quest for independence and change was paralleled by my mother's need to nurture. I found her pregnancy a bit extreme, not to mention dangerous at her age. She said that it wasn't planned. At age seven, having a younger brother or sister would have been understandable. But in my mid-twenties? As it turned out, Oliver is one of the most special little boys, and I don't mean in a *special* way.

When people are first introduced to my family, they must automatically assume that my father traded in his first wife for the younger model. Mom hardly looks her age.

I picked up the phone and found myself dialing Mom's number.

"Mom?" I asked. There had been no greeting, just a flustered woman misdirecting a baffled housekeeper.

"Emily," she said assuredly. "I was just speaking about you, literally just hung up with your Aunt Sophie. She mentioned that you and Anne saw one another at some museum thing last night?" This was a prompt to tell her about my social life.

"Yes," I quickly said, not eager to rehash last night's catastrophe. "How would you and Oliver like to meet me at The Museum of New York this morning?"

"What an excellent idea. But Emily, small technicality: Oliver's in school."

"Can't you pull him out? Besides, it will be an educational day. And he's sharper than that inane teacher of his—please, she's just biding her time before she snatches a divorced dad."

"I don't know if I really like the sound of this. It's just too disruptive and may not be good for Oliver at this time."

"What do you mean, 'at this time'? "

"Well his choice of Halloween costume has been a bit peculiar. He wants to dress up as a Muslim terrorist."

"Mom, you can't let him be a terrorist! His teachers will freak, not to mention that this is not healthy. You should restrict his time on the Internet. Where does he get these ideas from?"

"He also was considering being a skyscraper."

"Whatever happened to cutting two peepholes in a sheet—or a cowboy or Indian?"

"I figured that I would just indulge him with the Muslim-y costume and tell people that he is one of the three wise men."

"You really have become soft in your old age. I remember wanting to be a hermaphrodite and you forbade it."

"But that's because you were going through that tomboy period and I was worried that, well, you know."

"No, *I don't know*," I snarled. "Just because I'm not as 'girlie' as my cousin Anne doesn't make me some freak."

"Yes, interesting that you mention Anne. She really does put herself together impeccably." Mom could be so callous.

"Please, Mother, not this conversation again." But she was on a roll. It's another form of voice-mail therapy, speaking to herself with no consideration of who's on the other end. The worst part is that there is no delete button.

"I don't see why you can't put on a little eye makeup or blush or something. Maybe you can ask Anne for some help?"

"So you can't pull Oliver from class?" I said, again steering away from any counterproductive topics.

"I'd rather not. Take him on Saturday."

"Very well."

"Besides, don't you have some work to do? I can never understand this freelance life of yours. I thought the purpose of this studio was to keep yourself busier."

And what was the purpose of this call, I started to wonder.

"Decided to make it a late morning. Long night," I rambled.

"Oh, right, that museum thing. Well why don't you meet Sophie, Anne and me for lunch today at Doubles?"

"Sorry, I do have an assignment to submit. The music company is expecting samples by the end of the day and the finished work needs to be completed by Thursday."

"And what is the assignment this time?" asked Mom, in what sounded like genuine interest.

"A CD for some new girlie band. Otherwise I would have been thrilled to do the lunch thing. Next time perhaps?" Just a little white lie. The idea of two helmet-headed ladies and my cousin with her fishing-line silky hair and little outfit, pushing steamed vegetables and shrimp around on their dessert plates, was the last thing that appealed to me. Besides, I was hungover and in need of real food.

"Is Oliver there?" I asked. "I could use a morning pick-me-up that doesn't involve harmful chemicals."

"No, Dorit took him to school already."

Dorit is our housekeeper, a loose term considering that she is the family nanny—raised me, now Oliver, and always my mother, who needs the nannying more than anyone.

"Oliver did seem a bit down today," Mom said.

"Pray tell."

"He's been pressuring your father to invest in an innovative little solar energy company. Eco-friendly, and keeps us from depending on the Mideast. Your father thinks that it's a bit too vanguard at this time. I don't know if I agree with him."

"Who? Dad or Oliver?"

"Your father, of course."

Right, how could Mother ever support the man who decided to marry her?

"And how old is Oliver again?"

"Eight," she said, not realizing it was an agenda question.

I said good-bye, hung up and looked at my watch. It was just after 9:00 A.M. The only real priority was to come up with a few of those CD sketches. The label was trying to market the band as the new Go-Go's, calling them Fast Forward. The music was pretty mass-produced and I can never understand this navel baring, neon look that the girls are sporting on their promotional card. What was it with today's youth? Britney Spears? Please. It's all lip gloss and sit-ups. And what was wrong with me? I was beginning to sound like Mom. Decaf! I needed decaf to properly function. I made a coffee/breakfast run to the comfort food restaurant right across Lexington Avenue.

"Hey, Joe," I said to the guy who gives me my fruit salad and large hazelnut decaf coffee every morning.

"Morning, Emily. The usual?"

"Sure. And add a bacon and egg biscuit as well." Hangover food.

Almost forgetting, I quickly inserted "with cheese." It'd been a while since I'd been this wrecked during a workweek.

"What, rough night?" he asked with a naughty smirk.

"I would say so." I reached for the aluminum carry-out container with one hand, holding my coffee in the other.

I walked back at a slower pace, in order to balance the loose sunglasses perched on top of my head and keep my breakfast from littering the street. I couldn't quite reach into my jacket pocket for my keys without knocking my glasses past my nose; they rested on my lips as I gained access to my building. I made it up the four flights without losing my breakfast or my glasses and happily traipsed into my studio, which I had left unlocked. In my hilariously small kitchen, which nestled behind the bar that divided it from my workspace, there were two cabinets filled with every fat-free product imaginable, a kitchen sink and a deluxe-size refrigerator from my dorm days at school.

I poured the fruit salad into a bowl and added Cinnamon Life, two packets of Equal and two scoops of fat-free Dannon yogurt, vanilla flavored. I then added a drop of skim milk to my coffee and placed it in the microwave, punching in fifty-five seconds. I like it hot. I like the double punching sensation. Then I added some more Equal. (I forgot whether Joe had already put some in.)

Setting my breakfast on my easel, I opened the plastic covering over the aluminum dish, where lay the bacon, egg, and cheese biscuit with a garnish of tomato and lettuce. Eating lettuce and tomato with bacon, egg, and cheese is a little like having a Diet Coke with your Double Whopper and deluxe fries. Inhaling the greasy comfort fumes, I tossed the food in the garbage. What, you thought I'd actually consume all of those unnecessary calories when I preferred the taste of my yogurt and cereal? It was all about the smell and comforting feeling. I really should have gotten a dog for all the pizzas, grilled cheeses and other greasy food that I wasted.

I stared out the window absently, trying to come up with ideas for this not-of-legal-age-to-vote band. The band members looked like the kind of girls you'd find working behind a bar at some sports-restaurant franchise. The title of the disc was *Totem* so I was trying to fine-tune an idea I'd had while crossing the street— the girls arranged in a cheerleader-type totem pole. Or perhaps I should just sketch them naked, even if that has nothing to do with the album or their music—it's sure to sell records.

The phone rang. Oh, great, a diversion.

"Hi, Emily."

It was Daphne Carlton, now Daphne Trefry, my best friend from forever ago. We've known each other before Delta Thetas would come home from class to nuke up vegetable lasagna Lean Cuisines and watch Luke and Laura on GH.

Since I don't really have any friends, interaction with Daphne was a priority that trumped work. Having few friends was a deliberate choice. There had been a period where I went out almost nightly, trying to maintain relations with newly made acquaintances over margaritas. It became too tiresome and all of those drinks were beginning to have an effect on my morning runs.

Now friends were treated the same as bed linens. I put the time into shopping for them, never settled and spared no expense. I took great care of them, and they took care of me, lasted forever, put me at ease through comfort and pain. And I only had one high-quality set.

With Daphne it was family. Easy. No petty jealousies, weird games, or second-guesses, which some girls were programmed to do. She was not a girlie-girl, yet she was highly feminine. Always thin, blonde and well groomed—a knockout without all the maintenance. But her husband spoiled her, noticed upon a wave of her hand. Her skeletal fingers weighed down with jewels from her husband that were even more impressive than her four-carat engagement starter ring.

For Daph everything went according to plan. She got her boobs the summer that string bikinis made a comeback. Was accepted to Princeton early admission. Got her first job offer after her first job interview. Married the first guy she felt "comfortable with" in her first postgraduate relationship. Though she's never gone on record, simple math shows that she even conceived during her honeymoon.

I could picture Daphne at this very moment. The cordless tucked under one ear, her hands apple-picking about the kitchen, drinking her coffee while navigating about despite the encumbrance of a pregnant bulge, attending to Emily's sippy cup and assisting her with the most difficult choice of the morning—between the Cheerios, Rice Krispies and rows of kid-friendly low-sugar cereals neatly stacked and alphabetized like books on a library shelf.

Emily is her two-year-old and my extraordinary goddaughter. Thank god she's a gorgeous little girl and not some freak of nature I'd have to pretend was adorable.

"Daphne!" I beamed into the receiver. "And how is my precious gift of faith in the future?"

"Mommy's on the phone," said Daphne, bypassing my complimentary chitchat in a muted voice. "I'm speaking with your Aunt Emily," she then said, obviously directed to Emily Jr.

"Naked!" screamed Emily in the background.

"What's that about?" I started to wonder what really was going down in the Trefry house.

"Emily is going through her nude phase. First she stripped all of her dolls and toys of any clothing, now she can't even keep a dress on. I really hope it gets colder soon so she actually needs her clothes. I just don't have the patience for this one."

"I wish I had that problem. Would save me a lot of cash and would probably be conducive to a more active sex life."

"Sometimes I envy your life. This is just too much," she moaned, then shrieked. "Emily!"

"What. What!" I said in a panic.

Just then I heard a little manipulative giggle.

"No, not you. Little Em. She gurgled her chocolate milk and spit it out on me. Apparently she thinks this is funny. I now have this chocolate-milky substance all over my new sweater. It's cashmere from the Barneys' maternity line. Does chocolate milk stain cashmere?"

"Attend to it immediately with a Shout Wipe-It," I said, gathering that Emily had figured past the intended purposes of her sippy cup.

"You're really upsetting Mommy," Daphne scolded in that sweet mommy way. Probably wiping her sweater and then mopping up the mess Emily made. "Do I have to call a time out? Don't make me call a time out."

"Emily?" she asked.

"Big one or little one?"

"You. Do you have any use for a misbehaved kid?

"And I'm over with being fat. Does being pregnant mean that there is a big silhouetted hand on my tummy that beckons 'Rub Me,' because I really am getting that impression—from everyone to the doorman to my mother-in-law this stomach has been rubbed more times than the Blarney Stone kissed. I've just about had it."

Daphne said this kind of thing, trying to establish the travails of pregnancy—motherhood—but she really was that mom we all wish we had, or still really wanted. She's great at it. And she's not the kind of mom with all those kid bags and Ziplocs filled with cut carrots and mashed Oreos. She had too much style for that, never chancing a juice box commingling with a Smythson daily planner for fear of an explosion.

I took another sip of my coffee before it got too cold.

"Large decaf hazelnut?" asked Daphne, identifying my slurp.

"Absolutely."

"How many Equals?"

"Two," I said, lying. There's the three I put in, who knows how many Joe added.

"Emily, we've gone over this. Andrew said that the stuff is the devil's doing. You should really cut back."

Andrew is Emily's husband. A doctor, pretty much a dolt but smart and good-looking enough for the gene pool. He basically provided her with a life that suited her and was quite useful for all of those essential medical questions—like which artificial sweetener caused cancer and which caused cellulose. Hmm.

"Remind me. Which one causes cellulose, which cancer?"

"Sweet 'N Low—cellulose. Equal—cancer."

"Phew. Can't have the cellulose."

"Why don't you use real sugar, just fourteen calories a serving. Or, even better, use brown sugar."

"Nope. Don't like the taste of it, not sweet enough." I'm beyond reform.

"So," she continued. "Did you end up going to the museum thing with Dash?"

"Yes," I mumbled sadly.

"Oh, this doesn't sound good. What—too many gimlets?"

"Exactly. And what was even worse was that Anne was there."

"Ouch."

I wanted to stay away from the issue of Stewie Berkowitz, even with someone as familial as Daphne, which was something I couldn't even admit to myself.

"I don't see why you make yourself go to these little events. All of those tiresome people in one place."

"I know, I know—I wish I'd stayed in."

"Oh stop it, you're beginning to sound like Lizzie Grubman."

"Oh, please spare me that! But I am feeling this pressure."

"Pressure?"

"Well, after being with Stewie Berkowitz, Dash giving us this assignment to find The One."

Even though I deliberately muddled the Stewie Berkowitz part, Daphne couldn't be one to trail, not letting me get off this one.

"Stewie Berkowitz? Wait a minute, you had more than professional dealings with Stewie Berkowitz?"

Hearing the name aloud was pretty bad, right up there with cancer and premature aging.

"I did not have proper relations with Mr. Berkowitz," I said in Bill Clinton delivery.

"Oh, Em, he's truly hideous."

"Well, he is—" I said, until Daph cut me off.

"And don't give me that 'he's cute-in-a-pug-cute kind of way' defense," she said.

But Stewie really did look like a pug.

"Agreed. I made a mistake. But what's even worse is that Dash may have ended his quest in finding The One."

"Ouch. Really, really ouch. This is horrible. Who's Dash's *femme du jour*?"

"Now this is the absolute worst part, do you remember Katrina von Friedrich?"

"I hate her," wailed Daphne.

I loved Daphne.

"Yeah, she pulled the whole working at the United Nations, speaking a dozen languages crap."

"I hate her," she repeated in that derisive tone, hanging on my every word with the precision of an interrogator.

"She's a part of that whole group of Page Sixers who always look like they'd rather be someplace else. Then go to that place! But Dash couldn't possibly be interested in something like that. He's far too critical of the scene."

"No," I assured her, despondent, "he seems pretty into her. I was like the art on the walls, not even noticed."

"It won't last. Besides, haven't we always said that we don't like Dash for you? We've had this conversation, oh, maybe eighteen hundred times? He's just too, what's the word?" She paused. "Suburban!" she exclaimed, happy with herself for remembering. "Smart, cute and all, but a bit of a crowd pleaser. He was always supposed to be your safety. And you, my dear," her voice became sprightly and I did actually start to feel like a catch, "you are too smart and stunning to depend on a safety. You need someone strong."

"Not the point." I added a histrionic sigh. Loved that I could feel sorry for myself with Daph.

"I know. I know. You don't want him but that doesn't mean he can have someone else. I hear you."

Exactly.

"Hey," I said, diverting the conversation, which was beginning to irritate me. "How would you and Emily like to meet me at The Museum of the City of New York in, say, two hours?"

"What is it with you and that place? As much as I always love to indulge your need for nostalgia, I have to go to Dr. Snyder's office."

"Dr. Snyder?" I asked in surprise. "I thought your OB/GYN was Dr. Reed."

"It was Dr. Reed but I switched to Snyder so I could give birth at Cornell; it's like comparing an Ian Schraeger hotel to a Holiday Inn. Plus they come in these adorable little cotton nighties and caps."

"What comes in with nighties and caps?"

"The baby!" she said brightly.

Oh sure. Right.

"So it's time for another ultrasound. I've started a scrapbook with all of the pictures. It's in the prettiest suede blue, matches the plush lining of the nursery."

Anne was at eight months now, expecting a boy. One girl. One boy. Remember, for Daphne things happened according to plan.

If I didn't love her so much I'd hate her because she's hardly showing. She's a ladybug, sort of round in the middle but with the tiniest of legs. And she camouflages it stylishly without having to wear those promotionally trendy Liz Lange outfits that most New York moms buy into. Showing off their pregnancy in these fitted shirts, trying to make a trend out of Buddha bellies. But, really, they have fat stomachs and should just come to terms with an unfashionable silhouette for a few months and spare us all. Emily either wears Andrew's shirts or oversized cable knit sweaters—occasionally picking up the needed elastic waist jean or staple pant at maternity Gap.

"How about we meet up later this afternoon. It's a beautiful day and we can find some outdoor café. Mojito for you, fruit slush for me. What do you say?"

"Maybe later this week. I really should finish these drawings before I forget my sense of responsibility—I do need to stay on top of my financial flow now that I have this studio to carry."

"Okay. Big kiss then and we'll catch up later. I'll need details on the Katrina/Dash affair."

After we hung up, I looked at my watch. It was already 11:00 A.M. Where did the morning go? The intention of this studio was to keep me focused and yet I still managed to find diversions. I looked around my new space and was quite pleased with myself. I had the walls painted a light, creamy, honeysuckle yellow, the lightness intensified by windows that were bigger than the front door and a marbled fireplace that I would probably never use considering the mess it would create. The only decorative items I contributed were a crystal chandelier I borrowed indefinitely from storage in the Bridgehampton house, an antique gilded mirror hung above the fireplace and my easel. I had a Todd Hase couch on order that would be placed behind a sushi-level coffee table in birch. Clutter clutters the mind, so I pared down to the necessities. I tossed all my books and also those unnecessary knickknacks girls who love to shop unnecessarily find the need to buy—like lab beakers used as bud vases.

I turned the ringer off and jotted a few sketches. They were really quite good, up to my standards. My style focused more on the color and clothes of the animated figures rather than their faces, which were just ovals of peach with two raisin-dappled eyes. I took the latest fashions and carefully illustrated the trend, accenting with a high pony or chopped-up pixie cut—beauty trends, another skill I had to keep up on, justifying my $500 a month hair allowance. I kept forgetting to ask my accountant whether it could be considered a write-off.

My first sketch was of the girls dressing one another in more haute, less trashy outfits (which I can change if the client prefers the sex-with-a-minor look). The second was the totem pole idea, which showed a little innocent cleavage. The last, my favorite, was an homage to the *Beauty and the Beat* album cover with the band members wrapped in towels, faces blotted with olive-toned mud. That my market was probably newly embarking on their college years and may not get the Go-Go's reference was a sad announcement on today's youth culture.

When I was this age I actually had to use the Dewey decimal system—the World Wide Web didn't render the school library useless. A shame, really, considering that some of my most memorable sexual conquests occurred during finals week. The library stacks were the ideal location for a number of illicit trysts. I remembered feigning study, finding a suitable diversion from my studies (fables of unrequited love; breathing patterns of weeds). Nights living off instant coffee and secondhand smoke. Quick study breaks outside the glass-encased entrance obstructed by a celebrity-alumni-donated piece of modern sculpture.

Great. 11:37 A.M. on the microwave clock. Just faxed through the work and went off to the museum; another day with my extraordinary company. Work hard, work smart. Well done, Emily.

I took off my pajama workday uniform and headed for the Upper East Side—where half a 10021-zipped lady's day is spent preparing for such an outing. I walked the entire way, almost sixty blocks. It took me less than two hours, including the mandatory stop at Barneys (there was a sale and it was a Tuesday).

4

The only energy I wanted to use when I came back to my apartment was in deciding between takeout from Sushi Samba or East and in trading my constraining outfit for a fluffy bathrobe. Seven messages on the machine—I hit play and began to strip (but, trust me, it was hardly sexy. In fact it was quite spastic and would turn off a shipwrecked porn addict).

The first message was from the record people; they wanted to go with the sketch of the girls dressing one another. They also liked the *Beauty and the Beat* idea but didn't want to deal with any potential copyright problems. And they mentioned that I should make the girls a little more "trendy." Meaning "trashy," skin-exposure heavy. So much for trying.

Daphne called to say that she was e-mailing a picture of the sonogram. She thinks he looks like her father.

Oliver called saying that he'd really like to take up drums but Mom wouldn't allow it, preferring him to choose a more "gentler, quieter" instrument.

The next four were from Dash. Dash asking why I wasn't in my studio. Dash asking where I was. Dash asking why I didn't have my cell on. (I avoid cell phones the way I avoid fried food. Only used for important things, such as chatting with friends to cope with downtime caused by traffic.) And then Dash really wanting to discuss last night.

So do I or don't I return Dash's call? I was really looking forward to my relaxing night and calling Dash would throw off that plan; but if I didn't call Dash I'd be fraught with curiosity wondering what happened between him and Katrina . . . which would also disrupt my night of relaxation.

I quickly dialed Dash's number at work.

"Emily! Where were you? I was beginning to get worried."

"Just came back from The Museum of the City of New York."

"What is it with you and that place? And what happened to your working so hard in your new office studio?

"I was there from six to eleven." (Just one of my harmless lies.)

"Not one for conventional hours. And why weren't you around before eleven?"

"You have to ask?"

"Of course. You were with Serena von blah blah."

"Katrina," he corrected. "She loves you. Couldn't stop saying how cool and pretty you are. That she's always admired you from afar."

Yeah, right. Now she was working Dash on that angle. Trying to show how nice she was, then she'd ice me once she fully reeled him in. She was good—a real professional.

"So, what happened?" I asked cagily.

"We ended up going to her place. Did you know she lives near you? On East Twenty-first."

"Right, of course," I said. Let's get to the real issue here.

"Hey, why don't we meet at Florent, I'd be psyched to see you."

"Well," I folded. "Did you sleep with her?"

"No." He then wandered off dreamily, "but it was the most surreal evening. Can you meet me at Florent?"

Somewhat relieved but still anxious, I would have preferred to get the entire story immediately, but food also sounded good.

Dash and I love diners: the *W* magazine-size menus, some of the best service in New York and a bill that's remarkably under $40. We could eat at diners every night even though we always ordered the same things. And I really wanted the story in person. I'd miss too much over the phone, not uncovering the pertinent details one gains when forced to spend hours with someone over a table of food. But I just wasn't capable of heading over to the West Side.

"Do you mind just meeting me at Sunflower instead? Recovering from a heavy travel day."

"See you there in forty-five?"

"Perfect."

I looked in the mirror. My face was a disaster but workable. The crazy ponytail I had assembled on top of my head looked like a knitting ball after a cat had attacked it. It was beyond help and I had no time to take a shower. I added some fresh red lipstick and wore my favorite broken-in jeans, along with a suede coat, red Tod loafers and my Birkin bag. I was suitable for public display.

Removing the clump of clothes laid out on my To Do chair, I grabbed my keys and wallet and inspected myself one last time in the hall mirror. I headed around the corner to first make a stop at Madame Wu's to deliver my dry cleaning.

"You look sooo pwetty today," chimed Madame Wu with a smile and excitable whirlwind of hands. She relieved me of my bundle, thoroughly evaluating each item of clothing.

"Such nice things," she said, singing my praises again. "Fwiday good?"

"Perfect. Thanks, Madame Wu," I said with a toothy grin—she always lifted my spirits. I then skipped over to Sunflower, spotting the side of Dash's head through the picture window. He was already seated at our regular spot. He must have gotten off the phone and into a taxi right after we hung up.

His face was dazed, staring out the diner window and focusing on scenes of banality—the regular New Yorkers traipsing back and forth going to wherever it is they had to go. There was the bag lady with pigtails and a tutu, the foppish dandy dressed as if he were off to an awards show—some of the more dynamic regulars. And as usual the area was infested with nannies, dog walkers and couples destined for Darien.

The maitre d' returned my smile with a flirty wink and then pointed to Dash. Once he noticed me, Dash's expression went from blah to beaming. I think my smile broadened as well. He stood up, gave me the polite peck on the cheek, and we both sank into the kind of booth that I imagined would be on Japanese high-speed trains.

We were silent. We looked around the diner aimlessly: we couldn't tackle the issue at hand until the ordering was out of the way. Our usual waiter came and asked if we needed menus. He was a small man, and had a great body with a sort of sexy mysticism. I suspected he was Greek—at any rate, he spoke little English. In all the years he'd waited on me he'd never said a complete sentence, just a few nouns subsidized by nods and blinks.

"Menus?" he asked with that delicious accent.

"No, thank you," Dash said. "We're ready to order. I'll have tuna fish on lightly toasted rye—no mayonnaise, just mustard—tomato on the side, and a big pickle. The biggest one you have," he stressed, the big pickle having curiously developed extreme importance. "And a lentil soup to start." The waiter assured Dash with his nods and blinks, and looked over to me. Tilted his head to me with a sense of accomplishment—the signal that it was my turn.

"Hi," I began. He blinked, meaning "hi" back. "I would like the Cobb salad with balsamic vinegar, steamed vegetables and a baked potato. A dish of Grey Poupon and a black-and-white milkshake." I paused, about to speak again, but Dash interrupted.

"Please don't order a cheeseburger," he whined. "After you smell it, it's going to sit there and then I'll have to eat it. I really don't want to be piggish today."

Dash could be such a girl. It irritated me that I ate more than he did. That he was as much a calorie counter as I was. The *big* pickle. His stupid tuna with mustard on rye—he was going to get the mayonnaise anyway. How the hell did they make the tuna fish?

On one of our ski weekends in Vermont, when we used to do the ski cabin share thing, we'd left the city late on a Friday night. I remember being starved and pulling over to the roadside diner where we regularly stopped for refurbishment, Dash ordering his damn tuna to go with the *big* pickle. Inspecting his food in the car, he had cautiously lifted the bread like the sheet over a body on a hospital gurney. "Oh, shit!" he shrieked. I was driving (so Dash could eat his food) and I automatically swerved into the slower lane, almost hitting a car that was too small for highways intended for ski weekend travelers. He didn't even notice that I was almost the cause of a four-car pile-up.

"What? Did I miss an exit or something?" I asked in a panic.

"No," he pouted. "Damn boonie people. They put mayonnaise on my sandwich." He then whined like a Page Sixer. "Do you mind turning around?" Since we were running really late, and we were both so tired of driving, I ended up splitting my turkey sandwich without mayonnaise.

"I wasn't going to order a cheeseburger," I protested. "French fries please," I said, smiling to the waiter.

"Emily!" pleaded Dash.

"Fine. Cancel the French fries."

Slightly annoyed, I decided to check out the other diners rather than indulge Dash's ache to rehash his evening with Katrina.

"So," he said, securing my attention from the humdrum diner scene. "This Katrina is really something special."

I took my napkin from my lap and began to fold it into a fan. Having no use for a fan, I placed it on the table and pleated it like an accordion. In, then out. In, then out. Faster—in, out, in, out. Dash slammed his hand on the accordion, squashing it.

"Would you stop it," he snapped. "I mean, it's just so distracting," he added apologetically.

The waiter came with our water glasses. Ice shaped like large Chiclets bobbed on the surface. I smiled and then quickly took a sip to avoid accepting Dash's feeble apology for squashing my napkin.

The water dribbled from the sides of my mouth, as the glass was filled too high and I was sipping too quickly. I took the crumpled napkin to wipe the sides of my mouth, and returned it to my lap.

Finally I broke down. "Did you fool around with her?"

"What? You mean did I get to third base?" He started to laugh—there was even a snort that stunned us both a bit. "Are we like—oh my god—still in junior high!

"Emily, we ended up talking for, like, hours. We have so much in common. She's a big skier, hates the whole social thing but deals anyway, really into traveling."

That didn't answer my question. He continued as if he had

been pent up all day just waiting to share these supposed fascinating pieces of information.

"She even started this scholarship that awards inner-city kids summers studying art in Italy. We know a lot of the same people. She mentioned your cousin Anne, but I don't think they get along. She's actually very similar to you."

Spare me.

"Did you know that she speaks five languages?"

"It was mentioned a few times."

"And, no, I didn't go down her pants. We just kissed. Just kissed—! It was so late I forgot I should be making the moves on her. I just wanted to stare at her, get to know her."

Please.

"I left at about 7:00 A.M. and was so energized. I ended up walking all the way back to the Upper West Side. I'm still so up!"

"So how did you leave it?" I asked cautiously.

"We have plans tomorrow night. Any ideas where I should take her? I want something romantic, but not too romantic for fear I'll be trying too hard. And a place that's trendy but not too trendy for fear that I am trying too hard."

"You love Gotham. It's your favorite restaurant, just take her there."

"No. Never," he snapped almost condescendingly. "I can't take a girl like Katrina to a place that dated. That's a fourth or fifth date kind of place."

Ohhhh-kayyyy.

"I'm sure you'll figure it out," I said with a hint of indifference.

"Anyway I just want to thank you. If you hadn't gone with me to that party I would have never met Katrina. You know when—" He hesitated, looking into the air as if the sky were releasing the season's first flakes of snow. "You know when you just *know?* I am so psyched right now. You are the best." He laughed and threw his arms up. It was a goddamn Julie Andrews movie.

"Glad I can be of help." I looked out the window at a too-cute-to-be-true family.

"What do you think of Paul Lister?" Dash asked.

"I don't know. Not that attractive but somewhat appealing in that Steven Spielberg kind of way. Why do you ask?"

"He's the best pal of Katrina's. She thought it would be fun for us to all go out." He then moved in closer to me, leaning over the table, hands grasped at the edges. In a hushed, almost secretive voice, he said, "And, you know, Katrina has lots of single male friends—very eligible."

No, he didn't just say that. Dash just didn't say that. Now that he and Katrina are all couple-y, I'm going to become their sad pathetic project where they scheme dates on the sly for me (as I would never agree to a blind date), and all with boring banker types. What was it about couples that they continually want to pair off their friends? And since their selections will be *completely* wrong for me, it was going to become a "what's wrong with Emily" pity period. This sucked.

"Please," I scoffed. "I'm not interested in meeting anyone. Where did you get the impression that I wanted to meet someone?"

"Sorry, I just assumed. Well. Em. You never seem to want to meet anyone. True? And you're so opposed to blind dates. I just think you're ready but not projecting it."

The waiter arrived, decorating our table with many plates of food. I began with the salad and then spread the Grey Poupon over my potato, topping it with some steamed vegetables and shaking the pepper—apparently spastically, by Dash's annoyed stare. I started to cut the sides of my potato, including the skin and quickly ate my dinner, thankful that I was using my mouth for eating rather than speaking.

Dash checked his damn sandwich even though the cook is trained not to screw up with mayonnaise (after one mistake that I'm certain will never be forgotten). How many times does a customer meet with the cook to explain how a sandwich is prepared?

Dash happily munched on his sandwich having no idea that I was staring at him agitatedly, thinking about this past embarrassment.

"Can I have a sip of your shake?" he asked, pointing to my glass with one hand, sandwich held adjacent to his ear in the other.

"No way. You already took a bite of your tuna fish. I don't want all of that tuna residue-y stuff on my straw."

"Just pour some in here," he suggested, lifting his empty water glass.

"Nah ah, that's about five sips. Dash, we've gone over this. Get your own!"

"Forget it. I've got to be good tonight anyway. You know, the date tomorrow."

Dash really could be such a girl.

My plate was licked clean. Dash's platter was left with half of his big pickle and the crust of his sandwich. Offering me his side dish of coleslaw, which he knew I'd refuse, he then popped an Altoid into his mouth. He presented the sardine can lid up, but I declined his offer. Minty breath will not mix well with the Low-fat Fudge Brownie Ben and Jerry's I planned on having when I returned home. He then collected the bill from under the napkin holder. I threw a twenty onto the table. He picked it up, took some money from his wallet and handed me back a ten. This was the way we always paid for things. I never saw the bill, gave him whatever seemed appropriate, and he always gave me back more money than I was probably owed.

5

I have never understood why people read magazines in reception areas. Observing strangers was far more interesting than a quick read. Random people became real life entertainment. Picking up on their nuances, such as how they found momentary comfort in antiseptic office chairs. The most action happened when someone actually got up from a chair, exchanged a few polite words with the receptionist to gauge how much longer they'd be subjected to their resting station, and returned to their seat to find a way to occupy their time effectively.

Such situations demonstrated the true character of people. Were they antsy or productive? What clothes did they wear? Did they smile obsequiously when called for? I tended to fictionalize the missing elements.

I was particularly preoccupied with the hot bad boy, naturally gaining more stares over the pruned senior citizen in the latest St. John suit that might as well have been recycled from the mid-eighties. I kept returning back to that bad boy. He looked vaguely familiar. Or was it just that he looked like one of those babes in the Banana Republic ads—I wasn't one for their clothes but was definitely into their boys. He was unkempt but together; he would look perfect unshaven and in a tux. What did he do for a living? Model, fashion photographer, something with the Internet? Imagining what he'd be like to kiss, I was transported away from the reception area and into my bedroom. What if he was actually staring at me? Speculating about me the way I was him!

I purposely avoided looking at Banana Republic bad boy too much, so as not to be too obvious. My head then twirled about the room—another glance at St. John lady, at some young girl who should really eat something and at an older man who could use a pair of nose-hair clippers. Enough time went by to take a glance at Banana Republic bad boy. He didn't look too Euro. Yes, definitely Michael Schoeffling pretty without that touch of Guido. He was wearing a tan corduroy jacket with a black sweater and jeans—dark hair and mysterious eyes, absolutely stunning. But why didn't he show any indication that he noticed me? What was his problem? He wasn't even reading a damn magazine, he was staring at the floor in, I assumed, feigned deep thought. Surely I was more interesting to look at than the damn sisal-covered floor. Forget him. He was probably barely getting by. Didn't even know the difference between Patagonia the country and Patagonia the fleece jacket. What a loser.

"Ms. Briggs," called the receptionist, interrupting my mental diatribe. "Ms. Pierce can see you now."

"Thank you," I said in a velvety, 1-900 voice. Getting up from my seat I took extra note of my posture and tucked my clutch underneath my arm like a fifties film siren. Slowly turning to bad boy so he could have one last chance to make contact. If we held each other's gaze it was meant to be. Bad boy was still analyzing the rug. That damn rug. What? Was he trying to establish its thread count? What could possibly be so interesting in that rug?

In the uneventful reception area, I should be his focus, with my departure changing the dynamic of the sleepy room. But he remained transfixed with the damn sisal. Loser.

Joanna Pierce, built like a fire hydrant, and with the peppiness of a lacrosse couch, was as sprightly as ever, compensating her horsiness with long, perfectly groomed hair and hundreds of dollars worth of makeup drawn onto her peachy skin. Hailing from the South, though her accent adapted to the tune of a New Yorker, her claim to fame was being related to General Lee. Come to think of it, it seemed that every girl I've met from the

South was related to Robert E. Lee. He must have had a lot of offspring.

Joanna was my agent. She ran Pierce and Wilkinson with her partner, Casey Wilkinson. Her office had all the trappings of a high-powered professional. The uber-orchid, the thirty-second-floor view of midtown and black and white artsy photographs displayed in the chunky black frames you buy at one of those art galleries that make their money from corporate accounts.

"Emily!" she greeted me as she stood up from her chair, probably to showcase her Comme des Garcons pantsuit.

I took the seat opposite her desk while she slipped back into her chair and tilted her head on her hand like one of those cheesy portraits you have done at a Midwestern mall.

"Look at you, always so fit and radiant," she blurted in mock jealousy.

"Do you mind mentioning that to the babe waiting in reception?" I said, half seriously. Joanna looked at me somewhat confused and I just shrugged, not wanting to reveal my bizarre people-watching habit of picking guys up telepathically.

"So you've been going through a slow period and want some more assignments," she recounted worriedly, parroting my reason for scheduling the meeting.

"It's not that I've been slow, per se." This was a delicate one as I was about to say that she could hustle more on my behalf. "I just need to keep busy, especially now. More work and I become less neurotic. You know, I won't obsess on things that I would normally obsess over—going to the gym more, the holidays, boys."

"Are you still single?" she said, leaning over conspiratorially as if I suffered from some un-hyped illness.

"Why, yes." Could my pathetic single status have been that transparent?

"I really think you should take me seriously on this one, let me set you up with Henry Philips—he's totally divine. I don't understand why you never take me up on this. That's how I met Edward."

Oh yes, I recounted to myself—the illustrious Edward. Once Joanna turned forty, she feared being perceived as neutral (the soft term of describing a closet lesbian) or, worse, as another power woman lost to a career—until Edward came to her rescue. A goddamn modern day Prince Charming.

"I don't do the blind date thing, Joanna, but thanks for the offer."

"But he's sooo perfect for you," she purred. "So handsome. You guys would look great together. He is turbo talented and has that British sense of humor that you have. I really think you should meet him."

"Isn't there some kind of illustrator's event he can be at, which I can conveniently show up to?"

"Emily," she scoffed. "Every time I invite you to one of these once-every-year type of events you're a no-show. Not only is this bad for your career, it's bad for your love life. I'm giving Henry your number and I don't want to hear it."

"Fine. You win. And then after this forced tryst we can end this matchmaking game of yours. Okay?"

"Agreed. Expect a call this week and then let me know how it goes."

We gave the perfunctory air kiss and I left her office in a somewhat dour mood. Is Joanna being sincere or did she just want to avoid finding a reason to search for more work on my behalf? Whatever the reason, now I have another dreaded night to look forward to.

Henry Philips is a political cartoonist, also represented by Pierce and Wilkinson, so I've been following his work for some time. He is the creator of *Duncan-tics,* a syndicated cartoon that features Duncan, a reluctant congressman who abhors political life but finds that he becomes increasingly powerful despite his desire to leave politics. While he's genuine—and is commonly depicted rumbling beneath his breath about the louts he must contend with—everyone adores him even though he's not even trying to impress them. If anything, he continually explores ways that he can repel his constituents, but they just love him even more.

Joanna had been pitching Henry to me for ages—his brilliance, wit and self-deprecating charm. Never, never one for blind dates (I feel that they are too desperate, too contrived), I ordinarily would never have agreed to this. However, to be somewhat truthful, ever since Henry Philips had been mentioned to me my intrigue had been piqued. I had followed his syndicated cartoon and was impressed, finding myself falling for the cartoon hero as if it were his alter ego.

Henry Philips called just two days after Joanna's proposed setup.

"Is Emily there?" he asked politely.

"This is she," I answered with the proper etiquette I had been taught.

"Hi, I'm Henry Philips. Joanna Pierce may have mentioned me?"

"Sure. Hi there," I answered, reaching for a sketch pad and marker. Drawing during awkward conversations calms me. Otherwise I'd be spritzing my overly spritzed windows with Windex.

"Well, I wanted to know if you'd like to go out for dinner. I'd say drinks but I'm really not one for the drink thing. There's the bar and being around all of those 'let's meet up for drinks' people."

"I hear you," I said, creating a pineapple and now etching over its outline.

"Most people prefer drinks because then they're not committed to an entire evening together. But I love to eat out. If the company is bad—"

I cut him off with a laugh. "Are you insinuating that I'd be bad company?"

"No!" he protested. "I mean, I don't think so. Well, it's just that I really love to dine out. I don't cook. Dinner is good. Especially considering my friends always seem to be raving about some restaurant and I have no reviews of my own to contribute." He paused, probably to catch his breath. I wondered why he hasn't employed the drawing-as-a-soother method.

"Have you been to Porter's?" he asked in a more controlled tone.

"Actually, yes," I paused, then quickly added so not to disappoint, "but it was for a birthday party. There were so many of us and I only had a bite of my friend's appetizer. I thought it impolite to order too much because the birthday was my friend's fiancé's treat and I didn't want to be cheesy. I remember the appetizer being quite good."

"Oh!" he chirped, evidently pleased by my response. "So you wouldn't mind going there?"

"No, actually I'd be thrilled."

Henry Philips was adorable. In our brief conversation, I liked him.

"How's next Tuesday? I can pick you up."

"Where do you live?" I asked.

"On West Twelfth."

"Then I should meet you there. I live in Gramercy."

"Easy enough. I'll see you on Tuesday at eight. Porter's."

"See you then." I hung up.

Then I began to analyze, hoping that I didn't seem too pushy or strong-willed by nixing his suggestion to pick me up. If only he realized that I said this so he wouldn't be inconvenienced. *If only I had said that.* Maybe I should get his E-mail address from Joanna so I could explain what I meant by that comment? But then he'd think it weird that I was making such a big deal over one simple suggestion. *Emily, enough.*

6

I will spare you the details of my getting ready for the big date. Honestly, I am usually good about these things. During my morning runs I catalogue the contents of my closet and then choose the outfit along with two backups—always have a backup plan. If I need to buy something new I usually do that a few days before so I can give the outfit a test wear to make sure it's suitable. But tonight my outfit didn't look at all together. And the backups—the first, a gray shift dress with a tiny embroidered cashmere cardigan and the other, a red embroidered Tuleh dress—were too dressy. It would appear that I was trying too hard. Anything fur and leather was out of the question, since I had to find out Henry's position on animal rights before I went for any sure things. Calling Dash or Mom for their advice was also out of the question because my date with Henry would only be revealed on a need-to-know basis.

I ended up wearing my dependable black cigarette pants with Jimmy Choo burgundy stilettos and a fitted sweater with a red leather jacket—kind of boring but safe—and Daphne assured me that this was one of my sexier yet conservative outfits.

I was also running late. I never like to give myself too much time because then I end up sitting around, getting myself worked up and finding excuses to back out. Since I lost time reconstructing a new outfit, there was no way I could fit in a blowout, so my hair was an absolute disaster. I resorted to a low-slung ponytail. Boys hate hair pulled back even though we find it all so

Carolyn Bessette Kennedy. I then had to take a cab, and that made me feel even more sick. Luckily I still felt pretty. There must have been someone looking out for me since it was a thin day (only eating pears and tuna rolls for the past three days most certainly helped) and I had some natural color to my cheeks.

But nothing, *nothing* could have prepared me for what I saw when I entered the restaurant. There he was. Henry Philips smoking a cigarette. Henry Philips the Banana Republic bad boy from the reception area!

He instantly spotted me and returned my gaze with a smile that made Harrison Ford look like a once working actor who now sells tooth-whitening cream in a rumpled tie on infomercials. Henry looked around the room, stubbed his cigarette out on the bar and threw it in a half-finished beer, asked the bartender for a fresh Heineken and threw a twenty on the counter.

"Emily?" He asked carefully.

"Yes, hello." I beamed.

"Why, you're the girl from the reception area I saw the other week!"

And all that time I thought he hadn't noticed me.

"I knew I saw you before!" I responded excitedly. If he only knew. "What a relief, now the date is only semi-blind."

"We'll just say twenty/ten," he said. "Let's sit down. I believe our table is ready."

Henry gently put his hand to my back while I followed the hostess. Suddenly I began to question my ability to walk, and was thrilled to find that our table wasn't a trek across the restaurant. The not-so-pretty but well-dressed hostess pulled out a chair for me, while Henry seated himself.

"Ah, the man who will get us our drinks!" exclaimed Henry at the immediate presence of our waiter. He looked more like a broker than a waiter, with rusty tousled hair, a boyish grin and a one-too-many-late-night-pizzas gut.

"Are we allowed to smoke in here?" Henry reached for the pack of cigarettes in his shirt pocket.

"Uh, no," the waiter replied nervously.

"Just figured I'd try. Sorry, Emily, bad habit. Would see a hypnotist but not till after this big assignment I have to complete."

"Sounds interesting," I fished, not altogether pleased by the smoking. But looking at him, I could easily let it slide.

"Can I get you some drinks?" asked the waiter, clearly directed to me.

"How about two shots of tequila, a gimlet and a glass of water, please."

"Well, all right!" The waiter perked up.

"Great idea, Emily. Let's get absolutely smashed. I'll have the same," Henry said, which seemed to confuse pizza gut.

"So that's four shots of tequila, two gimlets and two glasses of water."

I did intend the shot order to be split, but what the hell.

"Indeed. You have it right. And I'd also like to see the wine list please."

"Okay," he said, still confused.

"So, Emily," started Henry, turning toward me with his hands clasped and a big smirk like the psychopathic villain from a Bruce Willis flick. "How do you like being represented by Pierce and Wilkinson? I believe Joanna is your agent?"

"Dicey subject," I began.

"Why? Because Joanna's gaze seems to be more directed at her image on the wall mirror across from her desk than at the person sitting in front of it?"

"Well, there most certainly is that, which I can let slide. This is the superficial business blah that you have to contend with. But I'm really more disappointed by her effect on my career. It's just so . . ." I hesitated. "So commercial."

"Commercial? The twenty-first century?"

I know, I know, I said without saying it.

Henry smiled. He knew too.

"She has gotten me the big accounts, but the work that I most enjoy are the jobs that I get on my own."

"And let me guess, those jobs don't nearly pay as well as those big accounts?"

"Well, yes, I suppose. But it's really more than Joanna's seeing me as revenue. I don't get the feeling that she's considering the long term—finding me an assignment that isn't merely appreciated today, forgotten tomorrow. I want to create something and

grow with it." I was realizing how therapeutic it was to communicate these thoughts for once.

"Have you told her this?"

"Er, no, I suppose not."

"That could be a good start. *Duncan-tics* wasn't my idea—embarrassed to confess—it was Casey's. I was in her face constantly
about how I deserved more than an occasional *New Yorker* cartoon. Was on her like the perfume spritzer at Saks. It was either
keep me sated or lose her mind."

"Interesting tactic."

"Whatever works. And I know you realize that opportunity
doesn't just fall in your lap. Before I had an agent, eighty per-
cent of my time was searching for business. I'm ashamed to ask,
but do you . . ." He paused.

What? Did I get private parts of my body shaved, have three-
ways, watch *The Bachelor*?

"Have you read *Duncan-tics*?"

Phew.

"Actually, I have. Just to keep up on some of Pierce and
Wilkinson's better deals."

Henry retreated into a hovel above his glass, consumed by the
bottom as if he were an alcoholic about to dive off the wagon.

"No, no. No!" I protested. "I love the column." He bubbled
up. "It's just that, a bit ashamed to admit it but you're looking at
the only New Yorker who doesn't buy any of the tabloids. I hate
myself for being behind on the *Times* and reading the gossips is
like drinking Starbucks, filling myself up with crap because
everyone says it's great."

"I couldn't agree with you more. But you can't beat syndication. Pays the bills and I can work in my pajamas."

"Me too! I won't ever work at a job unless the dress code calls
for men's PJ bottoms and Ugg slippers."

Music blasted from above—the new Beck song electrified the
atmosphere.

"Oh, excellent, drinks!" The waiter served us our alcohol and
asked if we were ready to order.

"Food? Why not," said Henry. "Emily, what would you like?"

"The antipasto to start, and I can't seem to decide on a main
course."

"The sole special is spectacular," suggested the waiter.

"Try saying that three times—'a sole special that's spectacular.' Well, forget about Emily here, I could really use one of those. And since it's a special, get me two—that may come in handy for the next life."

"I'm sorry?" said the waiter, apparently returning to his confused state.

"Just make it two soles," I directed.

"So that's one order of antipasto and two soles?"

"Wait a minute there, fella," said Henry. "I should have a starter. Can't be completely empty before coming into that 'spectacular sole.' I'll have the oysters," he said with a wink to me. "A little aphrodisiac with a spectacular sole, and a debauch bacchanalia aside, we're in for quite an evening!"

The waiter scurried away. Henry lifted his tequila, signaling me to do the same.

"To going after what you want," Henry said, waving the shot glass like a flag at a Fourth of July parade. I closed my eyes and drank it down.

"Round two?" I suggested.

"Why not," agreed Henry.

I lifted my glass, securing Henry's gaze. "To unexpected surprises,"

I toasted.

"Hear, hear," applauded Henry. He happily downed his shot and then reached for his drink. I was then given a moment where I could really take a look at him, realizing that this spectacular vision was not an apparition. His dark hair, fine features and the personality—he had the confidence of a candidate whose opponent had been caught with the office intern.

"So, Emily," he asked, tearing me away from my inappropriate stare. "How is it that a girl as charming and talented as you manages to stay single?"

"Once you get to know me you'll find that I am a complete high-maintenance controlling psycho bitch."

"Really!" laughed Henry, evidently pleased.

"Well, I am a bit independent," I said truthfully. "And fussy."

"Fussy? Pray tell."

"I only like men who ski, who would be happy eating sushi every night, who think that a day in nature does not mean Central Park, who can watch a movie with subtitles, and who are passionate about what they do. But, really, it's hard to find such qualities in Manhattan men. They're a little too slick for me."

The waiter rescued me, returning with the wine list and swiftly making his exit. Henry called him back softly while reviewing the list. My head began to cloud over with drink, a reminder that I had the unfair advantage of being a complete and utter lightweight.

"We'll have the Screaming Eagle Merlot," directed Henry.

"Excellent choice. Would you like to wait till your food arrives?"

"No, now is fine."

Moments later our waiter deftly opened the bottle, looking thrilled. Probably happy that his two-hour orientation in learning how to uncork a bottle compensated for his order-taking skills.

"Very good," Henry said after taking the requisite sip. The waiter slipped away, redeemed.

"I love wine. Drink it like water. Cheers." He lifted his glass again, instructing me to put more alcohol into my foodless body.

Our appetizers arrived and I found myself eating, because that is what one does when one's food arrives. I had caught such a quick buzz that my taste buds did not seem to be working.

"Delicious," mumbled Henry. "You must have an oyster." His fork was already in the air, ready for me to bite. I successfully snatched it with my tongue, soft-porn style.

After our appetizers and our soles, Henry asked if I was a dessert girl.

"Unless it comes in a Styrofoam container and has tons of chemicals, I am pretty much dessert-free."

"Great, I don't have much of a sweet tooth, either. Too fleeting, not substantive." Henry asked for the check.

"How about you," I quipped. "Any interesting relationships recently?"

"No," he said flatly. The most impassive response he had delivered all evening.

"Okay, I won't go there." I snickered.

"It's just that I've had some bad luck recently. I actually came to New York from San Francisco a few years ago, figuring that it was the place to be, the right place for a fresh start."

"Well, that's the truth."

"And I haven't had much luck with this sex and the city thing. I knew I should get out there a little more before my friends, family and colleagues labeled me as gay. Now I'm wondering why all of the fuss. You certainly make it easier than I had expected."

I smiled to myself. Words like this would have left skid marks back in my must make the five-point-list on potential boyfriend requirements but, from a guy that's better than the billboard, I was trembling.

The bill arrived and Henry attended to it effortlessly, paying cash so we didn't have to wait.

"Shall we go?" He got up from his chair.

"Sure," I answered. Though internally I was saying, *Just take me now. Surely we wouldn't be too obvious if we did it in the bathroom stall.*

Henry waited till I got up and, as before, he gently put his hand to my back. I received my coat from the check girl and Henry slid her a few dollars. Outside there was a cold misty drizzle, but it was seasonally warm for a November night.

"I'm not one for cabs, do you mind walking a bit?" he asked.

"I love walking!" Oops, may have been a bit overly anxious there as I saw pellets of my spit mingle with the drizzle. But Henry, a true gentleman, didn't even bother to wipe my saliva from his face—which may have been because the rain took care of that. Or, perhaps he imagined my saliva licking up his face later!

"But I have no umbrella. There should be a Korean deli around here somewhere."

"Don't bother, it's refreshing." Anything to sober me up. I was beginning to have concerns that my inebriated state would lead to some decisions that may not be conducive to a relationship. On my list (list of boys I've slept with) all the random entries have earned their mark due to near blackout evenings. After the particularly promiscuous summer of '96 I'd vowed to never again have sex under the influence on a first date. But here was Henry. If da Vinci were around, Henry would be his inspiration. He was so irresistible with that dark hair, blue eyes and perma-smile—a

WB actor ten years from now. Certainly I could amend some silly rule.

Henry took my hand without speaking and led me east. After a few blocks he turned to me, as it was apparent that the next stages of our plan needed to be assessed.

"I'd take you to a bar but I don't know about what kind of tolerance you have. I don't think I need another drink."

"Yes, I'm not one for late evenings at a bar. I find myself saying things and then having to repeat them to myself to make sense of what I just said," I said. Did that make sense?

Henry reached into his pocket and pulled out a crumpled pack of Marlboro reds.

"I hope you don't mind if I smoke?" he asked, cigarette in mouth being lit.

I did mind. I started to feel sick. The thought of nicotine in the air, mixed with everything that was circulating in my body— the evening could end with more than we expected.

Henry deeply inhaled his cigarette and exhaled away from us. I began talking about my parents, Oliver, Dash—I was like a television on in the background, jumbled words that added to the effect but didn't offer any insight.

When I began to speak about Daphne and her pregnancy I suddenly realized that there was indeed a live person next to me.

"Tic Tac?" offered Henry, displaying the container to me. He finished that cigarette quicker than a bag of nuts on an airplane.

"Yes, thank you," I said, softer, more composed.

"Love the sound of the container. Like one of those little beanie instruments you made in camp," he said, wiggling the mints.

We then arrived outside my apartment.

"How Edith Wharton of you," said Henry, admiring my building. "Hey, do you have keys to the park?"

I nodded while leaning on the front gate. It's funny, everyone seems to be so impressed with my having keys to Gramercy Park, when all it gives you access to is a bunch of park benches on gravel and almost no people-watching opportunities, which are the true merit of a Manhattan park.

"That's mine. Second floor with the window boxes. The ones with the lavender mums in them," I said, pointing to my window.

"I figured as much." Henry leaned over and then stopped, holding my gaze. After I became completely numb he put his hand around my waist, drawing me closer to him, and softly kissed my lips. I reached my arms around his neck and the kiss intensified. We rocked a little while, our tongues dancing and bodies moving closer together until I could feel the hard physique of his body. He gently pulled away and then softly butted his forehead to mine, gazing into my eyes.

"I'd really like to see you again."

Me too, I said telepathically.

"Kind of want to see you now." He paused. "How about I take you to breakfast tomorrow. Noon? Silver Spurs diner on Broadway."

I nodded spastically.

"Okay, I'll see you at my place. Silver Spurs."

He trickled his hand down my arm, lightly squeezing my hand and ending with a sailor's salute.

"See you tomorrow," he said, skipping away.

I unlocked the gate, looked out as I closed it and then ran into my building. Up the staircase, each stair creaking in a different tone like that of the keys of a piano being strummed with gliding fingertips.

Reaching the hall mirror outside my apartment I made an abrupt halt to inspect my late-night-after-many-drinks appearance. I was remarkably passable. I resumed my frantic pace into my bedroom, jumped onto my bed and practically fell off, which shook me to my senses. I didn't want to get evicted from my apartment so I tiptoed around my room giggling, getting ready for an evening where a sound night's sleep was, realistically, not about to happen.

I started to dust my bedroom and then moved into the kitchen, wiping the range of my never-been-used stove for what must have been its fourth cleaning today.

The buzzer startled me from my obsessive-compulsive behavior. The piercing sound shot to my heart and a warm, numbing sensation paralyzed me between my legs. I knew who it was.

It seemed like the buzzer was miles away. I tackled it hungrily.

"Emily. I should come up." It was Henry.

Nodding my spastic nod to no one, pressing the button to release the downstairs door, hearing its clunky push, feeling the pulsing throbs of his steps as he pounded up the stairs. Not fast enough.

Standing at the door—nervous, excited—the kind of passion I thought could only happen from a night suctioning beers from an illegally purchased keg, a night with a boy and a never-to-be-met curfew.

This was so going to happen.

Henry's boyish beauty searched my eyes as the height and weight of his body toppled over me. I suddenly realized how petite I was, as his tall powerful body overpowered me, delicately crushing me. Only the intensity of my kisses matched the power of his physical strength.

In the midst of our pawing one another and kicking off our shoes I managed to press play on my CD remote and navigated it to Roxy Music's "Dance Away," one of the all-time greatest. Henry's lips let go of mine.

"I absolutely love this song," he announced, then planted his mouth back onto mine.

He led me to my bedroom, as if he had been here before. Our clothes on fire, there was an urgent need to shed them—we frantically helped each other undress while our lips remained locked. Rolling over one another on the bed with such noise, I feared my neighbors would complain or just give me derisive looks the next time I saw them. I was feeling a real need to have sex, to forget the three-date rule. And so Henry penetrated me. A relief and thrill, but the mental overcame the physical: I really was feeling something for this boy and it made me want to scream out that I loved him.

After a few hours of drunk-induced sleep, Henry moved to the side of the bed and began to get dressed. I started to get up but he told me to stay put, gave me a peck on the head and slipped away.

Alone. The only thoughts that poisoned my head were bad ones. That Henry thought I was a total slut. Or was it my lack of preparation? I hadn't been wearing sex panties. His excitement for a silky thong had been met with a pair of cotton

Calvin's, the cut and feel of a Carter's cotton brief—the kind you wore with Grrranimals not low-slung jeans. I had been such an idiot in my selection of undergarments, assuming they'd be a deterrent from my having sex since I am one of the good ones and do not shed clothes on first dates. It was the damn underwear. Never again would I wear Carter's cotton briefs on a date. I fell back on my bed, crestfallen, thinking I might never see this incredible guy again because I hadn't worn proper date underwear.

7

I woke up early. Went for my run along the West Side and then lifted weights at the Equinox. Who was I kidding, I've never lifted more than twenty pounds, even the old ladies pull in more than me. This was partly because I like the way my arms look and am fearful of becoming too WWF. After showering and changing at the gym, I wondered if the Silver Spurs plan with Henry was still on or no longer a consideration because of the sex/Carter's underwear thing? I checked my cell and found a message from Mom. I dialed my home phone to retrieve those messages—one from Mom and then one from Henry. Henry was talking into my machine! Reminding me to meet him at Silver Spurs. He still wanted to see me despite the fact that I'd worn kid's underwear!

Sprinting with a speed that I hadn't known my body was capable of, I ran past Union Square, down University and arrived at Silver Spurs a little before noon. Henry, already seated, was occupied with the *Times*.

"There she is." He beamed as I approached the table. "The girl I can't get out of my head."

I smiled to try to prevent the flush of red from going any farther up my face and seated myself while he made an attempt to get up from the table.

"And here I wondered if I came on a bit too strong last night."

"Is that such a bad thing?" I said leeringly. He returned my look with a must-have-sex-now grin.

The table was already littered from what appeared to be

hours' worth of lollygagging. A tall finished cup of coffee with two broken plastic containers of half-and-half, assorted sections of the paper, a few copies of last week's *Variety* and the first edition of the *New York Standard*.

My eyes were struck by the *Standard*—a new weekly tabloid paper put out by publishing mogul Chet Wilson, solely created for his new young bride. She had quickly taken in her role as a high profile wife, the way a dinner roll sponges the gravy from its plate. As a wedding present she was given a cockatoo but it flew from the terrace of their Park Avenue residence. The wife became so distraught over this bad omen that Wilson was determined to get the cockatoo back—its distinguishing yellow mane of feathers and faux pearl choker from Bali made it easy to identify. Wilson allegedly created the paper for the column "Cock Around the Clock"—which reports regularly on Callie, the missing cockatoo. Today's edition had the cover line "Cock Adieu Adieu" with a picture of the bird "just minutes before it flew its coop." I homed in on the paper with a fiendish glance. I was suddenly distracted by Henry's presence, sensing that he was catching me in my shameless curiosity—sure enough, he was staring at me.

"I know," he laughed with a conciliatory smile. "And don't think I bought the rag for its twenty-five-cent price tag. In a city where its inhabitants are the spark plugs for all components of leading industries, I bet they're more interested in this talking parakeet than the latest advancements in the Middle East."

I then reached for the paper with the excuse of further examining the story. There were interviews with ornithologists on what to do if you saw the bird, numbers to call and a hefty reward of $50,000.

"I wonder how much my reward would be if I were missing?" I said to Henry without taking my eyes from the paper.

"I'd put up a hundred bills for you."

We ordered our food and ate and read. After he finished a section I would take it.

I looked up from the paper and saw a stillness in the room, similar to a late afternoon slumber on a hazy summer day. The once bustling restaurant with a line outside its door was now cleared out, except for a waitress sitting at the counter crunching numbers on a calculator. Henry had attended to our bill hours ago. It was just after 3:00 P.M.; so much lapsed time without my having to speak, when I had originally figured I'd have to share charming witticisms to impress this new boy. Henry, too, seemed to have just awakened from this introspective state.

We gathered the papers into one complete stack and left our seats. It was so natural, as if this were our regular routine. The waitress wished us a good day and we returned the gesture. Outside, papers and loose litter danced in the streets like loons on a riverbed. New Yorkers were bundled up with looks of haste, determined to enter a spot as cozy as the one we were leaving.

8

I was reading my three-week's-behind edition of the *New Yorker* but failed to register exactly what the piece was about. My eyes, going from word to word and sentence to sentence, were supposed to be transmitting expertly reported *New Yorker* information to my brain. Something by Adam Gopnick about a German restaurant in Chelsea that was the target of all sorts of controversy. Perhaps it was to be torn down for some new coffee chain restaurant. I loved the *New Yorker* and was humiliated by letting my reading slip behind so many weeks. It was similar to postponing a major project, reorganizing your closet for instance. There comes a point when the task becomes so overwhelming that you just say to hell with it and live with a messy closet. But I was not one of those people. I would read my *New Yorker*s and reassess my closet situation tomorrow.

So I began to read again. But suddenly my thoughts jumped from the page and into my freezer, where lay a half-eaten carton of Ben and Jerry's low-fat Blondies Are A Swirl's Best Friend. I visualized myself eagerly opening the freezer door, tearing off the lid and breaking into this cosmic flavor, the way an archaeologist would feel at the first dig of an anticipated excavation. I could actually taste the ice cream. I could feel the sensation of this fabulous delicacy, truly a girl's best friend, reaching my lips from a teaspoon. (Using a teaspoon prolongs the happy factor.) I wanted this pleasure immediately. Had to have it.

Emily—stop it! I scolded myself. I ate almost half the carton two nights ago and that was one night after binge night. Surely I couldn't go on like this or I would become that fat little girl I couldn't stand to look at. Just chill, three more days till another binge night. I could hold out. Get back to your reading. Reading would make me smarter and thinner. The phone rang. Thank God, a diversion from this demonic state.

"Emily, where have you been?" reprimanded Dash. "I've been calling you for over a week; have you gotten any of my messages?" I got up, cordless tucked under my ear and walked over to the freezer. But it was not what you think. I took the Ben and Jerry's and dumped it down the disposal.

"What's that noise? Is that a chain saw? Are you okay? Is someone torturing you? Just say mm-hmm if there's a gun to your head."

"Chill. It's just the disposal. I'm dumping Ben and Jerry."

"What is it about you and wasting perfectly good food?"

"I'm sorry for my being such a flake. I just haven't been around here that much," I said, scurrying out of the kitchen to distance myself from any bad influences and returning to my bed.

"Oh," said Dash, his tone considerably changed—more glum. "Is there something I should know about?"

"More like someone."

"Really?"

"You sound surprised."

"I just had no idea, I guess I'm caught a bit off guard. Who is he?"

"Well, since you did just help me break it off with Ben and Jerry." Burrowing my way under the covers, I continued. "They just came out with a new flavor. I've been stocking up my fridge with it because I fear they will discontinue this super-fantastic low-fat ice cream. And then I end up eating it all. I should really write them a letter."

"What are you talking about?" Dash sounded annoyed.

"Blondies Are A Swirl's Best Friend," I said. Isn't it obvious? "What? He's blond?"

"No, Ben and Jerry's. Ben and Jerry's Blondies," I repeated.

"Well, Ben and Jerry aren't blond—at least not that I know of—but it's hard to tell from the small picture on the carton.

And they're wearing hats—that makes it even harder to determine their hair color. Anyway, I'm referring to their newest flavor. Henry has brown hair. And I didn't want to mention anything about him until there was something to say."

"And what's to say?" Dash did not appear to be interested in discussing my obsession with low-fat ice cream.

"His name is Henry Philips and I think I am falling hard for this one. He's different, really special—and not in that misfit kind of way. It isn't like the times when I force, pretend to like someone because we share the same interests, they feed me well, they call me, they're polite enough to listen to my inane little stories and hear the scoop on the latest, including the scoop from Ben and Jerry's latest low-fat ice cream flavor," I chided.

"With Henry, my insides really do cave in when I see him. I'd happily give up a night with my favorite show and an extra large Tasti D-Lite, even when they have my favorite flavor."

"Chocolate Peanut Butter?"

"Chocolate Peanut Butter!"

"Wow, this is serious."

"And he just lets me be. I was beginning to think that such romance didn't happen at my jaded stage. Henry makes me burst out with an unexpected smile during my perfunctory walks. I find myself tolerating the rude lady at the gym and my mother's inane tirades. I am actually buying that sweater with someone in mind." I then paused, comprehending these extraordinary emotions, feelings of love that were more associated to a simpler time: when I licked the insides of a Double Stuf Oreo without thinking of the consequences, when the adorable boy at camp tugged my ponytail.

"So what's his story?" asked Dash feebly.

"He is the creator of *Duncan-tics*, actually."

"*Duncan-tics*. I love that cartoon," Dash blurted. "Emily, are you sure about this guy? Sounds like a real player."

"And why can't I play with a player?"

"Em, you know I think you're the ultimate prize, but these guys are professionals."

"And why don't you suppose that I'm a professional?"

"I'm just looking out for you."

"Dash, I appreciate your concern. Really. I do. But part of the reason why I've been laying low is that I hate it when I'm in a really good moment—a moment that will be shattered anytime by that impending AmEx bill or petty argument with my mother or gaining that extra three pounds. But right now I am truly happy and I'd like to extend that happy delirium as long as I possibly can. And if that means selfishly avoiding reality checks with close friends, so be it." I then picked up the remote to my CD player and selected Jacob Dylan's remake of "Heroes."

"Is that David Bowie?" chided Dash. "What's up with playing 'Heroes'? Dusted your CD collection recently?"

I was always dusting my CD collection.

"I love that song. One of the all-time greatest. But this is Jacob Dylan's version that Henry actually got for me."

"Oh, God, now he's giving you music!" Dash screamed, seemingly more to himself than me.

Decided not to indulge his childish histrionics. "I like this version not as much, but still like. Sort of similar to strawberries. I prefer blueberries, but if I eat blueberries every day it's nice when I have strawberries—to break it up."

Dash again steered away from my rambling on nothing. "First you start up with some player. Then you are MIA for almost a week and now you're listening to a David Bowie impersonator. What is up with you? I feel somewhat responsible," he griped. Did I handle the news of Katrina this poorly? Well, perhaps, but I hope I didn't vocalize in Dash's manner.

"Really, Dash," I scoffed. "Whatever has gotten into you?"

"Sorry, you're right," he said, calmer now. "Let me take you to lunch tomorrow."

"Can we have dinner instead?"

"Oh. Great. Let me guess, having lunch with the player?"

"Dash," I groaned.

"Fine. I will see you at Yama at eight P.M."

Henry was visiting me at my studio today. It was his idea, but I believe he wanted to acquaint himself with me through my work space. This was Henry's way. He didn't start a conversation or ask a question without an agenda. The other morning he was so perplexed about why I insisted on leaving for my run. Now, anyone who knows me realizes that I can't possibly function without my morning run. It's tantamount to my existence—it's my oxygen. Henry then stroked the side of my arm, the side of my breast and down to my waist before kissing me. I wasn't even self-conscious, felt aroused even. He whispered to me, saying how "phenomenally kicking" my body was. But I countered that running was more about my frame of mind than frame of body, though I can't complain about being 5' 5" and fitting into a size four.

I began to notice a pattern. From the way I ordered off a menu to how I handled a client, Henry's line of questions was becoming more in line with a reporter from the *New York Observer* than a boyfriend. Did I just call him a boyfriend?

I surveyed the studio proudly. No clutter. Every piece served a function, composing my most inviting, cheerful room. I loved the way it looked, how my spirits uplifted by just being there. The buzzer rang and I looked into the mirror above the fireplace. So this was shallow of me, my preoccupation with how I looked and how I was perceived in my place. But I lived in a critical world. And living in a critical world can make me do overly critical things.

"Hello," I sang into the buzzer.

"Ching, Chang, Wang, Foo—dewivery!" I buzzed Henry in.

Stomp, stomp, stomp. Henry sprinted up the three flights of stairs and then composed himself when he saw me at the door.

"Pour vous, mademoiselle." He presented me with a small box from behind his back, a size that would hold an engagement ring!

"What is this?"

"Well, I've always believed that when two people are really into each other, and they have great sex, there should be some sort of commitment that can only lead to more sex."

I hastily opened the box to find a pair of newly copied keys attached to a silver key chain.

"Henry!" I gushed. "Of course I will raid your apartment when you're not home and look through all of your things! You've been the only man who gives me the urge to snoop. Thank you and I will."

Henry then tilted his head suddenly like a puppy after hearing a high-pitched whistle. "Hmmm, not the response I pictured when going out and copying the keys, but you've made me a happy man." He leaned over and kissed my cheek.

"All I realized," he continued, "is that when I woke up the other morning when you hadn't spent the night, and when I didn't smell the whatever it is you wear smell on the pillow, I became insanely droopy."

I believed I just had my first orgasm without penetration.

He entered the studio and gazed about as if he were being shown an apartment by a realtor.

"Emily, this is absolutely perfect!"

"Thanks," I said, reaching for a vase in the kitchen and arranging the flowers that I bought earlier that morning from the canopied portion of my hazelnut decaf coffee place—yellow roses and irises. Henry sauntered over to my wall of artwork, a phalanx of my favorite illustrations that composed one large mural. He looked at them up close, moved back and then scrutinized them closer again as if he were analyzing a painting at a museum.

"You know, Emily," he said, still looking at the drawings. "You're quite good. And I don't mean that because I have a thing for the artist. I mean your illustrations have more style, depth and personality than the other illustrations that fill up magazine pages."

"Why, thank you." I kissed him on the cheek, en route to my desk, where I placed the flowers. "Actually, Joanna might set me up with an interesting project for once. A bedding line for ABC Carpet. The kind of job that has longevity, like we talked about."

"I still see more for you," he said, stuck on a picture of a girl with a miffed expression and a boy looking at her from behind. It was actually modeled after Dash and me.

Henry walked over to me and fastened his arms around my stomach from behind. He pulled me close and smoothed his cheek against mine as we both looked out the window. "You are exquisite," he whispered into my ear. "I could get used to you."

Oh my, my insides caved. This was a De Beers commercial with sound.

Henry turned to examine the items on my desk. Vellum paper, three black pencil holders from Moss—one with colored pencils, magic markers and pens—and two pictures, one of Oliver and Mom and one of Dash and me.

"Who's this?" he asked, picking up the picture of Mom and Oliver. "I didn't know you had a sister, I thought you only had a little brother."

"I do. That's him with my *mother.* Boy would she love you!"

"Very attractive. I now see where you get it from." He put down the frame and moved on to the one of Dash and me. It was taken at Daphne's annual Memorial Day clambake a few summers back. I remember Dash's feet being severely sunburned. Before going to the beach that day he slathered on his suntan lotion like wax to a car, but didn't smooth it in. But because his skin is so fair, and because it was his first exposure to the sun that season, by the end of the day he looked like a Ben and Jerry's cow in pink and white. He couldn't even wear flip-flops that night: his feet were so burned, they were too sore for shoes. I only added to his suffering by continually stepping on his toes with my Jack Rogers.

"Who's the Polo guy?" asked Henry indignantly.

"That's Dash."

"Not what I expected." He removed his hands from around my stomach.

"Really?"

"Really."

"Well, then." I paused to pick up the picture and reacquaint myself with the image of interest. "What did you expect?"

"Honestly, Emily, I don't know. Anyway, I'm starving. Take me to your place. The decaf hazelnut place."

"Great." I reached for my bag and keys. "Have you seen my cell phone?"

"I thought you were against cell phones because you didn't like the idea of always being reached."

"Trust me, my position on those traps hasn't changed, but Joanna says it's imperative that she be able to contact me today. If this ABC line happens then I will be a madwoman. They're looking to launch this next fall. Oh, here it is!" I said, fishing into my bag and presenting my phone.

Henry and I walked around the block so he could smoke a

cigarette. It's one thing after a meal, but before? His habit will definitely become an issue once we enter the not trying to impress period. As Henry flicked the butt into a trash can, I started to wonder if it might cause a fire, that we'd be partly responsible for destroying a historic section of Gramercy. Maybe I should do something?

Two girls stopped us. They were wearing all sorts of layered, tight, colored T-shirts, revealing ripped Britney Spear–styled bellies even though it was fifty degrees out. They had body glitter on the tops of their eyelids and it wasn't even noon.

"Excuse me," said the taller, purple-eyed one to Henry. "Do you know where Pete's Tavern is?" As we were standing directly beneath the Pete's Tavern sign, I could only assume that they were tourists or from Milburn, New Jersey.

"How much you got?" said Henry, motioning to purple glitter's pink patent bag.

"Excuse me?" she asked worriedly.

"You know how it works." Henry pointed to her bag.

Purple glitter looked in her bag and nudged her friend to do the same.

"Well, I have a twenty, but I need this for the train back. But I do have half a roll of Mentos."

"Forget it. I'm a Tic Tac man myself." Eyeing her open wallet, he added, "I do take credit cards."

"But my mom said that I should only use this in case of an emergency," whimpered Purple Eye.

"Fine. Pete's Tavern is right there." Henry pointed to the restaurant sign above her. "The holiday season has moved me. This one's on the house."

The glitter girls looked to one another with a faint expression of relief and scurried in the direction of Pete's. Henry lit another cigarette, took an intense drag as if it was from a bong and then stubbed it on the sole of his Blunnie.

"Well, that was charitable of you." I snickered.

"Something about this new time of my life."

My cell phone began to vibrate, completely startling me.

"Hello?" I answered sheepishly. It was Dash.

"Emily! Right on, girl, it's about time you put your minutes to use. I gather our little chat had an impact."

Henry looked at me curiously.

"It's Dash," I said to Henry, covering the phone with my hand, feigning an annoyed expression to show that I didn't want to deal.

"Emily, are you there? Is this a bad time? Are you with someone?"

"I'm here and, no, it's just Henry."

Henry looked annoyed.

"I mean Henry and I are just getting something to eat."

"Oh, well, about eating. I'm afraid I have to cancel tonight. Katrina is leaving for some conference in Davos tomorrow and I promised to take her out. Can we have lunch tomorrow instead? Possibly near my office because I'm a bit crazed at work."

"Sure, that's no problem."

"Great, thanks as always, Em. And I'll call you in the morning."

"Okay, then. Bye." I hung up.

"What was that about?" asked Henry, smoking another cigarette.

"Dash just cancelled dinner."

"Oh, love," he purred. "All is not lost. That gives me an opportunity to take you to wherever you'd like to go."

"Well, I kind of had my heart set on Yama."

"Yama mia! I could eat there for breakfast, lunch and dinner, Monday through Saturday. Excellent choice."

We walked into the deli, a deli I frequent more than my own apartment, but today was different. I've never been so proud to be there, showcasing this exquisite person who was with me. Sharing a place that is an essential part of my life with a person whom I hope will become an essential part of my life.

Henry was constantly touching my back. As he paid for our coffees and some enormously large muffin that was really more like a cake with all sorts of crumbles on top, I caught the stare of an older woman and held her gaze. She acknowledged me with a smile that said she liked what she saw. We were definitely a couple, Henry and me; we looked good together.

Since it was a particularly warm winter day, Henry and I walked over to Gramercy Park to drink our coffees. I unlocked the gate and led Henry to the bench in front of my building.

The bench that is an object of so many of my dreamy gazes, never used, just a focus point when I want to let my mind drift off outside my Gramercy existence.

After Henry opened the bag and determined our drinks by the markings on the lids, we became instantly quiet—steadily focused on our coffees. Two pigeons pecking one another became the object of focus. Even though I was not looking at Henry I knew that he, too, was fixated by these pigeons.

"Do you think they love each other or are trying to kill each other?" Henry asked, breaking the silence.

"Probably both."

"So they're a couple, you assume?"

"Oh, sure. But I think they really care for each other. At least they're getting it all out, expressing their feelings. I believe that's healthy."

"Even if one of them loses an eye?"

"It won't get to that." I took a sip of my coffee and then looked at Henry. "You know," I said, pausing in fear of how my next question would be received.

"What is it, Emily?"

"Well, you know that I don't even take aspirin if I have a headache, that I try to be as natural as possible."

"Sure, I love that you're so natural."

"Well, thanks, but that's not it. I've just been thinking that you're using condoms all the time. Well, you know, it could be more fun if I was protected."

"You mean you're not on the pill!" His wail was so abrupt that some spit flew from his mouth and into my coffee. I put my coffee down and pushed it aside.

"Chill. And why the sudden melodrama? It's not like we haven't been careful."

"Emily, I think we really need to be careful. *Really* careful!"

"We are. I am. Why do you think I am bringing this up? What's gotten into you?"

"Sorry. I'm just so thrilled with how things are going that if there were anything to spoil it . . ." He paused, gathering his next thought. "And I didn't realize. Didn't know that you weren't on the pill."

"Fine. It's settled then. I will start taking it after my period."

"You mean you have your period now?" he said, sounding noticeably relieved.

"Yes," I scoffed acerbically. "I just got it this morning. Little embarrassing talking about these girl things with you."

"Emily, I just gave you keys to my apartment. I want you to be able to open up to me."

This made me smile. I was thankful that the conversation was over and wanted to finish my coffee. Figuring that I'd had more than a speck of Henry's spit in my mouth, I lifted the cup and took a sip, but found that it was too cold to finish. When I put the cup down Henry took my hand and pulled it to his side without looking at me. He was watching the pigeons. They now were huddled side by side. I guess they, too, settled whatever needed to be settled. Another pigeon flew down to join them, which prompted the pair to fly away.

9

Waiting in the requisite line at Yama, I was not as anxious to be seated as usual. Henry was telling me about a neighbor from his building with white hair, Malcolm X glasses, mustache and teardrop beard, who seemed to be the double of Colonel Sanders. The neighbor was in the custom of stopping Henry to give him advice. Today it was about women. How a good woman was like your dependable wool hat. Sure, they could look ridiculous and itched like hell, but they most certainly kept you warm and protected. Without one you were bound to catch your death.

I smiled sweetly as Henry moved about spastically like a little kid vying for his parents' attention. It wasn't so much what he was saying but how he was saying it—so spirited and confident.

"A wool hat? I suppose we've been compared to worse." I happened to look toward the entranceway and was shocked to see Dash and Katrina entering. What was even more shocking was the expressions on the other people in the line, because Katrina was wearing some fur muff. Where does one find such an accessory?

"Emily?" asked Dash carefully, like it had been years since we'd last seen each other. "How funny to see you here."

"Dash. Katrina. Hey," I said unevenly. Henry looked crestfallen.

"Dash and Katrina, this is Henry Philips." Henry shook Dash's hand while Katrina removed her hand from that weird muff. She met Henry's extended hand while it was momentarily left dry.

"Have you been waiting long?" asked Dash.

"I don't really know. Have we been waiting long, Henry?"

"No, not really," he said to them. "Why don't I ask the hostess if we can all sit together?"

"No, no—we wouldn't want to impose. I know how Emily gets when her blood sugar goes down," Dash said.

"Really?" I never realized that my blood sugar level was such an issue for Dash. "Well, I'm completely balanced now."

"Oh, Dash," moaned Katrina, smoothing alongside him like a cat grazing her master's leg. "We're all here, of course we should dine together."

Henry made the decision for us by speaking with the hostess, who soon escorted us to the back of the restaurant, presenting two small tables pushed together. The hostess pulled a chair out for me while Dash seated Katrina. This seemed to annoy Henry. He then whispered to the hostess, patted her on the back and seated himself, giving each person at the table a singular smile.

The waiter took our orders and Henry added a few appetizers for the table to share.

"That's quite a muff you have!" said Henry to Katrina. I put my hand to the side of my temple and began to rub vigorous circles.

"I don't think that came out right," I sneered to Henry.

Katrina laughed while Dash slipped her a sly smirk. "Dash's been mocking me about my muff all night! It's that one accessory that really comforts me—keeps me so cozy and warm."

"Yes, muffs are indeed comforting," said Henry, causing me to panic.

"And a moment ago Henry was trying to tell me that a good woman was like a wool hat." I threw my hands into the air. "That must mean that a great woman is like a warm muff!"

"Cheers to that!" Henry gleefully lifted his saki. "Emily, my pet, I am buying you a muff. Where does one get a muff?" he asked Katrina.

"Well, this one happened to be given to me by my god-mother."

And all of this time I thought that fairy godmothers were anti-fur.

"Yet I believe it even belonged to her mother. I suppose women can't part with their muffs." She looked all sappy into Dash's eyes. "I just love the clothes from this period. The delicate gloves, embroidered bags—such detail and craftsmanship."

As Katrina was speaking my eyes turned to Henry and Dash. Dash looking at Katrina with such admiration, while Henry seemed perplexed by her. However, we were all, remarkably, at ease. As the appetizers arrived, everyone shared the dishes without pretense, cooing with mutual delight at a particularly inventive dish of cod in ginger sauce.

"So when do you return from Davos?" I asked Katrina. Leaning toward Henry I whispered loudly, "Katrina works for the U.N. She speaks seven languages."

"Five!" laughed Katrina. "And I return late Sunday evening. In time for the Monday nine A.M. yoga class at Om."

"With Marcus Ryser?" asked Henry excitedly. "I love his class."

"Yes, I am addicted. I will even be late for work just for that class."

"I am rarely up in time to make that one," laughed Henry. They chatted in yoga speak, a topic foreign to Dash and me, so we quietly spoke between ourselves. I told him how well our accidental meeting turned out, so thoughtful of Katrina to forfeit her last night with him for an unexpected foursome. He smiled and looked at me happily, not saying anything about Henry. We were different—Dash and I—strained. Perhaps it would be better if it were just the two of us, if we were able to say and act as we were accustomed. But now it was as if we had company over and we had to act respectfully so that our guests didn't feel uncomfortable in our relaxed demeanor with each other. Besides, Katrina was now the one with the rights to Dash's intimacy. She would be the first person he'd call if we were under a terrorist attack.

"Emily!" squealed Katrina, barging in on my internal monologue, as if she were listening to my thoughts and reinforcing her new hold on Dash's affections. "You really should take Ryser's class with me. You know, I could even take the entire morning off and we could have breakfast afterward."

This is a typical assumption by conventional professionals. Just because I don't have a time card to punch, they think I can squander a day that's convenient to their schedule.

"Oh, no," I responded. "The idea of willingly stretching my body as if it were a piece of chewed bubble gum—my framework is not designed for that sort of thing."

"It really is not that difficult. Focuses more on breathing," she said.

"Breathing? I guess I could breathe," I said to myself out loud. "Well, then, why not."

The check arrived, instantly directed to Henry as he stealthily handed his credit card to the waiter and sent him off approvingly.

I then felt a foot thumping on my Todded toes, which I discovered was Dash's after glancing covertly beneath the table. Meeting his gaze, I saw he had a shattered expression. I hadn't ever seen this look before.

He then composed himself. "Henry, you mustn't. Please, at least allow me to pay half," Dash said with a forced smile.

"No, no—dinner was my imposition. Besides, this allows us to get together again—then you can return the favor. Ideally at a nicer restaurant!"

"Agreed!" conceded Dash. "Emily and I will arrange something, hopefully soon, before the holiday." And I was certain that Dash would choose a pricey restaurant.

We left the restaurant as a group. The air seemed warmer than earlier. The light had a rosy glow. Making our way toward Park, Katrina and I led with Dash and Henry a few steps behind. She was speaking about our upcoming yoga class, how she had been searching for a fun partner to share her "special" exercise with. I believe we also made a plan to check in with one another on Sunday evening but I wasn't all that attentive because I was trying to overhear what Henry and Dash were discussing. But it was too jumbled, like trying to get reception from an out-of-range radio station.

Once we reached Park, Dash flagged down a cab. He opened the door, Katrina scooted to the far side and then he joined her. He should have offered to enter the cab first. Luckily she wasn't wearing a skirt because she would have been more perturbed than she currently appeared. She gathered her belongings from the passenger side—her bag, the muff—and smoothed her coat before the other seat was ready for Dash to enter. I wondered if this would be a petty argument during their ride.

"West Sixty-sixth, between Central Park West and Columbus," he directed the driver.

Henry closed the door for them and patted the windshield—Dash waved back while Katrina gave an inconvenienced smile, not waving, hands restrained inside her muff.

Henry put his hand to my back, leaned over and kissed my ear, though he probably intended my cheek.

"Well, that wasn't horrendous," I said, relieved that it was all over.

"And you were worried!"

"Worried? I think you have it a bit mixed up."

"After my muff comment you were worried!"

"Yes, that was a bit contentious, but it came off in that Henry way." We walked quietly for a few moments. "So, what do you think of Katrina?"

"Very sweet. Pretty easygoing. You know, she's one of those wedding girls."

"Wedding girls?"

"I don't have to explain the type. It's all about planning the big wedding, from the cut of the dress to the cake, dreaming of it from the moment when boys became more than germy petri dishes."

As we walked I examined the pavement. The sidewalks were really just big slabs of concrete with etched lines. Surely the city could afford to make more of a creative effort with our sidewalks? I began to wonder whether Katrina and Dash were discussing Henry and me. How was Henry being characterized? As some pompous creative type or as the brilliant, beautiful, quirky and sensitive person that I so admired? His mind was sparkling with possibilities. He was a force on this planet that actually could affect the way people thought. From a quiet moment reading the Sunday papers, a moment of comic relief. Henry touches many.

I supposed his assessment of Katrina had some validity but I was beginning to see more to her than just a wedding and a few society profiles in the glossies. The mere fact that she astounded me with kindness every time I saw her, while I secretly yearned for her to fail, must have meant something. Dash may have found his prize after all.

"Whatever happened to Cracker Jacks?" I asked Henry.

"Well if that isn't back to a time when Slinkys and rainbow suspenders weren't all the rage. Girls were either good at sports or just superfluous." He laughed. "I suppose caramel corn and nuts weren't tasty enough to justify a dinky plastic prize."

"I bet if they just made the Cracker Jacks without the nuts they'd still be around. I could never understand that. Nuts in general confuse me."

"They confuse a lot of people."

"No, really. Nuts in cookies. Nuts in ice cream. Nuts in brownies, for instance. Who thought of that? The brownie becomes more of a production than it's worth. By the time you pick through it, it looks more like a box of Krispy Kremes in a room full of potheads."

We continued to walk in silence. Our steps on the pavement, our controlled breathing and the ruffled sound of our coat sleeves syncopated to our movements echoed on an uncannily quiet side street.

Henry reached into his coat pocket for his pack of Marlboros, tapped one into his hand and then motioned the package to me. I nodded with an Emily face of disapproval. Why couldn't he have gone for the Tic Tacs?

"Do you think Katrina is pretty?" I asked, my voice seemingly louder on the undisturbed city block.

Purposely tilting his head away from me, he blew a cloud of silky smoke into the night air.

"Now how did I know that was coming?"

"Well, she is a prize."

With hair of melted butter, eyelashes that would make a giraffe envious, and legs that go up to her earlobes, Katrina really was quite attractive, but not in that supermodel way. Whenever I'm around models I always feel ten inches too short and ten pounds too heavy. They are these freaks of nature with such un-

realistic features, bestowed to them without the assistance of ma-
terials used to make Tupperware—the velvet skin, boobs like
water balloons and a muscle-perforated stomach resembling a
Carr's cracker. I don't have any close friends who are models.

"She's pretty pretty. Almost too sweet."

"What do you mean?" My voice quavered uncontrollably in
that insecure tone I so hate.

More assertively, he continued. "I mean she looks like the
kind of girl who could pacify a family of bears after breaking into
their den and wrecking their furniture, rock-star-hotel-room
style, while still having the audacity to eat their food!"

"I know. That's exactly what I thought!"

"You did? Exactly?" He flicked his spent cigarette into a sorry-
looking patch of impatiens, wilted like week-old lettuce.

"Well, perhaps not *exactly,* but I do find her to have that whole
fairy-tale illustrated look going on. Very easy to draw—simple
and pretty."

"But the lips are a bit of a throw off. I kind of find them alarming," he said.

"Me too! Like one of those weird plastic Halloween-mask
snouts permanently implanted on her face."

We continued to walk, our silence not as uncomfortable as before.

Henry's voice then punched into the quiet. "And she does wear
a little too much makeup. There's also the weird accessories and,
really, what was up with that muff?"

Fully relegating Henry into the Katrina-was-not-his-type cate-
gory, I began to wonder what he did find attractive. Did he go
more for the supermodel type? What type was Henry's type?

10

I collapsed onto Henry's sleigh bed with the kind of tired you get after driving in traffic for over three hours when the trip should have clocked in under two. The bed was the only place in the room intended to sit comfortably, as it also masqueraded as a couch. It was dressed in a fitted bed sheet, with coordinating pillows and a headrest in a striped pattern that could have been from the cover of a Beach Boys album. The colors were sienna orange, electric blue and the exact moss green of his doors, window frames and wainscoting.

My body's impact immediately caused the covers to rumple. I used one of the pillows to prop up a *Hollywood Reporter* that I'd picked up from a floor littered with other trades and magazines. Turning to the gossip column, I was not all that interested in what I was reading. Especially since I knew this was just something to do, making downtime go by quicker before having sex. I could hear Henry brushing his teeth in the bathroom. I gazed over to his bedside table, evaluating who received picture frame placement. There was the one of the parents on a golf course, pretty tame. Henry and a few Matt Damon/Ben Affleck types posed on a ski mountain—typical.

I heard Henry gargling so I took a peek inside his bedside drawer. Surely a bedside drawer was meant to be opened? I mean, just look at what we had in here—fine-tipped pins and vellum paper, naturally; some little piece of clear rock, which looked as if it were dipped in purple. (I believe it was one of those crystal things for good luck.) Very nice. Two condoms—I wonder if he had those there before I was in the picture? Tic Tacs, which I opened, tapping two pellets into my hand and then crunching them in my mouth without sucking on them. And, lining the drawer, there was a card of a rock climber making his way up some mountain. One of those cards that the Sierra Club sends you for free so you feel obligated to give them money. A loose picture fell from the card when I opened it. It was Henry with some girl—a very pretty girl. I couldn't find any fault with her. She was a supermodel girl. She looked like Claudia goddamn Schiffer in fleece without all of the makeup. I started to hate her. It appeared as if they were away somewhere. Somewhere warm, indicated by the palm trees in the background. I never knew that Henry liked places with palm trees. I loathed palm trees.

Inside the card was written, "To the top you go," and in messy handwriting, "xo, TS." I heard a door shut within the bathroom so I quickly threw the card back into the drawer, closed it and returned to my original reading position, just a little closer to the end table.

Henry came from the door wearing drawstring pajama bottoms and no top with a towel wrapped around his neck. He was not hard on the eyes.

Taking his towel he started poking his ear with such intensity, if it were me something useful would break. This is definitely a boy thing, this towel testosterone rubbing your ear thing. *Ever heard of a Q-Tip?*

"What's you doing, me pet?" He sat next to me and kissed me on my head. *Ah, snooping,* I said to myself. I feared that he knew what I was up to. What I was really thinking was, Who the hell is this Claudia goddamn Schiffer person and what the hell was she doing in his bedside drawer? But I couldn't ask him. Of course I couldn't. Then he would know that I had been looking through his things, that I had felt justified in snooping. But being that there was a girl in there—something to hide—was it justified?

"What's up with *The Hollywood Reporter?* I am so lost by this." I pointed at a random page in the magazine. This smooth save scared me. I was becoming the expert psycho girl that I'd always prided myself in never being.

"Interesting that you ask. *Duncan-tics* is being considered for a pilot."

"Henry!" I squealed.

"I wasn't going to say anything because it will probably amount to nothing. The people I've met are all TV people. I don't get TV people."

"No, this is a brilliant idea. You can't get sidetracked just because you're in unfamiliar territory. I am so proud of you."

"We shall see. I am actually meeting with FOX tomorrow. The meeting is at ten thirty A.M. For God's sake, who can function that early in the morning?"

"I believe most of America, love."

"Well, if you don't mind, I should try to get some sleep."

We then both looked upward; the tenant who lived above him seemed to be moving furniture around with lots of *thumps, pows, oofs* and other sounds shown in a bubble from the original *Batman* series. As I thought about it, there were a lot of loud noises from above.

"What is it with the guy who lives above you? Does he train dancing elephants?"

Henry just responded with a smile, probably too tired to make the effort with a laugh.

I got up from the bed and began peeling off my clothes, dressing in Henry's pajama top, which was laid out on his chair. He puts it there on purpose, in perfect view of the bed, so he can watch me dress without it being too porno-watching sleazy.

I turned around because I had that sense that Henry was staring at me. He was.

11

Henry awoke at 9:00 A.M. on the nose. He was a human alarm clock, always waking at the top of the hour no matter when.

He slipped out of bed and into his robe and lit a cigarette while lifting the window (my influence). Since spending more time at Henry's, I have set a few rules, most of them regarding Henry's smoking and the rest of them regarding cleanliness. Windows must be opened while smoking. No ashtrays. He will eventually have to contend with an irate super, due to the plumbing problems caused by all the butts flushed down the toilet. And his reclusive neighbor in the garden apartment will, come spring, be welcomed to the new season with a mound of cigarettes outside his door.

Henry put on his Blunnies, fumbled with his keys and went down to the lobby to retrieve the morning papers.

I took Henry's momentary absence to use the bathroom unobserved. Despite my new rules, the bathroom was still a mess. His medicine cabinet was filled with various herbal drops, pellets of arnica contained in a ChapStick-size container, Tiger Balm and elixirs and lotions of brands unknown to me, which were packaged in sapphire blue bottles like vials from an apothecary's chest. Stacks of glycerin soaps had melded together, probably from the summer's unseemly hot days, the soaps overpowering my senses with scents of peach and vanilla. I used some Burt's Bees lip balm and a runny face cream that curdled like spoiled milk when it hit the palm of my hand.

Henry's demeanor when he returned to the apartment was noticeably changed from when he had left moments ago—venting about his stolen paper and how he would now have to trek to an out-of-the-way newsstand.

Someone had been swiping his *Variety*. Normally he could do without it but it was essential that he stay on top of Hollywood on this particular day. Henry shared his embarrassment in reluctantly moving outside the front door in the menacing cold, glancing from side to side as if his missing paper would suddenly materialize.

"Goddamn it," he had mumbled aloud, putting out his cigarette on the banister and flicking it toward the trash cans. As he was jumping about to both search for his day's attire and warm his chilled body that was lost to the cold air, I was already dressed in last night's clothes—it was time to leave anyway.

Henry slid into his jeans, a black cable knit sweater with a high turtleneck and an orange parka. He checked the insides of his wallet and stuffed it into his back pocket. We left the apartment together, parted outside with a respectful kiss, and headed in opposite directions.

Right before Broadway I decided to turn back toward University to try out Dean & Deluca's version of flavored decaf. I whisked through a line of people in professional attire, was handed a cup of coffee over a plastic partition and enjoyed the warmth of the extra large container.

At the end of the line there was a huddle around the sugar and cream, so I sashayed in between the crowd and picked up two Equals. There was also a crowd at the bar alongside the window, where I commandeered an end seat by clearing a few forgotten papers. A drop of coffee slid down the cup, which I wiped back upward with my tongue and I caught another drip with my middle finger before it reached the counter. Inserting my finger into my mouth I savored the liquid, holding my finger at the edge of my tongue, letting it dissipate. Kissing the finger slowly, delicately, I noticed that I still had the taste of Henry on my hands. Suddenly I felt like I was being watched by the perv next to me, a guy in a cheap suit carrying a Coach briefcase (which, from the look of it, was probably a gift from a 1989 college graduation). I took my hand out of my mouth and instead entered my comatose/daydreaming state.

Among the bustle along University, I was surprised to see Henry, a dramatic contrast from the New Yorkers who surrounded him. Henry's rugged looks stood out and his clothes were noticeably brighter than the crowd. The guy belonged on a ski mountain. Seeing Henry unexpectedly was like seeing someone you recognized but couldn't place. His large hands crushed a newly bought pack of Marlboro reds and he tore the top adroitly. Before I could tap the window, he escaped my vision. I couldn't even see the blur of his bright orange coat. It was funny, catching someone in a regular moment.

12

As I finished my run I could hear my phone ring from outside the apartment door. The added stress made me fumble with my keys, miss the lock and then drop them to the floor. As I opened the door a beam of sunlight illuminated the dark hallway, creating askew Hitchcock shadows. I burst into the apartment without even taking off my sneakers, just missing the call, naturally.

"Goddamn it," I shouted to the phone. Punching into voice mail, I was comforted by the natural light that warmed the living room to a summer temperature. Two messages were from Joanna with "big news," one was from Henry and the last one was Dash confirming lunch.

I couldn't have asked for better messages, especially since I had only been gone for two hours. I felt the way I did when I'd found a $20 bill in a neglected pair of jeans. I speed-dialed Joanna while returning to the hallway to take off my shoes. Seeing and hearing no signs of my neighbor, I clapped the sneakers together to remove any trapped dirt. Joanna's assistant answered and put me on hold. I happily sauntered back through the living room and into my bedroom—opening my closet and surveyed my wardrobe, deciding which clothes would compose the day's outfit.

"Emily!" chirped Joanna, in that chirpy Joanna way. "I have wonderful news. Are you free for lunch?"

"Actually, I have plans. What's up? Has the bedding line been approved?"

"No. That's been suspended till the spring. But don't worry about that. I have even better news." She didn't seem aware that I might be craving more details here.

"*Vogue* loved your Ingersoll illustrations so much that they want to start a new column or, rather, a cartoon of such. Very Cathy meets twenty-first century. And without all of that feminist, girl power plastered onto a coffee mug thing going on." I could picture Joanna's face contort into something fierce by the potential following the character could have from women who cushion their butts on fuzzy toilet seat covers and buy evening dresses from catalogues.

"It would be about a fashion victim who is really quite clever but has a tendency to obsess over superficial things. Kind of like you!"

"Get out of here!" I yelled, jumping up and down.

"The pay is decent but I took a cut to ensure that you have creative control of your character, in case you want to franchise it. That's where the big payoff is."

"No way!" I danced around in circles to each corner of my room. "This is exactly the kind of project I've been harping to you about. Joanna, you are the best. So what happens from here?"

"Call Sadie Burke immediately, the features editor. I believe she wants to introduce this in the next issue. I'd also prepare some sketches and, if you're up to it, come up with a storyline. But don't get your hopes up—they may have someone else in mind to write this."

"Great," I said, grabbing my sketch pad to outline a few ideas. "Thanks, Joanna."

"Oh, shit," I groaned as I hung up the phone. I had just less than an hour before meeting Dash, which left me only enough time for a refresher shower. I decided to wear a head scarf and thread-thin gold hoop earrings so as not to contend with my ponytail-waved hair.

I successfully hailed a cab outside my apartment, frustrated that I couldn't fit in a walk.

I arrived just five minutes late to Michael's. Dash was at one of the side booths, appearing busy by punching at his Blackberry.

"Hello," I said, leaning over him from behind and planting a kiss on his cheek.

"Hello. You're looking stunning. Walked over, didn't you? With those new freckles adding to the constellations on your cheek."

"Or is it that I did something new to my hair?" I smiled, tugging at my scarf. I carefully slid into the vacant side of the booth, like a little girl awkwardly shimmying into a cab so as not to show her panties from beneath her party dress. I kept my eyes on Dash, who was watching my every movement.

"So, last night was a bit weird?" started Dash.

"Weird? I suppose—more, really, uncomfortable at first, but then very natural. I think there is a possibility for us as a group after all."

Dash picked up his fork and started to etch the prongs into the linen. He appeared pensive, losing his earlier joviality.

"You know, I wasn't all that keen on Katrina at first. Just wrote her off as one of those Page Sixers. But I now realize I was too quick to judge. She's so easy to hang with."

Dash looked to me with a forced smile. "I'm glad." He returned to his sketching on the table. Since he hadn't used the opportunity to relay his comments about Henry, I left it alone.

We sat for what seemed to be hours in an uncomfortable silence. Dash began tapping the table with his fork to the theme song from *Spiderman*. Then he began humming along. I glanced up from the menu and raised my eyebrow.

"Sorry." Dash put the fork down, carefully setting it into its original place. He took up his menu for the third time, possibly even more considering that he had been looking at the menu when I had arrived.

"What are you having?" he asked, meeting my gaze.

"I don't know—maybe something decadent." I cut off his protest by immediately adding, "Don't worry, not something I will throw away. I have some news to celebrate."

"Really?" he said, an octave perkier than before.

"Actually, yes. You're the first person I'm telling this to, as a matter of fact. Apparently *Vogue* likes my work so much they're beginning a column based on a character I will create. Joanna said it will be loosely based upon life as I know it."

"Emily! That's amazing. I am so proud of you. This is exactly what you deserve." He stood from his seat and came around to my side. He put one hand on the back of the booth and the other on the table, enclosing me in my seat, then leaned over and gently kissed my cheek.

"Well done, Emily," he whispered softly, back to his grave and serious tone.

We ate in silence. There was a lot of silence between the two of us lately.

"There's been a lot of silence between the two of us lately," I said, which sounded all the more dramatic because it had been so silent before I said it.

"Can I ask you something?" Dash asked. This seemed serious.

"Okay."

"Do you think that true love lasts?"

I remembered reading one of those damn E-mail chain letters—the one where if you didn't irritate ten of your friends by forwarding it within six minutes you would be hit by a bus—that eulogized going for true love, for only then would you be true to yourself. It irritated me because I'd been doing precisely that and it'd gotten me *nowhere*. The E-mail also said that when someone asks you a question you don't want to answer, smile and ask, "Why do you want to know?"

I smiled and asked, "Why do you want to know?"

"No reason," he replied unconvincingly. And I left it at that.

I offered to walk Dash back to his office. We had to be especially cautious as the streets were pulsing with holiday shoppers; the added bags made the sidewalks more difficult to navigate. Dash appeared even more introspective than he had in the restaurant, unable to look at me as we walked. I watched him stare at his feet, which were sporting those ridiculous Prada slip-on shoes.

"What the hell are those!" I pointed at the shoes.

"Oh," he mumbled with a forced smile. "I needed something comfortable to wear to the office because my knee has been kinking out on me, after that rock climb I did a few weekends ago in New Paltz."

"They're hideous. Like you're about to go surfing. Let me guess, Katrina's doing?"

"She did pick them out, but I kind of like them."

We walked beneath a billboard as big as a Sagaponack house—an image of a couple in their underwear having a pillow fight.

"You know," I said, looking up toward the billboard to direct Dash's gaze, "for many months I'd hoped to have a boyfriend just so I could look at that damn billboard and say, 'Yes, that was inspired by my Sunday mornings.' But I've never had the urge to hang around in sexy underwear and have a pillow fight with Henry. We're either too exhausted or itching to get out of the apartment and start the day."

Dash's smile widened.

"Do you spend many mornings with Henry?" he asked sheepishly.

"I suppose. Definitely prefer his place to mine because of the being in control thing. But I would never get ready there. There's all sorts of stuff growing in that shower."

"Ew, gross," he moaned.

"It's better, though, now that he's gotten a maid. Henry was so happy with this big change, so impressed that she cleaned the shampoo bottles. The littlest things can make that boy giddy with pleasure." I looked to see if Dash was still smiling. He was. "And it wasn't even my idea."

Dash decelerated his pace as we approached his office building. "What wasn't your idea?"

"Getting the maid. That was all Henry's doing. He really has this way about him, kind of picking up on things about me and then doing what I want. Maybe it's the Far Eastern thing. He has this Taoism thing going on."

"Taoism? That's the Coca-Cola of religion."

"Hey, whatever works." We arrived outside his building. Dash was looking at me wide-eyed.

"Thanks for walking with me, Emily."

"Thanks for lunch."

"You really are so talented," he said into my ear, and then did the soft-kiss-to-my-cheek thing.

As Dash walked into his building, I found myself staring after him. Chaos began to enclose my pitched space. New Yorkers with schedules to keep flurried about in random directions while I stood completely still, deep in thought, like the subject of a Doisneau photograph. It was suddenly different with Dash. His petty bantering had morphed into something sincere, honest. But it was not the affection of a brother or even a best friend. I couldn't understand my feelings. Did I like this new attention, or did I miss what we once had?

As I started walking toward home, I replayed our lunch and Dash's changed attitude toward me. Something was different between us and I was afraid to discover the source of his new demeanor. He was less snarky than usual. His eyes had been fixed on me even when he evaluated the lunch crowd. A slight blush warmed his face when I had leaned over to give him a friendly kiss. There was something familiar about Dash. Safe.

13

Mr. Silvano was Henry's eighty-eight-year-old neighbor whom we periodically—*periodically*—checked up on, for fear of his inevitable death (which might otherwise be detected by a bulging mailbox or, worse, the smell of a decaying body). Walking up the stairs with an energetic bounce, I caused the faultily lined wood-paneled floor to creak in alarm. The warning sounds spurred Mr. Silvano to peek through a chain-link lock just as I was about to make it to Henry's door. Deciding that I was worthy of interrogation, Mr. Silvano unhinged the lock. *Jeopardy* played in the background, and a whiff of fried steak and onions seeped into the hallway. His slippered feet baby-stepped to the entranceway. He looked frail, his khaki pants belted with a leather strap tightened to its farthest notch, his heavy flannel shirt tucked in—a boy in his father's clothes.

"Did you get it, Maggie?" he asked intently, tugging on the fur-lined trim of my cashmere coat. I twisted my head so quickly, my neck popped an uncomfortable crick that sounded borderline dangerous. There was no Maggie present, no other person besides me, in fact. So today I was Maggie.

"Did I get . . ."

"The ginger snaps!" Right. Of course. The ginger snaps.

"Uh." I hesitated. "No. Sorry." I fished through my bag. "But I remembered the Tic Tacs!" I took the candy from my bag and shook the container in front of him. He looked at me suspiciously, crossing his arms and folding his mouth into a you're-lucky-for-now grin. I extended the Tic Tacs, which he swiped with a vein-popping liver-spotted witch's hand.

"Ginger snaps!" he shouted, slamming the door behind him.

Amazed that I had gotten so far relatively unharmed. Now it was Henry's door that flung open, releasing the smell of heavy incense, the kind you buy off the street from men in African dhurries. It was a dramatically different olfactory sensation from that of steak and onions. And the sprightly exuberance of Henry's demeanor also dramatically different from his neighbor's.

My eyes glistened, the rims of my mouth curved to the clouds. I was in the midst of a perfect afternoon with not a care in the world.

"You got a little sidetracked by my neighbor."

"What is up with Mr. Silvano's family? Alzheimer's is a serious disease and requires professional care. If it weren't for your Tic Tacs, which I can't return to you by the way, who knows what would could have happened?"

"Yeah. Attacked by a decrepit man—you're lucky he didn't torture you with stories from back in the day, when vigilant Mafiosi were the best method of crime prevention, movies cost a quarter, and you could buy iguanas at the Kmart on Fourteeth Street." He showed me into his incense-laden den, musically highlighted by what appeared to be one of a thousand new CDs spilling from a Tower Records bag.

"So!" he exclaimed, clapping his hands together. "Where should we dine tonight?"

It dawned on me that I ate only a Power Bar all day; being fraught from nerves about Henry's meeting at FOX had suppressed my appetite—mental appetite suppressants the natural way to go, always a good thing. I really want it to happen for him but I can't help but wonder if—once Henry becomes Mr. Fabulous—he'll just dump me for one of Justin Timberlake's leftovers because that will be his new best bud.

Falling onto Henry's bed/couch, I could have slipped into a comfortable nap. The music sounded familiar, vaguely familiar. It was a band that I had never heard before, but they were singing Roxy Music's "Dance Away." It was always a treat to listen to one of the all-time greats, but I began to crave the original. It's like Hollywood trying to remake *Sabrina,* they should just steer away from the classics.

Henry's smile was in tune with my thoughts.

"Pretty lame band. A British import," he said, filling in the details. "So? Are you hungry?" He joined me on the bed/couch.

"I'm so tired," I whimpered, head falling onto his lap. Henry stroked my hair. He loved my hair, always commenting on how soft it was. It was soft because I didn't bleach and damage my hair to a color that God hadn't given me. My hair's not the texture of a girl who gets it colored every three weeks at Brad Johns'.

"You know, Henry, you never mentioned how it went at FOX."

"Right. How funny. I guess I didn't."

"Well?" I really hated this.

"You know. I think it went really well. The guy was a bit slick but he had passion, quite smart actually. He does think Duncan has great potential."

"Of course Duncan has potential." I lifted myself up from his lap to stare into his eyes. "Just look at his dad!"

Henry swiped his hand along my cheek. I touched it like a sultry screen star, the kind that knew her man, but then I felt an itch and started to worry that I may have had a rash, which would have been completely senseless of me if it were contagious and gave Henry this horrible itchy infection, so I turned back a bit.

"Perhaps we can just pick something up? Maybe even cook something?" I nestled my head back into the pillow of his denim-covered legs.

Henry had the expression of a little boy who had lost his mommy in a department store. "Cook?"

"Food. Preparation. Fire. Eat. The human species has been doing it since evolution."

"It's just that I don't know how."

"To cook? Well, neither do I. I don't even have a viable stove—it provides, as you know, a useful function as a liquor cabinet. But the grocery store can do all of that for us. We can just buy salad stuff and ready-made fare."

Henry's jaw dropped.

"You do know what a grocery store is?"

"Of course I do. I just don't know where one is."

"You mean that in all the years you've lived here, you've *never* been to your local grocery store?"

"Do I really need to?"

"How do you function? Things like milk, fruit—toilet paper and toothpaste."

"Restaurants, delivery service, the Korean place around the corner," he said uncertainly, a student unsure of his answers.

"Henry! You are so coddled. We must go shopping. I believe there is a D'Agostino on University."

Henry still appeared flummoxed.

"Come on," I said, finding, in this new challenge, the energy to get up from his bed. I took his hand. "This will be a good experience."

We left quietly to avoid Mr. Silvano, and walked west toward the D'Agostino.

"This is a shopping cart," I instructed Henry, pulling it from a stack of other carts. We wandered through the sections, mindlessly tossing boxes and cans into the cart. As we turned into the cereal aisle Henry's eyes bulged like a balloon about to burst.

"Can you believe all of these selections! Cookie crunch, banana bread—dessert in a breakfast bowl." Henry reached for a box of Kellogg's Smart Start.

"I heard about this one," he said, plopping it into our cart, which was dangerously close to overflowing.

A man the shape of a paper clip, with a long strip of hair slicked over his bald spot, leaned on his shopping cart like an elderly person on a walker. Munching from a bag of cherries, he spit the pits into his hand, then snuck them into his pants pocket.

"Henry," I said, nudging his rib. "Did you see that? That man is stealing cherries!"

"Stealing cherries?" he huffed. "Doesn't seem the type."

Four hours and seven bags of groceries later, it seemed like we had depleted the shelves of their stock. Henry took four of the heavier packages and I suggested we have the rest delivered.

"They even take ATM cards!" Henry roared excitedly.

"Okay, George Bush Senior."

Just outside the door, I stopped mid-step.

"Damn! I forgot something."

Henry appeared confused. "How could you have possibly forgotten something? We have more food than the supplies on that truck." He put down the grocery bags and pointed to the food truck backing into the store's garage.

"Just wait a minute."

I balanced my bags against Henry's, then dashed inside to the cookie aisle, jumped and tapped a box of ginger snaps from the top shelf so it fell into my arms, caught it, and ran to the express lane. I handed the cashier a five, didn't take a bag, and didn't wait for change.

Now I knew what I could accomplish in the amount of time it took Henry to finish a cigarette. His butt was so spent it was practically singeing his fingers and he flicked it away like a piece of lint from a sweater. He eyed the box of ginger snaps and broke into a warm smile.

On the way to Henry's apartment, I arranged the box daintily against Mr. Silvano's door.

Henry unloaded the bags of food onto his table: a ring of shrimp, cut carrots, flimsy plastic containers of hummus, olives and salsa. Aside from his smoking habit he really was quite healthy.

I removed the soy sauce packets and menus from his kitchen's bottom shelf and stocked the cabinet with Irish oatmeal, Wasa crackers, green tea, cans of black beans and jars of vegetables. They added some color and gave the kitchen a lived-in feel.

14

I left Henry's earlier than usual. It was Saturday, the weekend before Christmas, and I was not in my usual holiday spirit—probably because I had bought most of my presents on-line this year. There was something about interacting with the clueless tourists and fans wearing antler hats outside of *The Today Show* that captured the true spirit of the season.

The naked branches and the leaves circling on the ground outside my kitchen window provided me with some comfort as I cozily puttered about. I was dressed in my pale blue Natori slip adorned with creamy lace; the gown was prettier than the dresses some girls donned at black ties.

I went to the closet and pulled on my Blunnies and big shearling coat, a coat I had purchased especially for ski holidays and moments like these. It provided instant warmth while I collected the morning paper and mail.

I loved this. The way I felt, the look of my bulky coat over a pretty, delicate undergarment. Sure, I would be momentarily inconvenienced by the outdoors, but that would heighten my appreciation of the comfort of my kitchen.

I sorted through the mail as I climbed my stairs, irritated by the overwhelming bundle of red and green envelopes. Christmas yuletide goddamn cheer from people that I hadn't sent cards to. Now I'd have to send even more cards to compensate.

I tossed the cards onto the table so I could make my breakfast, spilling the last of the Cinnamon Life into a bowl. I opened a new box which advertised a chance to win a trip to Disney World, only to find that the inside said "Sorry, you're a loser." "Great. Now tell me something I don't know," I mumbled to myself. I poured three packets of Equal over my cereal and mixed it with blueberry yogurt. I then pressed the play button on my answering machine to hear "You have no new messages." I was in masochistic mode.

I brought the holiday envelopes to my dining table/work desk and spread the cards out one by one with my forefinger, creating a red and green tableau on the marble countertop. As I moved a particularly large card, I noticed the name Hardy on the return address. Hardy was the married name of Louisa Cotter, my roommate from my junior year abroad in Florence. This one intrigued me. Last year's annual photo had been of her two girls, Haley, three, and Madeline, ten months (their ages had been embossed on the card in shamrock green writing). They were especially peculiar looking, like the Oompa Loompas from *Charlie and the Chocolate Factory* but without the berry-stained faces.

Louisa had married Lionel Hardy who, like Louisa, had grown up in New Canaan. There are a lot of those—couples from New Canaan who tended to meet up after college, get married, and live that life all over again. It was as inbred as West Virginia.

Lionel was not the most attractive choice. He almost looked like a character from *Sesame Street:* he was pudgy all over, with bulging eyes. However, he was a guaranteed earner, with a position at his father's law practice.

I opened the card and was as surprised as I would have been if I had won that trip to Disney World. The two girls were beautiful. Their two doll-sized bodies fit perfectly into an Adirondack chair, and they were dressed in matching snowflake sweaters. Their hair was pulled to their sides with big red bows in the style of a young Caroline Kennedy in Hyannis. Madeline was looking at her gingerbread man while Haley hugged hers protectively.

I could just imagine Louisa styling the photo as fanatically as the girls from *Vogue* on a fashion shoot—from the baking of the cookies to waiting for the perfect day to take the picture. Thoughts of my current life polluted my head. What if I had ended up with Scott Bankstrom? My first serious postgraduate boyfriend. Would

I have two adorable creatures to show for it? To give me some deeper purpose in this world?

I went into the kitchen, rinsed off my bowl, and placed it in the dishwasher. I absently picked up the phone and found myself dialing Louisa's number.

"Hello," she answered hurriedly.

"Louisa? Hi. It's Emily. I just received your card."

"Really, already? My sister didn't even get hers and she's in Westport." Okay, was this a matter for the Fairfield County postal system?

"They're adorable, Haley and Madeline. So how are things?" Which really meant, "How's life? Are you truly happy with that drone of a husband of yours? And is having the new Lexus SUV really worth it all for a professional marriage?"

"A bit crazy," Louisa responded. "Haley's hand is currently stuck in a jar of pickles."

"Pickles?"

"Pickles are not breakfast food," she said in a muted voice directed to Haley.

"So, what's new for you?" Changing to a tone that was less motherly, more in confidence. "Is there a man in your life?" She always asked me this. But I could never be completely certain if it was out of concern or out of intrigue, considering that I'm the last of her group who was still unattached.

"Actually, there is, but who really knows. It's all a bit early now."

"Just remember that love doesn't last," she instructed. "You've always been such a romantic. Lionel is just a good friend. That's what you need."

I couldn't help but wonder if this was friendly advice or a stab at my attempt to find real happiness. I'm too happy to be miserable.

"So. How is Lionel, the kids?" Mind if we turned this conversation back to my line of questioning? It was on my phone bill.

She started in with that insouciant tone. "The same. But sometimes I wonder if I'd be better off getting that call one night with news that he's been in a car accident. That would just fix everything." She said this as naturally as if we were talking about a vacation to the islands. "We actually rented a house in Bridgehampton this summer. I was going to call you, but the kids were so sick." Her kids always seemed to be sick, even in the healthy summer months. "Listen, the contractor is over right now and Haley has pickle juice all over her new shirt. I'll have to catch you later."

The conversation had been less cordial than usual. I could never guess whether Louisa was curious about my life, the way I was about hers, or if I bored her. I hung up the phone and it instantly rang.

"What is it with you?" It was Henry. "How can you not have call waiting? That's so nineteen ninety."

"I think it's rude."

"Sorry. You're in a mood."

"No, not you, call waiting. But I am in a bit of a foul mood."

"I gathered from the indent on your pillow. You didn't even leave an unopened packet of Equal."

"Really? Well, it's not you, just the holidays. Or, more appropriately, lack of them. And here I am, staring at all of these Christmas card photos of kids I don't even know."

"I hate those," Henry said. "I always feel obligated to keep them, peg them to the refrigerator or something, but really, I have no care for strange little people whom I have no connection to. But throwing them out seems so wasteful. I mean, they did make the effort with the film and all."

"Well, I just toss them," I said, dumping the unopened cards into the trash.

"So why don't we do something Christmassy today?"

Before Henry called I had been considering a plan with Daphne—it was embarrassing how long it had been since I'd last seen her. And she always lifted my spirits, especially with the season approaching and with her giving me a legitimate reason—little Emily—to go to FAO Schwatz.

"You've never met Daphne," I said. "My best friend and the mother of my goddaughter Emily."

Henry didn't respond.

"You know, Daphne. The one who's pregnant? I've mentioned her a few times to you. The last time I saw her, hissing at people wearing fur was all the rage."

"I had another idea. How about taking that little brother of yours skating at Rockefeller Center?"

*   *   *

Henry was more than brilliant. Not only had he picked the perfect thing to do but also had taken care of an issue I'd avoided like midtown traffic—his meeting the family. The policy with family and boys had always been on a need-to-know basis, ideally when Dad needed to report for duty and escort me down the aisle. At the same time I would like to keep Mom from sending me clippings from the *Times* wedding section where past relations are marked in a yellow highlighter pen.

Now there wouldn't be this big introduction, since we actually had a purpose in visiting them, which saved us from a brunch filled with polite little stories about what kind of child I was and how respectable our family was.

15

Once Henry arrived we agreed that taking the subway was the best route, to avoid the weekend shopping madness. On the subway we stood next to another young couple, who were also circled around the silver pole. I had put on quite a show for Henry around one of these silver poles a few drunken nights ago. The subway can be quite illicit after midnight.

"They're holding a Christmas party at the Central Park Zoo in honor of that damn missing bird," said Henry, opening his section of *The Standard* to the "Cock Around the Clock" page.

"We should go," I said mockingly.

The subway stopped at 86th and Lex. Or "Whitey-six," as a do-ragged skateboarder shouted, surely directed to Henry, the other couple, and me as we made our exit.

I despised this part of the city. Nannies, dog walkers and college kids living in dormitory-styled apartment buildings. Walk four blocks west and the tone would change. You'd find New Yorkers who make the city their permanent address, couples in matching Barbour jackets with children dressed in European styles, purchased from one of the many specialty boutiques in the area.

I rarely visit my parents because venturing uptown was as inconvenient as heading to the suburbs. They live in a town house right off of the Met. Christmas wreaths with velvet bows decorated each window, and at night the wreaths were lit with red lights. Sergio, my mother's handyman, set them up every year.

My father is as clueless about the household as a Park Avenue doyen.

"This is where you grew up?" asked Henry, looking up at the house.

"No, I'm not one of those city kids. I grew up in Westchester."

"Oh, right."

We walked through the hallway leading toward the kitchen in the back of the house. I went straight for the refrigerator and opened the door to probe its contents. I always do this when I visit my parents. Something about a stocked fridge—the four kinds of mustard, the wrapped up leftovers from Ferrier, the sodas that you need a bottle opener to open, and, best of all, the kid food. The Snack Pack puddings next to the wedge of Jarlsberg cheese undermined the prestige of the real estate.

"Want a Snack Pack?" I held the two puddings up by their cardboard top.

"No, thanks," Henry answered, pulling a bar stool from beneath the kitchen island. He took off his *Easy Rider* motorcycle jacket, draping it on the chair next to his. He was wearing his black-ribbed turtleneck sweater, and the removal of the jacket was like adding a blazer to a polo shirt: two dramatically different effects with the absence/addition of a coat. He could have been dressed in more suitable attire considering this showroom to Scalamadre, and he appeared uncomfortable, aimlessly looking about the room.

It was a warm, inviting kitchen with a glass wall that opened to a terraced garden. My mother was not one for the steel trend—all appliances were white but you wouldn't know it by the refrigerator, which was covered by Oliver's test papers with ink-red A's visible from across the room. The cedar walls were painted white and the upper portion of the walls were wainscoted with blue and white striped wallpaper. The stool's fabric matched the wallpaper. The floors were sanded to a dusty white.

"Are you sure?" I asked Henry again, waving the package of pudding. "Fat-free!"

He nodded that he was fine. I peeled open the foil, licked it and threw it in the trash. Opening a drawer built into the island table, I took a teaspoon and began to eat the pudding.

"I thought I heard something in here," said my mother, entering the room. She looked like she had just whacked a few ducks—wearing a tweed jacket over a plaid shirt and fitted tan corduroys with crocodile riding boots tucked under. I wondered about the alligator that had given up his life to style my mother's feet and felt underdressed in my jeans and cashmere turtleneck sweater.

"Hi, Mom," I said as she leaned toward me and offered her cheek. I pecked it while she reached into the fridge for a bottled water.

"Aren't you going to offer your friend a drink?" she asked, acknowledging Henry.

"Well, I offered him a pudding." So Henry may have preferred a drink. "This is Henry Philips."

"Pleased to meet you, Henry. I'm Catherine Briggs."

"We're going to take Oliver ice-skating at Rock Center."

"But, Emily," she said, in the *But, Emily* way. "He has stock club today."

"What the hell is stock club?"

"A group of his school friends choose companies to invest in and go over the percentages on Saturdays. And watch that language, Miss Emily." This is what my mother does, she either offers the kind of hospitality that she feels the world should benefit from or she directs people to the kind of world she is accustomed to.

"Whatever happened to a Saturday of soccer practice and going to a movie?"

"It's quite extraordinary," she continued as if I were not there, "what these young boys are up to. Your father even made some good investments based on Oliver's advice."

Henry looked at my mother in amused bewilderment, smiling at me in a conspiratorial way. I must have had an agitated Emily look on my face.

"Besides," continued my mother, "he's much too old for skating at Rockefeller Center."

"How can Oliver be too old for ice-skating when I'm not even too old for it?"

"Well, that's something we'll save for the psychiatrists," my mother said with a smirk, tossing her water bottle into a bin for recyclables.

"Emily!" yelped Oliver from the kitchen door entrance. It was hard to see him as he was one big blue blur, like the Road Runner being chased by the coyote and all you could make from the dust cloud were some eyeballs and a blue feather. I caught him in my arms and rocked him back and forth.

"Hey, finance geek, you were almost saved from dork club. My friend Henry and I were going to take you ice-skating."

"Ice-skating!" he exclaimed.

"Mom, I thought you said Oliver was too old?"

She was evidently agitated. "Well, perhaps another time." She seated Oliver and began preparing him a ham sandwich on pumpernickel.

"Hey, what's going on here?" I tousled Oliver's hair, which was so long he looked like one of the Hanson brothers. This made Oliver uncomfortable, enough to pull his head away from my touch.

"Don't go there, Emily. Oliver won't hear of having his hair cut," said my mother. It sounded like a heated issue that had not yet found a resolution. "He's learning about the American Revolution in school right now, is inspired by the founding fathers, and would like to grow his hair long enough so that it can be pulled in a ponytail and ribbon."

"A ponytail and ribbon? Are you sure he's not getting all Village People on us?"

"Oh, no!" gasped Mom. "More a radical politician than some common plebian."

"What I mean is the Village People." I enunciated the band's name. Then I sang, "It's fun to stay at the YMCA," while making the YMCA sign. Mom looked at me dumbfounded. Oliver also looked at me curiously. I leaned over and kissed his cheek.

"Very patriotic of you," I said, and he broke into an irresistible smile.

"And, Mom, you need to get Oliver a secretary. It's harder to get some time in with him than an appointment at Bliss."

"Hi, Henry," said Oliver, turning the conversation to Henry who, all this time, had been out of character in his quietness.

"Hey, Oliver," Henry said with a casual wave.

"Henry draws comics," I said to Oliver.

"Nah-ah. Prove it," Oliver said, presenting a pen and phone pad to Henry. Henry took the pen and stared at his subject, pen cap in mouth. Oliver kneeled on his stool, which appeared to make Mom nervous, and then head-butted Henry, smiling.

Henry laughed, smoothed his forehead, and jotted a sketch. Mother placed the sandwich in front of Oliver, molding him into a proper dining position like a piece of hard clay.

"No lettuce," said Oliver, inspecting the inside of his sandwich by lifting up the bread.

"Of course not, Oliver, you'd think I'd have gotten it right by now. What do you want to drink?"

"YooHoo!" This makes Oliver very excited.

"YooHoo? That's a kid's drink, back from the Cracker Jacks era," I said. "You're too old for YooHoo."

"He loves YooHoo," Mom set the bottle by his sandwich. "Wow, that's really good," she said to Henry, sneaking a look at his drawing.

"Let me see." Oliver scrambled onto the table, almost knocking his YooHoo over. Mom saved it from being spilled—Mom was doing a lot of Oliver coddling.

"Wow!" Oliver's eyes widened like saucers. He took the picture to the fridge, pulled off one of his A-graded tests, and used the magnet to pin up the sketch. I joined Oliver and inspected the cartoon. The drawing was of Oliver running over to me in a flurry; I was all smiles—arms wide open. Henry had captured the moment perfectly.

"You really are quite good," Mom said. "Your style looks familiar, from a card I've seen or something."

"I create a column called *Duncan-tics,*" said Henry.

"You wouldn't know it, Mom, it's only in the *Daily News.*" To Henry I said, "Ever since Liz moved to the *Post,* Catherine's cancelled her subscription."

"Of course I know *Duncan-tics,*" Mom said, defending herself. "How wonderful!"

Oliver hopped back up on his stool and stared at Henry approvingly. He couldn't take his eyes off him.

"Want to come to stock club?" Oliver asked Henry.

"Nothing would please me more, but I've already promised your sister a holiday-filled day."

"Jeepers!" Mom said as she looked at her watch.

"What the hell is 'jeepers'?" I asked to no one.

"You watch your mouth, and you," she pointed to Oliver, "you get ready. I get so disoriented on Dorit's day off. Into your tan corduroys and Bon Point coat," she continued to Oliver. "We're running late and I have to pick up some last minute presents."

"Bye, Henry," Oliver said, offering him a high five.

"Right." Henry slapped his hand. "Next time we meet, it will be with ice skates on."

"Cool!" said Oliver, skipping out of the room.

"And Emily," Mom said, "you know that shearling coat at Searle you asked for on your Christmas list?" We still make Christmas lists in our family—complete with sizes, URL addresses, and the packages are delivered with gift receipts in case we still get it wrong.

"Yeah, what's wrong? Is it still available, I hope?"

"No, it's not that. I know the one you're referring to. You see, that's the problem, I don't like it. The style is all wrong—not very flattering."

"I am not asking you to like it. I am asking you to buy it."

"Why don't I get you one of those pastel cropped coats they have?"

"Because my name is not Mary Kate or Ashley and the weather in New York is a bit cooler than LA."

"You can be so practical," she said derogatorily. "We'll see about the coat. I'd just rather get you something a little more feminine, softer."

"You know, forget about the coat," I snapped. "Christmas is not about transactions on other people's credit cards anyway."

"Great!" She gloated as if she had just won match point at the club tennis finals. She then walked over to me, her dewy forehead creased into lines resembling cross-country ski tracks. Squeezing her hands around my chin like a vise, causing me to make fish lips, she looked at me in her disapproving way.

"What?" I asked in that annoyed, Mom-leave-me-alone way.

"I just don't know why you can't give in to me on this one little thing."

"Not now, Mother."

She turned to Henry. "Emily's always been a pretty girl, but a little makeup could make a big difference."

"Goddamn it!" I threw my head into my palms.

"Very well." She morphed back into her high-energy mode.

"I'm off, then. And nice meeting you, Henry. Lovely picture."
She sauntered out of the room.

"Forget reception areas," I said to Henry, seating myself in the
stool where Oliver had been just moments ago. "Enough material here?"

"I like Oliver. A reluctant genius. And your mom is just being
a mom, though she could use a week in Beirut."

"Well, I'm a bit mommed out after that." I took Henry's hand
and pulled each finger individually till there was a soft crack.

"And I don't think you should wear that face dirt." He leaned
in to kiss me. The kiss intensified. I suddenly felt the urge to
have sex with him; however, regressing to a time when I brought
a boy home and worried that my parents would walk in, I pulled
back and became coy.

"Shall I give you a tour while we're here?" He popped off his
chair eagerly and followed me out of the kitchen. I detected
overzealous curiosity in Henry's sudden interest in exploring
the home.

I led him up the staircase just as Oliver and Mom tumbled
past us like dogs on the loose. We quickly moved to the side of
the wall for protection.

"Bye, kids," Mom said to us. "Bye, Jed!" she yelled up the stairs
while closing the front door. "We have to skidoo!" Skidoo? Both
Henry and I looked to each other, sharing silent laughter.

I made certain that Henry and I were always touching while I
guided him through this fabled house. We first entered the living room—the hearth of the house. There was a black marble
fireplace with a Duraflame log in it; the log would only be lit on
Christmas Eve due to the ashy mess it would create. A Turner
painting of the Hudson Valley hung above the mantel (fire-
places were in every far room of the town house). Both modern
and American art decorated the walls, but it all seamlessly
blended together, since each painting had a touch of hunter
green and the walls above the chocolate mahogany paneling
were also hunter green. The couch and all of the sitting chairs
were upholstered in black and white stripes, while one large
zebra-striped ottoman centered the room. I noticed a camel
cashmere throw—that was new. The Christmas tree was also up
and decorated: every year it appeared bigger. I had a pang of

nostalgia when looking at the ornaments. While the house was always going through some form of renovation, the ornaments were preserved like Egyptian artifacts. Every Christmas, a new ornament with the date on it was added to the collection. My particular favorites were a painted wooden Uncle Sam from 1976 and a quilted Beefeater from London with 1990 sewn into his hat.

Henry rested at the credenza behind the couch, which displayed the family pictures. Most of them were taken in the summer, aside from one ski picture, a family group shot from one of our annual trips to Jackson Hole.

He seemed stuck on a photo of our family in Daphne's boat, drinking margaritas with sombreros on. "That's my friend Daphne," I said.

He didn't comment. Perhaps I looked ridiculous. He lifted the picture of Lisa and me in matching Christmas dresses from when I was, I believe, seven. "Who's this?"

I realized that the image might appear curious to someone not versed on my background. Lisa was Dorit's daughter. Dorit was our *house*keeper, literally. Basically she was the woman who had raised me and, now, was basically doing the same job with Oliver. Dorit had come to the United States from Jamaica in the early seventies, a single mom with her daughter Lisa and my mother had hired her from an agency when we had moved back from London.

Lisa was a year younger than I and basically lived with us in Rye through the golden years of childhood right into teendom. We had walked to school together, played on the same athletic teams, even applied to the same colleges. Lisa attended Stanford and now lived in Portland. Though she was as close to me as a sister, we were not in regular contact due to the encumbrance of distance.

"Don't worry, my father didn't do the Thomas Jefferson thing. That's Lisa. She's Dorit's daughter. We essentially grew up together."

"Where is she now?"

"She works in the marketing department at Nike. In Portland." He put the frame down, shimmying it into is original place, which was difficult to determine since there was no dust imprint to go by. He gave me a faint smile, which was my cue to continue the tour.

I took his hand and pulled him along, up the staircase, where the walls were decorated with framed floral prints pulled from an antique book. The matting of each picture had the same tone of yellow as each flower's petal, seamlessly blended with the chiffon-colored walls. (Mom was real big on seamlessly blending.) The rug had flecks of leaves that matched the leaf-motifed border along the ceiling, a Bruswig and Fils touted pattern. I was suddenly overcome with embarrassment by the utter perfection of it all. I found myself squeezing the circulation out of Henry's hand, which had gone momentarily white.

There was no room for error in the decor of this house. It was maintained by specialty Manhattan services—companies that did on-site couch cleaning, companies that steamed drapes, even a company that bleached our particular type of Italian marble (yes, leave it to Mother to find such a cleaner)—and all of them were on the kitchen phone's speed dial. There were no quirky flea-market finds, not even a whimsical piece of art bought at auction, no personality pieces, no souvenirs (unless you count the teak four-poster bed in the guest bedroom that Mom and Dad bought on a trip to Thailand).

On the next floor, the door to my parents' bedroom was closed and Oliver's was open. If we were to go into my parents' room, it would probably stump Henry, as it was devoid of any personality. It was so flawlessly kept, it might as well have been replicated from a suite at the Ritz-Carlton.

It had wall-to-wall carpeting with the trim of Astroturf, but softer in texture. The cappuccino hue of the rug was lined by linen-white walls, which became more yellowish in tint when gilded by daytime sunlight. Pratesi sheets were trimmed with two golden, heavily stitched lines, which were ironed and changed almost daily. (The hallway linen closet stowed about six matching sets.) It was quite a distance to get from the door to the bed, to the bathroom and then to the closet; whereas in my bedroom all you had to do to reach my queen-size bed was open the door.

Their wardrobe was another adventure in peculiarly perfect standards. The closet, really another room, could happily house a college graduate looking for a studio. Lined in cedar, it was broken into two sections. The first was my father's. One side of his section was devoted to gray flannel suits, with ties hanging on specially constructed pegs resembling a Victorian game set. Beneath were cedar drawers—the top drawer for his boxers and pajamas, the remainder storing his collection of Oxford broadcloth shirts. All the drawers were color coded, one with blue, the other white, the third with petal-colored pastels for the warmer months; and the shirts were folded with tissue and preserved in plastic as if just returned from the cleaner's, which they probably were.

Across from the suits were father's sport coats, with racks of shoes beneath. The periphery of the ceiling held extra shelving for his sweaters, primarily navy blue, black and gray cashmere V-necks from Brooks Brothers and a few bulkier ski sweaters in similar colors. The door at the end of father's section led to my mother's section, while the light switch turned on both overheads—though light was not necessary on Mom's side during the day because there was a bay window at the closet's end, with a golden upholstered cushion built into the seating. A pincushion of an ottoman in the same material was the only piece of furniture, which was centered in the middle.

One rack of clothes was lined with mother's pressed blazers, khakis and jeans. Dorit was doing a lot of daily pressing. The other rack had a selection of dresses—couture evening wear at the far end, working up to more day dresses. The wall next to the door was constructed in cubbyholes for her hundreds of pairs of shoes. If only I wore the same size. And, adjacent to this homage to Ferragamo, Manolo and anything else Italian leather, were her drawers. Like father's, they were also color-coded, to give her blouses, summer pique shirts and even lingerie the feel of a Barneys showroom. Giving some thought to both my parents' styles, I realized that I'd never seen Mom or Dad in any prints or patterns. And all of the trendy clothes I'd given to Mom throughout the years—the striped pajamas and so on—had probably been donated to the Housing Works Thrift Shop so they wouldn't interfere with the scheme of her wardrobe space.

Across the hall you would go from the daytime feel to one of evening, as Oliver's room had Concord grape–blue walls and celestial scenes on the ceiling, modeled after Grand Central Station.

A few of the constellations had lights that gave the effect of stars, which could be illuminated and adjusted with a dimmer. Clothes littered everywhere made it hard to distinguish the room's other features.

"Dorit spoils Oliver," I said as we surveyed the disaster site. "Everyone spoils Oliver," I mumbled, entranced by the dimmer and as I brought the lightness in the room down to a cavernous dusk. "I would never have been able to get away with such a mess. She basically picks up after him without any complaints. She was the disciplinarian with me and the doting grandparent with Oliver. Who knows how he'll turn out?"

As I said this aloud I began to wonder how Oliver's pampered upbringing would affect him in later years. Luckily he was a genuinely considerate, loving kid. I just hoped he would not turn into one of those boys who would be wearing pink shirts his freshman year because he hadn't separated his red socks from his whites.

The fourth floor was my father's study, the only room I ever really saw him in, and a room that my mother rarely set foot in. I knew she took issue with the big leather chair behind the desk— extremely comfortable but devoid of any aesthetic value. The chair was the cause of one of their four arguments, none of which I'd seen. Just heard, rehashed in hushed banter over a polite family dinner. They must have traveled miles away to a remote place when they needed to settle any disagreements, so as never to expose any discord.

The chair quandary was settled by renovating the attic into a study—strictly to my father's taste—and detaching it from the rest of the house where design-conscious guests could not discover it.

It was similar to the living room in its dark wood paneling, but the walls were painted in a cranberry red as opposed to a forest green. Letters from past presidents whom my father admired, notably Abe Lincoln and Teddy Roosevelt, were preserved in bloodred acid-free mats with heavy mahogany-framed borders. The far wall had a built-in bookcase with a mobile ladder. Most of the books were first editions, with many war series encyclopedic hard bounds. Within the bookcase was a tiny stained-glass window the size of a legal-size envelope. His desk was larger than Oliver's bed, littered with documents, bills, and all of the other paperwork that kept the family financially sound and secure.

Aside from Oliver's room and the contents of the garbage bins, this was the only other room in the house in which you could see objects that were not in a decorator-approved place. Again, some arrangement must have been made in which Mother was allowing the men of her home to have an outlet for their unkemptness. The shared spaces were strictly maintained. Even the kitchen junk drawer was organized with divisions that had special compartments for tape, pens and those momentary clippings that would be systematically tossed out like old E-mail.

Though I had only snooped in Dad's desk once, I had been dissatisfied with its lack of anything interesting—the juicy material was probably kept in a wall safe somewhere in the house. His hidden messiness was like a health nut having a box of Twinkies beneath the bed. I was struck by the number of junk drawers he had.

Aside from the crumpled papers and bills, family pictures in silver frames edged the desk, like a city skyline. But these particular pictures were in black and white—Mom's touch. Even photos that were originally shot in color were developed in black and white. The hand and foot imprints taken from when Oliver was born were in eye's view of the big chair that, ironically, rarely received the implant of my father's cheeks, as he was always standing (appearing to be on the brink of a sudden escape). The prints always made me smile. I had been a tomboy, but Mom was able to get the real thing with Oliver.

The study's only modern feature was a flat screen Compaq and two plasma TVs adjacent to the handprints, which were always tuned to CNN and CNBC. Behind his desk was a picture window looking onto a small terrace, which bulged out like an Adam's apple and at the moment had a Christmas tree with red bows and lights. Garlands encased the window, the scent of pine mixing with the musty books.

My father was tall, distinguished in that Attorney General John Ashcroft way. One of those men who looked better as he aged, a source of both appreciation and competitive contention to my Pilates-pampered mother.

He was wearing a tan corduroy jacket with tweedy pants, the reverse of what Mom was wearing today—she must have planned it deliberately, probably assembling his clothes each morning on the bed the way she did for Oliver.

"Hi, Dad," I said, finding him with his nose in a leaflet. He put his finger to the page and looked at us. I dropped Henry's hand.

He bumbled in that absentminded away. "Uh, yes. Hello." He paused, confused.

"Dad. It's Emily!"

"Right. Of course. Emily. Well, this is most certainly an unexpected surprise. Does your mother know you're here?"

You mean, was Mom here to save you from interruptions?

"Yes, we just saw her." I leaned over and gave him a quick kiss on the cheek.

"Right, then," he said, again clumsily.

"Dad, this is Henry Philips. Henry, my father, Jed Briggs."

"Henry, good to meet you," he said, extending his arm the way I imagine he would to a new business colleague.

"Hello, Mr. Briggs," said Henry.

"Jed. Please call me Jed. So, um?"

"Emily!" I blurted.

"Right, then. Emily. How's your squash game?"

"I haven't played squash since college. But I'm going to try a yoga class tomorrow."

"Right, that hippie exercise."

"Madonna does it."

Suddenly my father regained his ability to communicate. "I could never understand how that woman could have the audacity to make a mockery of religion by choosing that name. Travesty."

"Okay, then, we'll be downstairs if you need us. Bye, Dad," I said, cueing Henry to leave.

"Bye, Mr. Briggs. Nice meeting you," said Henry.

"Jed, please call me Jed."

"Right then. Bye, Jed."

"And kids, help yourself to anything in the kitchen."

"Thanks, Dad. We will."

I led Henry to the living room, where we plopped ourselves onto the big couch.

"Thank God that's over with." Henry looked equally at ease

now that it was all over. "Or, more thankfully, over for Father Jed. He really is out of his element with me. And he's always asking me about my squash game."

"Why is it that you two, uh . . ." Henry hesitated, not wanting to probe.

"It's okay. With Mom and me, well, we used to have a stronger relationship. But once I got boobs—that changes everything between a girl and her father."

"Huh!" Henry's face was overly animated.

"Please, what do you take him for? Nothing Oedipal. It's just that the father/daughter relationship becomes strained when he doesn't know what to make of boyfriends—the protective father deal."

I thought of Dad and tennis. Parading me out on the court at the club, holding two rackets that I had just a few inches on. He'd given me a few basic pointers, checked my laces—Dad was always a doer, throw-the-kid-in-the-deep-end-and-see-if-they-don't-drown type of instructor. Once he bobbed that ball in a strobe of Kermit the Frog green light and smashed it to my side, I returned it to his awed surprise. Though it was probably from an act of self-defense, I managed to keep up with him, even inherited his talent on keeping the volley going with all of the passion and strength I had.

On the tennis court we had a communication of exchanged lobs and grunts. He never lowered his playing level, knowing what I could accomplish. It worked for us during this time when a girl would happily give up a Saturday afternoon to be with her father until she finds trawling for boys on the beach a bit more exciting.

"When I was away at school, letter-writing helped, that is until he found the need to deface all my letters in red ink and send the corrections back FedEx. Nope, from that point on it's been quite professional. And cards that say happy holiday with a 'Love, Emily' are the way to go."

"Your parents," continued Henry, again cautiously. "Not really like you."

"God, no! We have such different approaches. Politics for example—Dad treats the Middle East like it's a game of *Survivor*, rooting for his favorite team. And as long as there are no more terrorist attacks to disrupt Mom's little world, she sees no need to follow what's going on in the rest of it."

Henry's head bobbed up, down and then around to fully take in the room.

"What is it with this house? I feel like we're in one of those rooms blocked off with a velvet rope at the Met."

He held my hand closer to his and rubbed his thumb against my palm. "So now what would you like to do, my pet? I do want to spend the day with you, especially since next week I am beyond crazed. Even if I were offered a fat, high-paying job to produce, direct, and star in the Christmas yule log on Channel Eleven, I'd have to turn it down."

"Does this have anything to do with the FOX thing?" Henry had not brought the subject up since his meeting. I realized that discussing it with him could make him more anxious.

"Actually, yes. Thanks for not getting in my face about that. I'd rather reveal everything on a need-to-know basis."

"Agreed," I said, smiling knowingly.

"Still up for ice-skating?"

"I'm a bit mentally exhausted by the Briggs'. Hmm." I looked around the unfamiliar space we were currently sharing. "The only use for this room is to drink and fool around. Want to drink and maybe see if you get lucky?"

"Why not."

"Okay, then." I walked to the liquor cabinet. "Let's see what we have. A lot of bourbon, scotch and whiskey—want to play quarters with shots of whiskey?"

"Or we could just go to the Stanhope and get smashed. Less of a hangover when we have control of what we drink."

This was an excellent idea that I approved with a smile. I lifted my creaky legs from the couch and extended my arm to Henry, pulling him to his feet. We ran down the stairs—something about those stairs invited running—and collected our coats from the hall closet. We rushed outside the front door, giggling as if we were guilty of doing something naughty.

"Bye, Dad!" I shouted into an intercom, which had probably been installed during the Carter administration.

16

We detoured toward Madison before going to the Stanhope. Henry still needed to buy Christmas presents for his mother and nephew. Approaching Searle I quickened my pace, finally stopping to ogle the display window. One of the headless mannequins was wearing the coat that I was not going to be given for Christmas.

"That's it," I said sadly to Henry, pointing to the coat.

"Well, I think you'd look absolutely sexy in that."

"Why, thank you," I said, embarrassed, feeling my face blush.

I weaved my arm through his like a pretzel and we continued down the street. I found myself smiling, thinking about past relationships in which I'd had to convince myself to try to make an effort, to not be so "fussy," as mother liked to say; relationships which I would break off over anything that irritated me.

We approached a children's boutique that I had shopped at as a girl, and I saw it still sold children's clothes but was under different ownership. The space was crammed with clothes. Clothing lines clamped with wooden pins displayed miniature sweaters and shirts from above to conserve space. The store was full of blinding pinwheel colors, accessories adorned with bows and Lilliputian furniture just a size up from dollhouse pieces. There were party dresses in timeless century-old styles, rubber boots built to seize puddles, and corduroy blazers with suede elbow patches for an afternoon with Granny.

Bumping through moms with vanilla-marbled hair madly sifting through the racks with Grinch-sized grins, Henry and I both fell under the spell of a navy rolled-neck sweater with a red lobster emblem.

The store owner came over to us. Though she could have been related to any of the other ladies infesting the boutique, her smile was softer, without affectations.

"It really is precious," she said to us both.

"Reminds me of when I was a boy," Henry said. "It's just that he is six. Will this be too small?"

"We sell from infant to six, so you just made it." She winked. "These clothes are a wonderful excuse to have more children, aren't they?"

My face heated up to the same red as the knitted lobster and my head dropped to conceal my embarrassment. I had the sense Henry was doing the same.

We next stopped at a hilariously small antique shop across the street from the trendy stores. Old bureaus, chairs and other furniture created corridors throughout the store. On top of the furniture, smaller items were on display—glass paperweights magnifying molten beads, pieces of china that must have once been part of a remarkable set and other bric-a-brac. One person's treasure and another's junk.

He inspected an umbrella holder, a grizzly bear carved from a wooden trunk. "The search is over," he said ecstatically. "My mother loves bears, but not the teddy bear kind."

The aloof salesperson became suspiciously accommodating, probably realizing that a young couple dressed for an afternoon of ice-skating might actually spend money in a store like this. Henry made the purchase and arranged to have the bear shipped by Christmas with "not to be opened till December 25" written on the package.

Henry's cheek was red with cold by the time we arrived at the Stanhope. I kissed it and found it frosty to the touch.

"You're an icicle." I ran my forefinger across his cheek.

"Yes, you're frozen as well," he said, pulling off his gloves and stroking my cheek with his fingers. "Hello, do you have any warm drinks?" he asked the bartender.

Moments later we were served the most delicious cocktail; it had a warm rum spice taste, like drinking a Chamonix chalet.

"Do you ever find it strange that we both essentially do the same thing for a living?" I asked, once we were fully settled into our seats.

"Never really given it much thought. What do you mean?"

"I mean, speaking for myself, I can be rather competitive."

"Oh, really!" He laughed mockingly.

"No, seriously. But with you I am different."

"But we're not different in the big picture, which is what makes us so right for each other."

This was the first time Henry had commented on our relationship. I was suddenly shivering and it wasn't from the cold.

"Here's a little game," continued Henry. "Favorite city?"

Excited by this, I immediately fell into his gimmick. "After New York?"

"Yes."

"London. And yours?"

"Saint-Tropez."

"Favorite television show?"

"*90210,* the Brenda years. Otherwise, *Northern Exposure.*"

"Mine's *Twin Peaks.* Favorite children's book?"

"*James and the Giant Peach.*"

"Ah! We're getting closer," said Henry. "Mine is also Dahl— *Charlie and the Chocolate Factory.*"

"Okay," I said, finally understanding the gist of the exercise. Taking my chewed-up cocktail straw from my mouth, I asked the next question.

"You're favorite cartoon, including any superhero strip?"

"Easy. Felix the Cat."

"Over Superman?"

"I always had issues with the validity of that one. Any villain who can't tell the difference between Clark Kent and Superman, really, what kind of criminal mind is that? What's yours? Favorite comic?"

"Peanuts, of course. But I also had a few issues with this. Like what is up with Charlie Brown having no hair? I know they call him Blockhead, but is he suffering from some sort of disease or something? And I always had a few questions regarding Peppermint Patty."

"What do you make of her?"

"A little field hockey butch, to be honest."

"And," Henry prodded.

"And what?" I said, not biting.

"So you suppose she likes chicks," he said.

Hmm. I needed a moment to take this one in. As a child and you didn't think of Paul Lynde . . . what was he, besides making guest appearances on campy shows and always getting the center square on *Hollywood Squares*? At that age you didn't realize that he along with the Village People were gay. And in cartoons? Peppermint Patty?

"No," I said confidently.

Henry looked at me skeptically. "Took you a minute to say no."

"It's just that she was so hot for Charlie Brown. I played field hockey, and there were some girls that were masculine but still into boys. They just dominate the relationship. Peppermint Patty probably ended up with some feeble accountant type. But Marcy, her nose in the books, perfect math scores on the SATs— I bet she turned out to be an Upper West Side Zabar's patron intellectual lesbo."

"Interesting theory. Though I still have my suspicions about Patty, I do agree with you on Marcy." He took a sip of his drink. "You see, Emily, this is precisely what I mean by you and I understanding one another. We're different but have the same approach. We have respect for each other's talent; we understand our passion but execute differently."

"Also," I continued, not wanting to put an end to our game, "remember the Island of Misfit Toys?"

"Of course, from our pal Rudolph—I believe an annual CBS special during our time. Pre-cable overplay."

"Well, what was wrong with the doll—there was a train with square wheels, a cowboy with a gun that squirted jelly—but what was wrong with that little doll?"

"Sexually molested," he said evenly. I threw my chewed-up straw at him.

The bartender asked if we'd like another round of those spiced rum drinks. I looked at Henry to gauge his order—to see if this would turn into a drunken afternoon or just a quick drink.

"Not for me, thank you. A beer would be great, however. Whatever you have on tap."

"Certainly," said the bartender. "And for you?"

"A gimlet, please."

Henry began to put his coat back on. "Don't go anywhere," he said in haste. "We'll be right back," he added, as if he were an announcer coming on before a commercial break.

"What?" I was surprised by his sudden motion to leave me. "Henry—where on God's earth are you going?" But all that was left was his moistened cocktail napkin.

So now, here I was, alone. Sitting at the bar. Staring at the people. Alone. At the bar. No drink. Staring.

"Here you are," said the bartender, serving my drink and placing Henry's fresh beer beside it.

"Great. Thanks." Now I could drink my drink and stare around the room. Alone at the bar. With my drink. At the bar. My cell phone started to ring, which surprised me, since I never keep my cell phone on. Also, mine has more of a tune than a ring.

I reached into my bag and it was Henry's phone. He had asked me to hold it for him because he didn't want to have it in his pants pocket when we went ice-skating.

So? Do I answer it? Normally I wouldn't have even considered such a gesture, but since I was abandoned with nothing to do, at a bar no less, I really needed to make myself useful.

"Hello?" I answered inquisitively.

"Hello?" asked the caller, also in surprise. It was a girl's voice. She sounded annoyingly pretty. "Is Henry there?"

"No. He just stepped out for a moment," I said, then became confused by my own response. It's not like this was a home phone.

"Oh. Okay. Well, then can you tell him that Tina called and I wanted to confirm what day he'll be arriving next week."

"Sure. No problem."

"Great, then. Bye." Click.

What the hell was that all about? "Coming next week." Christmas week. A girl. A supermodel girl. Calling Henry to confirm next week?

I looked up dumbfounded. All I could do was return my gaze to the uneventful bar and attempt to make sense of this new situation. Then Henry returned to the lounge with a shopping bag as big as one of those pumpkin garbage bags filled with leaves. He had this big, goofy grin on his face. Seating himself back at his stool, he flashed me his goofy smile. I looked to the bag and noticed that it was from Searle.

"Henry!" I shouted like a little girl being told that she can have a pony.

He stuffed the bag into my embrace. "Open it. You don't have to wait till Christmas."

I tore open the bag and it was, indeed, the coat that Mom wouldn't get for me.

"Henry, you are a prize," I gushed.

"Try it on!" he said, helping me take off my coat.

The shearling fit me perfectly. "It looks great on you," he approved, and I happened to agree with him.

"Thank you. I can't imagine how you ever guessed what I wanted!"

I pulled off my cashmere sweater revealing a fitted white Theory top, to keep me cooler so I could wear my new coat while we sat and drank. I stared around the room, with Henry beside me, smiling.

"Oh, I almost forgot," I said. "I answered your phone while you were out." Then I started to mumble many words into one: "Thought-it-was-my-phone-ringing-but-it-was-yours. Anyway," I continued in coherent English, "Tina called to confirm next week."

"Really? Thanks," he said, as if this were totally normal. Completely normal that some supermodel phone sex girl would be calling to check in on his Christmas week arrangements.

I decided not to make an issue of this, not even a simple "Who's Tina?" Amazing what a great present can do.

Our new drinks finished, Henry made another departure— this time to the men's room. I've never been comfortable seated at a bar by myself, even if it's just the momentary absence of a companion. It's wasted time that I could be putting to proper use. If I had something to read, I'd be reading. Something to eat, eating. But now I could only observe, which I did enjoy, although that fact that others might notice me not doing anything—even though I was mentally active—was somewhat unsettling.

So I found something action-oriented to attend to. Usually this entailed interaction with the bartender and arranging for more drinks. But, considering that I was sufficiently buzzed and one more drink would lead to uncontrollable actions, and considering that I wasn't one for using a cell phone in public, I had no other options but to rifle through my bag to find some device to occupy myself—or at least appear to be looking for something.

I took off my new coat, which I needed to do regardless as I was becoming quite hot. This coat really worked. And then Henry saved me from having to do nothing.

"Let's sit over in that banquette," he suggested from behind. "Bartender," he said, acknowledged by the bartender's nod. "Two shots of tequila."

My legs felt fatigued, as if it were the day after I'd tried a new exercise. I wobbled over to the banquette and Henry followed me with the two shots, which could not have been intended for me. I knew my limit.

"Here, I'll scoot in first," he said, holding the two shots carefully in the air as if he waded through the ocean trying to protect his sunglasses and camera.

"I really can't have one of those," I warned.

"No problem." Now comfortably seated, he lifted one glass to me, said "Cheers," and downed it. Then he downed the next one as if it were medication.

Since we were both seated on the same side of the banquette, I extended my feet to the other side. Henry put his arm around my head and we lounged as if we were staring at a movie.

I shook my head for some brain oxygen. Had I napped a bit? Luckily there was no drool on my shoulder. Even though it was Henry, it would still be embarrassing.

Henry looked at me intently, but his focus not at eye level. He was transfixed on my breasts. I followed his gaze and noticed that one of my buttons had come undone. I was wearing a tight blouse. My version of the tube top when I am going for the sexy look, it had a bit of a stretch to it, quite form-fitting. My breasts were exposed in the shape of two crescent moons, cupped by the lace of a demi bra. La Perla. I always wore my best lingerie with Henry. Now that I had a boyfriend, the delicate-lingerie half of my linen drawer had been getting more play than the cotton-Calvin half.

The only other people in the lounge were an older Midwestern couple trying too hard in evening wear at five in the afternoon, and an older man—probably gorge in his day sporting a crew cut and football uniform in his yearbook photo—accompanied by a significantly younger woman who looked like a former beauty queen battling a drug problem. Between the dated wallpaper and the dated people, I had a sudden flashback to a time when drinking liquid lunches and in bar cars were routine.

Washed-up beauty queen was wearing a sequined halter top that was too tight for her two-Pilates-classes-and-one-power-walk-in-Central-Park-a-week physique, my preppy sexy look quite conservative in comparison. I undid another button while Henry watched in amazement. He looked at me all sexy.

"I must have you now," he said, pulling me into him, breathing deeply into my ear sounding like a Sleestak from the *Land of the Lost*. I wondered if Henry might have had a cold, hoping that I wouldn't catch anything.

Henry's breathing accelerated into the canine family. Though I was able to justify undoing another button, the thought of having sex in a banquette a bit too Carrie Bradshaw for me. I was about to kill the moment with an explanation of etiquette and sex in public spaces when Henry led me out of the booth.

Our heated moment briefly lapsed as we gathered our things and my new coat; then I silently followed him to the front desk. He was so hot. I started to feel numb between my legs.

"We'd like a room, please," he said to a clerk named Coleman, identified by his name tag.

"Certainly. Would you like a suite or double?" While Henry conducted business with Coleman, I slipped away so Coleman couldn't register me as the tawdry affair type. I went to the ladies room to relieve myself and made sure that everything was in check, then meandered over to the elevator where Henry awaited me.

In the elevator Henry pushed me against the back wall. I was thinking the hotel surveillance would be in for a good show.

With one deft maneuver he undid my blouse, fully exposing my bra, now justifying the $300 I had spent for swept up factory floor remnants of silk and lace. He rubbed between my legs; my hand slid from his chest to the front of his pants. He was so hard. Our hands met and then he bound mine together as if they were tied, guiding them above my head with such force that they pounded against the wall and shook the elevator car. We gyrated like a cheesy couple getting it on on the dance floor of a cheesy dance club. Appropriate for one of those trendy clubs in Miami—where J. Lo and Justin Timberlake are spotted celebrating some fab celeb birthday party that I would never go to. (Well, actually, would love to go but never openly admit to something like this.)

Outside room 714 he fumbled with the key card while we kissed with the urgency of an adulterous couple having an impromptu tryst. We managed to get the door open while maintaining locked lips, then we fell to the ground. The heavy door shut on its own. Once my panties were forcefully pulled down— causing the fabric to tear—and his jeans were below his knees, we had sex. Each penetration I returned was increasingly harder, removing any thoughts of Tina from his head. This was controlling sex. Quick. Powerful. Mind-altering. Sex.

17

I lifted myself out of my bed, wobbly, and put on my pajama bottoms. This would be one of those mornings where I abandoned routine and gave in to the serendipity of freelance life—one of those mornings when I couldn't remember how many gimlets I'd had the night before. I lifted my hair into a messy knot, to get it out of my eyes and I slid my feet into my Ugg slippers. Walking in these caves of cotton like walking on a floor padded with sheep hair.

Decaf. I needed decaf.

Even though I drank decaf (the effects of caffeine can cause a cocaine-like reaction), there was something about the potency of that warm hazelnut flavor that gave me the kind of energy I imagined a Chihuahua would have after being scented by a runaway Rottweiler.

A container of coffee leftover from the other day smiled to me from the top shelf of my fridge, intentionally kept for mornings such as these. I placed it in the microwave, pressed "Soup/Beverage" and added my two Equals. (Four packets but I tore them open so quickly I justified that only the contents of three made it into my decaf.)

I arranged today's assignment on my marble-topped table. It was my second installment for *Vogue,* which I called "Wall Flower," derived from a character named Lily and the painted lily on her bedroom wall. Though Lily was an amiable, intelligent and successful booking agent at a modeling agency, her vocation and the people whom she worked with bored her. She tried to find meaning and substance in a life where those she interacted with found a museum's main function to be granting access for a photo shoot or holding a really great party.

Yes, *Vogue* had loved my storylines. Granted me carte blanche in both writing and illustrating the entire strip. The first piece hadn't been stressful; I had been taking a chance and was prepared for the worst. But it had been received well, and now that I had expectations to maintain, the second strip was proving to be a challenge. There was no room for a bad drawing day.

Sitting and gazing glassy-eyed at the sketches on my pad, I felt my head shaking and yawning. These sketches were horrendous. I'd seen better drawings on a paper tablecloth at a kid-friendly restaurant.

The phone rang as if summoned from my mental powers of procrastination.

"Hello?"

"Well, hello!" exclaimed Henry. "I must say I am a bit surprised you're up after the night you had!"

"Oh yes, last night. I am a bit befuddled about that. For one— how did I get home?"

"How did *you* get home? That's a bit malapert considering that *you* wouldn't be home if there was no *me.*"

"But why didn't we just stay at the hotel?" I've always loved the idea of spending a night of luxury in my own city."

"I believe you mentioned something about how disappointed you were not to have your running sneakers and Gramercy Park across the avenue."

"Oh." How Emily of me to be so focused on my stringent habits in that kind of a situation.

"You were about as useless as a museum in Times Square."

"Thanks. I feel much better right now, especially since I've been thinking about abandoning my career."

"There's no use in entertaining such thoughts. Besides, what is it that you would do instead?"

"Well," happy to share a dream I'd entertained, "I was toying with the idea of becoming a professional tennis player—working really hard during the peak tournament months and spending the off season doing endorsements and making appearances in desirable places. That's a life that would work for me."

"And this is coming from a girl who hasn't picked up a racket since college?"

"No. Get it right. That was squash! I haven't played tennis since I was in pigtails wearing a double layer of alligator shirts. But you do bring up a valid point. I may be a tad rusty."

"A *tad*?"

"Okay, rustier than a vintage Pepsi sign. So then there's option two."

"I'm afraid to ask."

"Become a rock star. Now there's a life that would suit me nicely."

"Emily, take no offense, but you're tone deaf. A basset hound sounds better groaning for its dog chow."

"You think Britney Spears has a voice? Please. One month at pop star training camp and I'll out-market all of those sit-up slaves." I began redrawing Lily's stomach a shade thinner than usual. At least one of us should have a thin day. "And really. Those concerts she has? Please, they're just a long aerobics class. Do you know I used to coach swimming in the summers?"

"And Bob Dylan?" Now entering a phenomenon that had always perplexed me. "What's his deal? He looks like a calico-jacket-wearing lesbian and sounds like a dying crane."

"You've heard a dying crane?" pressed Henry.

"Well. No. But he sounds like what I would *imagine* a dying crane to sound like."

"For now you may want to focus on your current assignment and leave some room for me later. It's important that I see you today."

"Oh," I teased his suddenly earnest tone. "Who's been diagnosed?"

"I would just really like to see you."

His gravity was beginning to scare me. "Fine."

"Fine, then."

Before he could set his phone on the receiver, I said, "Not so fine. Time and place?"

"Oh. Right. How about I come by at around seven P.M.?"

"Okay. Fine." I hung up. The boy was going to give me the shaft.

And why did I make it so easy for him to meet up with me? Perhaps I should have made an excuse that I couldn't make it, kept blowing him off until he came to realize that I was impossible to give the heave-ho to.

The phone rang again.

"Henry!" I said excitedly.

"Why don't you have call waiting?" demanded Andrew, Daphne's husband. "That's so," he paused, "so out of touch."

"Andrew, my God, is Daphne all right?"

"All right? She just gave birth to our son—Henry Holden Trefry. And how did you know we named him Henry? We just decided about twenty minutes ago."

"Huh?" Then I realized what I'd said. "Oh, right. Sorry—thought you were someone else. So can I see them!"

"Daphne's asking for you."

"I'll be there as soon as possible."

I raced to my bedroom mirror to see if I was presentable. Just barely. I threw my cell phone, Tic Tacs swiped from Henry, and Steiff elephant into a bag. As I ran out to the street I unsuccessfully tried to hail a vacant cab—must be out of practice—and dialed Henry's number.

"Hello," he answered.

"Henry, I am on my way to see Daphne at the hospital. She just had a boy, his name is Henry!"

"Really," he said in a tone more dour than when he had picked up.

"Sorry, but can we meet up tomorrow?"

"Okay. How about Silver Spurs for breakfast?"

"Would love to but committed to that damn yoga class with Katrina."

"Well, I have another meeting at FOX tomorrow afternoon and I really want, need to meet up with you."

"Yes, you've made that quite clear."

"Just come to FOX. They're on 6th and 55th. At four thirty P.M."

"Fine," I said aloofly, abruptly punching the end button on the phone. What the hell was his problem?

I looked to the street. Cabs were circling Gramercy Park like bees to a hive but not one of them was available.

18

I couldn't have been happier for Daphne. Truthfully. It was just that seeing her with that bundle of dough being tucked into its nubby blue blanket, it was hard not to reassess my situation.

Daphne was in a different place from me. A settled, happy place—secure in the knowledge that the little people she brought into this world would someday grow up and continue the cycle, so she wouldn't be without traditional plans come the holiday season. Holidays put together in her renovated kitchen where medleys of rice cultivated from the fields of Vietnam add a decorative yet utilitarian touch to the stone, steel and glass decor.

I gave little Henry the Steiff elephant. It was a sentimental gift since Daphne and I had both been given Steiff elephants by my mother when we were born. I had also given one to Emily on her birthday. But since Henry was unable to use his hands, and the elephant was about twice his size, his current purpose was to remind me of my feeble future. Soon he would be able to smile, produce cooing sounds with adorable expressions to match, and might actually find amusement in that stuffed toy.

The next day I woke up earlier than ususal—both my face and brain puffed like a cotton ball—and went for a short run so that I could process the rest of my problems and ensure that my cynical angst would not throw off the healthy karma of this touted yoga class.

I couldn't remember the last time I had gone to bed and awoken the next morning in the same clothes. Even in my most drunken of stupors I had still been able to robotically process my evening routine. Perhaps it was the combination of exposure to hospital air, the psychological trauma of the impending Henry-wanting-to-break-up-with-me conversation and mental fatigue at the prospect of having to twist into not-meant-for-human-body positions for this yoga class with Miss Muff.

Katrina was annoyingly perky for this time of the morning. Typical. She also looked great. Hair upswept into a neat pony-tail; drawsting orange pants, coordinated little yoga-y shoes and tank top over her tiny figure—I attributed her appearance to the fact that she must still be on Swiss time.

After we went through all of the pleasant "how was your trip?" "Daphne had a healthy little boy" chitchat, she instructed me on the different mats and handed me a Mexican throw that was distinctly similar to a blanket from the Deta Epsilon living room at Dartmouth. That particular blanket had had such a stench of bong water, its primary function was to cover the tears of a couch that had been in the fraternity since the days pledges went on panty raids and were spanked with lettered wooden paddles.

Katrina and I situated ourselves toward the back of the class. I was grateful for this. She positioned herself like one of those wooden Tibetan prayer statues, hands lifted to her side as if she were attempting to push the air upward. Roping her stringy legs around the minuscule waist—defying genetics—a move that could only be viewed otherwise by paying an extra five dollars for access to a roped off section at a carnival. I just lounged back, feeling especially sloppy and unkempt next to all her little flut-ters and quick breaths.

A very little man entered the room. Katrina stopped her pe-culiar movements and focused on this tiny person who, if dressed in a pointy hat and shoes, would have looked like he was on break from the Radio City Christmas show. He started hum-ming sounds that had the overtones of a Moroccan medina dur-ing prayer time. This elfin man was like an oboe—strange sounds emanating from a strange package, yet achieving a soothing tran-quillity.

We were told to draw our mind blank, close our eyes and breathe. I was sitting in that Buddha-like position trying to do something that I didn't need to be told how to do, and wondering if I was I really learning how to breathe. I didn't think you learned to do this. Wasn't breathing instinctive?

I opened my eyes and surreptitiously scanned the room to see if I could get any indication whether I was breathing correctly.

The Keebler cookie-maker caught me looking around, but he just smiled and went on to the next pose. He was probably too spiritual and kind-hearted to make an example out of me.

We moved into various positions, which increased in difficulty. I couldn't understand why he kept reminding me to breathe. What was he thinking? That I would stop breathing altogether? My most intense focus was now on the clock above the instructor. In ten minutes we would be at the halfway mark. Ten minutes later and the clock's hands were in the same place. The clock was not moving! I wondered if I should say something.

Pose after pose and I felt like a stranger in my own body. This Lilliputian yoga instructor was probably not helping me because it would be counterproductive for the rest of the class. I was grateful for that.

Finally—after the class had chanted some words that sounded like "you have to stay," which caused me a brief moment of utter panic—I was free to go.

Katrina reached for a water bottle and tiny white towel and lightly dabbed her head of nonexistent sweat. "Well. Didn't you just love it?" she said, as if we had just seen a fabulous movie or shared a great sushi dinner.

"It just flew by," I said, as enthusiastically as possible.

We showered and changed. I desperately wanted to do a cellulite check on Katrina but was nervous that it would be a bit too lesbo. And obvious.

Katrina wanted to make a quick stop at Jefferson Market. She was considering making coq au vin for Dash this evening. Please, that was just an excuse to use your leftover Chardonnay. Cooking for Dash? She would have had to use her stove to do that. That was a point in her favor, I supposed. "I use five different kinds of mushrooms," she was saying. Okay, you might have gotten Dash on the five languages/five mushrooms lure, but all she really had to do to get five mushrooms was slightly shift her hand into a different basket.

We decided to put off the mushroom shopping, as it would

have cut into our "special" time together. Instead Katrina suggested that we stop off at her place while she picked up a few things. This idea pleased me, as I would be able to observe Katrina's home and gain a more complete picture.

She lived a block away from my apartment, in one of those historic Gramercy buildings with an elevator. Before entering her apartment she did the Mr. Rogers thing and hung her coat on a pine peg coatrack, trading it in for a dainty black cashmere cardigan. She then removed her sneakers, sliding her feet into a pair of slippers secured by a strap of black feathers. Her red pedicured toes were so shiny I feared they would smudge to the touch.

"Should I take off my shoes?" I asked, relieved that I had a new pair of Polo Sport socks on.

"If you'd like," she said, which meant no sole that had touched a dog-walked, gum-glued street must ever touch her sacred floors. I took off my shoes.

It was a spacious apartment. Overly decorated. Lots of coordinating fabrics and rooms stuffed with bridal registry knick-knacks. I wondered if she'd been married. No, I would have read about it.

A credenza showcasing black and white pictures framed in checkerboard pearl and black onyx was the only item that distinguished this as an apartment and not a home-furnishings room at Bergdorf.

I asked Katrina if I could use her bathroom. She nodded and directed me down a narrow hall, then checked her phone messages. I overheard her assistant going over the afternoon itinerary as I shut the door.

The bathroom, also spacious by New York standards, had an antique white paint-chipped medicine cabinet and rusted chair with fluffy towels stacked on top. I wondered if Dash had used one of those towels. Probably to Katrina's consternation, as they were only meant for display. Hmm, where would she have kept Dash's towels? I looked inside the medicine cabinet. But surely the medicine cabinet couldn't fit towels? Since I had already opened the cabinet, I decided to check out what drugs Katrina was on. Just an assortment of creams, pretty tame—more like an ad for Mario Bandescu. And, please, what was with all of the

Crème de la Mer products? Like that stuff really worked. One hundred and fifty dollars for less than an eighth of an ounce of cream with the same properties as a jar of Ponds. "Beauty victim," I sang to myself with a diva delivery.

Hearing Katrina just outside the door fidgeting with the CD player, I flushed the toilet and quietly shut the cabinet door.

"Oh, hi Katrina," I said as I exited the bathroom. "You really have a decorator's eye. Love the whitewashed iron chair."

"Thanks!" she responded, exalted. "I found it at a flea market in Paris."

Well, of course she had. Why bother going to Chelsea when Paris sounded so alluring? I was sure she had suckered Dash on this one.

"You wouldn't believe it, even with shipping it cost me considerably less than if I had found one in Chelsea. It was something like seventy dollars!"

Leading me back into the bathroom she asked, "Do you mind if I get ready with you here before we go out?"

"No, not at all. I am pretty much ready anyway." I was curious about what else she needed to do—I thought we had already gotten ready, back at the gym. And it wasn't like we were going to a party or meeting up with the boys or anything. It was food with another chick.

Squeezing onto a window side-counter so I could comfortably sit and chat, and feeling a bit awkward at this exposure of her more intimate side, I watched Katrina powder the forehead of her unblemished face. Even after an unlimited spree at the makeup counters at Barneys and a day at a spa, I still would never have been able to look as pulled together as she did.

She was wearing dark denim Seven jeans with a crisp just-pulled-out-of-the-shopping-bag white fitted shirt. A black duster sweater coat with a draw-string waist was on top. Not my style, but I was eyeing it as it really did add some flair to basic jeans and a white shirt.

Her little black mules were made especially for her lipstick red toes, her feet impeccably dotted like a vase with tea roses. I'd been fixated by this enameled touch that must have cost her hours at a salon each week, time that I just didn't have. I made a mental note to schedule an appointment at Rescue. Aside from a few blonde hairs magnetized onto her sweater, she was completely flawless.

Katrina applied her eye makeup with as much skill and precision as I used when creating an illustration. I looked on with the same awed amazement that I had for those little gymnast freaks when they twisted into the air. She began outlining her cat lips with a plummy lip liner—swerving up, down—in the same motion as script-writing. Smacking her lips together, she reached for a Lorac lipstick of a more fiery hue. After one application she added another coat of a different lipstick, still Lorac but just a shade darker. I wondered if no lipstick existed in the color that she was going for, or if it was all about the different coats.

"Katrina?" I asked quietly so as not to completely break her from her makeup zone. "If Lorac came out with the shade you are trying to achieve, would you still add on more layers?"

"If it were the summer, no." She took a makeup brush and dusted on some bronzing powder. "But I need the added help in the winter months. The two-ply process really stays on."

"Oh." I tried to sound like I had registered the information and was happy to learn something new. Katrina undoubtedly took her makeup seriously and I didn't want to belittle its importance by asking flippant questions.

Still looking in the mirror, she said, "You're so lucky. Being so naturally pretty without all of this effort."

Was this a come-on? I was secretly aroused.

She then pulled out a metal contraption, some type of mobile torture device, and suctioned it onto her eyelashes. This completely fascinated me, but I couldn't follow its high degree of technical difficulty.

"Are you ready?" she asked, putting the last of her tools in her animal-print makeup case.

"Sure," I said, jumping from the counter.

"Let's just go to the Irving coffee place, if you don't mind. There shouldn't be a wait at this time and it's quite cozy."

We politely discussed inane topics during our walk to the restaurant. The only other patrons were an older woman who was reading the paper with Philip Johnson glasses and a patchwork quilt of a scarf wrapped many times around her neck, and someone who looked like an unemployed screenwriter, about to head cross-country on his bumper-stickered skateboard. Or could he have been a cutting edge/in-line skating clothing designer? I began to feel that being born in 1970 had put me out of touch with the new millennium.

We put our bags down at a table near the artsy lady and went to the counter. The only food offered were trays of fattening pastries and a few bagels, which looked hardened. The breakfast crowd had probably taken the best of the bunch.

Katrina attracted the attention of the clerk and asked if they had any more fat-free angel food lemon muffins. He apologized, and she settled on a poppy seed pound cake with an Earl Gray tea.

"No worries," she said, appearing dejected when the plate of cake was handed to her from above the glass divider. "We just exercised," she added, convincing herself that it was okay to devour something as evil as poppy seed cake.

No decaf hazelnut. I ordered a vanilla Chai tea.

As I reached for my wallet, the cashier said that my tea had already been paid for. Katrina had handled that one slyly.

At the table Katrina was reeling her tea bag into the hollow end of her spoon, twirling the string around the bag a few times and squeezing so tight that the remaining concentrated tea trickled into her mug.

I excused myself and returned to the counter for more Equal, bringing back a few extra packets in case she wanted some. Katrina placed her mug on the lopsided table and broke her pound cake in half, popping a broken piece into her mouth.

"Would you like some?" she offered.

I shook my head that I was fine.

We continued discussing all things girly—our unhealthy obsession with the lives of people on reality TV shows, estimations on when we'd be reading about the breakups in *Us* magazine, buying doubles of outfits that we had no room for in our limited closet space.

"So," she said in a tone that signified a more pressing agenda. "How is it with you and Henry?"

Katrina was the first person to address the subject of Henry since our awkward "we need to talk" conversation. I was suddenly filled with relief and gratitude. Maybe I would get something out of this obligatory breakfast after all.

"Well," I said in a tone more upbeat than before. "It's been great, that is until a day ago. Out of nowhere and Henry called me all concerned saying that we needed to talk—in that 'we need to talk' tone. I've been driving myself mad trying to figure out what I did to spur this."

I took a sip from my tea, taking in what I was verbalizing. Henry and I were still in that stage where small gestures revealed a lot.

"Just two days ago he gave me the most thoughtful gift," I prattled.

"What was the gift?"

"A fitted Searle shearling."

"Oh, I love those!"

"I know. I was so thrilled!"

Pretty impressed that Katrina knew to give the gift some concerted attention.

"Well, maybe you're overreacting. Since you yourself said that nothing really happened to spur this reaction," she rationalized.

"Yes. That's true. He did, however, meet my family earlier that day and perhaps when he realized what kind of family I'm connected to, he just freaked."

"Did he meet your cousin Anne?"

"No, thank God! Then I would really know where this was coming from. How did you know my cousin Anne was such a liability?"

"Emily, that girl is out more than a publicist with a new lip gloss to promote. She befriends journalists just so they can write about her. Frankly, I was shocked to know that you two were related. You both are so different."

"Thank you," I gasped in relief.

"I hope you don't mind my being so forthright?"

"Not at all, it's actually reassuring."

"But your family is utterly charming," she said, her affected European accent less pronounced. "My father adores your father. Says that he is highly respected at the club and that every year the players on the tennis ladder are dying to be his doubles partner. That he's an extraordinary player."

"Really?" I had forgotten about his prowess on the court. "And how do you know so much about this? My family?"

"I'm afraid that I'm guilty. When I started dating Dash and gathered that you two were so close I did some probing."

Suddenly I was silent, amazed that Katrina was so blatant in her checking up on me. I again became impressed, even touched. Though obviously if she had issues with her discoveries, she wouldn't have fessed up.

"I'm sorry. Was I being impertinent again?"

"Katrina, you never cease to impress me. I suppose I did some checking up on you as well. And, since we're being so honest with one another, I was really looking for the bad things. I feel sort of bitchy, in that superficial sorority girl sort of way."

"Please, Emily—that's not superficial, that's just plain rational. But enough of that. I believe the real issue is this sudden mystery you've stumbled onto. Surely there must be a few clues that have you completely stumped?"

"As a matter of fact, there are. Like who's the picture of this girl in his bedside drawer? Why doesn't he have any interest in meeting Daphne? Is it just me or do the Olson twins look like Teletubbies? Why the hell didn't Frida Kahlo ever shave that mustache? Why do men with hairy backs still insist on wearing wife beater tees at the gym?"

"Okay, slow down here. The Olson twins are an image perpetuated by an obsequious society that just buys into whatever image is spun, sort of like *The Emperor's New Clothes*. Frida Kahlo was a freaky artist who looked to her mustache the way Lauren Hutton looks to the gap between her teeth. Men showing off their hairy backs are delusional. And who's this girl in the bedside drawer and what's up with Daphne?"

"I found a picture of some phenomenally insane beauty in Henry's drawer. It was in a card signed with the initials TS. And then a Tina called Henry on his cell on Saturday, asking about his trip next week. None of this bodes well, especially considering the current change in his attitude toward me. What I do know is that Henry left California over a relationship."

"What about the Daphne connection?"

"He just doesn't seem all that enthused to meet her, or even indulge my discussing her in the way that he tolerates my talking about everyone else in my life. I don't know, maybe my investigative skills are based more on paranoia, but I sense something."

"From what I can see, you appear quite controlled and justified in your assessments, aside from your worry about his trip next week. It is the holidays, after all. But he should discuss these issues with you. Luckily you two are meeting today and you can get some questions answered. Just be open and honest, not like these other girls who play all these games until they get the rock. That doesn't seem your style."

"Please. I am too opinionated, independent and obstinate to act like that. And, Katrina," I said respectfully, "thanks for this. I mean it's been so nice and refreshing to speak to you."

"I really don't know if I did anything."

"More than you realize." I looked at my watch and it was already 2:00 P.M. I had to meet Henry in less than three hours.

"I have to meet Henry in less than three hours."

"Don't fret, it will be okay. I should get going as well. A good idea to make an appearance at the office. But whatever happens today, I need an update."

"Yes. And thanks again. Oh, one more thing."

"Sure. Anything."

"Well, since we're being so honest with one another, I didn't really love the yoga thing."

She smiled.

"I figured as much! Not to worry, it's always like that in the beginning."

The beginning? I moaned to myself. Does she really think I would put myself through that again?

We gathered our things and did the air kiss outside the café. A cab pulled to the curb as if it had been called especially for Katrina. She slid in and then rolled down the window.

"Call me," she shouted from the departing cab. I just waved her on.

Now, standing alone at the curb, I considered what to do next. The day was basically wasted and the idea of trying to do work before this impending conversation would be futile. I could have gotten a manicure or done something girlie but the idea of mustering dead time with a perky pedicurist was a bit too much.

I decided to walk over to Barnes and Noble for some inspiration. An hour there could go by in minutes.

Turning the corner toward the bookstore, it was Katrina, not Henry, who suddenly fixated me. Granted, we are all experts on other people's problems, but I really was intrigued by her sensitivity. I was even starting to like her.

19

There was a book about tree houses that particularly fascinated me. It reminded me of the tree house that I once had
at the house in Bridgehampton. I called it the "French Shack."
Derived from French toast, French kiss, French manicure—by
just adding French to something simple it was suddenly chic.

The tree house was basic in design—a few floorboards and an
antique sill that had been saved from our house when it was
being renovated. The French Shack was the site of many mile-
stones, especially during the summer months.

I had my first stitches after showing my neighbor James
Burton that I could jump out of the tree just as Wonder Woman
could. It wasn't the fall that caused the gash but the rake I
landed on. James just gawked and I was too much of a superhero
to cry. One butterfly stitch on the bottom of my foot, but the real
disappointment was in not being able to swim for three weeks.
Luckily it was late August and the summer would be over after
the weekend.

Many afternoons were spent doodling and painting water-
colors in the French Shack. Daphne and I had our first bong hit
there. It was where Susie Forseman taught us how to give a blow
job, using a bottle of Moosehead. And it was where I had sex
with the first boy that I loved. I knew Mark Pierce from Rye, but
he spent his summers in East Hampton. I believe my infatuation
began when he would shoot spitballs at me through a milk straw.
Mark had a lot of girlfriends. He was the most handsome boy I

had ever known. And he had the good fortune of traipsing through his growing years with ease. I was an awkward, bumbling girl, especially in his presence, and I was never considered a catch in my preteen years. I was a late bloomer who pleaded with my chest to grow something, finding it cruel and unfair that the other girls had a reason to wear training bras. But in the summer after my sophomore year, I had filled out and in—newly acquired boobs are a wonder for self-esteem.

The summer before I left for Dartmouth, Mark and I would always find one another at the end of a party. He'd walk me home in a roundabout way so we could hit some neighbors' backyards to pool hop, kiss and fool around. Mark always persisted in trying to get me to sleep with him and I started to wonder why he even bothered. I made it quite clear that it wasn't ever going to be an option. Now that I think of it, that's probably why he tried so hard.

It was the night before I had to return to Rye, to pack and get ready to leave for Dartmouth. I was one of the first from our group to leave for school because I had to arrive early for field hockey tryouts. Mark and I left Daphne's earlier than everyone, even though the party was given in honor of my departure. We made our way up to the French Shack and went about our fooling around on the pool cushion and tartan throw padding the splintery floor. Mark asked to sleep with me again and this time I just went along with it. The entire ride up to school I replayed that night.

I spent the summer after my freshman year in Nantucket with friends from Dartmouth. The following summer I returned to Bridgehampton. The French Shack was demolished since Mom thought I had outgrown it. That same summer I reconnected with Mark. He told me that he loved me, always had, and he even had the confidence to profess that I was the one he'd marry. I wasn't all that interested because I was on a break with the lead-scorer lacrosse captain—the Dartmouth equivalent of dating a rock star. But, come to think of it, in my dysfunctional way, I might have been a bit wigged on the forwardness of Mark's proposed marriage plans.

Mark and I met up once again after graduation, in the city this time, and he just wasn't the Mark Pierce whom I had been in love with for most of my life. The last I heard of him he had married some girl he met from work and moved back to Rye.

I closed the book but not the memories. It was already 3:15 P.M. Barely enough time to survey the Saks makeup counter for a last-minute face check, as I also intended to walk to the FOX offices.

It was chillier outside than before. I took my scarf from my gym bag and wrapped it around my neck a few times, tying it in the front in a loose knot. I was wearing a heather blue duster coat, denim pencil skirt, and Dior denim stiletto boots. Well, the heel wasn't quite stiletto, but for my purposes they were as stiletto as I would ever get. The point is that I looked good. And who was Henry to pull this we-need-to-talk BS on me. I had sex with Mark Pierce in my tree house. I had a life before Henry Philips, and there most certainly would be a life after Henry Philips. I kept walking but I wasn't able to smile. Maybe I was suffering from that lack-of-light syndrome.

Making my quick, mandatory detour to the Saks shoe department, I was immediately drawn to a pair of Chanel shearling boots. They were the only shoes in the room, the way a cute boy stands out in a crowd of sad, dweeby-looking things at a party. Certainly those boots would make up for any lack-of-light syndrome relapses in the ensuing winter months. Etched in blue ink on a Saks sticker, the price was $3,800. Yes, there was indeed another 0 after the 380. Okay. I twirled those tootsies around quicker than a bad picture of myself in a roll of Mother's Christmas pictures. Guess those boots couldn't be justified as a health expense.

At the FOX offices a woman who looked as if she were on Anna Wintour's waiting list before getting the call to become one of her many assistants greeted me at reception.

I asked for Henry and she handed me the phone while dialing his extension, as if she had been instructed to do this. She shot me an annoyed look, agitated that I was tying up her phone.

"Hello?" I said cautiously into the receiver.

"Hey, Em. I'll be out in a second. Laveda and I are finishing something up."

"Okay," I answered. "No rush." I returned the phone to the receptionist, who gave me a snide little smile.

What gave? And who was Laveda? Was that a name or a hair product? Her real name was probably Linda but she had changed it to Laveda and dropped her last name.

"This is Laveda Hayes," Henry said, suddenly appearing from behind the glass divider, along with the girl in question.

"Hey, there," she said, waving to me.

Laveda Hayes had a nose ring, no bra and a tiny tee that had a McDonald's M but said "marijuana" beneath, and "over 2 billion stoned." She looked like she lived on a diet of trail mix but traded it in for tekka rolls once she moved to New York. Her jet fuel silky black hair was pulled up into two Minnie Mouse ear buns and it appeared that she took makeup tips from *National Geographic*—the smudged black eyeliner inspired by the current cover of a panda bear. As she reached for her coat partially exposing her underarm, I could see that it had been a week since she'd last shaved. In Europe that's just plain gross. In America it was absolutely unsanitary. What, you think you're so cool and into such important things that you don't have time to shave your underarms? Well, in my opinion, you're just dirty. Take a shower. And isn't there some sort of company policy about dressing in such inappropriate office attire? I know you work in television, but really.

Laveda's face was not yet plagued with a wrinkle, a telltale sign that she spent her summers working in a video store. With the way she dragged her "a" and that cool-climate complexion, she probably grew up in *Fargo* country.

She extended her hand. I doubted she was telepathic so I looked at her warmly and returned her shake.

"Heard a lot about you," said Laveda, revealing another earring on her tongue. E-A-R ring. Do these people understand the meaning of this type of jewelry? Does Cartier or Harry Winston have a tongue ring line? And how does she blow her nose or taste food? Who would want to make out with a girl with a tongue ring? And why has she heard a lot about me when I've heard nothing, *nothing* about her? More secrets.

"What a lovely tongue ring," I said as sincerely as possible. "I've always wondered, does that get in the way of . . ." I hesitated.

"Kissing," she assisted. Maybe she *was* telepathic. Henry began to laugh but I disregarded him, as he was currently out of my favor and I remained focused on Laveda.

"Well, that too," I said, "but even simpler things, like eating sushi."

"No. I guess it's similar to braces, but I've never had those."

"Yes, you do have beautiful teeth."

"O-*kay* then. Anyway, I better bolt. Nice meeting you, Emily," she said sweetly, in that Fargo-esque voice. Yes, she must have been from Minnesota.

"Nice meeting you, as well."

Laveda scooted to the elevator banks, caught me staring at her and waved. I waved back just as she entered the open elevator. Then I glared at the reason why I was there. Henry was looking at me in that naughty way, like we were about to have kinky sex, but I knew that was not the reason.

"What?" I huffed.

"You were judging again."

"And who are you to judge that I was judging." I paused, crossing my eyebrows for effect before continuing. "And, if you must know, I've always been intrigued about body piercing. How it affects the senses."

"Yeah, right. Anyhow, we should go. Maybe get an early dinner somewhere. There're a few good sushi places on West Fifty-fifth."

"Come to think of it, I haven't really eaten yet. Sure, I'd be up for sushi." I said this despite having no appetite.

We walked in silence to the restaurant. Typically I am the one to instigate the random chitchat but with the suffocation of this impending talk separating us, my cocktail party ability to muster inane conversation eluded me now. Checking out Henry to see what may be going on in his head, I noticed an expression that was new to me—he had a pensiveness laced with melancholy.

At the restaurant we were immediately seated, probably because we were the only patrons. We were given menus as soon as we were seated, but I intended to order my usual and assumed that Henry would do the same. After the waiter took our usual list of rolls and edamame, I folded my arms and gave Henry a harsh stare.

"So. What gives?"

"All right, Emily, I have some weird news and I'll just get right to it. Remember that woman I mentioned to you, the reason I left California?"

Oh, God, it was coming. Just stay in control, Emily. So I nodded, unsure if my voice was working.

"Well, she kind of sprung some news on me. Apparently she feels that issues between us are unresolved."

"She?" Come on, Henry, who did you take me for?

"Em, I never had closure on this one."

Oh, God. He wasn't pulling the guy freak-out crap.

"Oh, God, you're not pulling the guy freak-out crap!"

"A lot's happened to Tina since I left. She had this life-altering trip to Tibet. Really shook her from her coddled world. She's even taken up her photography again. She is pretty talented, when she applies herself."

Was Henry speaking to me about Tina as if I were some friend and he wanted coaching on the love of his life? What, I was supposed to be impressed by some gimmicky trip promoted from a recent *People* magazine cover story on stars and their holiday destinations? Where it takes a few orange-robed bald men with sweet smiles to break a psychopath from her psychotic world? Sorry, wasn't buying it.

"And she recently made a trip to Yosemite. Climbed El Capitan!"

"Great. I am so happy for her." After saying this, I realized I sounded a bit sarcastic.

"Emily, this whole New York intensity thing has been a bit . . ." he trailed off. "A bit intense. My timing. *Our* timing is off."

I wanted to throw a drink in his face—real melodramatic Aaron Spelling *Dynasty* style, back when television had substance. But my arms must remain intact otherwise they would knock off the little Daphne angel perched on one shoulder and the Mom angel on the other. Both were telling me to remain calm, to show Henry how strong and confident I was—that I was the catch here.

My hands flew in the air wildly without throwing my brain completely off guard, drenching those angels with the shock of champagne thrown into their sweet little faces.

"Our timing off! If that's not a load of Tibetan lama crap. And Taoism is the McDonald's of spirituality."

I was now sitting silently in this Japanese restaurant that I would never be able to eat at again because it was now the *Henry and Emily talk place.* Staring at this boy whom I was mad about, I started to realize that I couldn't move, not even to blink my eyes. I supposed my body was still operating, with healthy working cells and organs, but I wasn't certain of it. I felt swelled, numb. Please don't let there be a fire or terrorist attack because I wouldn't be able to run.

"Emily. Are you all right?" Henry looked terribly worried.

"Let's see." I paused. What were the right words? "What would you do if a pink flamingo with a black leather biker's hat came over to you, took a seat, and asked what your position was on eugenics?"

"I don't know. I guess I'd be pretty shocked."

"Not as shocked as I am!" My throat began to get scratchy, in need of echinacea. I was raising my voice quite a bit and hoped that I wasn't coming down with something. Being sick and dumped would be too much to handle. Dumped—such a horrible, pathetic word—currently applied to me. This was not at all good.

"Listen, Em, try to see it from my perspective. Suddenly I fall completely for someone and, just as I was ready to forfeit everything to the throes of happiness, the reason why I left my old life comes knocking. If I don't deal with this now, it will always haunt me, it will always be there—between us. This is the right thing for me to do. I am not like you, Emily. I need to face my realities, deal with my emotions."

"That's purely asinine! What a cheap tactic. You've gone Kraft Mac and Cheese low here—you've gone tabloids-wouldn't-even-sniff-it low. Press-on-nails-and-thongs-in-Jacuzzis low."

I stopped, tried to catch my breath. I couldn't think of any more lows and my voice was really going. I wished I could have controlled my damn breathing. Why the hell didn't I take that yoga class more seriously? Just as I was about to continue, Henry started in again.

"I just need some time," he said, real smooth this time. So straightforward—it was a little scary, in fact.

Henry twirled his head about the room as if I had been his mistress and he was worried that his wife was about to enter. I then saw the Henry that I knew.

"I went through the kind of hurt that I wouldn't wish upon my worst enemy. I never told you the full story."

I stared at him, waiting for the full story.

"I'm listening."

"Tina became pregnant even though she was on the pill. She then miscarried."

Wow, that was a bit heavy. Kind of glad she miscarried. Oh, God, I would be struck down for certain for having such evil thoughts. Please, forgive me, supreme Almighty who never sold out for a Pepsi commercial.

"I really can't believe that I am about to confess this but . . ."

There was more? How could there be more after that Lifetime Movie of the Week?

"It's okay," I soothed.

"I was so relieved that she miscarried. How horrible is that?"

Pretty horrible. Praise you, Lord.

"And after the miscarriage things got pretty out of hand. When we'd go out she would blatantly flirt with guys. She was picking up bartenders and bringing them home. For the life of me I couldn't get what she was trying to accomplish here. I started getting violent, not with her, of course, with myself, the wall. I punched a few walls.

"She then turned to alcohol and I started fooling around. That's what she wanted me to do."

A little too much information here.

"She was always going out, getting drunk, and I was picking up everyone and their mother."

This was pretty ugly.

"This is pretty ugly," I let slip. But I don't believe Henry was even listening to me. He was going through these hypnotic motions.

"I went through women the way Tina went through tequila—quickly and it wasn't always pretty."

Okay, okay—got the picture Raymond Chandler.

"Okay, okay. Got it—you did the womanizing thing to get back at her. Tina victimized herself to get back at you. And as a result of both of your messed up actions, you hurt each other and your-selves. But what does this have to do with us?"

Completely disregarding the us part, Henry continued, still in a trance. "She made it clear that one of us had to leave San Francisco and that was, as you know, me."

"And this was a bad thing?"

"Emily, you can't just leave all of that behind in another city. That kind of emotional stuff stays with you. Haunts you. A flight across the country and you're not over it."

Finally his eyes searched mine. I nodded my head to show that I understood.

"So what do you intend to do now?" Real sweet and composed, as I believed Henry was attempting to be intimate here.

"First, I will be going to San Francisco. I have a nine A.M. flight tomorrow. Then and there will I figure things out. Take things as they happen."

"So. Us?" Again, bringing up the issue of him and me. "Are we . . ." I couldn't bring myself to say it. Luckily Henry relieved me of the task.

"I just need this time and space to sort through things."

"Yes, you've made that fairly clear."

"I've also made arrangements with FOX to work in LA for this pilot. I want you to know that I have never met anyone like you." I gulped so hard and loud you could have seen the bulb of saliva shoot down my throat like a turkey swallowing a golf ball.

Henry continued while I stroked my neck, mildly concerned by my current condition.

"When I thought I was incapable of love, I found myself easily falling for you. I laugh at not-made-to-be-laughed-at commercials. I fill once-vacant thoughts with images of you. I finally get why man and woman come together. But this is not the time to preoccupy myself with such frivolities. Two days ago I was the happiest I've ever been. Yesterday that all changed. My sordid past fuddled my bright future."

I was back to my numbed state. This was a premeditated breakup speech.

"Emily, are you all right?" Henry had that worried look on again. I must have looked like Dominic Dunne at the OJ verdict.

"How and where should I begin? Or is there even a point, considering that you had this all figured out and that I am some distraction? And, goddamn it, I thought I was finally going to have a boyfriend during the winter months. Looks like another cold season where I get really psyched for the Lifetime Movie of the Week."

"I want you to be able to talk to me."

"And I would've liked the same from you, Henry. It's called a relationship. You're not being truthful with me right now. Are you even being straight with me?"

"What do you mean?"

"How can I know what to believe? Two days ago I was talking to some Tina chick who brings up your travel plans, which appear to have been made well before you claimed to know all of this. There are a lot of curious things that I can't make sense of."

"I was always going to go to California for the holidays. My family is from Carmel. Tina didn't want to spring this all on me when I showed up. She thought it would distract me. Ruin my Christmas."

"How considerate of her."

"That didn't come out right. You have to realize that there's more ethics here than justifying taking someone's laundry out of the machine."

Bad analogy. I send my laundry out.

"If I don't deal with this now who knows if I will ever deal with it."

I looked at the table for the first time in what seemed like hours. The food was on the table. I didn't remember the waiter serving our meal. I didn't even remember ordering. I had such an emptiness in my stomach, but the thought of holding down a piece of raw fish seemed too difficult. I felt like I had been crying for hours, rendering it impossible to swallow.

Henry took what appeared to be the last bite of his toro roll. Great, the boy still had an appetite. Eat food? I can't eat food. How is it that he can eat food—this was completely unfair.

What would he say if I asked him for a bite? Was he one of those people who would say, Sorry, it's my last bite? So what if it's your last bite, I still want it. Does that make me the selfish one? Was he the selfish one? Or were we both being selfish?

I got up from my seat weakly, balancing my hand on the edge of the table. I kneeled down to Henry's side with no available chair to sit on.

"I love you," I said, intently looking into his eyes. Never would

I have imagined that my first time saying this to him would be under such circumstances. "And now I will let you go." My heart felt scorched and then exposed to a pounding hail storm. Returning to my things, I gathered them as controlled and as quickly as possible.

"Wait!" he wailed. "Remember Cat Woman—real naughty but oh so hot. I always thought she was just going through a confused period; that eventually she'd come around. She really was a pussycat beneath it all. And Batman was real into her. If Bob Kane continued the series—"

"Bob Kane?" I asked. Who the hell was Bob Kane?

"The creator of our beloved Caped Crusader."

Like I should have known that.

"So if Kane went further with Cat Woman—and all of us young boys so wanted it that way—she would have had some epiphany and then they would have been together."

He took a moment, dreamily. "Cat Woman was so layered—by far the most provocative of any Batman character. I always thought you kind of looked like her."

Was this some kind of joke? Some bizarre sexual fantasy? I really wasn't up for one of our little games right now. Was he saying that I was like Cat Woman? I supposed that would be kind of cool.

"What are you saying here? Because this may come as a surprise, but I am kind of not in the mood to analyze some campy strip so that I can understand your feelings on our relationship."

Then I tossed my final pitch. "By the way, I snooped in your bedside drawer and, in hindsight, I don't feel all that bad about it."

I left the table, intentionally not looking at Henry. Outside the restaurant, I intentionally did not look back.

It was dark—the air moist and windy, threatening rain. I didn't have an umbrella and felt it unfair to mistreat expensive Dior boots, and the idea of going underground to catch a subway was too depressing. I sprinted up the street to catch a cab that had pulled over to let a couple out. I slid in and the taxi began to drive away. The driver then looked back, startled by my presence, apparently unaware that I had slipped in.

"Where to, miss?"

"Gramercy Park, please."

I propped my arm alongside the sill, placing my chin on top and gazed out the window. The streets were glistening. It must have just rained. The evening glow from the lit buildings gave the streets a pinkish reflection that sometimes refracted into purple, like a hologram. The ride was particularly smooth, luckily my driver didn't do the jerk and accelerate thing, competing with the other cars as if they were racing for points in a video game. And there was no cheap disinfectant spray and no nauseating smells emanating from a cardboard pine tree. It was a clean smell. The window across from me must have been left open by another passenger, allowing for cool, dewy air to create a cross-ventilation effect. WQXR was on the radio—no 1010 news with that annoying ticker sound that always induced my cab sickness. I believe Brahms was playing. Normally I found Brahms dull but right then it lulled me into a spacey trance, like I had awakened from a massage. I didn't want to think, just wanted to escape. If I knew how to meditate I would have been meditating. But since I didn't know how, and had never watched Buddhists meditating in the park long enough to understand the method—that would be rude, sort of like staring at nuns—I looked for other diversions.

On the floor of the cab I noticed a copy of the *New York Standard*. I picked it up and turned to "Cock Around the Clock." There was an image of bloody white feathers on a sidewalk with the headline reading, "Doesn't Look Good, Callie the Cock Feared Dead."

20

It was over two months since I'd spoken to Henry Philips. It was over two months since I'd spoken to anyone. There were a lot of concerned messages from friends—I had intentionally kept this from everyone—more diva dramatic this way. Conveniently it was the winter months, which, to my favor, was a more suitable time to hibernate and wear Carter's cut cotton underwear. I felt okay, just those understandable meltdowns like crying after mistakenly buying my vitamins without iron, claiming single on my tax return.

I wasn't keeping especially busy, wasn't adding more assignments as I typically did, but rather maintained my current projects and the cartoon with *Vogue* (which, by the way, turned out to be a dramatic success and even received more hits on their Web site than their gossip column). There was also a lot of press surrounding the character Lily. Was she my alter ego? "Page Six" speculated. Joanna was trying to persuade me to get a PR agent but that really wasn't my thing. And it was especially not my thing at that time. All I had to show for those past two months were five extra pounds and a few extra inches of hair. So it probably wasn't wise to accept that lunch date with my mother for the coming Thursday, as she would have a lot to complain about. And I should really have stopped all the whining—so Long Island housewife. Which didn't seem such a bad option, considering.

Walking to my studio, I passed a telephone booth covered in

handmade flyers, typical announcements—photographer head-shots, dog walkers, apartment rentals. But as I was not an actor, didn't have a dog and would never leave my apartment, only one announcement compelled me enough to stop: a grad school student offering $20 therapy sessions for the experience. I had never considered therapy, a little too *Ordinary People*—the book turned movie with Timothy Hutton—not that I was above ordinary people. In the past the idea of talking to some stranger about my random problems had seemed so self-absorbed. And I would have rather used the time to watch bad television. I looked around to make sure that no one I knew saw me, and then tore off one of the phone numbers at the flyer's edge.

I sprinted up the last flight of stairs to my studio, prompted by my phone's ringing. Right as I was about to reach for the receiver, a fumbled click echoed from the machine—typical. That was so rude. If the caller had left a message, it would have given me added time to pick up the phone. But, who was I kidding, I would have screened the call.

Thyme Garner, the tenant from across the hall, creaked open her door, probably to determine the source of my disruptive entrance. To be caught in a conversation with Thyme right now would be quite a setback and I could only hear so many stories about her days as a Studio 54 fixture and her former marriage to a fashion photographer who announced that he was gay back when being HIV-positive was in vogue.

It was really quite sad, actually, to have had four explosive years and only to be remembered by an *E! True Hollywood Story* or sought out by a magazine editor looking for a quote about the return of all things discotheque.

Thyme now cashed in on the only currency that a past life had—writing her memoirs and working with one of her "endless" contacts on trying to get her story on Broadway. She had a remarkable talent of sliding extremely powerful names into mundane conversations. I would never admit to knowing any of these names and would be brought up to speed later by a Xeroxed newspaper clip slid beneath my door.

My door was wide open and we shared glances.

"Emily! I haven't seen you in ages," exploded Thyme.

There may have been a reason for that.

"Come over for a second, I want to give you something."

Unable to come up with an excuse fast enough, I found myself walking into her studio. She touched my arm, her hands skeletal, a flimsy piece of skin sealing her bones like cellophane. Her peck to my cheek revealed a whiff of whiskey on her breath. There was something alarming about the smell of whiskey on one's breath in the late morning.

Her studio was considerably smaller than mine. The walls were painted in the same shades of purple and magenta as the folding chairs at Madison Square Garden. Pictures of rainbows, unicorns and other psychedelic motifs adorned her walls, making them look like the sides of long-ago vans. Coating the disassembled wooden floorboards was a shag carpet that looked like it was once white and had been painted with a purple magic marker to camouflage red wine stains. A sad-looking cactus sat in the window. It was really more of a foamy piece of vegetation propped up in soil and should have been thrown out. This room was either a product of extremely bad taste or it all came together under hallucinogenics.

"I saved this for you," said Thyme, holding out a pack of Fruit Striped Gum. Suddenly I was touched by her gesture. That she actually recalled a conversation we had when I shared my childhood addiction to Fruit Striped Gum and was so disappointed at never being able to find it.

"That is so sweet!" I opened the package, unwrapping a piece and popping the velvety stick into my mouth. The artificial burst of orange was momentary but effective. I extended the pack to Thyme. She pulled out a grape stick and inserted it into her pants pocket. Probably to be saved in one of her thousands of boxes of mementos.

"I found it at that candy shop, the one near Dean & Deluca. Do you shop there?"

"Sometimes. They have great premade dinners and champagne grapes. Love those. But I tend to find the divorced dads a bit distracting. I always seem to be getting hit on."

"Oh," she said, as if this were the most disturbing thing she'd ever heard. "I could see how that would be disruptive."

"Thank you, Thyme, for the gum and everything. Well, I'd better be going—a few deadlines to deliver."

She waved me off and I was finally able to unload my bag of folders. I had to sit down for a moment because I had a sudden head rush from the exposure to cleaner air and the change in temperature.

The studio was rather hot, felt like getting into a car after it had been soaking up rays for a few hours in a beach parking lot. It was nice to be here—this special place that I came to so I could create my special worlds, I thought to myself, as I extended my legs in a stretching position till I heard a muscle crack.

Just think if I was Lost in Thyme, living in New Canaan, with a husband whose idea of ending a good week would be to say, "Honey, I'm taking you to the Olive Garden!" The buzzer interrupted my "What If" exercise. I didn't remember ordering anything and I hadn't expected anyone in over two months.

"Hello?"

"Hey, Emily. It's me with little Emily. Let us up."

I buzzed Daphne in. How strange it was for her to be here. I basically sent out a mass E-mail explaining to everyone that I was traveling a lot and under extraordinary deadline pressure, which is why I'd be out of commission for a while.

But here was Daphne, apparently disobeying my request. How amazing of her! I suddenly felt exhilarated by the thought of conversing with someone aside from loony neighbors.

Daphne showed up looking as radiant as ever, which made me feel as unkempt as ever. Little Emily peeked from behind her mom's legs. She was wearing a pumpkin costume.

"Well, hello, you two! And Emily, I'm sorry but I really don't know if I have any Halloween candy leftovers. What's up with the pumpkin outfit?" I asked Daphne.

"It's been a little crazed at the Trefry house. And to further compound things, I'm in between housekeepers. So I had to do my first laundry in months this afternoon and this is the only clean outfit I had for Emily. I thought we'd be okay just staying at home, but I forgot this is our special day."

"What special day?"

Daphne leaned in closer to me. "Emily," she said, intended for her daughter, "please sit down for a minute and take out one of your coloring books. Mommy needs to talk to Aunt Emily for a second." Little Emily's face scrunched into confusion; it appeared that she was about to make a fuss. I knew that face. I had it on for most of my childhood.

I walked over to my desk and chose a few colored pencils and some sheets of vellum paper. Emily scrambled onto the chair, which was much too big for her.

"Emily, do you know what would really please me? If you could draw me a pumpkin. Do you think you could do that for me?"

This adorable creature looked at me with Little Lucy Loo Hoo eyes and perked her nose like a bunny wiggling its whiskers.

"Does it have to be a Halloween pumpkin?" she asked with the utmost professionalism.

"That's a good point. I'd actually prefer a magic pumpkin, like the one from Cinderella. Why don't you take your magic wands and make some magic."

Her eyes lit up like sparklers. She sat down and suddenly became quite excitable, looking out the window.

"Police!" she wailed, completely freaking me out. Was I about to be put under arrest? I started to wonder if there were any drug associations catching up with me from my Dartmouth days. No, that was completely absurd.

"What is it?" I asked.

"Sorry," Daphne said. "Emily started this new game during the cab ride over, Spot the Police Officer, which basically entails her shouting 'police' every time she sees an officer. Which is about every two seconds."

"What fun," I said sarcastically. I motioned Daphne over to the couch, where she fell down comfortably.

"Do you want anything?"

"I'd love some tea. Do you have chamomile?" She looked up to me as if I'd just offered her a year's service of free baby-sitting.

"Of course," I said, walking toward the kitchen. "And does Emily want anything?"

"Besides a porch swing, this sparkly dress at Calypso and to be an only child again?"

"Well, I was thinking more in the fruit juice/graham cracker kind of way."

"Yes, she'd love whatever fruit juice you have."

As I boiled some water and poured a glass of orange juice for

Emily, Daphne looked around the room. "Emily, it's wonderful. I can see why you don't ever want to leave your work. So modern, yet cozy. Very Victoria Hagan."

"Thanks, Daph. That means a lot coming from you." Placing Emily's juice on her desk I peered over her shoulder to evaluate the progress of her drawing. A wobbly circle, in more of an egg-plant shape really and a lot of sporadic lines that looked like witch's hair. Apparently Emily didn't have the drawing gene.

"Wow!" I feigned. "How pretty."

"Thank you," she replied as if she knew her work was utterly brilliant.

Now I could focus on Daphne, who was in daze mode.

"What is it Daphne, is everything okay?"

"Yes. No. Not at all. Everything has changed since Henry was born. Emily can't stand her brother—hence we have her special day. Andy is never around, which doesn't help things. The house is a disaster zone—I'm remodeling the kitchen."

"You redo your home the way I redo my hair."

"No!" she cried. "This is the last time. We're living in a dust bowl; we're sniffling constantly like ladies in distress. I've truly lost it. Maybe I am just experiencing that postpartum thing?"

"Emily, you are Madonna mother cool."

"Madonna Madonna or Madonna the mother of Jesus?"

"Well, considering how I haven't been to church in like a thousand years—Madonna Madonna. I don't think I could ever do it."

"Please, you will be the ultimate mom. You're the only one of my friends who can relate to Emily."

"That's just the problem. I am more on their level than a grown-up one. If I get one of those questions like why does the ocean smell funny, I continually question my intelligence be-cause I never know the correct answer."

"Thanks, Emily," she said, and began to cry. What had I said?

"Daphne, goodness, what did I say?" She looked up at me. Her mascara had created little dots on her upper and lower eyelids that made her look like a Raggedy Ann doll, which happened to be very in at that moment according to the spring fashion shows.

"I miss you!" she bawled. We then gave each other a warm

hug. I started to feel like one of those mean high school girls who dumped her old friend for the more popular girls and then proceeded to make her cry.

"Oh, my," I said, breaking from our hug. "I feel like the mean high school girl who just manipulated her friend into crying. What have I done?"

Daphne collected herself. "Is it my avoiding the subject of Henry? Are you upset about that?" she asked.

"Yes!" I roared. Daphne looked like she had just been told that she had to move to Darien. I suddenly realized it was little Henry that she was referring to.

"I mean, hell no, not your Henry—it's my Henry. That's why I've been out of the loop."

Daphne took a sip of her tea to clear her throat, speaking more clearly. "Now I feel like the bad friend. I never really kept up with you on your new relationship with Henry. Henry? What's his last name? God, I really suck, I don't even know his last name."

"I am so guilty as well, Daph. I guess I was a little sidled by your being a mom again, wondering if I really had a place in your new life. I sort of felt like . . ." I trailed off. "Like dark stockings on tan legs. There's really no need for them and they look and feel absolutely ridiculous."

"Well, then you are ridiculous!"

When had I regressed so much? In one month I went from nun to nymph. Then I lost my best friend. Then I gained a boyfriend. Then I lost the boyfriend. Then I lost all my best friends. This was not me, this was the character I put to paper. I really should have taken my mother's advice and moved to Park Avenue.

"Can I begin the insecure rant now?" Daphne asked, breaking into my mental ramble.

"Of course."

"I was a little jealous of you. Or, to be specific, your budding friendship with Katrina."

"Okay, now *you're* being ridiculous."

"But you really seem to be taken by her."

"Honestly, at first I was surprised by her. She is so not the Page Six we pegged her to be. You remember the joke about how a princess would never hear 'Attention all Kmart shoppers'? Then after going to the Kmart in Bridgehampton you learn how great it is."

"So Katrina is the Kmart here?"

"Sort of. It's that she made such an effort with me. It was like the most popular girl suddenly accepted the outcast art chick into her circle. While I always found it easier to categorize and hate her, because that's easier than saying, 'It's because I am not cool enough to be a part of her world.' I got to know her. And she's simply a sweet girl with different interests."

"Perhaps I misjudged her as well," Daphne said.

"But the real truth is that we are still very different. I mean Katrina is the kind of girl who sees each day as an opportunity to wear a melon colored scarf and she really does indulge in votive-lit bubble baths. Whereas I like the idea of taking baths in theory, but get bored and make mental lists in my head of what I should really be doing with the time once my fingers begin to prune."

"How do you know she takes votive-lit baths?"

"Well, I'm not entirely certain, but when I was in her bathroom I did notice that she stocked bath products and scented candles the way I keep Windex."

"What were you doing in her bathroom?"

"Snooping."

"Oh, right," she said, as if this were totally normal. "So, it seems that you two are friends now?"

"I have no friends now!"

This made Daphne's riddled face perk into a smile. Aside from the smudgy eye makeup, you'd never be able to tell that she had been crying just moments ago. Her cheeks had a natural rosy blush, while Chanel sunglasses held back her streaked hair, courtesy of Oscar. I could never have pulled off this look, as the glasses would have kept falling on my face.

"Well, maybe Katrina sees you as the cool, edgy artist type who is far too interested in other things than to make appearances at all the right parties and who is pursued by all the right boys—all because she happened to be the first girl to wear Gloria Vanderbilt jeans at Snowy Coleman's roller-skating party."

"Oh, my, remember those? But it was Misty Coleman's party

when we went to see *Annie!* Though you've got the Gloria Vander-bilt jeans right." I felt quite proud of my early style sensibility.

"Okay, right! And bad example, you were always a bit of a trendsetter but never a follower. Too secure, never one to com-promise yourself and act a certain way just to be a crowd pleaser. Get where I am going?"

I did, actually. During this self-isolation period, I'd thought a lot of things over. But it was as if I'd created a sketch in my head and had yet to commit it to paper. Actually communicating my feelings gave these sketches life.

How simple it seemed in the animal kingdom, where a koala bear is a koala and a panda bear is just a panda. You don't see the koala trying to hike up to China, nor does the panda have any desire to venture Down Under. They simply know who they are and leave it at that.

I couldn't believe I had now regressed into that judgmental seventeen-year-old who I never really had been. It was all so much easier for me then. Life had become a bit jumbled during the post-college, pre-married period. It was unfamiliar. Some girls went for the big wedding, but since that never interested me, I did the urban single thing. But the social stratosphere for this lifestyle didn't suit me either. So, I created this animated world—a few good characters and some funny dialogue. But then all the supporting characters I based this on began to frag-ment and I lost control of my special place. So I further re-treated into an imaginary place, this cartoon world. At least I had control here, ensuring a happy ending.

"I miss 1987!" I blurted.

"You and me both," she huffed

"Those summer days when our biggest dilemma was how to score some beer."

"Bartles and James, more specifically."

Of course, Daph and I hadn't been beer drinkers. Bartles and James wine coolers gave us the perfect pre-party buzz at a parent-free friend's house. I started to drift. 1987.

Turning toward Daphne with both of our feet propped up on the coffee table, it was as if we were two fussy ladies lounging pool-side, mai tais in hand. She was also deeply pensive, her thoughts probably focused on that momentous year that moved to the sounds of Erasure and New Order. When crushes overtook your body, eating and sleeping were rendered useless, and you were handicapped by the thrill of young love.

She met my gaze, as if I had just poked her out of a late afternoon slumber.

"Hey. Let's take a pottery class together."

"What a great idea," I said, sharing her enthusiasm. "So Demi Moore *Ghost*. I believe they offer some classes at The New School."

Though I was a bit of a minimalist and questioned the idea of creating some pottery that would only be used as throwaway gifts to distant relatives, I was intrigued by the idea of working with and shaping clay, branching out into new mediums—very Pablo of me. But clay was dirty. It would get all over my clothes, under my fingernails. I didn't even like the mud baths when I went to the Sonoma Mission Inn. And who even knows if this type of clay had soothing properties for the cuticles?

"Or maybe we can just meet weekly at a spa?" Daphne was truly my telepathic sister.

"Or maybe we can just meet up for margaritas at Rosa Mexicana?"

"You're two thoughts ahead of me! How have we gone so long without each other? It's like I've just had a bagel after zoning for three ridiculous months."

"Did you do the zone thing?" I asked.

"Well, if you don't count mashed potatoes, Carr's crackers and Cinnamon Life as carbs—yes. But I only lasted three days."

"Yeah, what's the point of cutting out Cinnamon Life? Then I wouldn't even like food."

"So? We never tackled the Henry issue. Your Henry. Is there anything you want to share?" As she said this I shifted closer into her so I could prop my head on her shoulder.

"It's all a bit complicated. He left me two months ago. Went back to San Francisco because he had some issues to take care of. The issue being a girl. A blonde girl. A goddamn Claudia goddamn Schiffer."

"Wait a minute. This is a bit of a stab in the dark, but what's Henry's last name again?"

"Philips."

"Holy hell. Henry Philips the cartoonist! I am so daft. Can't believe I never made the connection."

"Why, do you know him?"

"Yes, well, sort of. Indirectly. Who knows if he remembers me. When Andy was living in San Francisco, before he dated me, he was involved with this Tina something or other."

"Somers!"

"Yes, you know her?"

"No. Continue," I coaxed.

"Good, because she's a real psycho, that one." I loved Daphne. "And, no, I'm not just saying this because she's sort of attractive." She looked at me as if she were trying to get out of a speeding ticket.

"Sort of attractive?"

"She's a Dairy Queen. You know—has that whole Victoria's Secret trashy look, grew up in a middle American town with a lot of girls named Tammy, having sex with the boys behind the bleachers kind of thing. But it's really like sucking on a piece of granny candy. Looks all sweet and seductive on the outside, and then you chomp into it and some disgusting licorice flavor oozes out. Anyway, she pulled the whole missed-her-period and then went Winona Ryder, *Girl Interrupted*—real life, not the movie—psycho on Andy. Then Andy found a tampon wrapper in her trashcan and she went Winona Ryder, shopping-in-the-parking-lot-at-Saks psycho. Which was basically the best thing that ever happened to Andy because she then banished him to New York and into a stable girl's arms."

I believed I looked Winona-Ryder-being-arrested-and-caught-on-film shocked.

"Emily, are you okay? Those are *my* arms he fell into. This is all a good thing."

"No. I know. Sorry, but suddenly a lot of things are starting to make sense. First, did Andy and Henry know one another?"

"They met. We all met. As a matter of fact, we all had this psycho brunch together right after Andy proposed to me."

"I vaguely remember that. Going over what you'd wear for the big meeting with the ex that turned out to be a non-event."

"Exactly, the big meeting that turned out to be a non-event."

Daphne began to fill me in on the pertinent details, as they were now relevant.

"Tina and Henry had to come to New York for some work thing of his. And she became insistent with Andy that we all meet. I suppose to showcase Henry to Andy but, as you probably realize, how could that really work when Andy had me to flaunt—with my four-carat rock, may I add," Daphne then gazed at her ring, mesmerized. It was pretty spectacular.

She held her hand into the air so we could both bask in a glow only produced by four carats. "Naturally I found ways for my rocked finger to be easily noticed—you know, those girls who get the ring and then forget about the guy who gave it to her—I became that girl during that moment!" Daphne brought her hand back down to street level, plucking her diamond with a cunning smile.

"Understandably. So, what was she like?"

"After getting all worked up, I wasn't really impressed with her."

I loved Daphne.

"The hair was what first threw me off—this Krystle Carrington haircut that she probably had styled especially for her big trip to New York."

We both laughed. Mine was more guarded, since I was fraught with nerves, wondering if this was Daphne's way of avoiding the big issue—that Tina was a raving beauty.

"And? So did you think she was pretty?"

"She's pretty, in that common way, but had no sense of style. I think she was even wearing a shift dress. *To a brunch.* She's the kind of girl who has no problem wearing synthetic fibers and shopping at Ann Taylor. And I remember that she kept saying how cold she was. I mean it was the middle of a New York City heat wave. We were dining outside at one of those Madison Avenue bistros and she had a cardigan on, for God's sake. What's that all about?"

Daphne was on a roll, as if she had just remembered the events of a really great party after thinking she'd had a blackout. "Want to know what was really weird?"

I nodded spastically.

"Andy further infuriated my pre-jealous rage by mentioning

that Tina was this hot-shot architect. So while the boys were involved in some guy talk about Nagashami stereo systems, I had
her to myself for the Daphne crisp-to-the-middle grill. When I
asked her what she did for a living she blurted that she was a receptionist. And I was like, '*Receptionist*'? Her face paled in ghostly
horror, and she tried to conceal her blunder by saying that she
worked at a well-respected architecture firm, just a stepping-
stone, blah, blah, blah. But it was out there. The girl was a goddamn receptionist."

I felt like I had just found a ring next to the soap dish after
spending hours looking for it on the floor. Not that I'd ever mis-
placed a ring before.

"So, let me get this right. It's her job to answer the phone, put
the caller on hold and then transfer the call."

"Yes. I do believe those are the skills required of a receptionist."

We both shared an evil smile. This was too easy.

"And what was the dynamic between Tina and Henry?" I was a
little embarrassed in returning to my insecure questioning, even
though it was Daphne.

"It was all so uncomfortable. I was even being as nice as I
could because she just looked so damn frigid and miserable. She
kept giving that take-me-out-of-here stare to Henry. I bet he was
as uncomfortable as I was, and just wanted to get through this
brunch that she had set up."

"And how was Andy after all of this?"

"It actually brought us closer, realizing how lucky he was not
to end up with her. He basically said that coming to New York
was the best thing that he'd done. He was so shell-shocked after
his experience with her."

I smiled a smile that could only be created out of consumptive
bliss. Like getting that call from someone you like, or being told
by your accountant that you'd be receiving a big wad of cash
from the government when you thought you owed. Maybe Henry
would realize what Andy had realized!

Daphne continued, "I'm glad I pursued him as strongly as I
did. I was a bit of a husband hunter back then."

"Shameless."

"Successful. Hey, I knew he was the one. Never had a question in my mind."

I then shared my entire saga with Daphne. She nodded and added little details about her brief tryst to prove my theories correct. This was more than Henry's departure from my life, it pertained to my career choices, friends, lifestyle—it seemed that half my life had been trying to convince myself that everything was okay. And now I really knew that everything would be okay.

Suddenly the plastic guy on the wedding cake and the personalized Christmas cards with my own illustrations of my kids lost their urgency.

"Are you happy?" I asked Daphne.

"With Andy?"

"No, with your laundry service—yes, with Andy."

"Of course. I mean, we're no Carole and Clark, but the marriage works. I always knew it would. Andy is my partner. This is what I wanted. This is what I have—we have."

I looked absently at the toes of my new cashmere olive socks.

"I know you," laughed Daphne. "You want to be Jennifer Hart."

"You remembered!"

Daphne and I used to love watching *Hart to Hart* together. Back then I always assumed that I would become this fabulous beautiful lady married to some stud of a guy and we'd stumble onto all of these sexy crime-solving mysteries. I wonder why they never had kids?

"You know, Daph, that show didn't glamorize parenting. Interesting."

"So you now realize, I hope, that being Jennifer Hart is not an option?" She sounded concerned. Daphne could be a bit conservative in regard to these things.

"Of course," I lied. I still wanted to be Jennifer Hart. "But what else is there? I mean, besides you and Andy, who else has a cool marriage? Do your parents?"

"It's different with my parents. Remember that Poppy is eleven years older than my mother. He's still courting her and she loves it. They have separate bedrooms, for God's sake. He knocks on her door every evening with a bouquet of flowers."

Daphne's parents had always been eccentric. Her mother was Portuguese, very exotic and her father's family had the kind of American lineage that socialites make up to pad their resumes.

"How sweet. It's like Parisian chocolate shops and listening to Ella Fitzgerald."

"What about your parents?"

"What about them?" That didn't sound particularly upbeat.

"I don't know—are they satisfied with their laundry service?"

I knew what she meant, of course, I just didn't like going there.

"I suppose it's like toll collectors. Someday they will be replaced by machines, which will probably be more effective in the long run."

"I don't know about that. I can't ask a machine for directions, and they won't say 'Have a safe trip' as genuinely."

"You have a point. I missed you!"

Daphne hugged me so tightly her cheek brushed against mine. Her skin was so soft I began to resent her for being so vigilant all those summer afternoons when I baked myself with double album covers wrapped in aluminum foil. Daphne had sat in the shade, sunblocked and hatted, nose in a book.

"It would have made for a more stimulating two months if we'd checked in with each other earlier," I pointed out.

We stretched out before getting up from the couch. My body readjusted itself to the land of the ambulatory.

It was now dark outside and the room's only light came from the lamp on my desk and the city lights outside the window. Daphne looked at her watch.

"Oh, my, it's almost six. I've been here for almost five hours. *We've* been here for almost five hours." She turned her attention to Emily.

Emily was asleep on my desk, the tiny lamp spotlighting her storybook slumber. I had been at that very place many times. But there was one considerable difference—this was a child's sleep, her mind was being lulled by enchanting images and thoughts of promise.

Daphne gently tapped Emily's shoulder and instinctively enveloped her child in her arms, the way batter oozed into a pan.

She took her things quietly. The added movement awakened

Emily, but only enough for her to shoot me a lethargic smile. Mother and daughter quickly exited the studio.

It was so peaceful watching them walk down the stairs. Even listening to the front door slam was peaceful. I was so moved by their presence I couldn't bring myself to return to my studio.

Footsteps drummed up the stairs. They're returning! I thought. But it was Thyme. Thyme with many Dean & Deluca bags.

"Oh, hi," she said, apparently startled by my presence.

As she put down the bags to unlock the door, her white leopard fur flew open, revealing the kind of sexy halter-top that Bianca Jagger sported back in her Studio 54 days.

"Just wanted to try out those premade dinners you recommended." She picked up the groceries.

And possibly a few divorced dads?

21

What was it about answering the phone perfunctorily when your mind told you to let the machine get it? What was it about having a mother who chipped away at your self-esteem, like an unattended splinter infecting a finger?

"Oh, Emily," she started in, with that oh-Emily-what-could-I-possibly-have-done-again tone. "You've been a bit out of commission lately."

"Have not," I said. Blatant lie.

To disengage myself from her destructive insights, I perused my kitchen cabinets to determine what would be this evening's dinner. Since it was indeed a crazy Friday night, I decided to treat myself to a bowl, rather a box, of cereal. I chose Cinnamon Life, big surprise there, carefully putting a few fistfuls of cereal into a bowl so as not to reveal any audible activity and then sliced up some bananas.

"Yes, you have. Just spending time in your apartment, at your studio drawing and maybe an occasional foray to the bookstore."

Yup. That was about right. Was there a point to all of this?

"The point is you have to circulate, meet prospective significants. And how is it that I caught you at home on a Friday evening after eight P.M.?"

"I'm actually getting ready right now." Getting ready to splurge on cereal and bad television.

"You are not, dear. I refuse to allow you to dawdle your time at home eating cereal when you should be out circulating."

"What are you possibly talking about?" I asked incredulously, looking at my Life and wishing the one I had with my mother could just fade out like a forgettable character on one of my shows.

"Considering that I have an appointment at that new downtown micro-dermabrasion place that was written up in *Bazaar*, I will swing by tomorrow so we can go out for lunch."

"Are you going to Skin Trip?" I'd read the same article and was reminded that I needed to make an appointment.

"Yes, that's the one."

"Mom. That's all the way in TriBeCa—another city from where I live."

"You know me, anything south of Saks and I might as well book a hotel room."

"But wouldn't it be better if we just caught up later in the week?"

"I will pick you up at noon." If only getting the final word was as simple as winning an argument.

There's a reason to obsess over what to wear on a date. There's a reason to worry about dressing for a black-tie event. But nothing is as difficult as getting ready to meet your mother.

If I went the conservative route, she would say that I should make more of an effort. If I shopped for the occasion and arrived resplendent in the latest style she would say that I was too obsessed with fashion. Why did I even have to contend with this lunch, I wondered, staring at my closet. Nothing materialized magically.

Getting dressed was usually a matter of whimsy for me. First determining the color mood of choice and then reaching for a pair of pajama bottoms and a coordinating cashmere sweater. I now had to wrestle with an armful of clothes and dent my newly made bed with their weight.

Sorting them into little outfits like cutout silhouettes for a paper doll, my eyes fixated on my most prized possession—a pair of Levi's bought in Paris. Purchased over five years ago on a trip I was supposed to take with the boyfriend of the time. But, typical of romantic weekends that bear the burdens of travel abroad (not the burden of updating expired passports but the significance implied by a Paris getaway), we broke it off a week before the trip. I had the ticket he'd bought and my updated passport, so I still went, of course.

Part of my mission that weekend had been to buy a pair of Levi's, as the measurements are different in Europe. They're designed especially to a woman's proportions—lower slung and slightly looser around the hips. I remember finding a French tailor on a street that stemmed off of Avenue Foche. I stayed at a flat that belonged to friends of the family, who probably purchased it for the cachet that comes with saying you own a pied-a-terre off of Avenue Foche, its simple yet expensive décor had the appearance of a hastened decorating trip on the only available weekend that their New York decorator could make the trip.

I remembered how independent I'd felt. Liberated from the confines of a Christmas-card boy while staying in Paris without hotel conveniences. How happy I was to use my high school French to explain how I wanted my jeans tailored (slightly tapered and hemmed). I suppose my ability to communicate doesn't suffer from language barriers when discussing fashion. Even though I could recall the trip as clearly as what I had for breakfast (a teaspoon—half the jar—of Wonder Butter, a kiwi and hazelnut decaf), the pair of Levi's were showing their authentic signs of age, which no couture jeans could replicate. As society continually tries to skew perceptions on growing old, the only things that truly age gracefully are clapboard cottages, the two Hepburns and Levi's blue jeans.

Naturally bleached and broken in from thousands of washes and nights fooling around on the beach, even the insides of the jeans had lightened significantly from their original denim. Mom hates jeans. I settled on a pair of boot-cut almond colored corduroys with a suede blazer and calfskin boots in the same dusty brown as the jacket. The decision was conservative with a touch of trend.

It was 11:30 A.M. and my mother was the only person in New York who arrived fifteen minutes before, rather than after, the appointed time.

She was also the only other person who noticed used DVDs, significant papers, or other items muddling a room's neatness.

Even though I'd done the search-and-conceal sweep a few dozen times last night, I still made the necessary rounds through the apartment, straightening already straightened frames and wiping wiped counters.

Fully expecting the bell, 11:45 A.M. to the second, I pressed the buzzer to allow her in. This time I did not wait for her at the front door, to be greeted with gasping breaths more appropriate for the final ascent up K2.

She entered the apartment with all her usual melodrama—one hand clutched to her chest while she leaned over as if she were about to fall into a tumble—never avoiding the opportunity to show her displeasure at my living in a walk-up.

"It's not like you haven't walked up stairs before," I hissed.

She poked out her dermabrasioned cheek for me to kiss. This was standard Mother behavior—she got the kiss; you did the kissing. Her $300 an hour treated face then followed me as I grabbed my bag, ready to leave to avoid further scrutiny.

"I suppose you save gym time from not having to use the Stairmaster." She managed a jab despite her difficulty in breathing.

"This is coming from a woman who lives in a town house? How is this different?"

"Water," she gasped, avoiding the validity of my argument. As I walked toward the kitchen to get her some water—too bad I wasn't in possession of an oxygen tank—she seemed to get her energy back, skirting me as she beelined into the kitchen.

"Where are the glasses?" she asked, while opening and shutting cabinet doors, her gaze lingering on the pantry shelf in an overt display of inspection.

"Above the range." I pointed to the crystal highballs glimmering through the glass-encased shelving that had been the cause for a moment of decorating bliss.

"But that's so inconvenient."

We had this conversation every time she came to visit. Why shouldn't I store something that I use so infrequently in such an out of reach place? But, as I too am a victim of vanity, I stowed the glasses for the effect and just used my bottled water in the fridge regularly. Rather than explain this to my mother for the 1,800th time, I left her to get my keys.

In the two minutes she'd been in the kitchen, she managed to remove the entire contents of my pantry onto the once smudge-free countertop.

"Mom, I wish you wouldn't."

"But these chromed Dean & Deluca spices also have aesthetic value. I'll just do some quick transferring."

"But I actually use the spices, while the glasses are strictly for guests."

She shot me a piercing look. I'd hate to be the one who crosses my mother on a more serious issue.

Her face snapped back to a more human demeanor, the latest development in George Lucas technology.

"Also, Emily, what's this?" My mother held up a Glad bag of pot that I'd completely forgotten about, for those nights Henry and I wanted to chill.

"I found it in the fridge next to the jar of gherkin pickles." Her voice became mildly panicked, borderline sob.

"Is there something I should know about? We don't communicate. Is this . . ." she trailed. ". . . marijuana?"

"What are you talking about," I breezed, snatching the bag from her perfectly tipped nails. "Marijuana is for the flower children." I intentionally spoke in taboo terminology that Mom could never associate one of her kin with.

"Just some special herbs I bought in Chinatown, to help clear my pores. I just add a pinch to steaming water and let the vapors penetrate my skin."

"Really? Perhaps I should try it?"

"No. Not a good idea. I suffered from a horrible headache. Migraine to the max."

"Oh, look," she said, pointing to the digital microwave clock. "It's almost twelve fifteen and we have reservations for one P.M. We've been dawdling."

Dawdling?

"And where does the time go?" She capped with a sigh, one of her more theatrical ones.

Leaving the mess for me to contend with later, she mumbled something to the effect that she would never be able to understand my lifestyle choices.

Apparently doing her downtown trend reading in bulk, Mom made reservations at Gas Stop, the latest restaurant spotlighted in *New York Magazine*. It was modeled after a roadside diner with the prices of a four star restaurant. She was paying, what the hell.

The restaurant was on the edge of the meat-packing district, situated in a renovated garage. The pipes and exposed brick walls gave it that industrial chic effect. There were withered highway signs and broken traffic lights and other train-set detritus added to the mix. A row of gas tanks separated the bar from the restaurant, a junk shop discovery probably made by the hip restaurateur at a rest stop en route to Stratton (having the idea to open a restaurant called "Gas Stop" based on his need to purchase these souvenirs to pop culture that had no value aside from the aesthetic).

The Statue of Liberty blue banquettes, with their own jukebox and attached coatracks, probably also relieved that very dealer, who rescued them from a deserted trailer diner. If the restaurant failed I'm sure the restaurateur could peddle the wares to one of his contacts in the film business, encouraging them to remake *Giant*.

"Miss and Mrs. Briggs." Our maitre d' approached as if she was expecting us. "I've saved a special table for you; Moby ate there just last night." She was as obsequious as a fashion stylist assisting Gwyneth Paltrow in her selection of Oscar dresses.

"Who's Moby?" whispered my mother in my ear as we followed the maitre d' to our table. "Moby the whale?" She sounded bewildered.

"I believe she is referring to Moby the musician." Mom's face was still a big question mark.

Watching the Moby spotter lead us to our table, I couldn't help but notice (even though I'm not a lesbian) how round her butt was and how straight her legs were—two scoops of ice cream balancing on popsicle sticks. She was stunning. Most certainly collecting rent money and numbers of eligible men until she landed that role on *One Life to Live*. She was wearing stiletto boots with a logoed skirt and fitted sweater, not to mention glossy hair that looked like it had been shellacked, and her face was finished with just the right amount of makeup. I was not going to hear the end of this from Mother.

"Enjoy your lunch," said the aspiring soap star as she presented each of us with a silver menu adorned with patina-blue writing. Mother smiled to her conciliatorily. She had probably given the maitre d' the heads up on my *as if* attitude when she made the reservation.

"Isn't she lovely?"

"A real knockout, straight from the French royal goddamn family."

Mother gave me that Oh, Emily perturbed look.

I gave her an Emily smirk.

"Emily. Stop it with that smirk. You'll add another wrinkle," she said.

And this was assuming that I had how many wrinkles already?

"It's just that I don't see why we have to get into this. I've already failed your little makeup tests and it's about time you fail me from the course and move on. It's not like we're about to be snapped by some paparazzi."

"Well, you should be!" she screeched. "Be on constant alert due to your prominent status. You are such a pretty girl. Prettier than those other simpletons who are constantly being churned out as the next Grace Kelly, like you can manufacture style like some reality television show."

"What are your real opinions on this matter?"

She suppressed a sigh. "I will never understand your motives for anonymity."

I looked at her, stupefied. She couldn't be serious. I then looked about the room to analyze the crowd, anything to keep me from registering what she had just said.

"Sorry for the choice of lunch boites. Peggy Ritter suggested it, but it's a bit too—" she searched for the right word "—junky for me."

"That may have been the point, but what would I know?"

I opened my menu to avoid exerting energy on inane topics. Yum—fried zucchini. I hadn't ordered that since college, back when no matter what I ate or drank, my weight never broke from 105.

"Well, you look a bit tuckered out." And she continued from there. I just nodded and appeared transfixed with the menu. This was a game of tic-tac-toe and my strategy was not to play.

"Are you sleeping well?"

The real issue was that I wasn't sleeping with anyone.

"Yum—tuna melts, apple pie, and blueberry ice cream. This reminds me of a Sunday brunch at the Candy Kitchen!" How was that for a non sequitur? It worked. She immediately opened her menu in fear that there was nothing non-caloric to order.

"Are you ready to order, ladies?" Mom was mentally crunching calorie numbers. She then shimmied herself onto the edge of her seat like a schoolgirl asserting herself to the teacher because she knows the answer.

"Are you ready, Emily?"

I nodded.

"Then I will have the BLT on lightly toasted seven grain bread with no bacon and extra tomatoes. Oh, and a glass of iced tea."

"Mom, you can't call it a BLT without the B. What's the point, you're just ordering a bunch of condiments on two pieces of fancy bread."

"Oh, right," she said to the waiter. "Please make sure there is no mayonnaise or butter, but if you have honey mustard that will be fine." She apparently had the non sequitur thing down as well.

Eating disorder, I sang to myself.

I said, "I will have the BLT—extra bacon, less lettuce, lots of mayo—and the seared tuna with sautéed mesclun."

"Anything to drink?"

"Yes, please, a gimlet and glass of water, thank you."

The waiter appeared pleased with our choices and scooted from our table. I'm sure he'd seen his fair share of non-orders from anorexic ladies who lunch.

"Emily," said my mother in that disapproving tone that I am all too familiar with. "Please don't tell me you ordered that BLT just to smell it and then brush it aside; that's such a waste!"

"As much of a waste as it is to order rabbit food and pay the same price as an entree?"

"Fine, I'll just have him wrap it up for Oliver."

"Sensible plan."

The waiter presented me with my gimlet. I felt like I'd been just given a Tiffany blue box from a really cute boy. The drink didn't even have a moment to settle into its new resting place as I eagerly grabbed it.

"Is everything okay, dear? It is a bit early to be drinking."

"I'm not drinking. Unless you call a lime ricky a drink."

"That's not a lime ricky, you ordered a gimlet. And the last time I remember having one of those there was alcohol in it." I guzzled my drink as if I were seventeen in a Chinese restaurant draining blue Hawaiians before arriving at a party with really cute boys.

"Really? I meant to order a lime ricky."

"Oh, Emily. I never know if you're pulling my leg." She sighed.

"And what would be the point of that?"

She smirked. I smirked back.

"Well, I would like to say what a nice thing it was that you did for your cousin Anne."

"What did I do for Anne?"

"Introducing her to her boyfriend, of course."

"What boyfriend? I avoid Anne the way you avoid your last decorator."

"Her new *paramour.* Oh, what's his name?" She paused, pulling a runaway strand from her headband and draping it behind her ear.

"He went to Duke, Harvard Law. He had a position at Sullivan Cromwell before starting his own firm. The family summers in one of those little Cape Cod towns."

Aside from his SAT scores and annual salary, Mother seemed to have the more important details than his name.

"His mother is a Corning—of the St. Louis Cornings."

Opposed to the other Cornings? Is she describing a family or a breed of setter?

"But what's his name? James, Jonathan—Jason! Yes, Jason. Jason what's his name?"

"No way!" I shrieked.

"Yes, Emily, I believe his name is Jason but his last name escapes me right now."

"No, I mean no way because you couldn't possibly mean that

loser Christmas-card boy from the museum party. He is such a geek."

"Well, I do think he is the one but I don't know what you're referring to by his being a 'geek.' Sophie says that Anne says he is a 'complete stud' with the Wall Street crowd."

Mother, apparently taking out her aggression on packets of Equal, ripped apart two into her iced tea and wildly stirred it with her butter knife so it created a tornado-like fulcrum similar to a bath right before it drains.

"Well, if Wall Street studs are looking to get their Christmas card lists perfected, they're all losers to me."

She put her glass down, face returning to a question mark.

"Gosh, I can't believe Anne is with Jason what's his name. Watkins?" I paused, rehashing the countless times he had introduced himself to me. "Whitten!" I became overly excited in suddenly remembering.

"Yes, that's correct, Jason Whitten. Sophie suspects that Anne will be proposed to before Easter." Mother sounded as if she were discussing her landscaping plans.

"Oh, I can just see it. He'll take her to Deer Valley, in Park City and propose to her in the lodge—not on the mountain for fear that she'll get overly excited and drop the ring in the snow and he'll be completely freaked about the insurance and all. Then she'll come back to New York and give her notice to Christie's."

"William Doyle," Mom corrected.

"Right, William Doyle, because she'll need the time to plan the wedding. Oh, shit, there goes another summer weekend wasted."

"Emily, watch it."

"What, you don't think she'll have a summer wedding?"

"Well, I assume she will, but I really wish you'd avoid the vulgar language around me, love."

Our food was served. My drink finished.

"Would you like another gimlet?" asked the waiter.

I looked at my mother, who was inspecting the insides of her sandwich. What was it about people not trusting other people to get their orders right? I assumed it was a New York thing.

"Yes," I said to the waiter with a wink. "I would like another lime ricky," I enunciated. As Mother reached for the pepper, I then mouthed to the waiter, *gimlet*. He winked back. I loved him.

Taking a whiff of the BLT, I pulled my dish of tuna closer to me and grabbed the pepper once my mother had placed it back on the table.

"I don't know why you are always so down on your cousin Anne," she said, sipping her lemon-wedged water from a straw. The woman's cheeks became even more pronounced, showing the bony contours of her profile like a *Survivor* contestant's ribs on the final episode. "You two were raised like sisters. Since you and Oliver are so far apart in age, I always thought it would be nice if you had a close relationship with someone other than a friend."

"Are you referring to Daphne?"

"Of course you have strong relations with Daphne, but it's just not the same as family."

"But Anne and I could not be more diametrically opposed."

"I disagree. You have similar backgrounds, live in the city, spend summers at the beach and even share the same social coterie."

I raised my voice in reference to her last point. "We do not. You can't put two people together just because it's a visibly sensible match. That's so Tom and Penelope."

"Well, I like Anne," huffed Mother.

I was marking my X on the tic-tac-toe board; she roped me into this foolish game.

"Mom. Her idea of supporting a cause is to wear a tiny ribbon or pin."

"Whatever do you mean? She's on all of those benefit committees."

"She's on all those committees so she can get mentions in all the magazines."

"And what would be the point of that?" she said sarcastically.

"Anne is as plastic as a Hollywood actress after forty. It truly upsets me when you set her to be this model that I should strive toward."

"Do you really think that?" She looked hurt.

"Yes. I really think that." I imagine I looked hurt.

There was no point in discussing the issue of Anne's social

prowess with my mother. Sadly, I do think that she'd like me to be more like her. We seem to be continually putting a Band-Aid on this same sore, never properly treating the wound. A quivering line underscored Mother's expression. I'd seen this same face at funerals, during disrupted trips and after bad haircuts. It was disappointing to see her so agitated on my account. I lifted my fork to transfer priorities from debating to eating.

We ate in silence. Or, really, I munched and she tossed. For a tuna mesclun salad, which was pretty standard lunch bistro fare, it was actually quite original. I believe there was a touch of curry or a cumin-y something or other that really brought out a distinct flavor.

"Emily," my mother managed to say in a sigh. She placed her knife and fork in the waiter-please-take-this-enemy-away-from-me position over a plate of tomatoes and bread.

"How is everything with that cartoonist friend of yours? Henry." Here we go—X marks the upper left-hand square. And what was with her prefacing it by "cartoonist friend," as if I needed to be reminded of the men whom I slept with?

"Would he be potential wedding date material?"

She sounded noticeably livelier. Determined not to make this a contentious issue by the way she propped her two hands into a teepee on the table. Our eyes locked with a shared smile.

"Nope. Haven't spoken to him in a few months."

"Well, that's a shame. He seemed lovely, really encouraged your activity level." Were we discussing personal trainers or boyfriends?

"I guess he was okay," I stammered.

"Oh, he was more than okay. You two had something. I hadn't seen you so at ease with anyone since Dash."

"Dash and I were never a couple," I reminded her, for about the 1,800th time. Mother looked at me suspiciously.

"Who was that lovely boy you dated when you just graduated from school? The one with the bank job?"

"When I was twenty-one?"

"Right. When you returned to New York?"

"The year that I first went to a bar?"

She raised her voice, enunciating each word. "What was his name?"

"Scott Bankstrom."

"Exactly, the one from Darien."

"New Canaan."

"So whatever happened to him?"

"He's gay." A blatant lie. Mom's brow creased into a W. Complete shock.

Scott Bankstrom was a legitimate boyfriend. There was no shame in calling him six times a day to report on my discovery on how to remove the rust stains from my basin. (Bleach and rust remover.) Or that chewing gum after lunch was a great suppressant (especially Big Red). Or that, even though Shannen Doherty was a bitch in real life, we could agree that Brenda was much cooler than Jennie Garth's character on *90210*. Yes, Scott actually feigned interest in my value of the inane.

Though Scott did have a thing for Norwich Terriers and yellow cashmere socks, he was not gay. I made my point that living in Connecticut would be like living through a natural disaster, marriages that strummed their course to a loveless lull. He did the right thing, marrying his younger sister's best friend. A retired bridesmaid dress designer who, from the last I heard, was expecting their second child. (Third, if you counted that they had twins.)

After successfully chewing a rather large piece of lettuce, Mother continued her litany on the men of my life. "And then there is Dash. But I am registering that Dash is nothing more than a friend to you."

"How perceptive."

"I had the feeling that this Henry would be, well, possibly be your one. Both Oliver and your father seemed to have been quite taken by him as well."

"Really?"

"You sound surprised."

"I just didn't figure Henry as the sort you'd approve of."

"Sweetie, I'd approve of anyone who can tear you from your imaginary existence. You've always had the fairy-tale approach to romance. I suppose that's my fault, reading you too many bedtime stories."

"Dorit read me too many bedtime stories."

"The ones I told her to read to you. Anyway, that's what makes you so unique, not choosing this prescribed path. Sometimes I think it would be easier if you went along with the life I have tried to present to you."

For all of my mother's lopsided comments and toffee-nosed standards, she did seem to be attempting some rational insight here. And there was no one else's stomach who I could say was home to me for nine months. I guess I shouldn't be too hard on her.

"Henry needed to contend with a few past issues. He is in California right now." I was amazed at how much I was exposing to my mother/prosecutor, who would only use this information later to belittle me.

"Well, that doesn't seem too bad."

"You don't know the whole story."

"What I do know is that you are both single people, and this is the luxury that single people have. Before making a commitment you can choose yourself first. And only until you treat yourself with the fullest attention can you care for another. He may still be an option. In the meantime I suggest you date. And whatever happened to Dash as a potential . . ."

"Mother!" The entire restaurant was silent, music stopped, all focus was on me.

"Sorry, I should know better but I can't keep myself from picking up on some unresolved feelings on this one." The restaurant resumed normal activity.

"Even if I did want to pursue Dash, not to entertain any support to that rehashed little theory of yours, he's with somebody right now."

"Katrina von Friedrich."

I raised my voice bewilderingly. "What! How can you possibly know such things?"

"I read *WWD*. Besides, they aren't together anymore. I can't believe that I'm the one who has to tell you these things."

"*I* can't believe you're the one telling me this!" I took a sip from my gimlet but it was just a glass of melting ice with some cool limewater. This was all too surreal for me. My mother, whose idea of pleasing my father was to keep Clamato stocked in the pantry, was giving me advice on men.

"Just remember, a few of those so-called fabulous ladies that you see still circulating on those Sunday *Times* party pages, second-handing themselves by appearing to be with cradle-robbing news-casters—they were my Katrina von whatevers—and were all pursuing your father.

"And, Emily Carlson Briggs . . ." She was serious now, insert-ing the middle name—a name that indicated gravity in a conver-sation, prevented Mother from having to use a naughty word, kept her maiden name alive and acted as a password to access all of my accounts. "Don't pull that look on your face. Your father was a catch in his day. And, as dull as it may appear to you in your flying-fairies and magic-potioned world, I snagged him."

I was incredulous.

She looked at her watch. Her expertly treated face became jagged with lines of distress. Reaching into her bag and sliding a batch of magazine clippings across the table, I recognized the top one as something I'd already read, a profile of a childhood acquaintance who was written up because of her knockout wed-ding, now acquiring a name that I would continually be re-minded of every time I walked in the cereal aisle.

"I have to skedaddle," she said. Skedaddle?

Next I knew I was seeing my mother into her car. The hum of the electronic window from the backseat revealed her happy-go-lucky face. "Do you want a ride, dear?"

"I think I'll just walk, thank you."

"Oh, right, you never wear a heel higher than a kitten. Ho hum." Ho hum?

She was a Portuguese sonnet. What appeared wasn't always what was.

I noticed the clouds rumbling ominously, posing the threat of rain. One perfect drop fell on the top magazine clipping in my hand, making it bulge like a fresh mosquito bite. Enough to ruin a sheet of paper but not imposing to my calfskin boots, so I was still able to walk rather than take a cab.

Feeling inspired to draw, I had the urge to buy colored pen-cils. I walked east toward the Sam Flax store. The cashier was pre-occupied with a sheet of bubble wrap that I found quite annoying. Listening to the firecracker bursts I rationalized that if I were in possession of a fun sheet of bubble wrap, I'd probably be doing the same thing. I bought new pencils, paper and a random book with leather binding in a zebra pattern.

One thing had become clear in speaking with both Daphne and Mother—two different personalities with two shared perspectives—I needed to see things with a less fantastical perspective.

And I suddenly missed Dash. Interesting news about Dash. Dash. Dash? Dash!

22

I kept coming back to the same image. Some guy seated across from Lily with that Emily look on her face—a look that was completely perplexed by being interviewed for that lifetime role of mate.

Dating was similar to job interviews. You were selling yourself while hearing what the employer had to offer. I hated that dating was a series of interviews: going over the financial package, benefits and health plan—the vacation days that would make or break the deal. I just wanted the romance, the sex, the love—the Sunday mornings that never ended, getting out of bed only to attend to the food delivery.

So in the past month I'd been dating. Dating did not suit me. One guy was a fetus when the *Love Boat* was my Saturday night entertainment. He asked me to dinner, we went for Chinese—*cheap.*

Then there was the issue of semantics with two particular men—one fabulous, the other feckless. Mr. Fabulous could effortlessly swirl sommelier and chignon in the same sentence, which made me a tad suspicious. The culturally challenged one a retired professional lacrosse player (who even knew there was such a thing?) and I quickly lost interest when he thought Condolezza Rice was something you ordered from an Indian restaurant.

Last night had been an interesting one, an evening spent with an aspiring reality television personality. I knew, just knew I shouldn't offer, but suddenly I noticed my mouth moving, voice spewing out words to the effect that I'd speak with Dash about any possible leads.

We might as well have kicked the table over for the tackle that I received. Forget job interviewing on this one, this was all about his getting a contact. He did everything but take my cell phone and dial Dash's number for me.

He asked if he could call me again. While I found no laws prohibiting a person from calling someone, I did know that getting my phone number unlisted would be a wise move. Right, I needed to have my number unlisted. The phone rang. Was the telephone company telepathic? Technology!

"Hello," I answered.

"Oh, you sound pretty bummed." It was Daphne. "So how'd it go last night?"

"If hoping that you were the telephone company calling to have my number unlisted is any indicator . . . and I just polished off an entire box of Cinnamon Life."

"Ouch. That bad, huh?"

"I'd like to say that it's been an improvement but I seem to be finding comparable qualities of dismal, just in different scenarios."

I was looking into the fridge as my binge was just beginning. Dannon yogurt—expired two days ago. "What's the worst that could happen if I eat yogurt that's two days past its expiration date?"

"You sound like Melanie Griffith making a pitch to extend her contract with a cosmetics company. But I wouldn't worry."

I opened the yogurt. No funky smell, seemed edible. I unsealed a new box of Life and poured it into a bowl, blending in the yogurt and a fistful of raisins.

"What are you doing now? Want to go with Emily and me to see the new planetarium show at the Museum of Natural History and then head over to Serendipity's?"

Of course, Daphne knew how to entice me. Two places that never lose their luster to the dusts of time—the big whale and the only place you can get a malted made from an antique chrome blender used since the Eisenhower administration. As the world clocks in another day, everyone stays the same age at these two institutions.

I said while tearing open three Equals, "I could think of nothing I'd like to do better." Not quite pleased with the responsibility level of my answer, I added, "But I'm dealing with a deadline."

"What's Lily up to these days?"

"Oh, pretty much the same—feeling like a loser, dating in the big city, no idea what lies ahead for her in the future. *Vogue* is really into this single-city-girl-dating thing. What is it with people's interest in the single-city-girl-dating thing? 'Cause I can tell you, it really isn't that 'throw your hat in the air, I will make it after all' deal. First, I rarely wear hats. And, for the bad hair days when I do depend on a hat, I am not about to throw it into the city streets with the likelihood of it's getting squashed by a cab or my getting stared at by fellow bystanders."

Daphne's tone became more serious. "Can I ask you something?"

"Of course. Anything."

"Why do you think you are single?"

"Well, that's a question for the therapists. But, really, it has nothing to do with my being some modern feminist. I can't find allegiance in a group that finds billowy skirts and ugly rocks mounted as jewelry fashionable.

"And it's not that I am clocking in the hours to advance my career. Me? I take afternoon naps. And it's not that I am completely self-absorbed—though my mom may want to debate that one. Or that I enjoy the fast-paced sex life of being single; please, finding a suitable date in the city is like trying to find a fifteen-million-dollar movie actor who isn't into Scientology."

There was a silence at the other end of the line. I suppose this was a lot for Daphne to take in. Maybe *I* should have taken this in.

What was the answer to the everlasting relationship? Could love be like that vacation you didn't want to end? Or was this why Daphne wasn't immediately responding? The marriages that appear to work on the surface, which I find dull on the day to day—was that what a lifelong commitment was really all about?

Happily ever after was a long time when boobs begin to sag and hairlines recede—without the surgery and plugs.

Society wanted to put labels on people like me, spin off a show or book heroine whom others can relate to. The only thing I might share with other single women, and men for that matter, was that I would rather be with this person for life than just have them provide me with a life. I had a life. It might not appear to be much, but it worked. It was dependable.

I loved my little shopping sprees. I liked what I did for a living. I loved where I lived, although I could be into having a dog, but wouldn't raise one in the city. And if I did get a dog I'd want a big one, not one of those puntable barking cats but a mountain dog, a lab—something that if I threw a stick into the ocean, it wouldn't run the other way.

I was independent, so my options were less binding. Happiness and love trumped expense accounts and picking up dinner weekday nights from Healthy Pleasures (though I could get into the husband picking up my Barneys' bills).

"Daphne," I said, breaking the silence. "You seem to be continually playing Socrates with me on this issue. Do I sense some disapproval on your end? Are you pressuring me to assess my situation based on your constant questioning?"

"It's just that I have to wonder if what you're holding out for really exists."

"Well if it doesn't exist, then I don't want it."

"Emily!"

"Emily Shmemily." There was silence. My voice calmer, "I've been let down."

"Emily!" Daphne was going for the big breakthrough on this one.

"No more Emilys! I want. I want . . ." I hesitated.

"Not the hugged-from-behind thing again." Daphne never lets me get away with anything.

"Well. I can't help but hold out for being hugged from behind."

Sorry to disappoint, Daph, but ever since I've been hugged from behind it's been hard to settle for the hugged in front, loveless marriage, obligatory kind.

The hugged-from-behind syndrome began one Hampton summer, a summer before publicists created invitation lists printed on adhesive labels from an Excel program. You didn't get invited to a party by schmoozing with the right promoter or working your career as a social connection; it was simply a matter of going out with some friends.

Daphne and I vaguely knew the host throwing that summer's most debauch party but were considered suitable additions to a bouncer just uprooted from his loft in Sigma Alpha Epsilon to manning this all-night, all-you-could-drink-eat-and-swim-naked-until-the-police-put-an-end-to-all-its-hot-summer-fun party. (And why would the police ever want a job like that? Being the one who had to put an end to all of the parties?)

It was the same summer that I reconnected with Mark Pierce and, while I was in the middle of some cocktail chatter with acquaintances I only acquainted with over cocktails, Mark startled me, hugging me from behind. It was so unexpected—and sexy— I believe I had an orgasm right there, which actually happened fifteen minutes later beneath some privet hedge on a secluded side of the house.

Though Mark and I were never meant to be together, I will never forget the three-second fizzed-to-the-top champagne explosion I felt when Mark hugged me from behind that was better than the orgasm served on a bed of grass.

"Do you think Mark and I should've ever, you know . . ."

"Not this again, and the answer is no. Not unless you want to be on kid number three driving around somewhere with Connecticut plates, finding excuses to come into the city just to scope out my apartment's views and secretly resenting me because I have clouds slipping through my windows."

"Daphne!"

"Sorry, we've done the Mark Pierce could've, should've and good-thing-you-didn't to death."

"No. I mean, who's to say that I wouldn't have more clouds slipping through my windows?"

"Right. Sorry. But again, Emily, you've completely managed to avoid the real issue, which is your delusional being-hugged-from-behind fantasy. It's kind of like morning television, very sweet but a bit vapid if watched day to day."

Not fully grasping what Daphne was saying here, I was beginning to lose my patience.

"I found love. I found it with Henry. And even if that isn't an option I know how it felt and who's to say that it won't happen again?"

"But perhaps you glamorized your relationship with him. I'm not too impressed with how he left things. Has Henry even tried to contact you?"

"No," I fessed up ashamedly. "But I haven't been leaving my home answering machine on."

"Have you tried to make contact with him?"

I had, actually. When Henry left for San Francisco he left no address, not even an E-mail or his parents' information. I wanted to send him a note, just to check in, see if he was okay. My only resort was to go through Joanna. So I gave her a polite, quick letter that she passed on to Casey to forward to him.

All she delivered back to me was the message that Henry had given Casey explicit instructions that he should only be contacted for professional reasons. The words were a blow—directly intended for me. I felt like a girl snubbed by a haughty salesperson, giving me the once-over and determining that workout clothes were not suitable attire for serious shopping interaction.

"He didn't leave his forwarding address," I said, not lying while not divulging the entire truth. "And it's not like I am so pathetic as to be pining after this boy."

"You know what I think?" Daphne said as if she had this suddenly all figured out.

"What?" I implored.

"I think it's time that you just wash that man right out of your hair."

I made an Emily look.

"I know this may sound campy, but by simply figuring that he's wrong for you—you can effectively move on."

"But he's the batter that molds into my pan. The added color to my sketch. I don't want to wash Henry out of my hair!" Though my hair could benefit from a good wash.

Again, silence. Though Daphne is my best friend, this is where it was hard for her to play the supportive role. While we adored each other, got each other, we had those differences in lifestyles where it was difficult to give advice without speaking from what we knew.

"Weren't we just discussing my adventures in dating?" I said, changing the subject lightheartedly.

"True and, really, about that—whatever happened to that guy you met on your flight back from Jackson Hole? You said he was cute."

"Come on, Daph, you know there's more to a man than just being good-looking—money, the car he drives."

We both laughed.

"Well, you must be getting something out of all these dates, besides being fed properly?"

"Hmm." I tried to take the positive, what-I've-learned approach. I could be considered a dating expert in that I had dated almost twenty men in two months.

"The whole species will continue to baffle me," I said as a settlement.

"Well, maybe you just need a change of pace—not anyone serious, just a boy who will treat you nice."

Okay, sounded like a set-up coming.

"Are you trying to set me up?"

"Well, perhaps, but hear me out on this one."

I gave her my "I'm listening" silence.

"He went to medical school with Andy, became a vet and is currently in between."

"In between what?"

"He's a professional masseuse," she sputtered—real quick, as if by saying this bizarre fact fast I wouldn't be able to take it in. Before I could take it in, Daphne, again quickly, continued. "A professional dog masseuse."

"Please, Daphne!" I wailed. "Am I now so pathetic that I have to get it on with a professional dog patter? What do you take me for?"

"Okay, bad idea." She sighed. "But then how about Mr. Rio?"

Mmm, Mr. Rio! Mr. Rio was the Brazilian babe who worked out in my gym. He had dark muscle-rippled skin littered with tattoos and wore wife-beater T-shirts, but the clincher was the icy blue color of his eyes, similar to a Siberian husky's. Mr. Rio made me think of not-for-daytime television scenarios. Though flirting in the gym was strictly designated to the neon and spandex crowd, there was nothing better than to be motivated, athletically speaking of course, by a man who really made you want to get all worked up in a sweat.

"Has he asked you out yet?"

"I'm not really sure."

"Excuse me?"

"Well, he said he'd like to show me where to get a real workout."

"What! I know you two have something real hot going but isn't that a bit forward?"

"No, no. Some club near where he lives, in Queens I think, that has this real Gleason's Gym feel."

"Um, Em, what are you waiting for? Take him up on it!"

"Just that I'm a bit worried about all of our differences."

"What differences?"

"Religion to start."

"He's from Brazil. Believes in Santa Claus. What are you talking about?"

"I guess I'm just making excuses."

"You do keep mentioning how hot he is. I believe your exact words were 'penetration on sight.' Is he better looking than Henry?"

"No, hardly. I mean conventionally possibly but when I see Henry I am suddenly suffocated with desire. I can't even look him in the eye for fear of combustion."

"Boy, you really had it hard for him. I've never seen you like this." Daphne raised her voice. "Have sex with Mr. Rio, let him break the spell and move on."

"But that's so Upper East Side Bitch. And, regardless, I think I'm only seduced by the body—he kind of looks like the *amigo* who delivers my burrito."

"Since when have you eaten burrito?"

"Day after gimlet nights."

"Right, of course."

"But using him for his body could be considered just taking the guy approach. I don't know if I have it in me. For me, great sex has evolved into something deeper than penetration. At my stage, penetration of the mind is better foreplay than toe sucking. When you've had someone that stimulates you on all levels, biding your time with men who have one element of something is incomplete."

"I believe our Emily is growing up."

"Please, the other day my father was reprimanding me about how I completely flaked that my taxes were due. 'Emily dear,' he said in that professorial manner, 'this is not how an adult woman should handle things.' I was completely stuck on 'adult woman.' Adult woman? I will never be an *'adult woman.'* Maybe an adult child, due to the fact that I keep adding a year each birthday, goddamn it, but adult?"

"But you've grown, become more sensible with your approach to men. I wonder if your experience with Henry has had this impact on you? Maybe now you should seduce and have sex with Dash?"

If I had taken a sip of my drink, it would have been sprayed from my mouth.

"What are you getting at! Dash and I are pals. You've always said that he was a bit too suburban for me."

"Suburban is safe," she said evenly.

"Suburban is boring."

"Well, he's ended things with Katrina."

"How is it that everyone, including my mother, for God's sake, is up on this but me?"

"Because you're so hung up on reading the *New Yorker* before getting to the important things like Suzy and Page Six. That's the stock ticker in our business, sweetie."

"So. What do you know?"

"I just think he was tired of all the functions and family obligations, which I was told by one of the mothers at a birthday party for a friend of Emily's. And, speaking of Dash, that's exactly what I must do right now if we want to make the planetarium show. Sure you don't want to come along?"

"Thanks, but I really need to put in some Lily time."

"Okay, then. But I do have a great idea, can't believe I hadn't thought of it earlier. There's this adorable doctor friend of Andy's—"

I cut in, "Let me guess, he's finished with medicine and now wants to open up a dog spa?"

"No. No," she pleaded. "He's in plastics—good future."

Was she talking about a boy or reciting a line from *The Graduate?*

"Daphne, you know better."

"I promise it won't be a set-up. I'll get a group of us together this Friday night. We'll go to that new oyster bistro place in my neighborhood."

"Is he cute?"

"Beyond."

"*ER* cute?"

"Could pass as Noah Wyle's brother!"

"Well, I do have to go see my parents on Saturday, so I will be in the area."

"Great! I will make it happen," said Daphne, hanging up.

It appeared that I was getting the kind of attention one deserves if she were battling an eating disorder. Maybe they just didn't get it? The two women who have taken me on, after all, were in secure marriages. While Mom was from the station wagon–era standard of marriage, Daphne had the SUV version—same functions, updated ride.

Since I had abandoned the security of their perfunctory lifestyle, I assumed that their fears of my not taking the safe route were being projected onto me. And if I were to prove them wrong, what would that say about the choices they made?

I started to feel a bit callous in my questioning of their direction; it was my best friend and mother, after all.

For me to have evaluated Lily's debacle *du jour* was too much to take on at that moment. I felt like I gained three pounds and was on crisis mode in having to shed the extra weight. But you can't lose it all by obsessing. You needed to eat right, exercise and not dwell. So I decided to buy something expensive.

Remembering that I had recently justified dropping $1500 for a shirt at Dolce and Gabbana because it would be the one item that would separate me from being well-dressed to best-dressed I went for a run as a way to save money.

Sure, running helped shed those lingering pounds; I didn't get into it because it seemed like a really fun thing to do. It moved my active conscience to a tranquil blankness, the way you become when staring into the ocean mindlessly as minutes pass in hours. And it wasn't an artificial, alternate source of happiness, like knowing that it was good for you but you still yearn for the real thing, like the way I pawned off chemically produced fat-free ice cream as tastier than a scoop of Chunky Monkey. It was that with so many variables, running was the one thing that stayed on course. Your body became numb to the exercise because the mental brainpower took over the physical exertion. Thoughts were clear. The current crisis became trivialized. The only conflict was a sudden change in weather or particular soreness that hurt less than a bruise. I left reactive mode, became able to tolerate uptight New Yorkers. I lost the urge to push the inconsiderate Chinese deliveryman off his bicycle.

No, running was that Saturday-morning–*Sigmund the Sea Monster*–watching moment when nothing bad could harm you. That is, until you slowed down at the run's end and faced the next crisis.

23

Cousin Anne was getting married. I was truly pathetic. Cousin Anne getting married and not me? That was a good one for the old self-esteem.

I was now expected to share her utter enthusiasm, the kind of enthusiasm more associated with the first blueberries appearing at the market or stumbling onto *Breakfast at Tiffany's* while channel surfing. The date was set for midsummer, probably so Anne could nab Jason before he realized what he was truly in for.

Part of my role as maid of honor was to appear so enthused for my cousin that (1) It didn't appear that I was jealous of the bride, and (2) I would not be viewed as poor Emily, will she ever be capable of having a relationship like her cousin.

But Anne really had more in mind for me than just my being affectedly pleasant. Oh, no. She had it all outlined in her Smythson wedding planner, which she bought a decade ago. There were the food tastings, the reception scouting, the registries and the dress. Finding the dress would be a time killer. Whatever happened to planning the shower and making a clever toast? And the shower. I had already become a major disappointment. I threw parties, not showers. My suggestion to have it over cocktails at my apartment, a rather nice gesture I thought, was met with outward resistance since Anne was another one of those who rarely ventured south of Saks. And for fear that her friends would get lost, the shower brunch would be held at my mother's. I had been on wedding duty ever since finding out this news three days ago, with no time to focus on me and, more specifically, on my set-up with *ER* guy.

I decided to postpone the meeting with the family till the next day so I could have a self-absorbed, all-about-me day. It had been quite a while since I'd put any effort into myself. Even an afternoon would not be sufficient time to prep myself back to a period when I was conscious of my appearance. Would I get the desperately needed haircut, pedicure or facial? Would I buy something cute? I went for the massage.

Grateful for the cancellation of a potential client with a sudden nanny crisis at the office (yet another benefit to being single), I used the free time to surrender my body to the skillful hands of a very large man named Sven. Sven kneaded my muscles like pastry dough for over an hour, allowing me to pass out and have my mind drift into this remarkable place that allowed me to have sex with rock stars. This man's gifted touch had the effect of a troll that could spin yarn into gold. I completely fell under the spell of his magic touch—for all I knew he could have raped and robbed me. When he was finished, Sven thoughtfully thanked me, though I was the one who should have been doing the thanking. (Perhaps he did victimize me?)

Sven slipped from the room where I lay naked on the bed (expected to change). The idea of staying there forever, or at least until someone kicked me out, was enticing. I couldn't move. I assumed this was what a slug felt like in ninety-degree heat. My head was the first part of my body that showed it was indeed in working order. The slight movement trickled down to my arms and fingers and my legs began to flutter like a mermaid's tail.

I mechanically changed into my clothes and paid in a haze that was so clouded I was reminded of leaving a dentist's office post–laughing gas. Outside the spa I was reacquainted with the humdrum state of life. It was spring. The air filtered with the freshness of the season but still had that nip of winter, the in between weather causing an internal debate on what I should wear that night.

Walking past a new salon that seemed to have more stylists than customers, I went in to see if they could fit in a quick blowout.

"May I help you," some woman who needed to add carbs back into her diet inserted herself in front of my face.

"Just wondering if you had time for a quick trim."

"Sure. What is it that you would like to have done?"

Well I'd like to look like Christy Turlington but wasn't in the mood to be laughed at that particular moment.

As she started to lift pieces of my hair well above my chin, snipping the menacing shears like a mad dentist with pliers, I suddenly changed my mind. "Actually, got to go!"

Forty-five minutes, $150 poorer, and mousy hair later, I had at least saved money by not having to buy another outfit that I'd only wear once.

Getting dressed in my red cigarette pants and coordinating fitted cashmere cardigan, I just didn't have the Babe Paley look I was going for during my massage reverie. I had no idea what to wear, so I dialed Daphne.

"Backup!" she wailed into the phone. "You always need a backup."

I had high hopes for my sexy socialite outfit, only to be reacquainted with the reality of my hibernated body. Those last three winter pounds didn't slip off as easily as the extra clothes.

With Daphne's approval, I wore a pair of cream-colored Comme des Garcons pants with dusty suede Manolo Blahnik boots over them, a disco-eye-shadow blue sweater with a neck that could be pulled over my head with inches to spare, under a wrap that looked like it was bought in Santa Fe, but, being Ralph Lauren, had a few more 0s in its price.

My hair was not cooperating and I started to wonder if my choice of a massage was wise, versus dealing with my uncooperative hair. I thought of the pool of drool that had settled on the massage bed and was assured that it had been the right decision. I restrained my untamed strands into a ponytail.

After Daphne called to say she had arrived at the restaurant, I headed uptown. I was the last of our group to arrive; the entire table got up politely while Daphne introduced me.

The scene in the restaurant was young, spirited—pockets of friends meeting up after a week's worth of professional hit and misses. Fridays. Springtime in New York just added to the exuberance.

The energy of this destined-to-be-hot-then-forgotten restaurant was set by these sycophants to the social whirl, reawakened after a long winter and thrilled to set the pace of a new spot.

Preston Lewis, my set-up, was the kind who felt comfortable in saying he likes to go from zero to sixty in under a minute. Tawny hair slicked back, Ascot & Chang button-down, and slim-cut khakis. I appraised him not as a doctor stimulated by the rewards of practicing medicine, but as someone who wanted the life of a rock star without the scrutiny of fame. I could tell by the way he wisped my hand and lunged in for a kiss to the cheek that he was happy with what he saw. I, too, probably gave off a similar read. He was straight from *ER*, indeed, the one where surgeries and dramas are cared for in under an hour. A little more rugged, less boyish than Noah Wyle, but he would suitably pass as Harrison Ford's son without all the hair polish.

The other couple at our table was a Venezuelan doctor and his American wife. He also sported the same cool khaki look while she was more conservative in style than Daphne and me. It was the double strand of pearls worn with a Jean Paul Gaultier boho shirt that set off her attempt to achieve a singular style that no unlimited spree could achieve.

Andy and Preston ordered what appeared to be every item on the menu for the table to share, and the conversation did not become isolated between couples. The discussion was charged, debating the recent Supreme Court justice nomination. I was thankful that I happened to read the Op-Eds that morning.

Having the sudden sense that I was being stared at from across the room and amazed at how this sort of intuition worked, I turned and found that I was indeed the object of another person's observation. Dash was at the bar, his eyes unflinching as he gazed at me. I looked to him not with delight or surprise, but with a blank reaction. He took a sip of his drink, still holding his eye to me with a shared blank expression. I turned to Daphne, who noted my diverted attention. She smiled a smile that was spun from an engaging evening. When she noticed my suddenly changed demeanor, she had the sense to look to the cause and, sighting Dash, she turned to me with a *what-now* look. Now two people in our group dramatically lost the simpatico that had set the table's rhythm.

"Excuse me," I said, raising my bottom from my seat, Daphne's eyes following my ascent with genuine concern. The noise and animation that I assumed would be easy to break from was now completely silenced by my impending departure.

"You're not leaving, are you?" questioned Preston. Not since the moment we were introduced had we shared a one-on-one, which led to me believe that he would make an attempt once the group splintered off with mentions of baby-sitters at the evening's end.

"No, no," I promised. "I just need to use my phone to check in with my family."

The table returned to its heated motions while Preston winked to me with the self-confidence that underlined my assumptions of his planned seduction.

I then walked toward the front of the restaurant, in eye's view of the bar but separated by the dining area, noticing that Dash was also one of three couples. The girl who seemed to be attached to him was petite, blonde, typical. What was it with Dash and petite blondes?

My heart tapped to the nervous pace of a number two pencil before filling in ovals on a college entry exam. I was bewildered by the current effect Dash had over me.

Arriving at the entrance of the restaurant, I waited to use my cell phone, watching the slick couples enter and exit. Whom I was calling was not known to me, so I dialed my home number to check the messages. Something I'd have to contend with later anyway. I listened to a message from my mother, concerned about tomorrow's "family meeting" and how she would like to converse with me alone before everyone congregated. I then felt the tap on my shoulder that I was so desperately hoping for.

I turned to face the object of the touch and Dash indeed came for me.

"Your hair, it's longer," he said softly, sealing his index and middle finger together, magnetizing a runaway strand, which he smoothed behind my ear. A gesture I do a thousand times had never given me the shuddered response that I felt then.

"Yeah, it's been a long time," I said, concealing my awkwardness with syncopated giggles.

"You look great."

"So do you," I said, all girlish.

"Why has it been so long?"

Good question, and not one with an easy answer. I suppose I postponed contact with Dash because somewhere after Henry and Katrina, there was a Dash and Emily that had to be reassessed as a result of what we'd both experienced. And it would never be able to return to the same riddled relationship. And, if I took Henry's poke, I had this knack for not facing reality.

"Just a weird time, I, guess," I answered feebly.

"Heard about you and Henry."

"Heard about you and Katrina."

We looked at one another. Who would go next? Never good with that awkward silence, I asked, "Are you okay with your break?"

"Sure." He laughed, bouncing a hand into the air. "But my tux could use a bit more wearing."

"Well, that will change in no time. We're entering a new social season."

"So who's WB boy," he said, evidently referring to Preston.

"Just some guy who I was introduced to tonight. A friend of Daphne and Andy's."

He searched my eyes. "So, are you interested?"

"Sure. Well. I don't know. I just met him and I do sense that it would be hard to get involved with a guy who sees no problem in using the same hair gel as me."

This made Dash smile.

"And you. Are you seeing anyone?" My voice was working, but quavered in that insecure tone that I needed to learn how to adjust.

"Just dating, no one in particular."

"Ah, back in the Dash."

"I need to see you."

That came from where? Dash never had any intention of slipping into our usual banter. My comfortable rapport with the Dash I once knew intensified to a desire not felt by close friends. I wanted to move closer to him but my insides were quivering.

I was afraid that Dash would feel my trembling. I needed to come to terms with these uncertain feelings, perhaps by drawing when I returned home tonight, or perhaps on my morning's run. Or shopping! But Dash rendered this impossible. He took my yearning body and held me still. Pulling me into him so he could whisper into my ear.

"I must see you."

It was as if his words were an automated switch that turned off my ability to speak. How could I respond to someone I knew so well yet was a complete stranger to me in this new context? I nodded like one of those springy hula dancers that are made onto the dashboards of NYC cabs. He then faded from my side like a superhero with special powers.

"You know it was always about you," he shouted to me as he returned inside. "Once I heard about you and Henry, I broke it off with Katrina."

Dash was no longer in my presence while his words quaked inside me. I was a shaken soda can about to combust.

I called Daphne's cell phone but was instantly connected to her voice mail. Losing the ability to wax on socially would be a major challenge, considering my current state. I stood in the entranceway to scan the restaurant. Dash's party was now seated, fortuitously distanced from my table. I intentionally grapevined through the crowded bar to avoid further contact with him, and became held up by two old friends who dated in college. I couldn't say that I really knew them as all interaction between us had been made under a haze of Jagermeister. They were now married and, seemingly, had a kid on the way. I knew not to ask when the due date was since the last time I reconnected with them— assumed she was pregnant and asked the due date question— she said "What due date?"

After getting the tabs on past relations with no relevance to my current life, and being told how "spunky" I always had been, I broke away—considering a shot of tequila or, more appropriately, Jagermeister (in commemoration of the reunion) but decided against it due to time constraints and made it back to the table. The original seating plan was now broken up. It was the end of the meal, indicated by stained espresso cups and a half-eaten tiramisu with three forks resting on the side of its plate.

"So sorry," I mumbled to the table, looking at no one.

"Was it your mother?" asked Daphne. She was brilliant.

"Yes, actually!" I beamed. "Just concerning the big family gathering tomorrow." I seated myself back in my chair, rimmed by Preston's arm. He then moved his thumb to rub the back of my neck.

"Are you okay?" he whispered into my ear. His cologne immediately offended me.

"Oh, sure. Just an overanxious mother." I smiled, one of my more superficial ones.

"Yes, I'm familiar with the type," he said agreeably. "Everyone is getting ready to leave. I live downtown, should we share a cab?" Ah, Preston did indeed have a plan.

"That would be great, however, I promised my mother that I'd swing by. Probably spend the night, so I will just share a cab with Andy and Daphne. Thanks, though."

This seemed to flummox Preston. I'm sure that's not the reaction a plastic surgeon regularly seduced by beauty editors, aging actresses, and models was accustomed to.

"Oh," he said, disappointed. "Well, can I call you sometime?"

Here we go. Suddenly the idea of a man who attempted to perfect imperfections seemed incomplete. And I couldn't help but wonder if he really found upper lips that have the swell of an abused wife attractive.

"Sure," I said, unconvincingly.

As our group congregated outside, the Venezuelan and his wife took the first available cab. Daphne was edging to the side of the curb anticipating the next cab, to pin me with Preston, yet not realizing that Preston and I would not happen tonight. I mentioned to her that I was en route to my parents, which seemed to unsettle her.

"Are you sure you don't want to go home?"

"No. I might as well stay as truthful to my scheme as possible."

"Very well, then." Another cab slid to the curb. "Preston, you take this one," she directed, breaking up the conversation between Preston and her husband, leaving the three of us.

Once his cab fled from the curb, Daphne gave me the concerned look.

"And? So? How was it? You and Dash."

"Weird, exciting, confusing," I said as if I were giving Brazil a review while stoned.

A cab pulled up, which seemed to ease Andy, out of his element when it came to females and their crises. I scooted in first.

"Did you like Preston at least?" continued Daphne, once sandwiched in the middle. Andy handled the drop-off points with the driver, relieving himself with something to do.

"What do you think of him?" I asked.

"I think he's lovely."

"Almost too lovely. I'm a bit dubious."

"Emily! You have to stop looking for fresh blueberries in the winter."

But Whole Foods market had them, I recalled.

"Fine. But the plastic surgery player thing makes me a bit cautious. Plus Dash did make an advance and I am in a bit of a whirl at the moment."

"He did!" Daphne threw up her hands, hitting both Andy and me. He seemed pretty annoyed.

"Sorry," she mumbled.

"Yes. And I am unsure what to make of it. Make of Henry. Make of me. Make of everything."

"Did you just say Henry and mean Dash, or did you mean Henry?"

Uh.

"Dash. Of course Dash."

It was a short cab ride. We were all very tired.

"Well, you've had quite an evening, Emily Briggs. Hasn't she, Andy?" Andy made groaning sounds that showed he was in agreement.

"And don't be so quick to write off Preston. I love the idea of your becoming involved with one of our friends, it will keep our social circle tight. And he really was taken with you. Wasn't he, Andy?" she said, nudging his rib.

"Yeah, he thought you were really hot," he said, as if programmed.

"That's so sweet, thank you for telling me that." I leaned forward to make eye contact. He forced a smile. Poor guy was completely suffocated by the girliness of it all. In a cramped cab, no less.

Reaching my parents' house, I gave Daphne one final look.

"Big kiss to little Emily and Henry," I said, swiping the side of her cheek with my lips. "And thanks, Andy, for such a fun evening. Sorry that I am such a wacko."

"Oh, no such thing," he mumbled, but surely thinking that I was indeed a wacko.

"Andy," instructed Daphne with a hint of abhorrence. "Walk Emily to the door, make sure she gets in all right."

This really annoyed me. When my married friends have to use their husbands for these completely nonsensical tasks that just underlined my singleness and gave me this weak woe-is-me feeling. I mean, for God's sake, I've crawled home from more questionable nights in obliterated conditions and, to my astonishment, still haven't been violated.

The real issue however were those eighty awkward seconds I'd have to be alone with Andy, making nice conversation when all I'd be thinking was that he couldn't hold out for just a few minutes to give his wife a proper orgasm. And how much sexual information he knew about me per his gabby wife, the truly frightening reality. In fact, I couldn't think about that any further.

"Really!" I said a bit loud as they both planted their heads into the vinyl seat. "It's just to the door and there are these surveillance cameras, which I'm not quite sure how they work but they do something."

"Okay," said Daphne dubiously, while Andy looked utterly relieved.

24

I punched in the code of the alarm to let myself into the house and immediately set toward the kitchen freezer. Yes, Mother had Ben and Jerry's low-fat Chocolate Brownie, S'mores, Häagen-Dazs chocolate sorbet *and* chocolate Reddi-Whip. I wondered why I didn't come here more often.

The last time I spent the night at my parents' house was when I had my floors refinished. I had been a total wreck from having to relive an evening under my parents' rule, but it was all quite painless, pleasant even. They went out for the evening so Oliver and I ordered in from three different restaurants and watched some movie on Pay-Per-View that had as much nutritional value as my late night cravings.

"Emily?" asked my mother, wandering into the kitchen, rubbing her eyes. She was wearing Yves Delorme slippers with a co-ordinated robe over a silk nightgown—apparently dressing for bed with more of an effort than I dress for a date.

Reaching into the fridge, she pulled out a bottle of Hildon's sparkling water and then turned on the stove to warm the kettle. I finished making my low-fat chocolate creation and jumbled through the neatly stacked pile of *Architectural Digest*s.

"Redecorating again?" I asked.

"Just the basement. I want to turn it into a learning center for Oliver."

Learning center?

"Whatever happened to rec rooms with foozball and train sets?" I spooned a mound of drippy chocolate into my mouth.

"Emily!" she admonished. "What are you doing here at this time? Didn't you eat something?"

Now that I thought of it, I had missed dinner entirely. Daphne's friends must have thought I was a real freak.

"I just came from Biarritz."

"Excuse me?"

"Not the city, the new restaurant, just a few blocks from here."

"Yes, of course, your father and I have eaten there. I had a great salmon tartar."

"How could you have eaten there, it just opened a few weeks ago."

"We know the owner." It's humiliating that my parents have a more active social life than I do.

"The idea of going home to return uptown in a few hours seemed pointless. Do you still have my running shoes in the guest bedroom?"

"I don't know, Emily. You put such pressure on me with your damn sneakers."

My jaw dropped.

"I haven't touched them. So unless Dorit threw them out they should still be there."

"Great. I'd be really psyched to get in a Central Park run tomorrow morning."

"So how was your night? Rather late, isn't it?"

"Great. Interesting. I saw Dash."

"Really!" She appeared to awaken from her rudimentary motions. "Are you two . . . ?"

"Mother."

"Okay, fine," she said, tossing the Hildon bottle in the recycle bin.

"So. What's this big meeting about?"

"Oh, that." She sighed, pouring the hissing hot water over a bag of chamomile, then sitting herself on the stool next to me. She slid an issue of *Arch Digest* under her nose, blindly thumbing through the pages. "Well, your father has some big news to share. He's been offered a position to head Tel-Carlton. In Prague," she said, with an edge of disappointment. "He's ready for a change," she said somewhat curtly. You just knew those two had an issue on this one.

"Wow, how exciting! Go, Mom!" My attempt to try to be a cheerleader on this.

"Interesting that you see it that way. Emily, I'm too old for this. It was fine moving about the world when we were younger but now, with Oliver, I finally feel settled—complacent with Manhattan life. It's the perfect place for us at this time."

"How does Oliver feel about this?"

"Your father's won him over with the three D's."

"The three D's?"

"The three D's," she repeated indignantly, as if I should know this.

"Hmm? Delivery. Diet food. Driver."

"Oliver—not me," she snarled. "Dad, Dorit, and Dog. He tried to make it the four D's with drums, but I absolutely forbade it."

"So Dorit finds no problems in moving to Eastern Europe?"

"No, it's actually ideal for her. Lisa was recently offered a promotion with Nike, to be transferred to Paris."

"Yes, Lisa mentioned that to me in her last E-mail. Great for her."

"Yes, everything seems to be working out for everyone. Except me," she moaned.

"Me, too." I laughed.

"So. What do you make of all of this?"

"Well. What's Dad's POV?"

"He's completely invigorated. I haven't seen him this rallied since he outbid Leland Cole for a private tennis lesson with Pete Sampras at that charity auction."

"I remember that. So rarely do I see him so animated. Mom, I think this is a really exciting thing. Dad has really exposed you to a charmed life."

"Well, it's starting to lose its charm. There's Oliver's school, renovating the basement, my fund-raising responsibilities at the Met."

"Excuses, excuses, excuses."

She was making excuses the way I make daily To Do lists. Her work at the museum? Okay, that involved a meeting a month. And I've seen her business cards: CATHERINE BRIGGS NOT-FOR-PROFIT FUND-RAISER. Real convincing.

Oliver would love it. Living in London when I was a little girl was a life-altering experience—exposure to a culture that wasn't patterned after prime time television. That departure from the prescribed American life is part of the reason I was who I was. Am who I am.

This would be good for Oliver, for him to gain a perspective away from this New York–centric mindset—a place foreign to deliveries, dog walkers, and little girls named Haley.

"And Anne's wedding."

"Anne has a wedding planner, Aunt Sophie and the entire staff of *Martha Stewart Weddings* at her disposal. Not to mention my duties as maid of honor, which I am constantly reminded of by daily E-mail updates."

"I've been afraid to mention this to you, but your Aunt Sophie let on that Anne was a bit concerned about your duties. She's still disappointed on how you handled her thirtieth birthday."

"What?" I squirmed from shock. "I put together a really fun party for her at Float. Todd Oldham, Frederic Fekkai, and Chris Noth showed."

"I meant thirteenth birthday—when you went with the roller-skating theme and Anne didn't know how to stop. But her thirtieth? Come to think of it, she had been upset about that one as well—finding it a bit . . ." She paused. "Tawdry."

Right, this was Anne we were dealing with.

"Okay, fine. Let's forget Anne for now. Prague? I am all for it. Just give it a trial run, say, for six months. And then reassess the situation from there."

"Well, your father thinks that he needs to only be there for a year, eighteen months at most. And we intend to keep the town house here in the city. And they promised to provide us with the most elegant housing that Prague has to offer."

My mother, Princess Catherine.

"I think the decision is made."

"But Oliver?"

"Don't speak for Oliver. He'll relish in the experience. Exposure to a new culture, enabling him to have an ear for foreign languages."

"True." She was perking up.

"I'd go for it."

"Well, you have enlightened me." She looked at the digital clock on the stove, which read 2:53 A.M. "Good golly, look at the time!" She stuffed the tea bag down the disposable drain, placed the mug in the top rack of the dishwasher, restacked the magazines (clapping their edges into a perfect box) and kissed me on my head.

"Good night, love," she said. "And you look absolutely radiant this evening."

Left alone in the kitchen, I was illuminated by a track light beaming on me from above like a pathway to heaven.

25

A quill pen grazing my nose awakened me. The tickling sensation was followed by innocent giggles.

"Emily!" Oliver fell on top of me, causing the bed to bounce.
If only I could wake up to such euphoria every day.

"Hey, you," I quipped, stretching my arms over my head. "Still
into the Fathers of the Revolution?"

"Vaclav Havel."

"Havel?"

"He's my hero."

"Oh, so you're excited about Prague, are you?"

"I'm going to get a dog!" he erupted. "A mastiff."

"Mastiffs drool, which is what I was doing yesterday when I
had a massage."

"GrrrRoss! I will call him Cornelius," he declared.

"After Yukon Cornelius?"

"Nah-ah! Cornelius the Carthaginian general. Who's Yukon
Cornelius?"

"You're not watching enough television."

"Mom lets me watch the Discovery Channel."

"Please, you need to get the classics in."

I got up, wearing a pajama top of Dad's that I had snagged
from the top of a folded pile in the laundry room. It smelled like
Tide and Bounce, one of the most intoxicating aromas. Wandering
over to the closet, I spotted my running sneakers tucked away in
the corner of the closet.

"Hey, Olive you! Will you go ask Mom if she has a T-shirt and running pants I can borrow?"

"But it's sooo warm outside."

I walked over to the window, cracking it open. A breeze more suited to a warmer, rural environment slid beneath the frame. It was considerably hotter than the day before, as if I had just flown to Florida.

Excellent. My first run of the season where my legs would be exposed to air.

"Ask Mom if she has a pair of shorts, then. Want to come along with me while I run? You can ride your bike alongside me."

"Goody! Mommy!" he screamed wildly, running out of the room. "Mommy!" I heard the yelping fade down the hallway.

I went into the bathroom to brush my teeth with Tom's toothpaste. Now I know why I never stay here. Tom's toothpaste? As ecologically cool as the packaging seemed, it just didn't give me the same clean feeling as Colgate.

"Emily," said my mother with a tap to the door. "I left some running clothes for you on the bed. There's also a running bra, socks and cotton underwear."

"Um . . ."

"Don't worry dear, they're new underwear."

"Thanks, those will be useful." She closed the door to give me privacy, then peered in right as the door was about to shut.

"Are you sure you want Oliver to accompany you?"

"Of course. I'd love to spend time with my brother, especially considering that I won't be seeing him come a few months from now."

"Don't harp on the sadness of it all."

"Mom," I said firmly. "It'll be okay."

"Very well, then. Just make sure he keeps his helmet on."

My clothes had that tags-just-ripped-off feel and smell. Everything in this place was so new, like a hotel. Mom didn't keep anything longer than a few weeks.

Oliver, who looked ready to take a bike tour through wine country, greeted me by the front door after I'd done a few hasty stretches on the banister.

We walked to the park, and, once we hit the track, I began to jog at a slow pace while Oliver zoomed ahead. I focused on the fluorescent flag on his bike, which was supported by a long, bouncy fishing rod.

"Ol love," I shouted as loud as possible without bringing too much attention to myself. "Keep close, please."

His bicycle zigzagged among Roller Bladers, runners and other weekend warriors, probably the cause of much annoyance to, luckily for me, complete strangers. After I did my part pleading with him to remain close, I began to enter my running zone.

Oliver's *Star Wars* Storm Trooper helmet again reappeared, coming into clearer focus by the second.

"Em," he managed after a few puffs. "Dash," he made out. I then looked up and noticed Dash on Roller Blades. His face covered with one big grin. I'd say shit eating but somehow I couldn't imagine eating shit.

"So you're MIA for months and now I see you twice in under twenty-four. Have you finally realized that uptown isn't just about Barbour coats and champagne brunches?"

"Never," I said, surprisingly chipper considering that I had to stop my run. "With all of these social distractions I'll never clock my miles in."

"Of course—Emily's obsessive-compulsive running regimen. Well, don't let me keep you." Oliver followed our exchanges like a game of tennis. "How about I see you later, at your place. Free for dinner?"

"Sure!"

"See you at eight." He skated off confidently until he was a singular blur meshed with other blurs.

I started running, my pace accelerated substantially. The thoughts I had earlier were obsolete after seeing Dash. Now consumed by our brief encounter, I couldn't help but smile.

Oliver rode alongside me. He peddled, I treaded—both of us engrossed until we returned to our original starting point. We walked home in silence.

26

The smell of bacon and sound of laughter came from the kitchen—bacon, healthy or not, is the all-time best morning aroma. It said Sundays with the paper and *polite* family conversation. It should be bottled and marketed. Like those new-car-smell air fresheners, which I'm completely opposed to.

"Tweety!" shouted Dorit, her roly-poly physique framed by the narrow hallway. She was just a little grayer since the last I saw her, but not an added wrinkle to her dewy face.

She cupped my cheeks for a quick inspection and then pulled me in between her bosoms, which looked and felt like two sacks of sand—the safest place in the world.

"Dorit," I purred. Suctioning my head from the clamp of her breasts, I turned my face upward. "You're as smoking as ever."

She let out a thunderous laughter, her whole body shaking.

"Look at you, girl. Not an ounce of meat on you." She always said this, hence the name Tweety—I was too skinny, in her view, like a tweety bird.

"You get yourself cleaned up for breakfast. I've got eggs, bacon, bagels, fresh squeezed juice, and fruit. And I also made one of those weird Egg Beater omelets you somehow manage to eat."

"Yum!" The vision of a spread created by Dorit swelled in my head.

"And blueberries as big as marbles, especially for you."

We entered the kitchen, which was abuzz with Mom setting

various platters and Dad sifting through sections of the Sunday
Times.

"Oh, good, you're back," Mom said, sounding almost hostile
in comparison to Dorit's greeting.

"Okay, dear, you can begin," she directed Dad.

Without even noticing the banquet displayed before him, he
took the box of Familia Muesli next to his bowl, and poured
while his eyes remained fixed on the paper. Once the clatter of
falling cereal faded to a sound of a few coins dropping in a well,
he scooped a spoonful of sliced bananas from an adjacent bowl
and poured milk from the mouth of a ceramic cow, expertly ex-
ecuted even though he wasn't looking at what he was doing. His
actions reminded me of *Little House on the Prairie*, when Mary
learned how to feed herself after she lost her eyesight and without all of the histrionic tilting of the head. He then took a sip of
his already poured coffee and inserted some cereal into his
mouth.

Oliver ran over and tugged the rim of Mom's chocolate colored sweater, so snug it instantly snapped back to the rim of her
velvet paisley pants.

"H and H?" he asked excitably, peeking onto the counter at a
large ceramic dish of bagels.

"It *is* Sunday, Oliver."

"Yes!" Oliver took a poppy seed bagel, plopped it onto a plate,
and seated himself next to Dad, who continued to feed himself
with eyes transfixed on the "Money and Business" section.

The kitchen island covered with offerings that I could have
lived on for a month. My two forefingers made their way into the
large glass bowl of blueberries and I surreptitiously popped a
few into my mouth.

"Do you need to take a shower?" asked Mother haughtily. The
woman was a surveillance camera—nothing got past my mom,
who was raised on Emily Post the way kids today are raised on
videos.

"No, I'm fine. Didn't really get the workout I had hoped for."

"We saw Dash," Oliver said, cutting the bagel that was as big as
a Frisbee.

"Oh, really," said Mother in that nosy neighbor way.

"Yeah, no big deal."

"That boy still a-chasing you," chimed in Dorit. As my mouth opened, she said, "I know, I know, you two just friends. How about some coffee with those berries?"

"No, thanks. I'm fine," I said, starting to make a plate for myself.

"And here I go all the way over to The Vinegar Factory for that Vanilla Hazelnut decaf."

"Oh! In that case, I'd love some."

Now Oliver, Dad, and I were seated and happily consuming our favorite breakfast foods while Mother and Dorit were on duty to attend to any of our other needs. Mom was assisting Oliver with the application of strawberry cream cheese while Dorit replenished neglected platters with fresher choices.

After Dad finished his coffee he inserted his plates into the dishwasher and returned to his seat, picking through the paper for a few more sections.

"I'm off to my study" was his only announcement to the family. "Lovely to see you, Emily." He gave me a peck on my head.

Oliver, too, finished his breakfast, but left his plate behind. He grabbed a YooHoo from the fridge and vanished. His departure was heard by booming thumps up the stairs—Mother following his point of exit shortly thereafter.

Dorit and I were left to finish cleaning the kitchen. There was significantly more food left over than actually consumed.

"Please, I've got that," Dorit said, pointing to the Ziploc freezer bag I was unsealing for the remaining bagels, her arm jiggling with fat.

"You sure?"

"Absolutely. This is my favorite time. Between you and me, I pick at a little bit of everything while I put it away. My private feast."

"How fun. I'm like that late at night."

"Let me guess. Ben and Jerry's?"

"Of course!"

I left Dorit to take a shower—the water pressure noticeably stronger than the shower in my apartment. I came out smelling like a popsicle from all of the Origins fruity products I had slathered onto my body, so putting on last night's smoke-drenched clothes was a bit of a setback.

All Briggs members were now designated to their specified rooms. Before heading back home I decided to check in on Mom where she was standing, peering out the window as if she was expecting a visitor.

"Mom," I said tenderly so as not to startle her from her daze. She jumped and I noticed a cookie that she haplessly attempted to conceal behind her back.

"Is that a chocolate chip cookie?"

"No," she snapped, annoyed. "It's a Snackwell."

I approached her, plucking the cookie from her hand and sniffing the evidence.

"This is so not a Snackwell. This is a Duncan Hines chocolate chip cookie, all eight grams of fat of it—the only thing I found edible in my paper-bagged lunch days."

"Oh, Emily, what is it that you want?"

"Don't get all antagonistic. We do have our splurges."

"What's yours?" she huffed, still annoyed.

"Well, Ben and Jerry's, which you know about."

"And that's low fat."

"I do have a thing for ordering black-and-white milkshakes at diners."

"I love those too!" Her face brightened.

"Great Saturday morning fare." Especially the morning after a debauch night of too many gimlets and sex, but I didn't think she'd care for those details.

"Well, I just came to say good-bye, not to play detective on your daily calorie intake."

"I'm sorry, dear. It was so nice to have you here, so comfortable and pleasant when you're around." She wrapped her arms around me, which felt nothing like the embrace of Dorit—a wispy reed next to the solid oak of Dorit. At first I felt awkward, staring at my hands, momentarily forgetting how to use them; then I patted her back and surrendered into a tight embrace.

"Yeah, I know what you mean. It's comforting to be here." I broke from the hug.

"So you're really okay?"

"Sure, I'm okay. Just navigating the obstacles life routinely throws my way."

"I'm sorry," she said, shaking her day-after-blowout silky hair.

THE FABULOUS EMILY BRIGGS

"What I really meant was if you were okay with this big move of ours."

"Well, I assume I answered this, considering that, no offense to my love for you, Dad, and Oliver, I do have my own life now. I'm sure this sounds completely self-absorbed."

"Of course not, it sounds independent, something you've always been, ever since you used to live in that little tree house of yours saying that it was better that you have your own place. What? At the age of eight? It's funny, I see so much of myself in you."

D'oh!—my mind just screamed a Homer Simpson yelp. I mean, talk about taking the fizz from the champagne, bubble from your bath. How could she possibly see herself in me when we were *nothing* alike?

Worried that one of my faces gave me away, how this little Lane's Keepsake Hope Chest moment sputtered into a good idea but not at all in fit with the scheme of the John Pawson styled bedroom that I secretly fantasize sharing with my newlywed husband who could double for George Clooney, I had to say something so not to hurt Mom's feelings.

But perhaps if I woke up tomorrow morning and did everything I normally would do differently I'd change into something that would have no resemblance to my mother. That's it!

"Emily? Are you all right?"

"What's that?" I said, shaking my head like the dizzy blonde that I secretly wish I were.

"You look a bit flushed. I really do worry if you're using the right creams."

Right. Creams.

27

I walked home, keeping on Park to avoid the weekend shoppers on Madison but, really, to keep from wandering into every store. Dash would be arriving in about two hours—two episodes of *The Sopranos,* getting my hair trimmed at a $200-a-visit salon, a flight to Bermuda, or an afternoon nap after a night of drinking. I wanted to use the time to get in a workout and make sure that the apartment was in order. Nixing the workout idea, I focused on straightening up—both the apartment and me.

Feeding old Pearl Jam to the CD player, I wandered from room to room draining a bottle of Windex. I squirted counters, blemished walls and the edges of picture frames with one hand while I wiped the dust with a dishcloth in the other, purposely avoiding any windows—a useless effort that would just irritate me as a rushed clean surely couldn't remove the grime that accumulated on a New York City window. Sufficiently ensconced in the cleaning zone, I became obsessed by the reality that I had grimy windows. There was no way that this apartment would be presentable with such gritty windows.

The thought of my magnetic squeegee sponge I had purchased from QVC on a particularly sleepless night started to excite me. Sufficiently excited about the idea of using my new squeegee toy, I decided to give it a test try. My face reddening with excitement from imagining the effects of how the sponge would sop up layers of New York City grime from my windows. It would bring in more fresh light for an entirely new effect; the

$19.99 squeegee investment would triple the value of my apartment. I must watch and buy more home improvement items on QVC. Perhaps I should be one of those real-life presenters who says how the item had changed my life. I reached for my pad, scribbling this idea down, and set out to do my life-changing task.

Opening the living room window, I watched an alarmingly large fly, more suited for a third-world country, buzz right in. The damn pest was probably waiting for just such an opportunity to gain access. Damn bug completely distracted me from the mission of the moment. Twirling and snapping the dishcloth into a weapon, I unsuccessfully chased him around the apartment. Completely flummoxed I just watched as the nasty black bug ricocheted from far corner to far corner, taking a rest break on my mantel. I crept up to him, swatting the guy fatally, his crumpled body falling to the terra-cotta floor that rims the fireplace.

Sweeping him into a dustpan (and he must be a "him," very testosterone-y), I then flicked his remains into the hallway. Becoming mildly disgusted that such a filthy, germ-ridden pest had contaminated my apartment, I returned to the cleaning product bin beneath the kitchen sink and took out a can of Lysol, spraying every area that the pest touched. Not pleased with the antiseptic smell, I then pumped wildly across the room almost an entire bottle of Gardenia Mathias home fragrance (the absolute best). As I was about to eyedrop environmental oil onto the overhead lamp and light a few candles the phone interrupted me.

"Emily? It's Dash. I'm calling you from my cell because I've been trying to buzz you."

I lowered the stereo. "Sorry, I just had the CD on a bit too loud. Come on up!"

Throwing the products and cloth under the kitchen sink, I raced back into the living room for a quick inspection in the mirror above my mantel. Aside from a few wispy strands of hair that were too short for my high ponytail, I looked remarkably pulled together, especially considering that I had spent more energy on murdering a fly and primping the apartment than on myself.

"Hi," I said, out of breath, as Dash came through the door.

"Woo!" he shrieked, a bit too theatrically for my liking. "It smells like a candle shop in here—what's with the suffocating odor?"

"Yeah. I had to kill a big fly."

"And this answers my question *how?*"

Blowing off his apparent ineptitude on the germ-infested properties of a dead fly, the real issue at hand was the two bundles tucked under each of Dash's arms, both dramatically different, both causing dramatically different reactions.

His left had a bag from Healthy Pleasures—one of the best natural food stores in the city—the other had a hairless anorexic dog, like a miniature greyhound, which had reached the point of hospitalization and was in need of intravenous feeding.

"What the hell is that?"

"I know," he moaned apologetically, releasing the dog to the ground. She darted over to me with a woeful look for approval. I cautiously dabbed its head like it was hot food just removed from the oven. Realizing that she would not be receiving the accolades she was in search of, the creature pranced around the room like a quarter horse on crack.

"This is not a dog, it's a circus freak." The creature continued to parade about the living room with its openly effete histrionics apparently not aware of how ridiculous she looked. "I am amazed that you, of all people, would be in possession of such a puntable animal."

"All right already. It's Katrina's. Well, really, Katrina gave her to me, but I granted her custody of Fifi because of my crazy hours at work."

"Fifi. Her name is Fifi?" A salesperson at Gucci couldn't sound more snide. "Let me guess, you named the creature?"

"Katrina's building doesn't allow pets so I'm holding on to her until her aunt returns from Italy, who promised to care for her."

Lucky for the creature. Now I wouldn't have to slowly poison it.

"All right, then," I said, as if I had agreed to go along with an inconvenient plan. What I found most interesting about this animal—aside from the fact that a dog, which is not subjected to society's unreasonable standards on being thin and could indulge on as much food as possible, still remained anorexic—was that Katrina still had a hold on Dash through this yappy creature.

"So what's in the bag," I said, nose pointing to the bundle that was refreshingly absent of any movement. Dash removed a jar of Peanut Wonder from the bag, one of my all-time favorite foods. It's natural peanut butter without all of the evil qualities of Skippy—even yummier in its deficiency of the chemical aftertaste.

"Dash!" I gushed. He gained many points, leveraging his knowledge of my passion for low-fat junk food.

I took the jar into the kitchen while the creature trotted alongside me like a piece of annoying fluff magnetically held to my side. I believe she sensed the savory rewards held within the jar. But I didn't think peanut butter was appropriate dog food.

Returning to Dash, I found him remarkably at ease, having settled onto my couch. I was expected to join him, judging by his longing expression.

Once I sat down, the creature jumped onto my lap. (Luckily it's a shorthaired creature, otherwise my thoughts would have been on how I'd have to Dustbust the dog hairs later.)

I pushed her off me but it was like hitting a tennis ball on a rubber cord. I felt Dash staring at me, not at the dog that so annoyed me.

"Do you want anything?" I asked, pushing the creature off me again with such thrust that it slid quite a distance before regaining her legs and scurried into a corner.

Dash flashed me a wicked look, but not for mistreating the creature.

"To drink," I quipped. He clamped a wisp of my hair into two fingers like a curling iron and began to twirl it.

"You look really good with long hair," he said, and then went in for the kiss.

"Whoa!"

"What is it?" He pulled away in shock.

Though I was aware that the purpose of Dash's visit was to convert this relationship from friend to intimate, his advance was a bit sudden, especially considering that we were still sober.

"I thought we'd go get some food and take the creature for a walk. I don't know—it's a bit sudden to go from Dash best friend to Dash spit swapping without some kind of transitional moment."

"All right, then. Let's go for a walk." The creature perked up, bony tail thumping against the wall.

"We can't go for a walk now! Knowing that we'll just come back and return to this same awkward moment."

I was not annoyed with Dash, just disappointed in his method of seduction. As much as he had the inside track on getting me, he did have the challenge of shedding his previous puerile role.

"Okay, then. Thoughts?" He didn't sound particularly happy.

"I know," I said, getting up from the couch. "Shots. Let's do shots of tequila!"

"You make me out to be the old landowner taking away the virginal bride from her family. And that she's a wreck having to lose her virginity on her wedding night."

"Sounds about right, except for the virginal part."

"Let's just forget this happened."

I looked at him, wounded.

"No, I mean we started off badly. You're right—we can't just jump into bed together because we both want it to happen. You do want it to happen?"

I nodded, not entirely convinced.

"I would like to take you out for sushi. I know you like sushi. I know we like to eat sushi together. This is something that we do. So let's do it. Uh, go for some sushi, rather."

"Great," I said, pressure lifted. "But what about the creature? Will the creature be okay here on her own?"

"Fifi," he scolded. The creature then scampered over to his knees nervously. It was a very nervous creature.

"I'm sorry. I just can't help but wonder how you can say that name and act all serious."

Fifi then looked to me sadly. For God's sake the animal could understand what I was saying.

"You sure she'll be okay?" Thoughts of mini turds adding scale to my pony-skin ottoman began to scare me.

"She'll be fine. Or should we call for takeout?"

"I like that idea." I walked to the kitchen cordless and dialed East, reciting my order and then Dash's. "Did I forget anything?" He winked in approval while lifting the creature's ears like a gremlin. This made me laugh.

Reaching for some plates from the cabinet, I looked into my stove/liquor cabinet for a bottle of wine and was momentarily struck by the bottle of tequila. *Drink me,* it was calling. *Forget getting a glass, just unscrew my top and pour me down your throat.* I could have taken a quick swig right then—but then I may have reeked of the evidence—so I decided against it.

When I got up, Dash was directly in front of me, this time locking my lips. I fell into his seduction.

He lifted me up onto the counter. I wrapped my legs around his waist. His body was powerful, his swimming at 5:00 A.M. each weekday morning paying off. My hands raked his soft hair—possibly even softer than mine. What shampoo could he possibly be using? Tongues tickling one another interspersed by butterfly-wing-to-the-touch kisses. He was an excellent kisser. My hands slid down his back, beneath his khakis, aimed straight for his butt. He always had such a cute butt.

Bzzzz. The buzzer made that unctuous sound that's as rude as an uptown doyenne hissing at her help. I tried to get over to the buzzer but Dash had me firmly planted to the counter, jailed in between his arms. My thoughts were less intent on his kiss and now focused on the steaming miso soup that was getting cold.

"Dash," I whispered. "Food." Kiss. "Access." More kisses. "Buzzer." He stopped kissing me. Thank God.

"Right, then," he said. I buzzed the current object of my desire in while Dash walked over to his Burberry satchel, pulled out his wallet to attend to the takeout and padded the delivery man's palm with some cash.

"Do you have a bowl that is canine usable?" he asked, walking into the kitchen waving a Ziploc bag of kibbles that resembled Mother's breakfast.

"Hmmm," I wondered aloud, then transferred our rolls onto a platter patterned with blue and white dragons and pinwheels, sort of a Chinese *toile de Jouay,* which I had bought at Pearl River and had intended solely for sushi.

Rinsing the aluminum container, I handed it to Dash to use for the creature's dinner. I poured the miso into a ceramic bowl—another Pearl River find—and filled the plastic container with Fifi's water.

Dash smiled, presumably at my frugal inventiveness.

"You know what they say." He snickered, setting out the creature's food while her nose dove magnetically into the kibbles. "A maid in the kitchen, a whore in the bedroom."

"Who says this!" I freaked, throwing my hands into the air. Dash's deviant smile folded into a squiggly line. He bumbled like a cad.

"Uh. Joke?"

"Yeah, joke my ass."

I was actually not that mad. His blunder before dinner was an excuse to focus on our food, not having to return to our passionate moment.

I shot him a you're-lucky-for-now-buster face, placing the platter, soup, and plates onto a tray and returned to the living room.

"Will you get the pitcher of water in the fridge? And some glasses," I called to him. "Also choose a bottle of wine."

"In the stove/liquor cabinet?"

"Yes, please."

"Any preference?"

"Just something white."

I started transferring our meal from the tray onto the coffee table. When Dash joined me, the remote was immediately fastened to his hand in an action position, like webs shooting from the wrists of Spiderman. (Dash's current obsession—now over his dinosaur period).

As he absently surfed through the channels, I chose not to participate in this migraine-inducing ritual men endure. While he flipped, I reached for the new issue of *Bazaar* and turned the pages reflexively. He flipped through channels. I flipped through pages. Who was absorbing more useless knowledge was anyone's guess.

After dinner Dash helped me stack the plates back onto the tray. I awakened the creature from sleeping on my feet by wiggling my toes upward. She returned to her teetering movements, this time jostling her feet in place, alternating paws as if she were standing on hot sand.

"Should I make a Tasti D-Lite run?" asked Dash, evidently sucking up from his previous blunder. "I know how you love to put your Peanut Wonder on top of it." Interesting strategy—acknowledging his main success of the night with what I was sure was an attempt to lure me back into a heated moment.

"That's okay, love." I kissed his nose. "You can still screw me." Dash looked befuddled.

"Why so befuddled?"

"You're truly nuts, Em."

"You don't want to get me into bed?"

"I want to get you into bed!"

And so he lunged on top of me. This time there was no deliveryman to interfere. Just the creature pawing on top of us, newly energized by whatever it was Dash used to spike her kibbles.

Our hunger was sated, unless you count my current fixation with the jar of Peanut Wonder on the second shelf of the condiment cabinet and the half-eaten container of Ben and Jerry's low-fat Chocolate Brownie behind the bottles of Ketel One in the freezer. I think of how those two needed to be mixed together, like the old Reese's Peanut Butter Cup commercials that had two very perturbed individuals complaining, "Your chocolate is in my peanut butter!" "And your peanut butter is in my chocolate!"

Dash lifted me from the couch with gentle care, in an attempt to preserve my lying position the way you would use a spatula to lift a warm cookie from a baking sheet in hopes not to break it. Unfolding me onto my bed, we undressed one another in what seemed a routine act of foreplay after a mind-numbing workday. We were deep in the throes of fooling around, but Dash didn't attempt to sleep with me. We were two friends who shared the same bed together on a vacation, getting together the last night to relieve that pestering curiosity that was suppressed after a fantasy week, but succumbing to those suppressed desires knowing that the following morning we would return to everyday life.

Once Dash fell asleep—which I gathered after my staring at him for what seemed hours and detected by his flu-like breathing—I put on my pajama top and quietly lifted myself from bed. Every ripple of the sheet, crick from my bones sounded like car alarms. I held in my breathing, on the verge of suffocation.

Making my way through the hallway by the Martian green battery light emanating from the fire alarm, I reached the kitchen without causing any bruises from bumping into corners that I forgot existed. I opened the cabinet for the Peanut Wonder and quickly turned around, feeling suspiciously caught in the act.

The creature was wagging its crow hook of a tail. While annoyed by its presence, I was encouraged by its courtesy in not exposing me with any yelping sounds.

"I'd share some with you," I offered, twisting the lid till it made that lip smacking pop, releasing its captivating nutty aroma, "but I've heard of terrible things that happen to dogs when they consume peanut butter. Very, very bad things. The sad demise of a particular basset hound comes to mind."

The creature turned its head and lifted its paw into the air like it was auditioning for a chow commercial. I was suckered.

"All right," I folded. "There must be a Scooby snack somewhere in here." I unloaded my pantry of mustards, spices, tea, a box of Equal and jar of Sarabeth's strawberry preserves.

"Hmm. Maybe these crackers that come with this can of tuna?"

"Who are you talking to?"

"Gag-jeez!" I screamed, dropping the Bumble Bee lunch kit onto the counter, causing the creature to scamper to the corner.

"My God, Dash. You scared the bejeebers out of me!"

"Bejeebers?"

Oh, God, please don't let it be true. I didn't want to become my mother.

28

Dash was away on business in LA for a week, forcing us to communicate through E-mail. He was much sexier on E-mail. But not in that phone sex kind of way, asking things like "what are you wearing as you're typing this?" Since Dash very well knows that it would be pajama bottoms and a cashmere sweater serving the purpose of a sweatshirt, that line of questioning wouldn't really work.

It was more his sincere ways that brought a warm blush to my face, even in the seclusion of my studio.

"Are you aware of how gorgeous you are in the morning?" he wrote. While I responded in something sarcastic and immature, slightly insecure, he bounced back with a simple, "Em, I'm serious. You are beyond that, you make me want to create life."

And so our meeting up at his apartment on Saturday night had the pressure of a first kiss. Luckily I was drunk during my first kiss, which makes sense come to think of it as the two do go hand in hand.

Arriving at his apartment, I was greeted by Dash in a frantic rush. He needed to leave for the office to check on something late-breaking. Apologizing, he instructed me to wait behind as he didn't want to subject me to the obligations of his work.

I toyed with the idea of getting a drink somewhere, but this was a momentary thought as being in his apartment alone did hold some allure.

My first thought was to investigate his art nouveau bar trolley—accessorized with basket weaved crystal containing the kind of hard alcohol that only writers or men with abusive wives drink.

Above the bar there was a vintage photograph of a waiter in a tux, skating with a cocktail tray; framed in dark wood and heavily matted, the black and whites perfectly contrasted with the elephant-gray walls. A zebra skin throw on a black leather ottoman casually completed the makeshift bar area. Dash definitely had the Ralph Lauren TriBeCa series thing going on. But drinking alone really was a bit too barfly and was not as interesting as perusing the bedroom.

His bedroom was more an homage to the design team of the W hotel. The flat screen television had DVDs on hand that are played for background effect—notably a few James Bonds (with Sean Connery as 007) and two Cary Grant films (*North By Northwest* and *To Catch A Thief*). A sleek black console camouflaged the television and stereo equipment, like a sewing kit to a smattering of thread and needles. Bedside tables held industrial steel lamps with springy centers like the chord of a showerhead and a Huene photograph of a couple wearing retro bathing suits posed like statues, which dominated the wall above the black headboard.

Centering myself on the goose-down Pratesi linens bordered by two dark ski tracks, my body punctured the middle like a button sewn into a pillow. I made a snow angel, moving my arms and legs wildly to further crease the cloudlike bedding.

Inside his bedside drawer there was a notepad lifted from the Chateau Marmot, on which was written a phone number. After punching *69 and, luckily, receiving Dash's office voice mail, I dialed the number on the pad, which connected me to Shun Lee. I wasn't in the mood for Chinese so I hung up. All that remained were two Pilot fine-tipped pens and a rumpled dictionary. But by rifling farther to the back corners, I found a rectangular matchbox with "Hudson" etched in silver—no discriminating pictures, letters, drugs or condoms.

His bathroom was immaculate, the floor glistened like melted licorice. No smudgy footprints, not even a strand of his honey colored hair that could be found on tiles so black and shiny they made a piece of onyx look like coal.

The walls broke into a random black-and-white mosaic like a crossword puzzle. The mirrored shower stall and nickled bath seat gave the entire bathroom a Tamara Beckwith art deco effect. Going directly for the medicine cabinet, I discovered it was basically an ad for Kiehl's—Kiehl's coconut body lotion, shaving cream, grooming lotion for fine, flyaway hair, cucumber eye gel. Opening each container, I inspected their scents and textures—sampling those creams I'd consider using. The newsprint packaging kept in sync with the monochromatic scheme of the entire apartment. If it weren't for Dash's soft hair, which occasionally (frequently) was a source of jealousy on a particularly bad hair day, I would have attributed his choice of products purely to their harmonious design. Deriving no deviant pleasure from snooping on Dash, I decided I could get more of a rush eavesdropping on my parents' dinner conversations.

Returning to his bed, I glided my hand along the pearly buttons of my blouse, unbuttoning each with one hand, and unclasping my bra to fondle my breast with the other. I then swiped my hand past my navel like a credit card being put to its proper use. Reaching my pant button, I undid it greedily and pulled my jeans over my French blue silky thong adorned with heavily stitched flowers. Starting to feel moist between my legs, I slipped off my panties so they settled on my shed pants.

My fingers probed inside myself adeptly, feeling about in a tickly motion the way I'd flicker them for a dropped key beneath a grate. Laced in a goopy film that was even more concentrated than Dash's eye gel, I used my dry hand to clasp my bra, then pulled up my panties. Lifting myself from the bed in a ravenous haze, I traced my syrupy fingers along Dash's console, bureau—languidly moving into the hall, the last drop of olive oil spewing from its bottle. I traced the rims of picture frames, books—my slicked fingers touching anything personal.

The sound of a key jabbing into the front door shattered my reverie the way it did when I hit traffic driving well over the speed limit. Too late to return to my clothes, I just stood there, awaiting my inevitable demise.

Dash entered. His composed face in the routine of returning to his home suddenly morphed into one of surprise. I looked down at myself. Bra and panties exposed while a flimsy shirt was unbuttoned like a coat. I was a cheesy goddamn Victoria's Secret ad without the garter belt.

"Um, Emily?" he said, naturally in surprise.

"Hi, Dash," I responded, hand waving in the air ridiculously. "I'm sorry. I suddenly wanted to take a shower and forgot my bag. Here"—I scanned the room—"right there," I said, locating the bag in question and then pointing to it—inconveniently far from where I was standing. "It has my toothbrush and such."

God, I hoped I brought my toothbrush in case he pressed this further.

While I was trying to think of more organic excuses, I was met with what appeared to be an elated Dash. His smile widened, dropping his keys on the pewter dish next to the door that was solely intended for them. He approached me.

"You're apologizing for greeting me like this?" He grabbed my waist and thrust me into him. But, no, he did not go with the moment and bring me to the floor. Dash cupped my cheeks and led me to the bedroom. Just as well, the sisal would have left some nasty scratch marks on my back and bikini season was approaching.

I plunged back into his pillow of a bed as he dove after me with a beginning swimmer's hesitation at going into the deep end. Lower on the bed, he hastily climbed up my body like rungs on a ladder. He gripped my legs, navel, passing through each rest stop hungrily till he reached the point of destination, the Golden Arches. Once his head greeted mine, he left his hands on my breasts, pulsing them the way you would throb a tennis ball before making a serve. Honking my breasts and tonguing my mouth, this was not getting it on but a frat boy knowing that he had an audience to impress by a hidden camera. His squeezes showed his athleticism as a climber and I could feel the ensuing bruising by their aches. An entire vial of arnica won't care for the plum stains that will stain my breasts. I couldn't stop thinking about the amount of weeks till bikini season and when the bruises would be erased from my skin.

Erogenous zones! I hummed to myself.

"Erogenous zones!" I called out in annoyance, as a plea for help, but Dash took it differently. He looked to me as if he had just finished his Big Mac and was now onto the deluxe-size fries.

It was the go-ahead to start right in. But before taking in such a reward, he opened his side drawer, which lost me for a moment. Reaching for the dictionary? I found his timing to look up the meaning of a curious word inappropriate. But in the dictionary was a condom. It all made sense right now. I was a snooper. Katrina was probably a snooper. And I'm sure his mother who visited him a few weeks ago was a snooper. So pulling out the condom, probably filed under S for Safe, he did the responsible thing. No, Dash was not the kind of guy who got lost in a moment, had sex on the floor or had to deal with a knocked-up lover.

And so he entered me. It was rough, strong, the kind of service I imagined the ladies in Fairfield County get, at least in the beginning until their husbands strayed.

I just followed the strum of his pumping body, finding a visit to the gynecologist's office more of a turn on. My mind wandered into Dash's freezer, looking forward to getting this over with so we could have a post-sex splurge. He'd heat up his Shun Lee after I softened the Tasti D-Lite he bought for me solely for this purpose.

Running a race should be fast, not sex. Dash finished, coming in record time, which I noted by his post-workout pants huffed into my ear. I didn't even come—me, who can get an orgasm by sitting on top of a washing machine. I supposed I was so consumed by thoughts of Dash's well-stocked pantry, with the added luxury of sprinkles and chocolate sauce to indulge in (the kitchen cabinets covered in a previous snoop) that attempting an orgasm was not even an option from his sex-workout video routine.

He now cradled next to me in a fetal position. I was waiting, trying to find the right moment to suggest a visit to the kitchen.

"I am so into you," he said, turning back on top of me and cupping my head. Cupping was real big with him.

I responded with a smile. There was nothing to say. I was not an actress. To expound feelings of intimacy after that excuse for sex would be as artificial as the container of Tasti D-Lite my stomach currently craved. Is this how it would be? Everything that I'd been advised to do when choosing your lifetime mate was now playing into action. I mentally rewound to all of the

guidance that I'd been given from my mother, Daphne and the
Christmas card of Louisa's kids—go with Dash, get the kids on
the card without having to adopt a child from the Far East.

"Hey, let's go see what's in the kitchen!" suggested Dash. Suddenly Christmas cards and a passionless marriage seemed a viable
option. He strutted into his bathroom, allowing me to freely check
out his naked butt. He did have a very cute butt. Returning with
two fluffy bathrobes that he probably charged to his corporate
card after staying at a Four Seasons on one of his business trips,
we robed our naked bodies. Though I was not just massaged,
pedicured and facialed in that post-spa treatment daze, I did
love the way I felt in fluffy white.

Licking my lips and smoothing my hands together, I worked
my way around Dash's kitchen in the same comfortable familiarity that I do in my own. Knowing exactly where his Williams Sonoma white chili bowls were, the Calvin Klein stainless steel utensils
and tall water glasses from Crate and Barrel—all purchases made
with me after he moved into his apartment when we hired a car
and made all the requisite stops to furnish a kitchen in a Saturday
afternoon's time.

Reenacting my vision of gastronomic happiness that was pre-
occupying me during the deed—I softened the peanut butter
fudge Tasti D-Lite in the microwave (twenty-two seconds), added
a squirt of chocolate sauce, a dash of sprinkles and even Reddi
Whip, fat-free. I shook the can with the same glee a child would
have, though I gathered that the Reddi Whip was intended to be
used on me, not by me from the smirk on Dash's face.

"Oh, please, after the mess it would make on your Pratesi
sheets? And there's only enough in here to cover one breast."

Dash looked befuddled.

"Not that I have enormously large breasts. The contents of
this can are limited. I know this from the many times that I've
leaned my head back and how fast it takes to squirt the entire
can into my mouth."

I returned to my routine and took a seat on one of the tall
swivel stools.

The room was eerily quiet. In my apartment there were always
city sounds of cars and neighbors, their presence given away by

footsteps creaking from my ceiling or a muffled television through the walls. But Dash's apartment was built of titanic steel.

"Who are your neighbors?" I asked.

Dash looked up, his head tilted in wonderment. "I don't really know. There used to be a young couple, Kate and Bill. They moved, right about the time she became rather large. Pregnant. I think they live somewhere in Connecticut now."

"Right. Connecticut." I mindlessly flipped through an issue of *New York Magazine*. I watched Dash watching me as his pizza heated up. It was a frozen Wolfgang Puck vegetable pizza, no cheese. There was another 4:38 minutes to go, 4:38 minutes of Dash's either having to initiate conversation or my being stared at in this moment that, if I were alone with my Tasti D-Lite, I would have found literally better than sex.

He continued staring, that stare laced with questions and concern. Maybe now my silence was an indication of my doubts on what we were as a couple. My food became inedible. This was not enjoyable.

"Can I ask you something?" he asked. Oh, God, here it came.

"Which is better—getting it soft-serve or having it this way?" What did he mean? Oh, my God, I thought, looking at the Tasti D-Lite creation that I just inhaled. He was referring to the Tasti D-Lite!

"Soft-serve," I answered immediately. "Absolutely. It's creamier, has more flavor. It goes down faster even though the action takes the same amount of time and I eat it with a teaspoon—to prolong the experience. But, don't get me wrong, this is great too."

The microwave signaled that Dash's pizza was ready. He quickly slid it onto the plate so as not to scorch his fingers. Now the microwave showed that it was 1:42 A.M.

"I mean, you can't have soft-serve Tasti D-Lite at 1:42 A.M. All of those places close at 11:00 P.M."

"No, they don't," he asserted. "There's a World of Nuts in Times Square that's open 24/7. I've wandered in there a few times after late nights in the office."

"Really? A World of Nuts that's 24/7? I can't believe that I, of all people, did not know about this. I will have to swing by there the next time I have an after-hours World of Nuts soft-serve urge."

He looked at me peculiarly.

"You're silly," he said, out of nowhere.

"Silly?"

Dash nodded as if this were funny.

"Silly," I repeated for effect. "Waddling penguins are silly. What happened to being beautiful, smart, clever—all the things that men betray their countries for?"

Dash now sat himself next to me, starting his version of post-sex munchies whereas I finished mine two minutes after I started it. He stared at the wall while chewing on his pizza. I assumed he was taking in what I had just said.

"Yeah, I could see betraying a country for you."

This was the right thing to say, which was a good thing since I no longer had anything that tasted delightful. If I were alone, which I seemed to be continually hoping for, I would have gone for a second, third—as many servings as it took till my stomach hardened like a pit in an avocado. But I was with Dash and I needed to act properly. He remained focused on the chewing of his pizza. I looked at the remaining wedges on his plate—this cheeseless pizza—basically a piece of dough with vegetables slopped on top of it. Dash could be such a girl when it came to food.

I returned to the mind-numbing routine of flipping through magazine pages, struck by the party pictures of a particular social column vaguely recognizing the people and place. It was from Biarritz. Apparently the evening that we were there was its official opening night and, sure enough, there was a picture of Dash and me outside the restaurant. He was looking at me all lovesick and I, too, had a bewitched expression on my face. I didn't remember the picture being taken. How did that happen?

"Dash, did you know about this?" I held the page up to his face like it was a mirror.

He tilted his head to the picture, removing the magazine from my hands for closer inspection.

"Well, I'll be," he said, approvingly—a noticeable spark from his previous comments. "I was wondering why the publicist sent me the advance copy."

"You're on the publicist's advance copy list?"

"Sure. For some issues. When she's pitching me more investigative pieces—typically cover stories. But I was stumped by her sending the Spring Interior Design Issue until now."

Dash studied the picture as intensely as Mother looks for new wrinkles after a day outside gardening. He then flipped through the magazine, settling on a profile of a banker/artist in his Williamsburg loft. I now had nothing to read and just looked at him.

"Are you okay with this?" he asked without turning away from the magazine.

"Sure, why wouldn't I be?" I said, somewhat hostile, which I realized surprised me—that a dumb picture would actually irritate me this much.

"It's just that I know you. How you feel about these things—preferring the anonymity of your illustrated world to following the flashbulbs."

"Oh, don't be silly. It's just a postage-stamp picture in a magazine. No one will ever notice." I then got up and placed my bowl and spoon in the empty dishwasher.

"And what if they do?" he said again, for the effect, "What if they do notice? Do you have any issues with that?"

"Dash, it's a picture in a dumb magazine. It would be pretty silly to be upset by something like this. I mean, look at my cousin Anne. The girl would give up a perfectly great night to watch a new release on DVD with her fiancé, just for a photo-op like this."

I said this knowing that I'd actually prefer watching the new release and, as I detected from Dash's expression, that he was aware of this.

"All right, then," he said, unconvincingly. "Let's just go to bed."

I'd spent many late nights at Dash's apartment but, even if the sun was breaking into its new day, I had always returned home—to my own bed, sneakers and runs to the river. Dash did live conveniently close to the park, so leaving a pair of running shoes at his place could be a useful change of pace, so to speak.

Eyes closed, I was unable to sleep.

"Hey, are you asleep?" I shouted.

"Huh." I believe was his mumble. I woke him.

"Sorry, just seeing if you were up. Good night."

It was a mistake to wake him up; he reached his arm—he had a long arm—and pulled me into him for what made for the most uncomfortable spooning that I'd ever experienced.

29

Dash's bedroom had a dramatically different effect in the morning. It was like a crime drama, in which a witness to a murder fled from the murky blood-drenched scene, returning with the authorities only to find that the massacre had been concealed. The room was cheery, flooded with sunlight and the perpetrator had that *I don't know what you could possibly be referring to* look.

I was in the same recumbent position as when I had gone to bed, only now my eyes were open.

"Good morning!" Dash broadcasted, a morning-show delivery, as he rolled me over onto my other side.

Oh, God, how could I have forgotten? Dash was a morning person.

"I'd suggest that we go for a run in the park but I realize you don't have your sneakers." He really did have an expert understanding of me. "So how about we go over to my gym and get a light workout in before breakfast?"

"But what should I wear?" I propped my head on my folded arm, just like Dash.

"There's an athletic shop in the gym's lobby and one in the club. We can get you a little outfit."

"All right," I said dubiously. "But they better have thongs. I like to show off my butt."

Dash got up with a bounce that would have given me an instant head rush. He raked his hand through his sandy hair—

there wasn't a strand out of place from last night—and he disappeared into his walk-in closet, mumbling something about how
well he'd slept. Minutes later he emerged holding a bundle of
clothes, one of his three hundred pairs of identical khakis,
webbed sneakers (demonstrating his passion for all things
Spiderman), and a black Patagonia fleece. Wearing a pair of
royal Stewart plaid boxers, he turned back to the closet and I noticed his boxers had the Greek letters SAE stitched into the rear.

"You were a frat boy!" The humor of this instantly awoke me.

"What?" he asked, poking his head from the closet.

"You are so Steve Sanders frat boy. But instead of KEG you
were in SEX!" I was so loving this.

"SAE," he corrected, in obvious annoyance.

"I bet you were the vice president. Not president, because that
typically goes to someone more responsible."

"Social director. I was the social director."

Of course.

"I bet you still send money to the chapter, keep in touch with
the brothers." I started to giggle. Dash's this-is-not-at-all-funny
face propelled my giggle into such a rib-cracking roar it almost
caused me to fall from the bed.

"Is there a point to all of this?" Dash said, again in that this-is-
not-at-all-funny way.

I sat straight up, wiping a tear from my eye and trying to compose myself. We were both quiet, it was all over.

"And did you actually smack the butts of freshman maggots
with that SAE paddle I found under the bed last night while
snooping?" Dash tilted his head, pretending to be confused.

"What, you thought I was behaving myself, quietly reading,
while you were at the office last night?"

"What are you talking about?" Dash said, now playing along.

"That paddle is in my room at my mom's house."

I looked at him blankly.

"Um. Kidding!"

"Oh. Okay, right then."

"Mr. Social Director of SEX. I bet you were the real campus
wolf." I curled my hand and clawed it in the air for effect.

"Okay. Enough, Emily!"

"Oh, come on, Dash, those boxers have that crease of newness. You're over thirty, for God's sake, and still up on frat life. That is pretty amusing." His face was blank. "Isn't it?"

He looked down at his boxers, then met my gaze.

"Isn't it amusing?" I coaxed.

Dash finally conceded, letting out a forced laugh, and then threw his fleece into my face.

Though I could have pushed this even further, I decided to give it a rest. It wasn't as much fun since I was the only one getting the humor.

I put on last night's jeans, fitted cashmere sweater in the style of a T-shirt with a printed mud flap girl and, luckily, I had worn Pumas, so I could use them for the gym.

Dash concealed his boxers, stepping into his khakis as quickly as if he'd just heard his parents' car in the driveway.

"What's with the civilian clothes?" I asked. "You working out in khakis?"

"My gym clothes are in my locker. I'm an executive member." Of course he was.

After I brushed my teeth with my finger (I hadn't brought my own toothbrush), I found Dash by the doorway, thumbing through *The New York Times*. Once I approached him, ready to leave, he tossed the paper in a pull-out leather box beneath the table. He then plucked a stray hair that was electrically connected to my sweater, to which I responded with a flinch. His look of sheer exuberance from such a humdrum act irritated me.

"So we're off for a workout!" he said, again in that annoyingly chirpy tone.

I forced my mouth into a saccharine smile. I wanted to punch the perkiness right out of him.

30

We first shopped in the Reebok store of the gym's lobby. Since I didn't want to advertise a brand suited for girls who aerobicize in spandex and neon, we then tried the little boutique on the main floor of the club. I was more comfortable with their selection, a cross between Scoop and Capezio. I selected a pair of orange-y drawstring pants and an athletic gray fitted tank, more like the top of a bathing suit; it was particularly handy because it also had the function of a sports bra. I threw in a denim Theory shirt.

The clerk didn't accept my Visa card, nodding at Dash, who was sifting through a pile of hooded sweatshirts in the colors of autumn leaves. He must have arranged the sale while I was trying on the pants—another perk in paying an extra $15,000 to be an executive member. Executive members also dressed on another level. After he traced my lips with his finger, he directed me to the active entranceway of the women's locker room and arranged for us to reconnect outside the climbing wall "in ten."

In view of many naked bodies that were disturbingly thin, I felt similar to the way I had when exiting backstage after a fashion show, seeing all the models getting dressed with their flat bodies built like folding lounge chairs. I suddenly regretted having last night's Tasti D-Lite. I quickly got changed, for fear that prolonged exposure to flawless albeit plastically enhanced women might set off an unhealthy reaction.

I found Dash where he'd instructed us to meet. He was

dressed in black satiny basketball shorts which, with a few added bars of gold jewelry and a backward baseball hat, could have passed him off as one of P. Diddy's posse who just so happened to be playing on the basketball court.

Dash took me to the climbing wall, an amusement-park version of a tame hillside. A boy, covered in freckles and capped with a beanie that looked like the top of a sock, dangled precariously from a Play-Doh stone. His nanny, hands folded and eyebrows arched upward, looked on worriedly, while his mother interrogated the instructor, rambling something to the effect that this wasn't supposed to be dangerous.

"Are you sure you don't want to do this?" I asked Dash.

"Kid stuff," he said confidently.

We ascended another flight of stairs, the climbing wall still in our view from a cutout in the wall. The once dangling child now regained his footing, and was a few clay stones from catching up with us. Dash ushered me into a room with a row of treadmills and Cybex machines designed specifically for legs. There were two quad machines side by side—one seemed more advanced than the other, which I detected by the sleeker chrome detailing and padded headrest. Dash stacked a load of weights while I made a go on the flashier machine, weight-free. I ran six miles, almost daily, and the idea was not to build up my quads.

As I was comfortably doing my reps, Dash pumped away with the exertion of a superhero lifting a bus. His moans, disturbingly reminiscent of last night, supported my damn theory that sex was just another workout for him. He pumped. He groaned. He broke a sweat. I was his goddamn workout! No wonder he splurged on the late night pizza, probably validated it by all of the extra calories he'd burned. Then again, I had justified my Tasti D-Lite for the same reason. Though I was the girl here.

Finishing the last set on a machine that propelled my leg to my side like a dog relieving itself, I started to quiver from the unexpected degree of difficulty in exercising new muscles. I closed my eyes as techno-color blobs merged into one another.

Approaching Dash, wobbling, I tried to compose myself.

"I'm going to check out the other room," I said softly, so as not to interrupt his intense exertion on the leg presses.

"Wait," he said, unwaveringly, after securing the press with a jerk of his legs. "I'll come with you."

"No, no. No!" Perhaps I was protesting a bit too strongly. "I'd hate to interfere with your workout."

"Oh, don't be ridiculous. I love having you here."

We entered a spacious room geared to strength-training the upper body. After a man with a hairy back (who still found it appropriate to wear a flimsy tank) pounced on a machine Dash was approaching, he resorted to a piece of equipment that spread your arms out like wings. I chose a weight machine that moved like a rower. I pulled faster and faster, mentally escaping the enemy who floundered in the wake of my ripples. A strong tap on my shoulder startled me mid-tug.

"The rowing machines are in the other room," Dash advised, jokingly.

"Sorry, just having a little fun." Another reason why I preferred running—no outside criticism. So what if I could cause serious damage to myself?

Dash returned to his executive-privilege locker room. I wondered if he'd see P. Diddy in the flesh. I took a quick shower, a bit disappointed that a gym as chi-chi as this only carried brandless products.

Changing back into my sweater, I decided to keep on my new yoga pants since I hadn't broken a sweat and wasn't keen on wearing the same outfit for more than a twenty-four-hour period. Luckily the mud flap girl was in the same shade of tangerine as the pants.

I met Dash in the lobby, and we passed by the cafeteria-style café, which was buzzing with kids conferring over lunch orders and parents espousing the benefits of midday protein. So what if tofu smelled like a science project?

"Should we eat somewhere else?" suggested Dash.

Oh, God, yes.

"Sure," I said, exhausted, suddenly feeling the effects from last night's lack of sleep.

We headed toward his apartment. It was a spring weekend on the Upper West Side, sidewalks fashioned with Burberry-coordinated families and teletubbie elderly folk who—in a world of meals on wheels, TiVo and delivery services—were making their first rounds outdoors since fall.

Dash and I walked quietly, and I indulged in the freedom to take full inventory of his ensemble. He'd outgrown his weathered khakis and felt-soft broadcloths to a more pulled-together look, with creased khakis and an overpriced gingham shirt (overpriced, but still costing nowhere near what we girls would spend). His style was similar to when I had first met him, just matured.

We slowed our pace outside a diner/restaurant in the storefront lobby of Dash's building. His eyes widened, clearly exposing their deep blue hue.

"Is this okay?" he asked, looking to the awning, which happened to mirror the same color of Dash's magnificent eyes.

"I never realized people ate here."

Dash and I typically have brunch in Gramercy to avoid the Lincoln Center crowds. But things were different now. I'd walked by this diner the way I'd passed by rest stops on a highway, knowing that they were there but wondering if people actually used them.

It was a diner, I thought. Dash and I loved diners. I followed him into the restaurant. We were seated at a booth and given menus that we had no use for, other than serving as a distraction from having to converse.

"Tuna with mustard on rye," Dash directed our waiter, a bit too uptight for my liking.

"Do you need a few more minutes, madam?" the waiter asked. Since he was not scribbling on a pad, I made certain that we shared eye contact as I started to recite my order. "Steamed vegetables, a side salad with no dressing, a baked potato, and side of Grey Poupon." He seemed to have gotten it, which I should have realized, as waiters at diners tend to do this as a profession and not as a means of earning rent between auditions. "And a black-and-white milkshake." Dash eyed me suspiciously. "But no French fries. That would be wasteful considering they are really overly fried potatoes. And I am getting a baked potato."

Everyone seemed to agree by the round of smiles. Now seated, with no other task to tend to, I took a moment to check out the place. Standard bar-side swivel chairs, like the ones in Dash's apartment but lower and more authentic; cakes that no one orders displayed behind glass cases like priceless works of art; danishes, doughnuts, and muffins on a platter next to the register.

The patrons threw me off. They were the kind of diners who could be found at any West Palm Beach establishment offering an Early Bird Special. I was suddenly hot and it was not because I'd just had a non-workout.

"What is it with this place? I'm feeling unseasonably hot. I'm never hot."

"The heat's on," Dash answered, his eyes studying me.

"To about ninety degrees! Not to mention the fact that it's a springy sixty-five outside and I'm still wearing last night's cashmere."

Dash was weaving his fingers together, and stretching his arms out in front of him until his fingers tightened into a loud, almost terrifying snap. He then proceeded to pull his arms above his head, hands still locked, leaning to both sides, giving his back a stretch. You could hear his joints crackle, but not as dramatically as before.

"Well, look around you. Older people like the heat on."

"Yeah. About that. I gather this is the kind of place that gets a lot of prune juice orders." Indeed, our waiter walked past us with a tray filled with dark, syrupy drinks in juice glasses.

"Well, I gathered from your Emily face that you weren't up for crying kids and overreactive parents at the gym restaurant."

"Can't we just play with people our own age?"

"What's with you?" Dash broke. "You're being about as rude as the customers in Zabar's."

"I'm sorry. I guess it's this whole Upper West Side thing in general."

"So I take it that you and Henry were more downtown people?"

This was the first time Dash had mentioned Henry, even though he'd been with us ever since we'd been together.

"Well, if that didn't just come from nowhere."

Food! Our food was being served. Bringing truth to my theory that the too good to be true couples that are all about appearances get quicker service for fear that their semi-private moments might become tenuous. Any good waiter knows that helping customers eat rather than speak, and raising their sugar levels at the same time, will make for a more enjoyable experience which he will, hopefully, be compensated for.

"Sorry," I said, sprinkling my platters with pepper. "You've been so sweet to me and I've been acting a bit spoiled."

"No, I'm the one who should be apologizing." Why should he be apologizing?

The waiter delivered the check, which Dash snatched as quickly as a glop-faced girl taking a gift bag from a party. I was not expected to pay this time. It was all different now.

Considerably cooler outside, the temperature still didn't penetrate the bottled-up heat I'd stored from sitting in that furnace of a diner. Dash made an excuse to head to the office, preventing me from having to lie. All I wanted to do was go home, get in a run and take a nap. We ended the entire episode outside a vacant cab with a quick kiss and a reminder of a little "thing" we had to attend the following night. We agreed to an 8:00 P.M. pick-up time.

31

I have issues with my phone ringing at 8:30 A.M. Normal business hours begin at 9:00 A.M. (10:30 A.M. to be precise). So rather than have the offender begin his Monday with a grumpy Emily, I let the machine deal with the inconsiderate caller.

Arising to my mother's voice, disturbingly reminiscent of the days when I was a boarder in her house, I reminded myself that this was one of those when-you-live-on-your-own-Miss-Emily moments that I'd always dreamed of.

"Sweetheart, you've made your mom so proud." What could this possibly be about? "Sorry, darling, just holding back a sneeze for a moment there. Anyway not only are you looking quite stunning in this week's *New York Magazine,* though you could trim your hair a bit, you're pictured with Dash. I've always considered you both to be a handsome couple. Well, you're probably at your studio right now, taking advantage of the publicity. That's what it is, sweetie, free publicity. About time is what I say."

I dove under my pillow, wrapping it around my ears and kicking my legs like a spoiled child in a tantrum. "And. I. Said. That. No. One. Would. Notice!" I screamed, evidently to the consternation of the neighbor above, whose presence was made known by a loud creak emanating from the ceiling.

The phone rang again. It was her.

"You should call up that *New York Magazine,*" said Mom derisively. Voice mail therapy. "I don't understand how they could spell Briggs with one g. Really, a publication like *New York Magazine* should have fact checkers. And you're not at your studio." Thank you for bringing that to my attention.

As soon as the tape rewound, the phone rang again. This time I was seated at the side of my bed, to take this in fully.

"Perhaps I'll call the editor who handles this page about the mistake." God, no, don't call them! "I mean they should be versed on who you are. You are a gorgeous, world-renowned illustrator dating a very eligible man. Are you two dating?" God, no, not the imminent dating conversation. "Oh, strike the first part. I just put on my glasses and there are indeed two g's."

She probably scrutinized that damn picture as closely as she did the rim of her butt for cellulite.

Walking to my coffee place, I told myself that no one goes to the painstaking measures that my mother does in reading the tabloids.

Upon keying into my studio, I heard the ringing of the phone, a sound that I knew better than my own breath, which prompted me to make a clumsy scramble for the receiver. My decaf hazelnut spilled from the perforated gaps of its plastic lid and seeped into the cuff of my white blouse, but I had no time to get annoyed by this.

"Hello!" I gasped, successfully picking it up.

"Love the picture in *New York Magazine*." It was Daphne. "It's just that the situation is now a bit awkward, because remember Preston?"

"The Noah Wyle look-alike from the *ER*?"

"And all that time he thought you were embroiled in a family emergency."

"You mean Preston has seen this?" I said, taking a Shout Wipe-It from the top drawer of my cabinet and rigorously scrubbing the coffee stain.

"It's already eleven A.M., Emily. The regular world has all of their gossip read by nine A.M. sharp." I gathered she was right by the fact that there were eighteen messages pulsing on my machine.

"So what's up with you and Dash, anyway?"

Silence.

"Emily, are you okay there?"

"Well, I have a feeling that you may not approve of what I have to say."

"Uh-oh."

"Counting tiles on the ceiling," I whimpered.

I turned down the volume on the machine and pressed play to hear the damage. Eighteen acquaintances whom I hadn't spoken to in months—even an art director whom I once borderline stalked for assignments who now wanted me to illustrate a story on how beauticians have the real insight into celebrity gossip. All from a picture that was as big as the coffee stain set into my shirt (now destined to be a thrift shop donation).

Don't people have lives to lead rather than glimpse at silly ones, notably my own?

Daphne said, "Ugh, sex that bad, eh? I would have expected more, considering he's such an athlete."

"And you know me, I experienced my first orgasm at the ripe old age of thirteen—horseback riding. But with Dash?"

Daphne moaned into the phone, relieving me from having to continue rehashing this sorry situation.

"It's probably me—just not aroused by him. Sex is a routine in a packaged life."

"So. What now?"

"I just wish that he was one of those ineffective characters from one of our favorite shows—easily written off by sending him on some 'save the puffins' humanitarian mission in the tundra or something."

"Well, Preston still has a keen interest in you. What do you think?"

"Aside from a much needed hair appointment with Gaston, I think I need a break from anything male related."

"So you're okay with the idea of being single again?"

"Well." I paused. "Naturally I have those particularly self-conscious moments, having to shop alone at Hermes where the salespeople look at me like I'm wearing last season's runway rejects while the cute little couples get the star treatment."

Without feeding into my self-pity, she said dryly, "No, they're pretty much rude to everyone. Look, Em, just let me know if there is anything I can do."

"Thanks, Daph. I was worried what you would think."

"Hey, if the passion isn't there, it isn't there. No use in fitting a square peg into a round hole."

She seemed almost ready to hang up, having completely avoided the subject of Daphne. She rarely mentioned her personal issues, which I sometimes found disconcerting given the open intimacy, the most raw and true kind, that can only be shared by best friends, oldest friends.

I knew what Daphne looked like in a Capezio leotard, that unfortunate form-fitting style that came along when our boobs were swollen bumps no bigger than mosquito bites. I knew her as the one who'd bought a Vanilla Slim-Fast and a pregnancy test at the Bridgehampton drugstore after she'd had unprotected sex for the first time. The appearance of a weak blue line was worse than reading my rejection letter from Stanford. In a fearful panic, we immediately raced to the hospital only to discover that her splattered pee caused the incorrect reading. There were many past references, trials and shared moments to a relationship with roots deeper than a redwood.

Attempting to have Daphne "open up" was like fixing an uncooperative zipper, at first a thwarted struggle but with a bit of readjustment it would glide up and down. I didn't know if her withholding was a security measure, a symptom of her repressed upbringing, or a feeling that her problems were inconsequential. Everyone had a daily dilemma that could cause mind-invasive distress, no matter what the difference in scale.

"And how are Henry and Emily?" I broke in, figuring it was better to angle with her children and then go directly for the personal. "Relations between the siblings improving, I hope."

"Actually improving considerably!" she sang happily. "Ever since Emily discovered the benefit of having a partner in her deviant little schemes, the two have become quite the duo. I'm just concerned about the side effects from my slack discipline."

Parental neglect? Hardly. Daphne was the twenty-first century yummy mommy.

"Let's reacquaint ourselves with the Briggs of childhood past. Wherein Father allegedly called me Charlotte the first month of my life, until Mother reminded him that I was named after Emily, not Charlotte, Bronte. And remember the time when my mother didn't even realize that I'd run away from home and was

camping in the French Shack? It was three days after the fact.
And I was only discovered because Mom was wondering where
all of the bug spray had disappeared to. She even used my runaway letter as a grocery list, for God's sake." I paused, feeling momentarily postal. "I still have it, you know. That runaway/grocery
list letter."

Daphne responded coolly. "I love Catherine. Sometimes I
think you can be a little hard on your mother."

"This is the same mother who took me to her nutritionist
when I was twelve, when I was lectured that a bag of grapes was as
bad as a box of Junior Mints. I was twelve!"

"Look at how well you turned out," Daphne said, as if in a
final plea.

I scrunched up my face—the way it would be if I'd been asked
to eat moving larvae on *Survivor.*

"Look how great she is with Oliver."

"She does have a pretty consistent approach to parenting.
From not involved—me—to overly involved—Oliver. Makes you
wonder."

"Well, she does have enormous respect for you."

"The woman who measures my success by how many mentions
I get in the glossies?"

"You're overthinking that one."

"Debatable. How about you? How are things with Daphne?"

"Can't complain really. Ever since that birthday party I put on
for Emily's classmate at Chapin, it's practically become a full-
time stint. I've been catering everything from board meetings to
a booking for a wedding this summer on Shelter Island."

She paused, but I sensed that she had not exhausted the subject.

"It's funny how things can fall into place. There's all this talk
about working hard and going after your dream, but honestly,
Emily, sometimes I am tormented by how setting simpler standards
just works for me. A little dumb-blonde of me, don't ya think?"

If she were next to me I knew this would be easier for her.

"Or the joke's on everyone else, Daphne. I'd say you're pretty
brilliant, actually. Unlocking the secret to personal happiness is
no small feat."

"It's just that I never really wanted anything more than a respectable husband and to raise a family. My entire month can be made if a new specialty market replaces the tired old deli around the corner from our building."

"Well, something like that can make my year."

"You're too generous. Anyway, I am starting to enjoy the motivation of a new routine, having this little catering stint. It's fun, breaks up my day, and even improves relations with Andy. There are more interesting things to discuss than Henry's eye color and the touted shades of Nars nail polish. It's also not bad on the savings account."

"Daphne, that's great!"

"Hardly. An Ivy League education to bake cookies."

"Yeah, and I'm using mine to doodle all day."

We said our good-byes and I took to staring out the window. A man in a weathered motorcycle jacket, à la *Easy Rider*, crossed the street. His face was indecipherable—an oval of peach similar to the cartoon figures in the Saab commercials that had once influenced my style. It could have been Henry. Skipping across, coming to greet me with an irreverent story, sharing a guilty pleasure, or having a laugh at old senile Mr. Silvano's expense.

Here was a story for one of my magazines, how to return to reality when you once had the fantasy.

I opened the top drawer of my desk and reached in the back corner for the chain of Henry's keys, intently focused on their feel and how they connected to the rest of my body like a crystal with mystical effects. Rubbing the two keys together, I held them in front of me for closer inspection. If only I could have used them, gained access to the life I once had with Henry.

The phone broke me from my trance, a school bell ending my ennui.

"Hey, you."

It was Dash.

"Hi, there," I managed.

"Monday blues?"

"Yeah, pretty much."

"Well, I won't keep you, then," he said, meaning that he was slammed with work and wasn't up for a vacuous chat anyway.

"Is it okay if I pick you up at nine rather than eight? The event is on Broome Street, sort of en route for me."

"Sure. What are we going to again?"

"Some book party. See you tonight, look cute."

Look cute? Right, a relationship based on appearances.

I went on-line to the Page Six Web site to figure out the evening's itinerary. Samara, an androgynous model in her mid-twenties (twenty-nine), was angling her forced retirement into a career as a writer—celebrating the publication of her book on famous people's baby pictures, to be held at a gallery on Broome Street. I would rather pluck out all of my eyelashes and start a new ridiculous trend.

I opened my pad to the day's agenda, adding the final sketches for a new beauty line being launched by a TriBeCa dermatologist. This doctor was keener on the high profile opportunities from brand marketing than on upholding her clinical skills in helping people through medicine.

Typically I would spend the day meticulously developing the sketches. But the drawings were up to my standards, I didn't particularly respect this doctor, and I was in a rancid mood, so I called for a messenger and arranged for them to pick up the artwork from my decaf hazelnut coffee place across the street. I locked up and decided to take the rest of the day off to shop for something that would make me "look cute."

All my favorite stores failed me. Why would I ever lay down my plastic for shirts that appeared to be victims of a swarm of moths or for weirdly colored pants so tight that I might as well have strips of Fruit Roll-Up on my legs? Or for low-slung jeans that were made for girls with miles between their legs; even my healthy body type looked bizarre in them. They should attach a warning label to them: *Made for Britney Spears Proportions.* I resorted to a simple black halter from Armani E/X that I intended to pair with jeans—Levi's.

Since Gaston was booked, I made an appointment with my safety salon off of Fifth and Eighteenth for a blowout. It was housed in a loft above a café, where the owner had a litter of toy poodles, which made the place look like a dog groomer's.

The day was unseasonably humid. Blasts of steam were shooting from the crevices of the city streets. My blown-out hair went limp once I left the overly air-conditioned salon.

Navigating sweaty New Yorkers and feeling light-headed from

the uncompromising heat—which had better not be the forecast for the months ahead—I made a quick stop into Jo Malone for an air-conditioning break. I smelled something fabulously expensive. I dabbed bath oil to my wrists like perfume; the scent was of a boudoir from a Parisian madam, very *Belle du Jour.* I bought the bottle, which cost as much as a month's rent, and justified the expense by noting that the classic crystal decanter would have a second life as a bud holder. (But who was I kidding, after two weeks of the bottle monopolizing much-needed storage space, it would be tossed into recycling.)

While I intended to have a bath, I could find no reason to submerge myself in a tub of hot water when I could experience a steam treatment outside my apartment door.

I decided to take a nap, which turned out to be an entire night's sleep, and then had to frantically get ready in less than thirty minutes. After a quick shower, I removed the tags from my new shirt and decided on white Levi's. The hair was the trick. So I treated long hair as if it were short, styling it into a tight ponytail and finished with ten minutes to spare. Eyeing the box from Jo Malone, its butter colored packaging sealed with a black grosgrain ribbon, I pulled the bow so it unfolded into a long, creased ribbon—warmly reminding me of the days when I would wear ribbons in my hair as regularly as Dash wore gingham.

Never one for the leg warmer and bangle bracelet trends that were all the rage during my eighties youth, I was more a follower of madras and prep-motifed clothing—classics that set my current aesthetic. Sliding the ribbon over the rubber band of my ponytail and finishing it in a neat little bow, I was quite pleased with the result, even though my magazines hadn't hyped this look as fashionably acceptable.

32

Dash called me from his cell, alerting me to his presence in a Big Apple limousine outside my apartment. I gave him a two-minute estimated time of arrival, threw my things into a black evening clutch, slipped my feet into flip-flops strapped with black grosgrain, and then applied Givenchy's Rouge Noir lipstick. That spot of red to the lips is the handbag to the face. Trying unsuccessfully to prevent my shoes from clippity-clopping down the stairs, I stomped away as quickly as possible—happy that I had forgiving neighbors who didn't fuss over such trivialities.

Dash was in a dark jacket with blue jeans. If I didn't know better, I would have thought that he was considering leaving television for film production. He kissed my check, gave me all of the you-look-smashing pleasantries, and instructed the driver to head to the final stop.

The crowd spilling outside the gallery could have been a casting call for a new HBO series. Girls elbow to elbow with the dimensions of a Twizzler seemed to be in the midst of a contest—whoever smiles first loses—while their camera-ready escorts were looking everywhere but at their dates.

The flash of bulbs, a camera crew focused on a reporter having an aerosol spray break and the red carpet entrance gave this the look of a movie premiere. Dash glided us through security, and it took a half-dozen squealy blondes to check our names from a clipboard.

The white S-shaped walls, positioned about the room to re-semble a garden maze, were decorated with poster-size images from the book. I tore the invitation out of Dash's hand. It called for dressing in colors of baby blue or pink, but aside from Samara in a blue tulle skirt and pink tube top, the crowd predominantly wore black and white. I was happy to blend in as seamlessly as the images on the wall.

Julianne Moore, Christy Turlington, Matthew Broderick and other celebrities—whose baby bottoms, I assumed, were fea-tured in the book from the guest list on the invite—mingled with the likes of Mario Testino, Patricia Underwood and James Truman. Hollywood and fashion synchronized to the music of an old Duran Duran record.

Al D'Amato, fashionably unfashionable, approached us.

"Got your message, Dash," he said casually. "I'd be happy to discuss Star Wars on the record for the piece you're working on."

Star Wars, Al D'Amato? I know I'm not in television but shouldn't Dash be approaching George Lucas on this one? Oh, duh—SDI.

"Al, that's great!"

Dash, put your tongue back in your mouth. He introduced me to the former senator and then rambled with the excitement of a sixteen-year-old who just got his license. "It's just that with the president's position, and the report issued last week by Defense, I feel there is something bigger here."

Al looked on proudly, like a wise old tortoise admiring the buckaroo qualities of his protégé. I could have easily contributed to this conversation as I was well versed on SDI, having written my final paper on the subject for my Politics in Post Cold War America class at Dartmouth. Well, truthfully, Daphne wrote the paper for a similar class she took at Princeton. Since she'd re-ceived an A, I'd assumed it would be senseless to do all of that work twice. And it's not as if I were entering a related field, that researching the topic would be useful in my postgraduate life. This was also before E-mail so I had to transcribe the twelve-page paper myself, absorbing the information.

"I can also get you in touch with Rice," Al said imperiously.

I sort of wished they were discussing *Star Wars* the movie.

　　　　　　Jacqueline deMontravel

Suddenly a glare of white light blinded us like a car crash at night. I opened my eyes and the black and white surroundings were then fluorescently silhouetted in reverse. The camera that had been in my face shifted into regular view.

"Thanks," said the photographer, running off like a streaker to find his next victim.

A fresh-faced assistant, wearing a knock-off dress effectively pulled together with makeup, spiky little open-toed shoes and little red toes, asked for our names.

Both Al and Dash intuitively handed her their cards, keeping her pen suspended from the page of her spiraled reporter's pad. I tried to scamper away during the exchanges.

"And you," she called to me with the authority of an airline stewardess catching a passenger sneaking into First Class. Feeling wounded, I fumbled through my bag and handed her a business card that I had created solely for professional contacts. She was good. Access to some really cool parties probably compensated for her low-paying job.

Al crawled away like the hunchbacked turtle he so uncannily resembled.

"Look forward to touching base," he said to Dash mid-turn.

"And nice meeting you, Emily." He winked like a philandering politician.

"Isn't that great!" Dash beamed, embracing me with a squeeze so tight a few strands fell from my ponytail. "That was Al!"

I searched his eyes, trying to make out what all the fuss was about. "D'Amato," he implored weakly.

"I know. You introduced us."

We glided through the exhibit, gazing absently at the images on the wall. It wasn't easy to view the birthday cake–stained mouths of celebrities from an uncelebrated time, at a party that strummed to the snaps of the paparazzi, with a crowd hovering over the newest celebrity arrival like a wave about to crush the shoreline.

"Should I get us something from the bar?" offered Dash.

"Yes!" I answered, perhaps a bit too eagerly.

"If they don't have gimlets?"

"Anything hard is fine."

While Dash sashayed around black and white life-size chess

pieces, I took a closer look at a grainy picture of a young boy wearing a holster and cowboy hat, the caption reading: "A Young Fox—Michael J. Fox."

Having that sense I was being stared at, I turned to my side and confirmed the fact that I was, indeed, the object of a stranger's interest. His hair was somewhat synthetic and he had beady raisin eyes. The requisite black blazer he wore was in a shimmery viscose material, which caused me a brief moment of panic as his highly flammable sleeve moved dangerously close to a man's cigar. Luckily a waiter attended to the fire hazard by disposing of the man's cigar.

He noticed my being noticed noticing him, and moved diagonally across the floor—a knight coming to take me out, the doomed pawn. Oh, for God's sake.

"Hello," he said in a voice that could earn him a fat living from voice-over work.

"Hi," I answered coolly.

"I know. I know. You're wondering where you recognize me from. The problem of being a C-list celebrity—happens all the time."

I tilted my head back, trying to avoid the smell of his overly mint-infused breath.

"People approach me all the time, wondering if I was their son's camp counselor, or live in the same apartment building, or take the same spinning class. But you probably recognize me from my show, *Blau for Now.*"

I shrugged, not able to speak words to this oddity before me.

"*Blau for Now.* My nightly newscast on FOX?"

My shrug became more pronounced.

"FOX cable news. Nightcast. At one A.M.?"

"I'm sorry. I really don't watch television."

"But how do you get your news?"

"Newspapers. The Internet."

"Goddamn Internet." He laughed. "Well, I'm Gordon Blau." He extended his hand but it never reached me—a woman tripping from her stiletto boot fell into him.

I began a mental word association game. Gordon Blau. Then changed Gordon to Cordon, Blau to Blue. Cordon Blue. Chicken

Cordon Blue. He looked like Frank Perdue. Six degrees of sepa-
ration—answer, Gordon Blau is a chicken!

There was then a fierce, almost painful tap to my shoulder. It
was Anne. How thrilled I was to see Anne.

"Cousin Anne!" I pecked her lips with the impact of a head
butt.

She recoiled as if she'd just been kissed by her landscaper
after a day of hard labor drudgery in hundred-degree heat.

"Who's this?" She nodded haughtily to Gordon.

"Gordon Blau. News reporter." He made another attempt to
offer his hand. She just looked at him in that haughty way of hers.

"Anne," I whispered out of Gordon's earshot. "Do you mind
leaving with me? This scene is starting to tire me." My head
twirled about, cocktail chatter in stereo from the lofty gallery
space. "We can go to the Merc Bar and get a real drink, not some
Korbel in a plastic champagne flute."

It was her look of death, a reaction more suited to my taking
her stiletto heel of a weapon and bludgeoning Chicken Gordon
Blue with it.

"But I nearly just arrived," she whined.

"Please. I'll be your very best maid of honor!"

"Oh, yes, that. Why didn't you respond to today's E-mail report? About changing the date and place of the shower?"

"Sorry. I didn't go on-line today."

"I thought you got your news from the Internet!" Gordon interjected.

Now he really had Anne's attention.

"Gordon. Gordon Blau is it? *Blau for Now.* Well, then, bye for
now." She placed her hands on my shoulder, shifted me away
from Gordon and led me in the opposite direction.

Safely removed from his presence, she stopped. "Emily," she
scolded, "this is a perfectly respectable event to which you've
managed to find the most ghastly person to occupy yourself
with. I'm quite surprised, considering that you are in today's
New York Magazine. And now you have the audacity to want to
leave—with me?"

"Sorry. I don't know what's gotten over me." Tic-tac-toe, I said
like a mantra, and I chose not to play.

"Well, then. Since I am in a charitable mood this evening and given the lack of charity around us—I do prefer not-for-profit events—and given that we have to catch up on some very important shower planning, let me find Jason and let him know that you need some serious attention."

"Thank you!"

Anne kissed me on the cheek for effect—deliberately in view of the party photographer who slid right past us—and then placed her hands, again on my shoulders, for a complete inspection, to which I returned the scrutiny. Her lip appeared more plump to the touch, swelled like a bee sting. She didn't! The girl was slowly pumping collagen into her lips like a rubber raft needing hours to inflate. Year by year she'll add just a little more with the hope that it won't look as dramatic once she hits the big four-oh. I felt like the only human in a *Twilight Zone* episode where everyone, even your closest family members, were taken over by plastic.

"What's with the little bow?" she said condescendingly, flicking at my ribbon.

What's with the Silly Putty in the lip?

I went over to the bar to locate Dash. Finding him in an intense conversation with a blonde. The blonde turned to me when she saw Dash's jaw drop. It was Katrina. They both approached me as if on cue, and looked like they had just been caught, teensploitation-melodrama style. I was, however, completely unaffected by this. In fact, I was actually quite thrilled: (1) Maybe someone else showing interest in Dash, notably an ex that I once was envious of, would renew my arousal in that messed-up kind of way, and (2) Now I could safely leave this place and cause a little melodrama of my own, which I could cash in on later.

"Hello, Emily," purred Katrina with a kiss to my cheek. Rouge was completely unnecessary at these affairs with all of the lipstick grazing your cheek.

"Hi," I sweetly said to them both. Then slightly more bitchy, "Dash, I'm leaving."

"But why?" he pouted, a bit too girly.

Anne's timing couldn't have been more perfect. I was amazed

that her presence had not only saved me twice in one evening but that she, of all people, was the one person that night who I actually wanted to be with.

"Hello, Dash. Hello, Katrina," she said diplomatically. "Emily," she instructed. "You've got twenty minutes."

Like I was a goddamn news reporter allotted time with the president.

"Right, then. Later everyone." And we shuffled away.

After we maneuvered through the crowd outside the gallery, which had swelled about as much as Anne's new lips, she started in.

"So, what's the deal?"

"What do you mean?" I was trying to walk as quickly as possible toward the Merc despite the serious hindrance we had with Anne's skyscraper shoes.

"Should we get a cab? Taxi!" she yelled to an off duty cab. Flicking her diamond-fingered hand into the air, she radiated a glare that was as blinding as the flash from the cameras we had just escaped.

I suppressed a groan. "Anne, it's just a block away." She could be such a girl.

"You and your damn walking. Sometimes I wonder how we could be related."

You couldn't possibly wonder as much as me.

"Well, again, you've managed to avoid the topic on hand. You? And Dash! What is it, Emily, what's the deal here?"

"There is no deal," I said, hoping to just leave it at that.

Lucky that Anne was so self-absorbed and that we only had twenty minutes to discuss more pressing matters.

"Okay, then, let's get back to me. I've managed to get in an appointment with Selma for Friday at two thirty P.M. so I'll meet you there."

"Selma?" She sounds as if she's just secured brain surgery with the world's leading surgeon.

"Selma! The most ingenious cake designer—really, Emily, stop being so daft. And getting her to fit me in was a matter of pulling off many favors."

Oh, yes, the one-named cake designer who charges more for bread and flour than Anne's Vera Wang dress.

"And the shower will be planned for the Saturday after Memorial Day. When the inaugurating summer events dissipate into the quietness of June and before it sets in all over again on the Fourth, that's when our true friends will be in the Hamptons, excited and eager for a bridal shower."

Yes, we all await your shower with anticipation.

"It will be at your house. Auntie Catherine has already given me the assurance that the hydrangeas will be in bloom on your far deck. Do you think we should actually have blue hydrangea floral arrangements, or would that be cheesy?"

Okay, we've had the blue hydrangea floral arrangement conversation maybe about 1,800 times now. How could I get excited about something that I normally wouldn't even notice?

"Hydrangeas aren't cheesy," I said, flatly.

"Oh, Emily, sometimes I think you need to take a blood test to see if we are indeed related. Of course hydrangeas aren't cheesy, I just fear that it will look too picked-from-the-garden-homemakery, rather than have the appearance of a floral designer."

"No, the blue hydrangeas will be perfect. And they will have that 'floral artist' look you are going for. But my new policy is not to answer any more questions you've already asked me ten times. Ten times should sufficiently confirm my position."

"Good, I'm glad you think that, since I do want the blue hydrangeas. The light turquoise color of the flowers will go perfectly with my white Michael Kors pantsuit and the aquamarine necklace Jason bought me as an engagement present, the one featured on the cover of last month's *W*."

"He bought you an engagement present after that free-weight of a ring?"

Though Anne's five-carat Harry Winston brilliant cut platinum-set ring wouldn't enable me to do such things as open a door without causing some sort of accident, Anne was deftly able to gesticulate with her hands. Even those picketed fingernails—another hazard—were effective in functioning as a wire-tooth comb to brush away the loose strands of hair from my face that I was certain had been secretly agitating her all evening.

"Well, yes," she said matter-of-factly, avoiding eye contact. "It was given to me as amends after a particularly abrupt cancellation."

"What do you mean?"

"Well, there almost wasn't a wedding."

"What? You're kidding me."

"Kid?" She now looked to me gravely. "Emily, I don't *kid* about such things as my nuptials. In fact, *kid* is what got me into this mess to begin with."

My eyes searched hers for more information. Reaching the Merc Bar temporarily put a hold to the conversation.

"Goddamn it, Emily," she griped, lifting her foot into her palm. "If I get blisters with less than three months till my wedding, you're toast."

After Anne instructed the unobliging waitress to seat us in the back lounge, which we were told was exclusive to members and hotel guests, Anne plucked her phone, showcasing that Epcot Center globe of a diamond, and threatened to make a call to Mr. Schraeger—who just happened to be on her speed dial. The waitress turned from ingrate to gratuitous as quickly as a publicist learning that it was indeed Ben Affleck beneath the baseball cap and dark glasses. Graciously seated, I ordered my gimlet while Anne asked for a bottle of Cristal.

My drink and her bottle, served along with a plate of hors d'oeuvre things, were compliments of Mr. Schraeger. Since both of us were avoiding the food, I was able to fully focus on Anne. She was dressed in colors that complemented her ring—charcoal gray shift, sharkskin Birkin bag, slate suede blazer and those pythoned weapons entombing her feet.

"Okay, the business of my shower. You'll read today's E-mail when you return home tonight. Do you have any Advil? My ankles are starting to swell."

You mean your lips are swelled. If Anne thought her bony ankles were injured from walking an extra five steps from what she allotted for tonight in those shoes, she'd have to start taking something a lot stronger than Advil.

"Goddamn puffy ankles," she hissed at her feet.

"Anne," I managed to interrupt. "What we were discussing before. Can we continue?"

"Figures you'd badger me on this. All you need to know is that you will still be given the honor of being my maid of honor."

"Anne! The little matter we were discussing before—the broken engagement?"

"You can be such a little stickler. Jason had issues with the fact that I don't want to have children."

"I never knew that."

"Of course I don't want to have children—to be all fat like that? Please. But we've worked it out." She lifted her hand to ogle her ring.

"So you won't have children?"

"I'll supply the kids but, trust me on this one, for transporting that pumpkin of a package around for so many months—what is it six, seven months that you show—I will be appropriately compensated." Her stare was so penetrating I felt that she could see right through the cotton fibers of my shirt. "And I must be pregnant during the winter months, preferably with a late April due date."

I wondered if she realized that this was not as simple as setting a shower date.

"Anyway, Emily, you've again completely managed to sap up all of my time, and we haven't even gotten to the caterer."

"We're discussing your shower?" I asked, seriously hoping that she wasn't commandeering me into the wedding arrangements with two wedding planners, every living relative, and half the staff of *Martha Stewart Weddings* helping her.

"Of course not. You can be so daft. The shower! I would like Daphne to cater it."

This was the most sensible thing she said all night.

"That would be great. Daphne is so talented. She recently catered a children's tea party. So clever because she made grown-up delicacies into desserts—cannolis wrapped like sushi rolls, melted chocolate morsels and shortbread cookies as caviar and crackers. The girls felt so grown up."

She looked the way I imagined she would if Jason told her that he wanted to give up banking to follow his dream as a park ranger.

"Anne," I said, waving to her to awaken her from her shock.

"To be quite honest, Emily, I wasn't completely aware of all of Daphne's capabilities as a caterer. I was just told that she was quite creative and professional. I want her to do it because, between Jason and me, we have no young relations that can play the pivotal role as the flower girl. I so desperately need one to include this fairy-tale Thumbelina dress that I found at Spring Flowers in the ceremony. It will also add the most festive touch to the pictures. Since Oliver is a boy, that's not an option." She said it as if Mother had had a boy to disrupt her styling. "But Daphne's daughter. Oh, what's that damn girl's name?"

"Emily."

"Not you. I know your name, for God's sake."

"No. Daphne's daughter's name is Emily."

"Of course," she said, like she'd known this all along. "Emily. She'll look just perfect in this dress. It really is the most divine little frock."

Divine little frock?

"Empire waist, which is really a fine style for girls since they're flat-chested. Georgette silk in the colors of a hyacinth—petal white on top, snap pea green on the bottom."

Is she reading *Town and Country* or *House and Garden*?

"With a little garland atop her head it will most certainly be 'a midsummer night's dream.' "

I looked at her, stupefied.

"Oliver can also be in the party. We'll dress him in the same color scheme of the flowers," She directed. "He'll wear Bermudas, a navy blazer and a seersucker mint green bow tie, since you do have a thing for bows. What is it? This peculiar little style you're wearing?" She reached over my head to tug on my ribbon.

I avoided the question by draining the remainder of my gimlet.

"So that's how we can appease Daphne."

"I'm sorry?"

"Oh, Emily, how I wish you'd pay attention. Maybe you should be taking notes?"

I looked at her, stupefied again.

"Notes!" she screeched, snapping her fingers in front of my face like I needed to come out of hypnosis. "You are an artist, don't you have a little sketch pad on hand?"

Yeah, right here with my easel and palette of paints.

"Have Daphne cater my shower so I can have Emily in my wedding."

"I'm sure Daphne will agree to have Emily as your flower girl without having to cater your shower."

"Really?" she whiffed in that in-the-know way. "Well, that may work because I really don't like the sound of all of those fattening pastries she seems to serve. I mean, of course anything buttery, decadently chocolate and rich will go over well with kids. But for a Sunday wedding shower? In June no less? And some of those ladies will be in my wedding party, on a strict pre-wedding-day diet. By the way, no late night Ben and Jerry's for you till after the wedding."

Yeah, like that was going to happen. What? She was going to put surveillance cameras in my kitchen?

"I've arranged to have you meet with my trainer at Casa on Tuesdays. Your sessions will end with measurements."

She couldn't be serious.

"I'm serious, Emily. But you do manage to look like a bone every time I see you. God, why couldn't I share those genes of yours?" She slapped her face with her hand. "Anyway, perhaps we should have Loaves and Fishes cater this, since I really had more of a fruit, tea, and cucumber sandwich sort of thing in mind."

So that was indeed the issue here. Calorie count.

"But have you seen Daphne's fat-free menu?"

"No!" She yelped so loud the music stopped, patrons turned to us, and all activity was momentarily frozen. Amazing the kind of reaction the word "free" will have on a girl.

"It's quite clever, really—fat-free muffins, scones, salads and even tea biscuits. It will be just perfect!"

"Oh, I can just taste it already. Then it's settled. Daphne will cater my shower and I still won't have to grovel for her child. Perfect," she said, sliding up her jacket sleeve to peek at her Cartier Tank Francaise.

"Emily!" she shrieked for the 1,800th time tonight. "It's been almost an hour. Jason is sure to not marry me now.

"And," she continued after making a dramatic gasp and eyeing the crowd, "what in God's earth are we doing in a hotel bar?

This is only intended for women who are interested in a one-night stand."

Interesting point. I'd have to keep that in mind during my next dry spell.

"You really are trying to sabotage my wedding—on all counts."

Before I even had a moment to register that, her untouched glass of champagne and mist of Creed were the only signs left of her mad exit.

Slouched over a table as tiny as an elementary school desk, drink finished, I felt small. I was always particularly gawky and tomboyish in Anne's presence. I shifted to her seat before the bubbles from a perfectly good glass of Cristal went flat. My dry lips tingled with that refreshing nip, an unexpected spray heeling on a sailboat.

Leaning back with a smile, I took in the room and, for the second time that night, had the sense that I was being stared at—which I was. Maybe I had been out of the pick-up loop for some time, but I could never have imagined being so blatantly gawked at by someone I found attractive.

This overtly obscene gazer, with plugs that seemed more legitimate than Chicken Gordon Blue's, seemed like the kind of guy that you see on the news being arrested for picking up underage girls on the Internet. I slipped my fingers around my clutch and made a stealth exit from the hotel.

Before returning home I stopped at the studio to check my E-mail, figuring that I might as well end a bad day badly and begin fresh in the morning. In the same way that my answering machine had beleaguered me with useless messages that morning, forgotten acquaintances had contacted me via E-mail, with more than five subject lines reading "*New York Magazine.*" I systematically annihilated them with the delete button.

Anne's shower stipulations included measures that I hadn't even considered for my own (hopefully, someday) wedding. With three weekends before the event, her list, from flowers to a fortune-teller, was just not manageable. Rather than break it to her the next day, I decided I would fail the assignment and be reprimanded on the dreaded day.

I was enjoying the walk back home and a sudden breeze released the strands from my ponytail that Anne had made such a point to fix. A couple approached, definitely together but not married because they both shared that glow of an early romance. She was waving an ice cream, one of those Good Humor cones that you can buy from a Korean deli. She ripped the logoed paper from the stale waffle cone, uncovering a hard chocolate shell clinging to the creamy vanilla. She dangled the cone in front of her boyfriend's mouth like a news reporter using his microphone to get a comment.

He nipped at the ice cream, gulping it down in one quick swallow, hands in both pockets to add even more of a bulge to his pleated khakis. She laughed as a bead of vanilla ice cream dripped from his nose. He laughed too, removing a hand from his pocket to wipe his nose though I was sure that it was still laced with a sugary film. It was indeed new love, when something like food stuck to one's face could be the source of such humor.

I was alone on the next block with my thoughts still focused on that couple. More specifically, on the woman and why she would waste the calories on an ice cream, probably well past its expiration date, when right on 23rd Street there was a Tasti D-Lite. She could have had a soft-serve frozen yogurt dispensed straight from the machine and, notably, it would have been virtually fat free. I looked at my watch; it was almost 1:00 A.M. Perhaps I was wrong, perhaps she'd made a Tasti D-Lite attempt but since it was closed, she had to settle.

Turning the block I spotted a man talking to himself—or really to his satchel. "You godforsaken bag, how dare you crap out on me now!" The satchel was camouflage green, the same color and material as an army duffel. Probably part of a uniform given to him when he was an Eagle Scout, not a Boy Scout, because the bag was more vintage and the man looked as if he were in his late fifties. His name could have been etched on the side, printed in indelible black ink.

He next yelled at the strap, which appeared to be held together by two thick canvas threads, the remainder frayed like my unraveled hair. While I loved New York because of the anonymity, I believed that anyone who yelled at themselves, their animals, inanimate objects, or others abused the right to this privilege.

Late night stops to my studio had their consequences. Tomorrow I would buy a laptop.

33

Like all others influenced by fashion, I'd been known to squan-der an entire afternoon on the fifth floor of Bergdorf's. Just a few blocks west, CompUSA also had a devoted following, though dramatically different in appearance than women who can mix purple tweed with above-the-knee patent boots. At CompUSA the ultimate in chic was how much RAM your hard drive had.

Luckily I could "stealth shop," as I knew exactly what I wanted: Apple's sleek little iBook. I knew this not by reading up on the latest computer magazines, if there even were such publications, but by finding this particular model on an accessories page in *Elle*. Trying to avoid anyone in a blue pique CompUSA-logoed shirt, the human version of spamming (I was continually being solicited about some 1-800 number that would set me back an extra $350 just so I could talk to some pimply faced computer geek about computer geek issues), I bought a laptop and es-caped this horde of computer freaks.

The new equipment had the smell of Christmas back when it was fun—before Mom asked if receipts came with my gifts to her. I used my finger to pry the adapter and outlet from their molded Styrofoam, the sound causing me to flinch. Then I plugged in my computer, foolishly assuming that it was ready to go.

Typical. There were about 1,800 applications that I needed to contend with, notably E-mail, which, it appeared, I either had to buy or install. Reading the directions would be similar to speak-ing Mandarin. So I called the 1-800 number specified for this trial period and just eighty-nine minutes later (my phone digitally records how many minutes of your life you're wasting), after being shuffled around more times than a Conde Nast editor, I was connected to a live person, who said he needed to put me through to the right technician.

"If you transfer me one more time I am going to kill myself!" I said, a tad hostile. I went from feeling capable to being the dumb blonde, this computer geek unnerving me even further because I didn't know who my host provider was.

"Sorry, I've been particularly ineffective in hosted situations these days."

This neo-Nazi skinhead who would probably be profiled on *Dateline* for leading a satanic cult was currently finding his calling by working at a place where he was totally anonymous. Just wait till phones routinely had television monitors, his career would be over.

What seemed to be an entire month later, I had Internet access. Right as I clicked the receiver, the phone rang. I began to wonder why I needed to be reached in so many different ways when all I wanted to do was escape to the dreamy comfort of my bed.

"Emily!" Dash cried in surprise. "I've been trying to contact you all day. What is it with your phone, it's the first time I've heard a busy signal since I've been to my dead grandparents' cabin in New Hampshire."

Taking off my Uggs, I wondered if I should change into a fresh pair of men's PJs or stay with the ones I'd been wearing all day. I decided to keep the ones I'd been wearing because getting dressed while talking, even with a cordless, required some degree of skill.

"Sorry," I said coolly.

"Sorry? Sorry!" Apparently he was not satisfied by my flimsy excuse.

With an agitated Emily look on my face, I continued. "*Sorry*. I just got a laptop and had to get it all set up."

"But I've been calling you since eight A.M. this morning. It's now past nine thirty P.M."

"What—am I suddenly under house arrest?"

"So. Which one?"

"Which what?"

"Laptop!"

"The new iBook."

"I love those. So sleek and compact. I'm surprised you didn't have me help you with the purchase."

Like I really needed you to tell me which computers looked the cutest.

"Well, don't you think you could have called me sometime in between your little computer lessons?"

I didn't find this particularly funny. I also needed to use the phone to order lunch in between those little lessons. Lunch? Dinner? Aside from a handful of gummy fish I hadn't eaten since last night.

"Emily?" he boomed into the phone, probably assuming the line was dead. Which it should have been.

"I'm here," I said in annoyance, my disappointment heightening as I inspected my sparse refrigerator. Dash was really an interference at the moment.

"You left in quite a hurry the other night. I was worried."

Worried about my leaving in a hurry, or worried that I'd crucify him on the Katrina issue?

"Worried? I've managed to leave parties many times in such a hurry and I've been fine."

"It's just that . . ." He paused.

What? It's just that Katrina still pines for you and you think that I'm ready to stab an ice pick into her back and then fill your car tank with sugar water? If only Dash knew that I hadn't even considered this scenario until he brought it up.

"Yes?" I prodded. Let him squirm.

"Well, I didn't want you to get the wrong idea about Katrina."

"Fine," I said as casually as jeans and a tee.

"Fine?"

"Dash, I have no problems with this. What? You think that I assume you want to get back together with Katrina because you were talking to her at a party? Wouldn't that be pretty neurotic of me?"

"Oh," he said in surprise. Silence.

I picked at the vegetable tofu sandwich that I had left over from yesterday's lunch and swallowed the last bite, but wasn't sat-

isfied with lunch food for dinner. Breakfast as dinner was perfectly fine, however. Ideally I'd be up for sushi. But that was impossible because Dash was still tying up my line. I located my cell
and speed dialed East.

"Hello?" East answered.

"Hello," I said.

"I'm still here," said Dash.

"Hold on, Dash," I said to the phone. "Hi," I said to East on
my mobile, reciting my order, "Tekka don. Four yellowtail, two
shrimp, two toro sashimis and a miso soup. Charge to Emily Briggs.
Three Gramercy Park West. One hour? No sooner? Forget it.
Thanks, though, it's just that I'll be asleep by then. Hey, Dash."

"I don't think the people at East care whether or not you'll be
asleep."

Food was becoming too much of an effort. I now needed to
brush my teeth to remove the garlicky taste from some sort of
hummus-type spread from the sandwich.

"Well, that little computer lesson has made me very tired. I'm
also kind of bummed that I missed Must See TV. I'm going to
bed right now, though you are probably as interested in my
sleeping patterns tonight as the people from East."

No reply.

"Is it okay to want some sleep? Can I go to bed now?"

"Yeah. Of course. But wait!"

"*Yes,*" I said, dragging the word out like a Brahms concerto.

"What are you doing this weekend?" Good question considering that I had been thinking more about the weekend than
about opening Web pages and choosing background colors on
my new computer.

"I actually need to get a few things organized in Bridgehampton. Sorry if I seem uptight, but I am currently dealing
with a lot of pressure in planning this shower for Anne."

"Really!" Dash must have been thrilled, as it does give some insight toward my apathy with the Katrina situation—even though
the two have no connection.

"First she totally freaked when she came by yesterday to go
over colors for gift bags—"

"Gift bags for the wedding?" interrupted Dash.

"Gift bags for the shower," I said as if this were totally normal.

"Then she totally freaks because she had a few handfuls of popcorn I had microwaved. Could not get over the fact that I'd eat Paul Newman over Healthy Choice when, as I've been clearly versed, Healthy Choice tastes as good with less calories and fat grams.

"She then had to rush off to get an extra hour in at the gym, E-mailing me later instructions to set up everything but a god-damn five-piece orchestra. And, actually, she may indeed have that in mind, but after I saw the word 'harpist' I deleted her E-mail."

"That girl has some issues. We recently did a segment on up-coming brides seeing wedding therapists. She could really use a few sessions."

"Therapist or more like exorcist?"

"And that Birkin bag she was carrying the other night—don't those things go for something like fourteen grand? She must really be robbing this poor Jason guy."

Dash was beginning to annoy me. It was okay for me to berate my family, but he was not granted this privilege.

"What? You think she put a gun to his head and said 'buy me a birkin bag or else the marriage is off!' "

"Whoa there, Emily. But you're the one who always said that she was a professional husband hunter. That the poor lackey who falls for her trap is only destined to escape it once he real-izes what he's gotten into. Inevitably securing some wily lawyer who will leave her with nothing but a few souvenirs from Cartier and Hermes and a video of the blowout wedding."

"That's a bit harsh. It's not like Anne will be one of those pa-thetic divorcees whose survival will depend on selling off her married goods on eBay, or that Jason is destined to leave her for a woman who acts both her age and her bra size."

I couldn't believe I was defending Anne; and from Dash's si-lence, I think he was a bit sidled as well.

"Sorry," he said genuinely.

"No, I'm sorry. It's just that Anne does have her finer points, some of which she's been able to show despite the wedding melodrama."

I went into my bathroom and lifted the mouthpiece away so I could brush my teeth while still listening to Dash. "Are you brushing your teeth?" My attempt was somewhat unsuccessful.

Mouth foaming like I'd just eaten explosive soap, I slid the mouthpiece back so I could mumble "mm-hmm."

"Well, why don't we go together—to Bridgehampton. I could pick you up after work. I could also help you open the house, get settled. It will be fun."

I liked the "pick you up after work" part. Since I didn't have a car in the city, depending on the Jeep Wagoneer kept at the house, a ride was an attractive option. However, I also didn't want to become dependent on Dash for transportation. At that moment I realized I needed to have my own car.

"Great. You can actually help me buy a car. I want something fun, beachy—maybe even a little retro. A convertible that looks good with a bucket of sand lining the floor and a fresh suntan." The thought of a sandy car began to freak me out. "Well. Scratch the last part."

"Not retro?"

"Retro definitely. Maybe a finned Ford Thunderbird in pista-chio—definitely a twentieth-century not twenty-first century model—or one of those VW things. A Jeep could also be fun, and since I'll be buying American I'm sure my dad will help out. Actually, I'd really like a baby blue Ford Mustang convertible."

"And I'd like to lose ten pounds by the weekend."

This was Dash's way of being sarcastic.

"In this brief conversation I've managed to realize that I need to buy a car and I've honed it down to what I want." Not bad from a girl who needed over twelve hours to set up her E-mail.

I hung up the phone with this new project in mind. Had I even said good-bye to Dash?

Rid of him, I had renewed energy. Having a professional rea-son to use the Internet, I punched in a search for "Ford Mustang Convertible, Hamptons, Long Island." Remarkably there were a few results. Though some were referring to a horrifically boring car show to be held Memorial Day weekend, a man in Remsenburg was selling a Ford Mustang convertible. Though it was in white, not baby blue, I rationalized that white would go with more outfits. I E-mailed him to hopefully set up a time so Dash and I could see the car en route to Bridgehampton.

I then surfed for ideas for Anne's damn shower, wandering to a site that sold French beach accessories. I desperately needed more espadrilles. The site had a dozen, in more shades than there were colors of fruit on a farm stand. The same site also had these hilariously adorable beach cabanas in thick blue and white stripes. I bought one, adding another pair of espadrilles in the same marlin blue, and arranged for Saturday delivery.

Finishing the purchase, I already had two new messages waiting in my mailbox: one an instant message confirming my order and the other the Ford Mustang man in Remsenburg confirming his availability to meet me Friday evening.

All accomplished in twenty-seven minutes. When it came to shopping on-line I was a master.

34

Dash's Chevy Tahoe pulled alongside the hydrant across from my apartment. The car seemed exactly proportionate to my eat-in kitchen. I supposed this was for all of Dash's four-wheel driving needs, navigating potholed Manhattan streets to pay a parking fee equivalent to a midwestern home's rent.

He called from his cell phone to tell me to come down. I hoisted my three extra large Bean totes from a clutter of five, the Louis Vuitton luggage set for the thrifty, and I clippity-clopped downstairs in my pale blue Jack Rogers, again happy that I had forgiving neighbors.

Looking both ways, I ran across the street—more like wobbled. Dash looked as if he had just eaten something funky. "Do you have your entire apartment in those bags?" He eyeballed the totes with the distrust of an airport guard viewing a bulletproof guitar case.

"Just a few summer necessities."

"And what's with the outfit?"

I looked down at my striped silk pajama bottom pants. I was so devoted to them, almost forgot that I'd been wearing them for the past two days. With pants held up by a thick white sailing rope and paired with a snug marlin blue turtleneck sweater, I could have been dressed as the new cabana I was so excited to receive. The outfit was meant to complement my new Ford Mustang. I just shrugged at Dash.

He loaded the back of the Tahoe, that extra space proving to be especially useful, and he opened the passenger door as if he were my personal driver.

"Wait," I said. "I have two more bags and my laptop."

"How? Where? What?" He sounded like an Introduction to Journalism professor.

"Trust me, we have everything from titanium dioxide SPF 50 sunblock to soothing peppermint foot cream to care for sunburned feet," I said with a wink. He got it and allowed me to run off for the other things.

Dash was about three Rocky Mountain states away from me in the driver's seat, while I felt like a small child in a big person's chair, feet propped up unable to touch the floor.

"Do you know where we're going?" he asked.

He could be so anal.

"Sure," I said breezily.

He shot me one of his annoyed-with-Emily stares.

"What?"

"How should I say this without coming off harshly?" He then had no problem in coming off harshly. "You can be completely obtuse when it comes to directions."

"Whatever do you mean?"

"Which trip to Vermont should I begin with—your assumption that every sign should be directed on how to get back to New York."

"Well, shouldn't they be?"

"Not when you are in a sleepy little town almost two hundred miles from the city. You can be so New York–centric."

And he was saying this like it was a bad thing?

"Fine. Here," I retorted, throwing the directions at Dash.

He read them carefully and then started punching at his computerized map toy thing, which was actually kind of cool.

I reached into my new wicker basket bag and snapped the headphones of a portable CD player around my ears, preferring to listen to my tunes rather than contend with Spiderman flickering through every radio station. Dash was very top forty, preferring what I considered to be bullet-to-the-head music. Surfing through television channels was nauseating enough; jumbled stop and go whiny sounds in a moving vehicle that the marines would love to recruit, vomit-inducing.

"How antisocial of you!" he said, one hand on the wheel, the other hand flicking my headphones. (Figures that Dash would immediately have issues with this one.)

"It's just that I know you have this car/music zone thing going on."

"Don't be ridiculous. We'll listen to what you're listening to." He paused. "What are you listening to?"

"Alanis Morisette."

"You see, I find her new album very uplifting."

It wasn't gospel music, for God's sake.

"Sorry. It's *Jagged Little Pill.*"

"Great." Then he started sputtering. "Is that the one where she wants to castrate every man?"

"Indeed, you are correct."

"And isn't that music a bit outdated now?"

How could music be outdated? Ever listened to a tremendously untrendy composer known as Mozart? The Beatles? "Sorry, my eardrums never got the up-on-music trend memo."

Without exchanging anymore opinions on our differences in music, Dash returned to flicking the CD remote and I plopped the headset back around my ears.

Arriving at the final stretch of highway before reaching the one-lane road that would take us to Remsenburg, Dash handled the elbow turn with race car driver ability. The Tahoe suctioned to the road like lips to a straw while the sudden jerk shifted a container of Altoids from his side of the dashboard right into my lap. My cheek, pressed against the window, left a perspired smudge. Yet during this hairpin of a turn, Dash was still able to flick the remote of the CD player.

Upon entering the town of Remsenburg, Dash punched something into this digital map OnStar thing—boys and their damn gadgets—we found the house without a hitch. Perhaps their investments have more use than pretty tops and flirty skirts. Erasing this ridiculous thought from my head, I was lured under the spell of popcorn kernels crackling from his car rolling on the white gravel driveway, a dramatic contrast to the chemically enhanced green lawn and glass-encased ranch-style house. We could have been in Malibu circa 1967.

Pulling behind the rear of the Ford Mustang convertible, I was immediately in love—which Dash probably registered because he had that worried look on his face, like a press secretary prepping a hubristic president before he made a speech about his improprieties.

"Let me do the talking," he said, turning off the ignition.

I immediately skipped over to the car. The white leather top pulled back like a St. Tropez beach canopy. Bucket seats in white were trimmed with the sea blue color that I had initially been so keen on. The steering wheel wrapped in leather and an ancient AM/FM radio that you twirled the dial to adjust.

The owner stepped from his front door, the sound of us driving in having alerted him. He was dressed in a yellow cardigan over flat-fronted chinos in the same sky blue accent as my car— very Perry Como after a day of golf, evidenced by his sunburned face tipped in white, where his visor was probably perched.

"Hi, Emily," he said graciously. "Mr. Nickerson," he added with a handshake.

Dash was inspecting the tires, the inside of the vehicle—doing the guy thing.

"That's Dash." I pointed. The two men waved to one another and Dash then joined us.

"It appears so well restored," I began. "So is the top easy to work?"

"As easy as buckling a shoe," he replied as we headed over to the car, joining Dash midway so that we all returned to evaluate the car. He coiled the top up and latched the side. Dash's face returned to that worried look—he was really beginning to ruin this for me.

I avoided his gaze and continued speaking with Mr. Nickerson. "I was a bit hesitant about white. White cars can be so Miami Beach Mafioso, not to mention difficult to keep clean, but this one really has that AMC film classic flair."

"Emily," Dash called over to me, in that *you're so grounded* fatherly tone.

I walked over to him while Mr. Nickerson folded the top back down.

"I told you that I would do the talking and here you are babbling 'Will I look cute in this? Is white the in color this year?' These are not the requirements for buying a car. Let me handle it from here."

"Okay Mr. How-many-miles-to-the-gallon," I huffed. "Fine." I'd already made my decision to get the car.

Dash spoke with Mr. Nickerson in some foreign mechanic garble that eluded me. Once Mr. Nickerson returned indoors to get some documents that Dash had requested, Dash walked past me with a knowing smirk and lifted the hood of the car. I joined him beneath the hood, scanning the metal internal organs of the engine. I was actually impressed, quite impressed, not realizing that Dash had such automotive insight.

"Whatcha looking for?" I asked, flirtatiously for a change, twirling around and leaning my elbows against the car's front fender.

"Quite honestly, Emily, I have no idea." And we both shared a smile.

Mr. Nickerson handed Dash a blue book and some other documents, then suggested we take the car out for a spin. I jumped into the bucket seat, which enveloped me like a baseball in a glove. All I needed was an Hermes scarf, white leather driving gloves, owl-eyed sunglasses and a wave of my magic wand to turn Dash into a giant size poodle (a breed I particularly despised but I was going for the Slim Keith/C.Z. Guest effect here).

We made the Rice Krispie's snap, crackle, pop sound down the driveway while my free hand immediately clasped the radio dial, searching for the local oldies station on AM. Dash appeared curious as to why I was making such an effort with the tunes.

"Looking for The Beach Boys," I said, as if this should be obvious.

Driving to the purring hum, turning the vehicle that was a bit more stiff in feel than Dash's space terrain vehicle, I was now more convinced than ever that this would be my car. The thought of stepping on the brakes was sheer torment.

Rolling back up the drive slower than when we had departed, Dash turned to me with the seriousness of a wedding proposal.

"Who is your mechanic out here?"

"I don't know. Oh, yeah, I do," suddenly remembering the time I had a fender bender in the Wagoneer yet had been too drunk to remember how it happened. Sam's Auto was particularly helpful in being able to fix it in an afternoon.

"Sam's," I said proudly, finally feeling useful on the automotive front.

Dash reached into his pocket and dialed his cell, which was as big as a lipstick. Big cars, big TVs, small cell phones and small computers—I had now fully registered Dash's preferences in electronic sizes.

"Number for Sam's Auto." He covered the mouthpiece. "Which town?" he asked.

"East Hampton."

"East Hampton," he said to the phone.

He dialed the number, a dumb grin on his face when he connected.

"Great! You're still in. Can you inspect a car for me this weekend? Uh-huh. Uh-huh. Uh-huh."

"What!" I nudged. "It sounds like you're discussing the prognosis of cancer."

"Shhh." He flicked at me like I was some pesky bug.

"Okay, then, how does an extra hundred sound? Great!" He snapped the phone shut.

"Emily. The guys at Sam's are leaving for the evening but they said we can leave the car there overnight and insert the keys in the drop-off box. They're a bit swamped due to the impending holiday weekend but they'll fit us in tomorrow first thing. I can get a ride to Maidstone and pick up the car after."

"You're playing golf this weekend?"

"Of course I am. I'm sure I must have mentioned it. Did I mention it?"

I shook my head.

"Well, yes. Emily. I am playing golf tomorrow. With Luke," he carefully added.

"Luke plays golf?"

Luke was a mutual friend of ours whom we both had worked with at MTV. Apparently Dash was more proactive on maintaining the relationship. Luke had an unforgettable geek-chic style.

Baggy golf shirts, bucket hats in blinding colors and even comfortable enough to wear denim pants in brands advertised in alternative magazines. He was really into the Seattle grunge thing, the way preppies morphed into Dead Heads once they left the confined rules of parental pressures for campus life. I recalled his absolute conviction that Kurt Cobain's death sealed the fate of music's demise into something that could be packaged and spewed out as easy as a tall latte at Starbucks—which we also both despised, escaping for many coffee/decaf breaks to a Parisian-style café in Hell's Kitchen.

After he shared his despondency over the industry's pandering to hip-hop with the wrong guys in marketing, and after he struck up a relationship with our boss's assistant—a very sweet girl with great clothes and a bad haircut—he left television (was forced out) to pursue his dream of making rock documentaries.

Dash stroked a hand to his smooth chin, not an hour's worth of stubble. "He's an excellent player, not to mention he has access to all the clubs because of Salomon and all."

"Salomon? Wouldn't that be more of a lift ticket/ski boot kind of connection?"

"No!" He laughed. "Salomon Brothers Smith Barney. Where Luke started working, about a year after he left MTV."

I see. Interesting.

"Apparently you two haven't stayed in touch."

"Apparently not."

"What happened to him with that—what's her name? That clotheshorse assistant."

"Heather. They were married about three years ago, just bought a house in Cold Spring Harbor."

Interesting.

"So, it will be fun to play some golf, catch up on old times."

"That's grrr-reat," I said like Tony the Tiger. Now I could spend the day painting, running and doing my thing without having to worry about Dash.

After Dash made the arrangements with Mr. Nickerson, I returned to my new happy place, ready to drive my new car. The seat was still warm from our ride.

We caravanned back on the highway; I led the way. My Mustang was much smaller than the other cars—particularly noticeable when a Hummer sped past Dash, then spastically maneuvered into, then quickly out of, my space, just a side-view mirror away from an impact that would have shattered my dream of a topless Mustang summer. While the driver, hair as slick as his car, was one of many of a breed that would soon be infesting the area, along with the arrival of bloodsucking bugs, he looked at me as if I were the one in the wrong. I didn't contend with his type, and chose to focus on the view ahead.

Safely reaching the one lane that led through the little hamlets dotting the Hamptons, we meandered onto the more secluded Three Mile Harbor road. The fragrance of budded flowers mixed with fresh-cut grass was especially potent in a convertible.

After dropping off the car, we stopped at Citarella. We filled our cart with every picked-from-the-ground fruit and vegetable we could find, adding fancily jarred imports. Giving particular thought to rotisserie chicken and grilled vegetables, we agreed that they would make for a more satisfying dinner than our original plan to go out. Dash then insisted on stopping at an out of the way liquor store to get a bottle of wine he was keen to sample.

Reaching the narrow tree-lined drive that led to the house, my insides started to spatter with gymnastic kicks the same way it did when I was given the go-ahead to open my Christmas presents.

The house's epic presence came into view. Tara still standing after the war. Dash's foot barely touched the accelerator as we rolled past her, my eyes glued to the view until we were parked in the lot adjacent to the service entrance.

Our country house had survived hurricanes, a tenuous bidding war between my father and a builder who demolished old houses and built new homes resembling toilet paper holders glued to chopsticks, and more than a few raucous keg parties. I loved the fact that the only renovations made since we'd been here were to modernize the kitchen and bathrooms, up from outhouse standards. I loved that while the current summer home trend was to have side-by-side multi-fauceted showers, our outdoor shower was the one put to most use. I loved that while some Hamptoners retreated to their private screening rooms, we didn't even have a TV. I loved that my father refused to give up the clunker of a Wagoneer, which he christened Molly, when all our neighbors were updating their Lexus SUVs as regularly as my shoes.

Dash unloaded my bags with the care of a roadie removing equipment from a tour bus. I grabbed his overnight. He smiled a smile that said he'd contend with the baggage so I could run inside and scream "I'm home!" at the top of my lungs. I flung open the screen door, which banged against the house and then shut by itself, and took in the musty beach smell blended with weathered antiques. As far as olfactory aphrodisiacs go, it was right up there with cinnamon and apples.

Dropping Dash's bag on an antique oak bench, I sprinted up to my bedroom. My room was also preserved in a time before homes were electronically tuned, a time when bugs were collected in jam jars, not trawling the clubs. I was at a loss on what to do first. Out the window I could see Dash entering the house with the Citarella bags.

I cracked the window open. "I'll join you in a minute," I yelled down.

His head twirled about, then tilted once he located me. "Take your time. I have to call Luke."

I returned to the room. It was painted in a crisp white as fresh as newly laundered sheets; even the wide-planked floorboards were white. While it was smaller than most of the other rooms in the house, it had the most coveted piece of real estate: the corner turret. The odd undulated shape encircled by casement windows created a remarkably special quality that couldn't be replicated by four basic walls. I opened my shuttered closet doors, instantly soothed by a Henri Bendel hatbox in its trademark brown and white stripes. Its contents were those priceless pieces of memorabilia. I opened the box, ready to travel back in time.

The runaway letter/Mom's grocery list; invitations to summer parties; a barrette with a painted rainbow; and streams of colored ribbons, a mess of fabric like the hair of a rag doll. I loosened the knot and released the ribbons, which floated to my bed like ticker tape. They'd been purchased from a notions shop in

East Hampton, now a specialty food store selling a polenta and julienne vegetable spread (cornmeal and recycled vegetables) that cost more than my shoes.

Each striped ribbon was in hues taken from the color prep wheel. The vivid pink, yellow and green striped ribbon on a background of dark momentarily struck me as chocolate. I remembered being offended by the choice of brown as the dominant color. I'd purchased it because I already had every other pattern, so this was a needed addition to my collection.

The sunset, in swirls of a grape-orange popsicle, went from day to night with the instance of a light switch, making me turn on the cast-iron lamp on my bureau. That early summer nip in the evening air, which went perfectly with fires and extra blankets, sent a chill through my body.

I changed out of my baby blue Mustang ensemble into an old pair of brown suede Ralph Lauren jeans that I intentionally left out here. They were especially hip for casual Hampton nights but would just get lost in my crowded New York closet, where I owned ten other things that were either similar or more appropriate for urban dressing. I temporarily threw on a baby tee with an Indian wearing a headdress.

The funny brown ribbon edging my quilt had the effect of a decorative border. I pinched it between my fingers and then wrapped it around my ponytail. I wasn't satisfied with the result. If it hadn't worked in the past, why would it work now?

I checked on Dash, finding him seated on the wooden bench, legs crossed like a girl. His ear was to the phone and he was nodding robotically. He spotted me and raised his eyebrows in pleasurable relief. My anticipated arrival allowed him to escape the call and say his good-byes.

"Hey," he said, walking over to me, giving me a polite kiss on the cheek. "Don't you look cute."

"Thanks," I said, peeking through the Citarella bags until I found what I wanted.

"What are you looking for?"

"Grapes."

"In there." The grapes were in a colander in the sink, dappled with water like a model spritzed with sweat for a swimsuit spread.

I pulled off a bunch and began munching, instantly sated by their crispy coolness. I then took a seat at the kitchen table and read the car pamphlets Dash had requested from Mr. Nickerson.

Dash walked over to the bottle of wine and two glasses, which had been thoughtfully arranged.

"Where's the bottle opener?"

"The drawer next to the stove."

He pulled open the wrong drawer.

"On the left side."

He corked open the bottle with the skill of a sommelier and poured, the gurgling soothing sound whetting my palate. Dash swirled the glass with such a whirlpool effect that if I were to make such an attempt it would spill everywhere. He then took a cautionary sip, which generated a satisfied smile. He filled both glasses and handed one to me. I took a sip while he looked on intently. It was oak-y, dry—buzzwords thrown around from one of those affected wine-tasting parties I'd been dragged to. I suppose this was the result he was after but, to be honest, I would have preferred something sweeter, stronger. Perhaps a concentrated gimlet? I really hoped that Dash wasn't about to initiate some erudite conversation about wine. (1) I couldn't care less. (2) Why try wine when liquor is quicker.

"So Luke invited us to some party tonight. Want to go?"

My visions of an early night building a fire and reading neglected *New Yorker*s suddenly disappeared. "Sure," I said indifferently.

"Great! It's not too far away. Not too big. In Sagaponack. Some benefit to save the duck, piping plover, or some other feathered creature indigenous to the area."

"Uh-oh, that probably means we'll have a run-in with Cousin Anne."

"We don't have to go," he said in a tone that indicated that he really, really wanted to go.

"Don't be foolish. Let me just unpack and then we'll be on our way."

"Unpack?" he said worriedly. "Won't that take, like, nine days?"

* * *

Walking—hobbling—up the stairs with my bags, I suddenly questioned our sleeping arrangements. Though Dash had slept with me in my bed before, it was as a friend and would seem somewhat uncomfortable under the current circumstances. Entering my bedroom behind me, Dash unzipped his overnight on my bed. Looked like he'd made the decision for me.

"I'm going to use the bathroom," he said, exiting the room, Burberry toiletry bag in hand.

I arranged my tees and lingerie in the appropriate drawers and hung my dresses and stowed my sweaters on the shelf above. Pulling a snug brown cashmere sweater over my tee, I untied the Henry Bendel brown ribbon with white dots from the hatbox and tied it in my hair.

Relegated to brushing my teeth in my parents' bathroom, I yelled down the hall to Dash to say that I'd meet him downstairs. Moments later, Dash greeted me in the kitchen dressed in a navy blue cotton cable knit. The little red polo player on his sweater was coordinated to the red checks in his gingham shirt.

We walked to his car in silence, a silence that remained with us till we reached a house illuminated with cutout lights like a cruise ship at night.

The party was not to save some bird. It was a pre-summer kick-off party for a new gardening magazine that had a bird on the cover of its inaugural issue. The party was not small, it was a thousand people. The party was not intimate, it was padded with the phonies whom I went to great lengths to avoid—the cherry-cheeked plastic surgeon, the entertainment/fashion reporter from the local news station and the lingerie designer whose label was only justified by her eponymous NoHo boutique. The only thing enjoyable about the event was that I struck it up with the bartender, who graciously made me a fresh gimlet, leaving his bar duties for ingredients in the kitchen, to the consternation of thirsty guests.

Anne was there, of course. She invited herself over for dinner tomorrow night so she could scout out the space, as if her shower were to be as big as this cheesy party. I lost Anne to some fund-raiser who mentioned that she was in need of assistance for the building of a school for local children who live in Manhattan, which didn't quite make sense to me but I was afraid to ask.

I leaned back on a butter colored wall that was sure to have a noticeable scuff once I moved away. With drink in hand, I surveyed the view. Not the view of the crowd, which I'd registered in all of two seconds, but of the home's décor. I'd driven by this house many times. Once it had been a sublime potato field and then, within two weeks' time, it had become a house as big as Shea Stadium. Rather than an assembling of a mess of bleached Lincoln Logs glued with glass, the architect had followed the design of the antique gambreler homes that are in the true spirit of the area. It was really just another display of wealth that followed a vastly different approach to summer cottage living than my mother employed. We didn't even have air-conditioning (but Mom was not quick to point out her temperature-controlled bedroom, to which she mysteriously retreated on sultry summer days).

The home was decorated in that quintessentially Hampton way. Floors the color and shine of butterscotch, white-distressed furniture, and glass bowls the size of birdbaths filled with white seashells (courtesy of their decorator, not from days collecting shells at the beach—what would be the point of that when you could just pay someone to do it?). What did distinguish this home from the other estates in a ten-mile radius was the artwork: super-enlarged fruit and vegetables from the garden of the Jolly Green Giant himself; if Botero created still-lifes, these would be them. The paintings were either truly surreal or there was something stronger in my gimlet than gin.

I twirled my drink and gave it an expert sniff, only to be driven further into this drug-free acid trip by the most frightening surprise of the evening. More frightening than paintings of produce on steroids, more frightening than a feather-bra-wearing Hilton sister (I could never tell them apart because they just looked like trashy Upper East Side versions of one of the Playboy Playmate twins). It was Luke.

He was almost unrecognizable, wearing the same sweater as Dash but paired with khakis. No funky jeans, hat, or geek-chic accessory. He'd turned into a father. Which was somewhat true, as a very pregnant Heather in a very navy, very tent-like maternity dress was at his side. She was looking like she shouldn't have been sucking the meat out of a spicy chicken skewer. If she stepped on that dance floor she had better be prepared to give birth on it.

Their voices had a new accent as well. Drawn out vowels, which had probably occurred from too many days in county club sun. After catching up on our past five years in all of two minutes, my brain mentally screamed *save me*, with topics teetering from taxes to the public-versus-private dilemma, until Joanna rescued me.

Once we were separated from the inductees to the Cold Springs newcomers club, Joanna and I were snapped by the same photographer from the other night.

She reprimanded me on my lack of cell phone use, or at least not checking my cell phone messages. She'd been trying to call me all day (she'd probably attempted two calls) and was pleased with herself that she'd be able to share the good news in person.

"You're going to LA," she gloated, as if I was supposed to be happy about this.

"Whatever do you mean?" I gave my new drink a stronger sniff than before, suspecting that the bartender had been slipping in more than a few fresh limes.

"I mean you're going to LA! Two weeks from Wednesday. To meet with the people at FOX. Remember how we were discussing the options to segue *Wall Flower* into a series?"

"Uh," I said, knocking back my gimlet. "I think so."

"Well. This is it!"

While her news should have been met with cartwheels and a smile so wide the guests across the room could see how many cavities I had from the year I was addicted to Sweet Tarts, I couldn't help but have trepidations. This was suspiciously reminiscent of Henry and his deal that was crystallizing before he gave me the heave-ho.

How could I pose this with the utmost professionalism?

"What the hell does this mean! This sounds a bit too close to a certain deal being made with Henry, and that would be, would be just insane!" So much for diplomacy.

"Oh, Emily, don't make such a fuss. FOX is the ideal venue to option this. They are *the* network for this sort of the thing."

"Why do I feel like you're not giving me all the details?"

"Because you're letting your emotions get the better of you."

If she were a guy, which was somewhat true because I'd seen her make deals that could make a pit bull scamper, I'd say she was pulling the emotional-girl card.

Still nervous, I agreed that though I was indeed thrilled, a lot needed to be discussed. That we'd continue this conversation tomorrow, perhaps over drinks conveniently scheduled when Cousin Anne intended to harass me.

"Oh, look," she squealed. Right into my left ear. "It's Elvin Werner!"

Elvin Werner I just didn't get. A social scion based on nothing. The best way I could describe the Elvin phenomenon: *The Emperor's New Clothes.* A clueless cycle only perpetuated by this self-profligate mystique with the substance of moth dust.

Drug dealers had more character than Elvin—or what I imagined a drug dealer's personality—but here's a guy who sought the spotlight the way I avoided it. Parlaying entrée from the success of a few radio stations that he owned, not particularly good ones unless you're more interested in the gossip of the musicians' lives than the sound of their music. Elvin once courted rock stars who now court him. How? Because this Smurf-size guy, not three apples tall, had become a fat naked emperor who had the draw of something he was not.

Being at the same party as him, I realized that the evening's end was fast approaching. I must leave before I became one of the perpetrators who allowed this fat emperor to cavalierly show off his naked self while everyone thought it miraculous.

"Emily!" Joanna scoffed. "Why can't you make an effort to promote yourself? And why are you always making that face?" I must have had the face on. "Elvin is a great contact for you. For Lily—think of Lily."

Oh, yes, Lily. Some color splashed onto a page, a goddamn cartoon character. Okay, so I would talk to Satan's son because I had an obligation to Lily. Just call me selfless.

"Why are you so opposed to Elvin?" she whined.

"Because he is part of something I am not. Something that I don't understand."

"I know," she said motherly, her feigned attempt to be understanding. "He is quite the society star."

"No." What I was trying to get across to Joanna was just another game of tic-tac-toe. "He has no consideration of tradition—unless you count the age old trade of bartering. Notice how artificially white his teeth are, and how he features on-the-hour promotions for that celebrity dentist on WFYI?"

"Excuse me?"

"Or the ads for hair transplants? Just look at pictures of him from a few years back and notice how much hair he's grown since then. And I love it, all services to make him look even more like something he's not."

Elvin successfully reached us.

"Jo-ann-a," he sang, like an old Toto song. Elvin's hypnotic magnetism on Joanna, even on those around us, had the effect of Rasputin gripping the Russian monarch. I just stared at the effectiveness of his plugs and stilted shoes.

Joanna introduced us for about the 1,800th time and he extended a hand that was as limp as a jellyfish, which I expected to shake into shape. They did the Euro air kiss thing, then began a discussion about how wonderful and beautiful they were. Elvin's head was spinning like a basketball twirled on a finger, surveying the crowd, probably figuring he'd made sufficient contact with us. I ducked in between his head spins and made a furtive exit. I'd say that was enough schmoozing on Lily's behalf.

When the bartender was the best friend to be found at a party, you knew it was either time to drink yourself into darkness or go home. As my bartender attended to the demands of guests who appeared more panicked than plane crash survivors abandoning floatable cushions for a lifeboat, I took a glass of champagne off a tray, unbeknownst to a passing waiter, and began searching for Dash.

He was easy to find. Katrina's hair shone stronger than a fluorescent bulb.

As I approached them, it was a replay of earlier in the week—my presence, evidently a cause of unease, must be the reason for something only I could scheme.

"Hi," they both said nervously.

"Hey," I responded naturally.

"Well, I better be going," said Katrina. "Early golf lesson."

What was it with golf? I could just picture Katrina in her cute little shorts coordinated to the Burberry golf bag. Next to Dash on a trimmed course, his looking on while she went for a putt— they'd make for great cover models on some goddamn vacation brochure.

"Hi," said Dash, solo, again nervously.

"Hey," I again replied naturally.

"So, what was Joanna so flustered about?"

"It's actually pretty interesting stuff. She secured a meeting with FOX about *Wall Flower* possibly being developed into a show." .

His face brightened as if a camera's flash were directed on him.

"Emily, that's amazing. You are so amazing. And so talented!" He leaned into me with that comforting peck to the cheek.

As he stood before me I just looked at him looking at me, so gentle and caring. I found myself enjoying this, taking in great news by sharing it with a true friend. That he was sincerely proud made the accomplishment all the more satisfying. It was familiar. Somewhat uncanny that Dash had been the first person I saw after receiving the news about *Vogue* and now here he was, after I'd been told about its future possibilities.

"Listen," he said. "I'm pretty exhausted and we have a full day tomorrow. Do you mind if we get out of here?"

You couldn't get me out of here any faster!

Sounding indifferent. "Sure."

He was still for a moment, then scanned the room. He pushed my back lightly, indicating that I would have better skill directing us out of this people-obstructed room, and I maneuvered through the partygoers like a hiker cutting through wild vegetation.

We walked to the Tahoe, parked against a small foothill rimming the driveway. It was not intended for cars; Dash had to use the four-wheel drive and generate a lot of skidding noises to release the car.

Driving to the meditative hum of the vehicle, Dash sensibly did not turn on any music.

"What now?" he asked. *Why now?* I wondered. I was too exhausted to contend with the issue of our relationship.

"What's that?" I said, as sleepily as possible.

"With FOX, the next step?"

"Oh!" I sparked up. "Apparently I have to go to LA. A week from Monday for a meeting."

"The sixth?"

"I believe so."

"What timing. I have to be there for the Carson piece. We can go together. I already have a room at the Chateau Marmont."

"Perfect," I said with a smile. This was actually an immense relief. The thought of LA—La La Land Brad and Jen or was it Jen and Ben as the anointed royals, the plastically enhanced people—it all terrified me. Dash had a better understanding of this orbit and I could really use his expertise.

He was driving with such focus, probably on the lookout for a sudden deer that could jump into his fender, damaging this vehicle that he nurtured like a firstborn, but I gently intruded into his zone.

"Thank you," I said softly.

"For what?"

"Because you always have such insight on what's best for me. You help me go after the things that I don't seem to realize I want."

"It's just the little push. A father nudging his son's ball into the winning hole."

"Well, I appreciate it. And I really feel much better about LA knowing you'll be there."

He gave me a look. It was a nice one.

"You're such a good friend," I said, looking at him so he could see me for a change without one of my faces on.

Dash turned into the driveway with a look of such peace I could have ridden alongside him for another hour or, really, more like five minutes. We entered the backdoor with the quietness of two people trying not to disturb a house filled with sleepers. Passing right through the kitchen, I was not even considering the Ben and Jerry's in the freezer, heading directly to my room.

I slipped off my pants, draping them on their hanger in my closet and then took off my bra from beneath my shirt, Jennifer Beals *Flashdance* style. Dash undressed right down to his Brooks Brothers gingham boxers, forming his clothes into a neat little bundle on the top of my vanity. I then bounced onto my side of the bed and assumed my regular sleeping position. My back to his front with his outside arm draped around me, which would be lost somewhere in the middle of the night. Placement we've comfortably shared in the past.

35

•

The slam of the Tahoe's door outside my bedroom awakened me. Further pulling me from my early morning haze was the sound of Dash mumbling on his cell. I weakly shifted position and looked at the Cartier travel clock on my bedside—just before 7:00 A.M. God, if this was not horrendously early for a Saturday.

Pulling my hair back in its messy knot, I slipped into an old pair of orange pajama pants in a herringbone pattern that I remembered were too small on me, and I was happy to find that they were a bit loose. Leaving my Indian headdress tee on, I took the special bag of Dreesen's doughnuts I bought last night and greeted Dash on the terrace.

Rubbing my eyes with the free hand of a child carrying a tattered stuffed toy, I noticed Dash was showered, dressed, had probably gone for a six-mile run and pruned the hedges, as well as the neighbors' hedges. He was a neighborly kind of guy.

Why did he have to be such a morning person? If he said Good morning, up-and-at-'em, this would be the breakup moment.

"Good morning!" he crowed.

Okay. There was no up-and-at-'em! And I was having a skinny day so I could be more forgiving.

Not returning his gaze to what I was sure was a very large and happy grin, I instantly walked to the white paper lunch bag that better have a decaf hazelnut in it.

"Decaf crème caramel," informed Dash. "From The Golden Pear. I remembered how excited you were by that flavor the last time we were there."

He could happily crow all he wanted. Now, having complete trust in Dash's marketing skills, I seized the coffee without even having to ask if there were two Equals and a splash of skim.

Dash finished removing the items from a larger bag—a container of fruit salad, yogurt and granola, and two muffins. I took the fruit salad without asking.

"Hey," I said with a melon UHFing my tone, something that would have caused my mother to freak. "Want a Dreesen's doughnut!" I pushed the bag toward Dash.

He looked in the bag as if the head of his mother were in it—throwing the doughnuts into the pool that was slowly being filled with water.

What the hell was that!

"What the hell did you do that for?"

Incredulous, I ran over to the pool, leaning over the edge to watch the doughnuts bob up and down like a few Cheerios left soggy in a sea of milk. Scooping them with the cleaning net, I considered anonymously sending Dash brochures from an anger management class.

Hoisting the drowned doughnuts over the pool fence into the wooded area, I thought the poor things would at least make for a welcoming breakfast to overpopulated deer or to a dog that was making an escape from his city parents.

Dash joined me, playing the death plot with the same reverence I had when seeing the road-killed opossum on yesterday's run. The doughnuts' resemblance to the mauled opossum must have been some kind of weird foreshadowing.

"Sorry about that," he said feebly.

"Sorry is for stepping on my toes or getting the wrong coffee." Well, perhaps not the wrong coffee.

"But why all this anger over some defenseless doughnuts? You don't have to eat them—I never do."

"Then why do you buy them?"

And why are you so clueless?

"Why do you buy candy canes or make eggnog? Do you ever eat the candy canes or drink the eggnog? Dreesen's is part of a summer tradition. And there's nothing better than that smell emanating from Dreesen's, one of the storefronts that survived being pushed out by boutiques that sell scraps of lycra, put a $300 tag on it, and pawn it off as the new bikini.

"Watching them twirled, baked the old-fashioned way in the deli's window with the same delight as seeing the fabled Christmas scenes at Saks."

Dash's sweet expression showed that I sufficiently made my case. We moved our breakfast to the kitchen, and Dash mumbled something about taking his multi-vitamin. He dropped a *Times* on the table that had sections from tomorrow's edition.

"How did you get the advance sections?" I asked, then realized the answer. "Let me guess, you had your home delivery changed to this address for the weekend?"

"Guilty."

He could be so retentive. But his retentiveness was now being gulped down to my benefit as I reveled in my decaf crème caramel and sifted through the paper, pinching the "Arts & Leisure" section.

"Em, do you mind if I look at that first? I need to check out something in one of the television articles."

Suppressing my irritation, I slid the section to his side of the table. Did he just forget that he massacred a bag of doughnuts?

At the bottom of the *Times* was the *New York Standard*. Dash was not the *Standard*'s readership. I lifted it to his attention with a snide look.

"They have an excellent wine columnist."

"Since when have you become such a wine snob?"

"Katrina got me into it. You know her family has a vineyard in the Loire Valley?"

Of course they did.

"They're actually looking to purchase one on the North Fork. I think they are pretty close to securing the deal."

Of course they were.

Dash looked at his Swiss Army watch, his face befuddled with concern.

"Where the hell is Luke?" he said, I assumed to himself.

The sound of a large car rolled up the drive. It passed the bay window in the kitchen: Luke's navy Chevy Tahoe obstructed the entire view. What was it with these boys, they needed these monster trucks the way we needed the touted bag in the color of the season.

"Great," said Dash to the kitchen window. "Now listen, Emily. I will be picking up the Mustang in the early afternoon and will call you to tell you how it goes."

"Fine."

"And another thing." He paused while he picked up some goofy golf visor.

Yes, I was listening but couldn't get passed the goofy visor.

"I mentioned to Luke and a few other people last night that, since there doesn't seem to be anything going on tonight, they should stop by."

"No problem, I said the same to Joanna, and Anne invited herself." I did a mental count. "So they'll bring their significants, what do you expect—ten, maybe twelve people."

"More like twenty, maybe thirty." If I didn't suck my crème caramel as quickly as a gimlet, it would have been staining the *Standard* place-matted in front of me.

"God, Dash, what did you do, make flyers?"

"It won't be too bad. Just buy some vegetables, fish, grill stuff and I'll handle the cooking."

"Hardly, there are the appetizers, confirming a maid to clean up tomorrow, preparing the table setting." We both took a moment to absorb this. And then there was the alcohol. Alcohol!

"Alcohol!" I shrieked.

"Luke will get a keg. I will buy the wine."

"And," I prodded.

"And hard stuff."

I was now fine with the whole idea.

"In that case I might as well call Daphne and Andy, since I rarely get to see her in drunken scenarios."

"Sounds like a fun idea."

Luke opened the kitchen door hesitantly, as if he wasn't sure if this was the right house and feared that he was trespassing.

"Hey, you two. Dash. You ready?"

"Yep. My bag is outside. Bye, Em." He waved, followed by a wave from Luke. "I'll call you later, about the Mustang."

Right, I wasn't brain dead, I said to myself with a saccharine smile and a wave to the departing boys.

As the truck crackled out of the driveway, I fast-forwarded to six years from now. Luke would be slightly pudgier, less trendier and the Tahoe would be replaced by the newest model with a bumper sticker saying "Honor Student On Board."

All thoughts of a long run, light gardening, and needed pedicure were now decimated, along with my fruit salad and Dash's granola—I couldn't help myself, it being a skinny morning.

That it was just 8:00 A.M. relieved some anxiety, so I returned to my chair to read the papers and noticed a few magazines. Oh, *The Atlantic Monthly.* Perhaps I would just read an article to have my dose of smartness for the month. Good idea considering that there would be much cocktailing this weekend and I needed to impress those to impress with my charm and intelligence.

Skimming through the table of contents—an article on Cuban farming, um—pass. Comparison of the two Bushes? I don't need to read some *pedantic* article to figure that one. (Pretty impressed in my using the word "pedantic." Feeling smarter already.) Hmm. Some story using the word "adumbration," clearly intended to insult my intelligence. Wasn't the whole point of this to make me feel brilliant and sophisticated? I mean these stories are carving into an out-of-shape area of brain space here. For God's sake, not even one puff piece on the latest promising film. This was horrendous, adding much tedium to a lovely day primed for heavy social activity. Reading such material would take the light-hearted joviality from the intended functions that lay ahead. In no way should I bog down my mind with such frivolities. Oh! What a shame, the wind from the screen door opened the *Standard* to "Cock Around the Clock," a sign for me to read and investigate. Turning my attention to the piece it reported that the hunt for the once dead bird continued.

"Bloody white feathers allegedly from the boa of a battered Mr. Samuel Cortez, age 26, cross-dresser from Brooklyn. In a report released by Harley Tinley, a spokesperson for Wilson Communications, the search for Callie is still on. Reward increases to $60,000."

I thought of Callie, still out and about. I was peculiarly relieved in knowing that she was okay. Adding a bright spot to this obscure morning. Returning back to the *Standard* there was something new to the page—the strip of *Duncan-tics.*

This felt a bit odd. Like forgetting to throw away the copies of

Men's Journal that Henry had some excuse for never buying but deliciously devoured, his natural-haired toothbrush that remained in my rinse cup, stocking up on Smart Start because I knew he liked it even though Cinnamon Life was the far superior cereal. (Not that I actually did any of these things.) Besides, did Henry preserve traces of my existence the way I supposedly didn't? If he happened to be reading *Vogue*—a certain possibility because Daphne said he was probably sexually confused and she took two psych classes in college—would he turn to *Wall Flower?*

So I couldn't help but read *Duncan-tics,* obsess over that hot little number even if he was just made from Magic Marker—the jest being that Duncan was going to give up politics and go after something real.

36

Driving to the store in Dash's Tahoe I almost totaled a VW Cabrio, almost killed two absentminded New Yorkers crossing at the wrong section of the street (but I was deliberately aiming for them), and, sadly, there was now a tailless squirrel ricocheting from tree to tree in the town of Bridgehampton as a result of my driving.

I decided to shop at Schmidt's because the King Kullen, bigger than ten New York City blocks, frightened me. It was the behemoth to all things suburban. The fact that I was in this Suburban Utility Vehicle only added to my fears. Backing into a space, I knocked down a Harley. *Oops,* I said to myself.

Jumping out of the car, I nearly sprained my ankle. My unskilled assessment told me that the Harley was okay; so what if there were a few metally things that looked a bit out of place. And rather than add to this as-far-as-I-could-tell *unobserved* accident by trying to lift the bat bike back to its standing position, I noticed an open parking space conveniently available across from the bike. So I maneuvered into the open space, rationalizing that if the bike was indeed a bit scrambled it was probably to the owner's benefit as the roads on holiday weekends were particularly unsafe, being filled with city drivers like me.

Shopping quickly, I threw every premade hors d'oeuvre available and every nicely packaged condiment into the cart—garlic hummus, artichoke dip, eggplant salsa and a few mustards and jams with gingham clothed tops that would add some flare to a pantry vacant from the winter season.

Trying to market for over thirty people was more difficult to assess than the never-been-used alarm system. So I bought more appetizer kinds of food, freshly squeezed juice and pineapple, strawberries, bananas and all fruit meant to be mixed in a blender.

I waited on a line that took the same amount of time as it would have taken to have a pedicure. Buying food for a group was definitely not fun. I made a mental note that this was not something I would ever want to be in the practice of doing.

On the drive home I left messages on Joanna's, Anne's and Daphne's voice mails to go over the details of tonight's appetizer and drinks party. At the house I found an enormously large FedEx package blocking the kitchen side door.

Kicking the box over, I managed to get into the kitchen and place the grocery bags on the table. I stowed the perishables, even though my thoughts were more transfixed by the FedEx.

Taking a razor from the kitchen junk drawer, I sliced open the package. Giant-size popsicle sticks tumbled like Lincoln Logs, along with a roll of blue-and-white striped canvas. An eight-page instruction manual attached to the side of the paper, which read like a goddamn Chinese puzzle. I tossed the directions along with the brown paper.

The one phone in the house rang, inconveniently across the yard as I made a sprint for it and then remembered that Dad had it set to the last amount of rings.·

"Hello," I gasped.

"Hel. *Krrrrrrr.* It's Da. *Krrrrrrr.*"

Dash was on his cell phone, the reception a reason to consider taking valium.

"Dash, the reception?" I said in vain. "Have you Windexed it recently?"

"What?" he asked, coming in loud and clear.

Not that I would ever Windex my phone, but how else do you get the sand out of the dial?

His phone returned to a muffled reception. "Emily. *Krrrrrrr.* Car. *Krrrrrrr.* Trans. *Krrrrrrr.* Fluid. *Krrrrrrr.* Wipers. *Krrrrrrr.* New brake. *Krrrrrrr.* You can get the car."

"Great!" I hung up, having registered all that I really needed to hear.

Lifting open the oak bench, I took some SPF 50 titanium dioxide sunblock made especially for a twenty-first century nuclear holocaust and a hat with a brim that could shield a small family.

Back to the jumbled mess I'd created. The idea of putting together the cabana was just not fun anymore and I decided to leave it for Dash.

I then did the very domestic goddess thing and prepared for the evening ahead. I mixed pink powdered Crystal Light lemonade with water, pouring the less-than-one-calorie drink into four ice trays. I also chopped the fruit and removed the steel Osterizer from its winter hideaway up onto the island.

Crackling pebbles on the drive announced Dash's return. A quieter crackle. He was driving a more civilized car. The Mustang! The Mustang most certainly complemented the white clapboard house.

"It's here!"

"You did get my message," he said, trying to be all serious but finding it difficult to hold back a smile, since I was a little kid getting going for the giddy.

"The car just needs some transmission fluid and new brake pads. Otherwise she has another two decades in her."

What was he talking about? A granny after triple bypass surgery?

"You did hear what I was saying," he said, waving me from ogling the car.

"Uh. To be honest, all that I really gathered was that I could get the car."

He shook his head in annoyed disapproval.

"And I was able to get Mr. Nickerson to go down five hundred."

Now he was speaking a language I understood.

"Thanks, Dash. What now?"

"You have to get him a cashier's check. I said you'd call him to make the arrangements."

We walk inside to the kitchen, my head turned over my shoulder so as not to lose sight of my car. Inside, Dash inspected my marketing efforts as if I were being graded.

"You were pretty busy, I see," he said, butt sticking out, nose in the fridge.

I smiled, loving the way it felt to ace a test.

"I was actually hoping that you could help me with this cabana outside."

"Sure." He cracked open a Diet Coke, taking a sip while still probing the contents of the fridge.

"Emily?" he asked. "Just one thing. Where's the fish, vegetables—dinner food and such?"

"Oh, that. I decided that it would be too much of an effort. Crackers, chips and nibbly foods go better with heavy drinking anyway. I mean that's all that anyone really wants to eat anyway." He didn't look convinced. "Really," I added feebly. "Nibbly food."

"Emily, we have to feed them more than just bar food," he snapped.

"Fine. You don't have to get all hostile. I'll just call Schmidt's, they have an entire buffet menu for this kind of predicament. Or perhaps I should call the Seafood Shop for a clambake? That's more in sync with the theme of the weekend."

Dash's furrowed brow, which I'd been seeing a lot of lately, was now smoothed back to his Kiehl's treated face.

"I shouldn't have doubted you. Now where's that cabana?"

"To the side of the house." I pointed, while dialing the number for the Seafood Shop.

Dash began arranging the large wooden sticks like an urban castaway trying to figure out how to build a tree house from fallen coconut trees.

"Emily," he called. "Where are the directions for this, this"— he looked around the mess that I'd created earlier—"this extra large LL Bean tote thing, this insult to an MBA?"

"Uh. Directions?"

"Directions," he parroted sarcastically. "Instruction manual to guide you on how to put something together, usually coming in a paper pamphlet among the warranties and such."

"I threw them out. I am more of a learn by doing person, myself."

"You threw out the directions!"

"Don't be so literal," I said, searching through the mound of brown paper. "Here they are!" I presented the crumpled directions to Dash, which he snapped from my hand with that, again, very annoyed expression on his face.

"I notice that you have this selective thing going on," he said while smoothing out the directions. "Selective shopping, selective listening, selective reading."

"Can I help you with that," I said, as unhelpfully as possible.

"Throw me that mushroom-y peg."

There was only one peg but I didn't think it was the shape of a mushroom.

"This?"

"Yeah, throw it over."

"But it really doesn't look like a mushroom."

"Throw over the damn peg, please."

Considering that it looked like something more phallic, and I didn't want to go there with Dash, I just tossed over the peg, which he used to adjoin the poles together.

He then inserted a large stick into a carved out groove of a shorter one and started to begin with another pair.

"Do you require any further assistance?" I asked, again as unhelpfully as possible.

"No, this really isn't too difficult to put together. Once you have the directions, that is."

"Great. Well the Seafood Shop guys will be delivering the clams at around six. I pretty much prepped the drink stuff, and everything else is just a matter of tearing open a bag, opening up a container."

"Yes, you've clearly demonstrated your prowess for buying already assembled meals this weekend. Just wish you'd consider the same approach the next time you're marketing for cabanas."

Dash draped the canvas over the skeletal wooden frame. The cabana completely, absolutely adorable—I was almost as giddy as when I saw my Mustang.

"All right, then. I am just going to go for a quick run."

Dash added some tiebacks to the strips of canvas that roll in the front, which functioned as a door, and waved me off with the brush of his hand.

Changing into my running clothes I exited out the front door intentionally avoiding Dash in case he changed his mind about other projects that I could have assisted him with.

I loved my runs in Bridgehampton. Running through the endless stretches of potato fields—wide, open farmland—the heartland of America not even a hundred miles from Manhattan. Aside from the King Kullen super supermarket-size mansions that littered the landscape the way hotels barraged a Monopoly board, their disruptive dominance to the quiet natural beauty—grazing horses, the scent of flowers combined with ocean air and the occasional tractor to hold up rude convertible driving New Yorkers like me. It was easily my favorite place to run. Knocking off seven miles as if they were just three.

Leaving the section of Sagaponack that my father dubbed "Shantaponack"—think elaborate shanty houses with veils of glass and moonscape miles between them—a few turns and one main avenue led me to my road home. Fully taking in the healthy benefits of a new season though my skin, despite the super titanium dioxide lotion, I was crisped from the sun like dried tears. A mist of bugs followed my winded walk up the long drive toward my house. Swatting the air, Dash looked to me from the kitchen door all concerned. I supposed from his distance he couldn't see the swarm of bugs annoying me. He greeted me with a sneering smile, ice tray in hand.

"Pink ice cubes?" he jeered.

"Of course. So when they melt it won't water down your drink."

"Though I do feel in touch with all things feminine, I cannot have *pink* ice cubes floating around in my gin and tonic."

Of course he couldn't. I just looked at him. This was his issue, not mine.

"I'll make an ice run," he resolved. "I also noticed that we don't have any dessert." Hello! Ben and Jerry's low-fat brownie frozen yogurt.

"And I don't think there's enough Ben and Jerry's for us all," he huffed, banging the screen door behind him. With one final stretch to my quad, I opened the door, which was still shuddering from Dash's slam.

"I'll make the ice run while you make the ice cream run. Me—

ice. You—ice cream. Do you think you could do this?" Dash apparently didn't trust my marketing skills.

I answered with a bratty Emily look. "You ice, me ice cream." He had the icy thing going as if I were four.

"Easy enough?" His eyebrows flexed with concern.

"Right, I've got the ice."

His face erupted in anger.

"Ice cream!"

Dash didn't look amused.

"Hey," I added in a sweeter suck up tone. "Can you please make sure we have enough limes?"

"Between last night and today, you've bought almost two dozen."

"Please," I whimpered. "I have a feeling this will be a long night."

37

We both showered, coordinated the evening's plan, and then drove on our separate errands, though I was certainly the happier of the two considering that (1) I was going to Carvel, the Walt Disney World of dessert places, and (2) I was driving in my new ultra-cool car—top down, perfect night.

I returned home and was a bit annoyed to find Dash with his nose in that damn fridge. I was not in the mood to fail another one of his damn inspections.

My inevitable trial approached. Placing the plastic sand pail of chocolate fat-free soft-serve ice cream on the table, I balanced the Carvel box like a pizza and tried to make a detour around the kitchen island and away from an approaching Dash.

"Can I see what you have there?" I was so busted.

I awkwardly displayed the ice-cream cake—my face a big goofy grin to deflect attention from the box.

"Fudgie the Whale, Emily?" He didn't see the amusement in my dessert choice.

"What? You wanted some elegant little tart?"

"An apple pie would have sufficed."

I set the cake on the table and spun it so the tail was upright. "Come Christmas and you can use this mold to make the Santa ice-cream cake. Now if that's not Martha Stewart crafty?"

He wasn't buying it.

"Fine," I said, picking up the phone.

"Who are you calling?"

"Daphne. I'll just ask her to bring a pie."

"Hang up the phone, Emily." I did what he said.

"Well, I don't know why we're making such a fuss. Is there anything else I need to do?" Again in my unhelpful tone.

"No. I've got a handle on things, just finish getting ready."

Opening my mother's closet door I regressed to a little girl playing dress up. Her wardrobe was filled with Oscar, Chanel, Michael Kors and all things expensive—comparing her summer reserves to mine was like comparing the racks from Gucci to the Gap. As simple our approach was to summer life, this wardrobe showed her slipping to the other side.

So vastly different from the seasons when she wore the same shift every day to the beach, and nights were spent in an Irish knit turtleneck sweater that had a few years over me. With just three staple outfits, and a pair of bug-eyed glasses and a headscarf, she couldn't have been more chic. Though I was loving this Halston pearly white chiffon halter that celebrated the back. With the pencil-thin pants, I would be perfectly dressed to trawl Euro players at polo—*sans* the fake boobs. There was also a fitted one-button blazer, more conservative, more Mom—I left that dangling in the closet.

In a naughty mood, I tried on the Studio 54 ensemble and felt the kind of transformation that only a fat little flying fairy could create with the poof of her wand. I even made an effort with my hair, no bows tonight, just a simple little chignon. Slipping my feet into a pair of Mom's Manolos, this may have been pushing the effect to gold-digger extremes. It would also be a shame to end an evening with a fatality—I intended to drink a lot, and drinking in stilettos was a fatal combination, sort of like mixing margaritas and methadone. Luckily my new pair of slides adorned with seashells that I bought from a funky shop in town went perfectly.

Dash was freshly dressed, in his new favorite stance—behind a bottle of wine waiting to be uncorked. He was in orange gingham tonight, and his hair had a bizarre slicked back effect, parted to the side like he was from a goddamn F. Scott Fitzgerald novel. I couldn't help but stare at his hair, which glistened as brightly as the full moon outside.

Dash became very animated. "Wow! I'd say that all of your shortcomings today could be put aside with that outfit. You look absolutely stunning!"

My shortcomings?

"That may not have come out completely right," he said, going for a save.

Damn right it didn't come out right. But I couldn't help but agree with him, I had been bitchy. And I did look stunning.

"Okay, this should be a good one." He joined my side with a glass of wine, no affected wine twirling this time, just a deep smell like he was sucking up a wad of air before diving underwater.

He intently watched me take a sip. I couldn't really tell the difference from the glass we'd had last night.

"It's a local wine, Bedell, somewhat smoky with a hint of citrus. Don't you think?"

I thought he should have washed all the grease from his hair.

"The best Long Island chardonnays have a variety of fruity flavors with the right balance of acidity."

Blah, blah, blah, blah. He spewed out tasting notes as if it were a goddamn sonata.

Completely cutting him off from his wine rhetoric, I asked, "Where's the vodka?" Then dumped the wine down the bar sink.

Dash was not pleased by my disposing the wine and he sadly watched it drain. The turn of his head showed a more complete profile—I couldn't get over the hair.

"What's in your hair?" I asked, smoothing my hand through the side of his shellacked head, my fingers gelled with enough grease to lubricate an aged surfboard.

The lights of a car outside the big window disrupted us, causing us to both turn to the source. Following the approaching vehicle, considerably smaller in size than the monster trucks that have been courting the view for most of the day, was a zippy BMW convertible. Daphne's car, which I had been mentally summoning all evening.

"Yeah! Daphne's here."

"How can you tell?"

The screen door slammed open. I had to get that door fixed.

"Ah!" squealed Daphne.

"Ah!" I squealed back. Arms like tentacles, we reached around one another, hugging, cheek-grazing, and sharing all the affections that best friends on the verge of lesbianism do.

Andy and Preston broke up our outpouring of love, both of them shrouded by brown paper bags.

"More alcohol?" I asked Daphne. *Preston?* I asked her subliminally while I nodded over to him as he unloaded the bags, the boys doing their testosterone handshake with a slap to the back thing.

She nodded happily. Answering my question telepathically, I presumed.

"A full moon and an overnight nanny will cause tempest-causing commotion."

"So let's get started!" I pulsed the blender that was jammed with fruit and margarita mix and then I double poured a bottle of rum and tequila. I switched the blender's dial till it made a sound of a tape rewinding from a Betamax that was about to blow up, and became sole focus of the room due to the noise poison.

"Sorry. Any takers?" A line of thirsty puppies, paws in the air, tongues out.

Pouring the slurpy strawberry margaritas in Mexican glasses (which I'd given to my father [to me] last Father's Day), I suddenly remembered the key accessory.

"Wait!" I shrieked, practically causing Daphne to drop her glass. I skirted over to the cabinet door beneath the kitchen sink and reached for a few straws.

"Anyone want a Crazy Straw!"

Since there were only three, and Andy and Dash appeared the least interested by their curious stares, I plopped a straw into Daphne's, Preston's, and my glass.

"Music," I said with a snap. "Andy, will you and Preston handle the tunes?"

I directed them to the den where the CD player was. They seemed happy to have a task.

Once they left the room, a swarm of people I didn't know entered the kitchen. Happily occupying Dash.

"So!" I yapped to Daphne, wondering where my real voice escaped to. "Did you see my completely cool car?"

"Very beach babe. But not cheesy beach babe. Retro-chic beach babe."

We then left the room, which had a disturbing resemblance to a Southampton Hospital summer party. A pair of geezer glasses couldn't screen out all of the Pulitzer and pink.

Swiping the blender of margaritas, Daphne and I went out to the cabana and sat on two squashy cushioned Titanic steamers—officially beginning a night that's only certainty was that we wouldn't be sober.

"So? What do you think of my little party gift?"

"It's the cutest thing I've ever been given, but it may be a bit too early for it in the current climate."

"You haven't done it yet?"

"I'm afraid not."

The great thing about Daphne was that we have a special language where we can communicate with as few words as possible, understand one another and cover a lot of territory quickly. Daph and I were, of course, discussing Preston and my impending heave-ho with Dash.

"Emily. What are you waiting for?"

The car deal was pretty much done so I had a ride out of here. He'd set up the cabana. I really didn't know why I was postponing the big talk with Dash. I supposed we had been a bit busy that day.

"You're nervous," asserted Daphne.

"Well, how do you break up with a best friend? Isn't there some kind of manual for this kind of thing?"

Daphne slurped from her Crazy Straw, balls of red twirling about like an old barbershop sign.

"I know!" cried the oracle, my most wise and trusting advisor. "Just keep drinking, once you're completely ripped you'll be able to deal."

We clinked our glasses together, finishing off the last of the blender.

Returning inside we found the house filled with about 1,800 guests—about eight of whom I vaguely recognized.

"Who are all these people and what are they doing in my house?" I asked no one in particular.

Many similar versions of the same person were standing in the kitchen. Since we had left the blender outside, Daphne and I huddled in a vacant area of the kitchen that allowed us to covertly make gimlets with the pink Crystal Light ice cubes.

"Well, there you are," said someone who sounded pretty annoyed. Turning around I saw that it was Anne, with Jason hovering beside her.

"Hey, you two." I faced Jason as I wanted to see a friendly face. "I think Dash is in the den. I heard him mention something about cards and poker chips."

Jason's look of unease morphed into jubilance. "Thanks, Emily." He darted off faster than a cartoon character escaping an anvil.

Says Anne in the voice of a lecturer, "When you asked us to dinner I had no idea that it was an open invitation to all of the Hamptons. What, you announced this on one of those banners flown from a plane over Sagg Main beach?"

I asked *you* to dinner?

"I mean, you can do what you want, this is your home."

Thanks for the reminder.

"But a week from my shower? A little risky don't you think?"

It wasn't like people were hanging from the chandeliers and there was a pyre of furniture on the lawn. Just then we heard a large thunk, the source being a very large, New-York-Knicks-large guy bumping his head against the kitchen overhang.

"Anne," I said, determined not to have her kill my buzz. "Your shower will rival your wedding day, you have not a worry."

She then saw Daphne and her eyes jumped out of her head.

"Well, this most certainly makes up for it."

Daphne searched my eyes for a save.

"Hey, Anne," said Daphne weakly.

"No shower talk!" I demanded. "We know we're doing the fat-free menu, I spent the past day setting up a little cabana for you *and* I booked the Minez sisters."

"The Minez sisters!" Anne cried.

The Minez sisters are two cokeheads, probably the reason why they give the best damn massages, who run a trendy salon in TriBeCa. Their cheesy, albeit sexy, Victoria's Secret looks and gazillion write-ups have made them the allure to people like Anne. After I illustrated them for a piece in last month's *Bazaar,* they'd become my new best friends and, through voice mail conversation, they'd agreed to give massages at the shower. I thought it a perfectly redeemable replacement for some damn fortune-teller.

With half a pitcher of gimlets finished, Daphne and I agreed that we needed to pace ourselves with a water break, perfectly timed to Anne's drinking since she was abstaining from alcohol till the wedding, treating her big day as if she were preparing for the goddamn marathon.

Jason returned to Anne's side and I noticed that she had a few inches on him. Though Anne did have the unfair advantage in spiky heels. She even wore those clunky-heeled sandals to the beach. I suspected that she had horrible foot problems.

"What? No poker?" I said to Jason.

"No. I'm in the next game taking Preston's slot. By the way, he asked for you."

Daphne and I shared a secret look. Anne, never to miss sly innuendo, said, "What's going on, going from tabloid journalism to plastics?"

And this was coming from a girl who courted columnists and pricked liquid Tupperware in her lip?

Jason, following the banter, tugged on Anne's silk button-down, which she then made a point to smooth over. "Honey, can I have an Altoid?" he asked weakly.

She opened up a wicker bag sturdy enough to attach to the front of a bicycle and reached for the sardine can of mints. "There are only two left," she warned, as if instructing a child on how many chewable vitamins he could have.

"Don't worry," I said to Jason. "Dash can always reinforce you."

What was it with boys and their goddamn mints?

Daphne, looking a bit glossy eyed but still remaining composed, nodded to the side entrance when Anne was fixing Jason's collar. Preston was walking into the room. A room full of people couldn't interfere with a gaze so penetrating that I began to shudder.

"Anne," said Daphne. "I'd really love to discuss your shower menu with you. Do you have a moment?"

Did she *have* a moment? There were no gifts or gestures that I would ever be able to repay Daphne with—indebted to her for life like a knight to his king.

"Shall we go to the side porch, where the event will take place?" she said, taking Anne's hand.

"Well, the night may not be a thwarted waste after all," huffed Anne.

Anne followed Daphne out the sliding door, perfectly timed before Preston made his way to greet us.

"They're waiting for you, Jason," said Preston.

"Thanks." And a minted-breath collar-fixed Jason went to join the other men to discuss subjects of war, politics and SUVs.

The glass of water in my hand felt like a grenade that needed to be tossed. I eyed Preston's empty drink glass; its syrupy bottom was the color of liquid cinnamon like the remnants of an espresso cup.

"Rum and coke?" I asked.

"Jack and ginger."

Taking his glass, I nudged my way to the alcohol we stashed in the Crazy Straw cabinet, mixing his drink to random specifications similar to the days back in chem lab, when I had no idea what I was doing but managed to ace the class.

Returning to Preston, I delivered his fresh Jack and ginger, then filled my glass to a seasonal key lime color.

"Shall we go outside?" Preston said in a flash, leading me out the sliding door with no consideration whether I actually wanted to go outside, which I did.

We stood at the edge of two steamer chairs like we were at an overcrowded pool with no place to sit. Aside from a canoodling couple taking advantage of the effects from the full moon, we were alone. Most of the guests, not yet at hook-up point, still were inside encircling the drink sources.

Taking a sip and then returning my glass to holding position, Preston leaned in. I leaned back.

"Wait a minute there, fella," I rebuked.

"But I was under the impression that you liked me?" The sound of his pinky ring tapping his glass ticked like a bomb.

"Like you or not, I am kind of with someone right now."

"What do you mean 'kind of with someone'? How can you be 'kind of with someone'?"

Okay, I get it, he doesn't get the "kind of" part.

"I mean," I pleaded, trying to figure out what I did in fact mean. Then I realized that I was not the one who needed to explain myself. "I mean that I am with someone but on the verge of breaking it off."

"Who? That Ed Burns wannabe—what kind of name is Hyphen, anyway?"

"Hey!" I barked, suppressing a laugh. "It's Dash."

I stared inside my glass to distract myself from incoming hysterics.

"And he so does not look like Ed Burns," I mumbled. "Well, maybe the slitted-eye thing. But he happens to be a really great guy. And it's a bit more complicated than you could even realize."

"Complicated? Complicated how?"

"We happen to be the closest of friends for one. Then there's the issue of him helping me out with a few things." My trip to LA for starters—I then realized that I needed to string Dash along for another few weeks. Preston, seemingly unconvinced, leaned in again.

"Excuse me! I don't believe I've finished." I settled my hair back and tried to regain some composure.

"And how do you know that I'm even interested in you!" I said, composed.

"Because Daphne said something."

Daphne was so toast. But I never really said anything to Daphne. It was really more her pushing the issue of Preston onto me.

"Excuse me?"

"All right. I just get the idea you're interested."

"Well, even if I were interested, and I am not saying that I am, your timing couldn't be more inopportune. Whatever the selection of reasons, there is the very real issue that I have not settled matters with Dash. And I've never cheated on someone, not even a kiss."

I put my hands on the edge of the teak lounge chair, feeling the smoothness of the wood, so soft to the touch it couldn't possibly splinter. The chairs were new. Mom replaced the old white Savannah-styled wicker chairs last season finding them tired and uncomfortable.

"You've never cheated on anyone?" Preston asked in amazement.

"Of course I haven't cheated on anyone. And don't act like this is some sort of deviation. I am actually quite proud of this." It was that perfect record that I held right up there with paying my bills on time and never getting a DWI. I was so virtuous.

"No, of course not," I snapped. "It's not like this is some great feat to be proud of." My face muddled with angry lines. "Why. Have you been known to get some on the side?"

A look of melancholy scanned his face. "Been cheated on, not cheated to." He added brightly, "Who has the time!"

"Exactly," I purred happily. "Well, then you're a notch less sleazy than I originally thought."

"Sorry if I seem to be coming on a little strong."

"A little?"

"Okay, pretty strong. It's just," he paused. "It's just that dating in New York sucks." Apparently his hesitation wasn't to search for the right words.

Taking a final swig from his drink he perched the glass of melted ice on the porch banister. The removal of the drink from his hand seemed to have spurred some inner sincerity. He continued in a sexy whisper. "I don't know what is about you. I'm completely taken aback by you. I've met a lot of people and at my age you just know."

"You're not laying some thick one on me?"

"No, really. I really, *really* like you."

"Okay. In that case, don't move," I said, balancing my empty drink beside his and then darting back inside. Hearing stifled background sounds from Preston, something to the effect of where was I going.

I'm sure appearing as a blur of white, I scanned the blurry people in my house until Daphne came into focus.

"Whatever are you doing?" she asked worriedly.

"I have to break up with Dash so I can fool around with Preston. Have you seen him?"

"Last time I saw him he was by the bar in the living room," she said, completely naturally.

"Thanks," I said, clasping both my hands around her arms and planting a big kiss on her cheek.

I found Dash at the bar, speaking with a head of blonde, the theme of the week.

"Hey, Katrina." I waved. "Hey, Dash." I started to wonder if I should add the "can I talk to you" bit but felt that may have come off a bit too television drama.

"Can I talk to you?" said Dash.

"Sure!" I exclaimed.

Katrina looked at me as if I'd just been taken off Chanel's Sample Sale list.

Dash led me up the stairs and away from the social clatter. With each step the voices and occasional roar of laughter became less audible, the vacant hallway tranquil in comparison to the chaos just below.

He chose my parents' room and seated me on their bed.

"Emily," he began gravely. It sounded serious. The start of the breakup talk I was reciting in my head just moments ago. "How do you feel the past few weeks have been going?"

Interesting approach, very pragmatic—almost professional—I can see why Dash was good at managing people.

"Well, quite frankly," I said, as if I've been asked what my weaknesses were during a job interview. "It's been a bit . . . different."

The grave lines of worry smoothed to a softness.

"Precisely!" he said. Apparently I've aced this part of the interview. "You and I best friends, that works. But as a couple I just don't think we have what it takes."

And he was absolutely right. I thought back to all the advice I was given, to search for this partner in life, a safe harbor to dock your ship. Our friendship was safe and was so much based on this playful teasing. But once Dash assumed that other role, all playfulness aside, he was a major drone.

Dash's eyes searched mine, and I suddenly felt tremendously guilty because I think I was gloating.

"Will you excuse me for a second?"

Leaving Dash on the bed, both his hands firmly planted on his lap, I whizzed into my parents' bathroom and opened the medicine cabinet in search of some Visine. Surely there must have been some Visine left over from all the smoking pot days when I bought the drops in bulk. Goddamn it, I scolded myself as

I removed every Estee Lauder product imaginable. I really needed the drops so Dash could think I was crying. Now what?

So I took some of my mom's vitamin C liquid drops and squirted it into my eye, causing a painful sting.

"Ow!" I squealed.

A worried knock to the door.

"Are you okay in there, Emily?"

One eye shut as if it were sealed with Crazy Glue, the other could barely open from being intrinsically connected to the other. Not the look I was going for but it would have to do.

"Yeah, come on in," I moaned, turning on the cold water and cupping my hands, flushing my face by the bucketful.

The pain still stung but my unharmed eye felt ready to be opened.

"What's going on in here," he said, surveying the mess I'd created. "My God, what's happened to your eye? It looks like a cigar's been stubbed on it."

So much for the crying effect.

"People are going to think I'm a wife beater!"

I believed he was half serious.

Dash stood above me and pulled my head back gently as if he were an ophthalmologist actually knowing what to do. He reached for a washcloth, ran it under cold water, and then compressed it to my eye.

"Do you have any eyewash?"

Eyewash?

He read my look, realizing that there was probably no eyewash.

"Here," he said, placing my hand to the cloth, instructing me to hold the position. "We better go downstairs and get you an ice pack."

Remarkably, the party cleared out. I looked at my watch, it was just past two. It had been a long day.

The poker table was decorated with tattered cards, clay chips, butt out cigarettes, and a few nearly finished glasses of port—the remnants from the evening's games having the effect of an Irving Penn photograph. Label-torn beer bottles, emptied drinks, scuff marks on the floor, and air potent with smoke and alcohol were the main damages. The kitchen was in a bit more of a state. More empty glasses and ravaged bags of nibbly food. The kitchen table set with the clambake, however, virtually untouched.

Dash rummaged through the freezer for an ice pack while I viewed the kitchen mess with my good eye. Walking to the closet, I pulled out a trash bag intended for collecting leaves and started filling it with the bulkier garbage items.

"Emily, have the cleaners do this," soothed Dash, the large bucket of fat-free Carvel in hand. Yum, I wanted some but thought better of my craving considering the moment.

"Sorry, just attending to the main ant attractions. I'll sleep better knowing there's less of a mess down here."

"You and your quirks," he marveled, then returned to his systematic removal of frozen drink packets, bottles of vodka, and all the other goods that weren't used for the party.

Clearing the island we found the leftover Fudgie the Whale, the prized artifact from an Egyptian excavation. The victim of relentless binge eaters, all that was left was a bite of shimmery sapphire that glistened like blue glass in sunlight. It was nice to see that someone still had a good eye left after this sordid evening.

Daphne and Andy entered in from the back sliding door.

"There you two are!" exploded Daphne. "We just couldn't leave without knowing everything was settled."

Her ebullience so welcoming, she was the emblem of composure amidst the chaos that surrounded us. The woman was as solid as this house.

"My God, Emily! What happened to your eye?" I truly must have been a sight of a sore eye.

"Just a minor accident with the wrong eye cream," I mumbled. "Hey," I squeaked. "Where is everyone?"

"We told most of the people that the neighbors had complained about the noise level and that the police were on their way."

"But that didn't seem to work," reminded Andy.

"So we stashed all the alcohol."

"Thanks, you two. Really."

They started to exit the door, Andy not able to leave fast enough. I called to a nearly departed Daphne, "And sorry about Anne!"

"Think nothing of it." Her face popped through the screen door. "She's really not that bad. Couldn't be happier about the Minez sisters, nice touch." Her voice trailed, "She really has a lot of admiration for you."

"Really?"

"Really."

The sound of the car's engine outside the door, headlights illuminated the dark kitchen exit.

"And whatever happened to Preston?"

"He passed out in the backseat of the car."

"Uh-oh. Do you need a bucket?"

"No. We're okay." She now looked to both Dash and me. "Thanks, guys. Great party."

Now back to me. "I'll catch *you* tomorrow." But both Dash and I knew she just wanted the lowdown on what happened between us.

I seated myself, now in perfect view of the whale so brutally victimized, and Dash approached with ice pack in hand. He removed the wet cloth, tossed it into the sink, and applied the pack.

"Do you want anything? Are you hungry?"

"Well, I could have gone for some whale but that doesn't appear to be an option." I nodded at the ravaged creature. Dash smiled, then looked over to the untouched clambake.

"I guess you're right."

"Excuse me?"

"On what people really want to eat."

38

Mornings like this I remembered why the allure of drinking was not so alluring. Either you have to be perpetually drunk, becoming a professional alcoholic never to feel the pain, or you have to abstain. The sun's glare flooded the room, indicating that it was a beautiful day. I wished it were raining.

Dash walked over to me, which I detected from creaking footsteps. My head peeked from under the covers and slowly acclimated to the sunlight. My eyes squinted to make out an angel ascending to heaven, Patrick Swayze in his final scene from *Ghost*. Seating himself at the edge of the bed next to me, he smoothed my hair in that comforting mommying way. We slept in the same bed together, but did not sleep together, I was assured. This was not bad because (1) This is what we did as friends, and (2) I honestly had little recollection.

"Your eye," he said delicately. "It looks much better."

The night now came back to me, the memento that pulled me from my amnesia. My eye did feel better; it was just my entire head that now hurt.

"What time are the cleaners coming?" he asked.

"Nine."

He looked at his watch. "It's almost nine now. Should I go into town and get some breakfast?"

I then twirled around to sit up. Apparently I'd been okay enough last night to change into my pajamas.

"That's all right. Movement would be good for me. A breakfast at the Candy Kitchen even better."

"All right, then, I like this idea. You get ready and I'll handle the cleaners."

Getting ready was just a matter of changing T-shirts. I left on my orange herringbone pajama bottoms, which also served the function of sleepwear, beach bottoms, and hangover outfit. And then put on some orange espadrilles, which served the function of slippers, beach shoes, and hangover shoes. Wrapped a headscarf around my head that, aside from sleeping purposes which was debatable as it could hold in the benefits of a penetrating hair mask, it also served the function of the aforementioned activities.

Dash made the final arrangements in directing the cleaning service while I pulled out a pair of orange tinted aviators and keys to the Mustang from the drawer beneath the phone.

"Why don't you drive," I said, throwing the keys to the Mustang to Dash, which he caught in one hand by clawing the air.

"I'm honored," he said, bouncing them up like a golf ball. "You sure you want to take your car?"

"Oh, yeah," I said as if this were the obvious. "Convertible." Essential hangover transportation.

Driving gunshot next to Dash in the role of *girlfriend* (the entire concept still a bit strange to figure) didn't work the way a pelican shouldn't be flying too close to any jets. Sure the concept may appear innocent, quite amusing and natural even, but once that pelican hits that jet and the situation explodes, lives are at stake.

Dash and I whetted our curiosity. A cat playing its odds by brushing its paw against the gleam of toilet water and, any cat that falls into that pool of clean yet-something-frighteningly-gross about this particular well of water, realizes it just isn't for them. We can now put this behind us as one of those freakish mistakes that shouldn't have happened—like Lisa Marie Presley and Michael Jackson. (It should be emphasized that I am the Lisa Marie and not the Michael Jackson in this scenario.)

Sitting back in the driver's seat of my white Mustang, I was a bit too cold for the top down but along with all the other drivers who made the sensible decision to go topless, after a long winter any nice day is worth showing it off.

It was much better like this, with Dash and me, I even get my way more—listening to my radio stations, spitting on my orange canvassed toe to rub out a piece of brown grassy something. What could this horrible piece of icky crud mucking up my new espadrilles be? I pulled my foot into my chest looking like quite the professional yoga person (I could twist and stretch when the appropriate opportunity arose) and then realized that it would have been simpler if I just took off my shoe to have a proper inspection.

Little did I notice that we were parked, possibly for minutes, and Dash had that look, which said thank-you-God-for-not-giving-me-any-legal-spousal-responsibility to this questionable being.

It was much better like this.

I loved the Candy Kitchen the way I loved our old house. This was a soda shop, the real deal, not some hyped restaurant jammed with overpriced memorabilia that club owners attempted to recreate in the coolest Manhattan neighborhood of the week.

There were swivel chair that actually swiveled, a soda fountain that only a skilled tradesman could repair, and banquettes with Formica tables embellished with flecks of gold glitter. If Schraft's were still around, the Candy Kitchen would serve it. But their homemade ice cream was a calling to all things Americana—flavors of blueberry, bubble gum, and garbage can (a little bit of everything) and I could rationalize a holiday from my artificially inseminated yogurt despite the alarming number of calories.

The only person who might love the Candy Kitchen more than me was my father. Who came here as a boy and rekindles his childhood memories when soda fountains inhabited every city corner the way Starbucks does now. I wondered if in twenty years I would be longing for a Starbucks?

After waiting behind a line of cell phone chatterers in trendy outfits that will probably go out of fashion once we finished breakfast, Dash and I were seated at the center booth.

The waitress had an uncanny resemblance to my junior varsity field hockey coach, but I knew her more intimately as she's been taking my orders for years. She removed the club chit pencil from behind her ear and was ready to roll.

Dash ordered the bagel platter while I asked for a bacon, egg, and cheese biscuit on lightly toasted wheat, a decaf—extra Equals—and a black-and-white milkshake.

"And a fruit salad," added Dash. Oh, right, might as well. I nodded in affirmation.

She delivered our water glasses before we even had time to register that we wanted them and then, once the bustle of her pocketed polyester half apron faded from the table, we both evaluated the crowd. I was definitely the one who had the most adventurous evening, considering that I was wearing pajamas at a Bridgehampton restaurant.

The egg sandwich was spatulaed onto its bed of toast, delivered to my papered place mat and, right as it was about to hit my lips, Dash broke me from my trance.

"What? No smell then toss today?"

"Are you kidding me?" My mouth disruptively suspended from what it needed to be doing. "I don't think you realize how hurting I am."

He looked impressed and then allowed me to comfort my body.

We finished our breakfast. The waitress had the good timing, and experience, to serve me my black-and-white milkshake as dessert.

"Do you want the fruit salad?" she asked, noting the untouched mixture of melons and berries.

Do you want to see me throw up my breakfast right here on the table? I said to her without speaking. The thought of consuming healthy food would have had the same effect as a vegan being told her hummus spread was goose liver.

"Just leave it, thank you," said Dash politely, to excuse my abhorred face.

I then happily poured my black and white from its stainless steel container and into the fountain glass—Dash's face on the verge of squealing into something from that very disturbing *Deliverance* scene.

"No!" I exploded. "Get your own." Happily taking another sip from my glass without a trace of guilt.

Our waitress, suspiciously close to our table, said to Dash, "Can I get you anything else?"

"Another one of those," he mumbled, pointing to my shake in embarrassment.

Joanna burst onto our little scene like a diva coming onstage. Donned in equestrian gear, a vision of Hermes. I hadn't realized she rode.

"I never realized you rode."

"Just started. I mean, I did take lessons as a little girl but that was all so walking and trotting—being pulled on a pony country fair kind of thing."

Mm-hmm. I nodded, not quite certain what she was trying to go for here.

"So," she continued, looking at both Dash and me curiously. "Did you get my message last night?"

"What message?"

"I figured as much. I was a tad dubious when the gentleman who answered the phone couldn't read back my number when I asked him to. Edward and I had to go to some tiresome barbecue of a cousin of his. It was all the way in Quogue, for God's sake. I told Edward that we might as well just head back to the city we were so far west."

I looked at her, unfazed.

"It was a good time," saved Dash. "But I'm not so certain that Emily over here would have had any recollection of seeing you."

I shot him a smirk, and he returned with a smirk. We were being smirky.

"Well, great. I felt simply horrible and now I'm okay with this." I supposed I should be happy that I was not causing her any grief. She then started to make her exit.

"Hey, Joanna, what about LA?"

"There really is nothing to it. You have a meeting scheduled at FOX. You show up."

"Thanks," I said, not meaning it.

"Don't worry," said Dash when Joanna moved out of earshot, not that I really cared if she heard me spew mean things about her.

"You'll be fine. I will be there with you but it's not as if you have anything to be concerned about. They already love your work. How can they not love you?"

I was so relieved that Dash still intended to chaperone me to LA despite our new, old, relation.

"You don't love me."

My infantile pout seemed to have been taken the wrong way.

"I hope you're not serious?"

I wasn't serious. But I didn't mind his continuing this.

"You know I love you. Always will. But as I said last night it's simply that we don't have the same wants and needs to sustain a relationship." His face so saddened with hurt that I began to feel heartless.

"Dash!" I said. "I know. I was just fooling with you."

He looked relieved, no more furrowed line indented between his brows. "So we'll be okay?"

"I think so. But I'm a bit worried about you. They do say that sex changes everything." Not that I considered what we had as sex. "Are *you* fine with this?"

"Actually, Emily, our having sex could be the best thing that happened to us. It extinguished the curiosity of what we would be like together. I actually think that all best friends should sleep together, put the curiosity past them and move on."

I shifted to a more serious tone. "You realize, Dash, that you are my first true friend in adult life. What we have can never be lost."

"I am with you exactly on this one." He then slurped the last sip and made an obnoxious vacuuming sound—*Dash!* I screamed with a look. He managed another unctuous slurp.

"Would you quit it? That's as grating as a car alarm."

He stopped and then poured more of his shake into a glass.

"So what about *ER* guy? He seems pretty cool."

"I don't know about that one. It seems that I'm only attracted to him after I've had many drinks and, after last night, I don't think I make for a good regular drinker."

Dash gave me a sly smile.

"So what's the lowdown with you and Katrina?"

"I was wondering if you'd bring that up."

I was bringing it up, get to it.

"She's just really sweet."

"And so is your black and white, but you don't indulge that regularly. What does this mean? Are you going to start things up again?"

"We'll see. Possibly."

That, I gathered, was a big yes. And I couldn't be happier for them, unless Katrina would interfere with our friendship.

"Does Katrina know about us?"

"Funny you mention that. I hope you don't take this the wrong way but I've just been telling her that we've been spending a lot of time together. That you're in a funny place right now—just so there is no weirdness between us all."

Phew! I sighed.

Not letting him in on my relief, I said, "Unless you told her that I've been institutionalized or gone stalker crazy."

"Well, I did . . ." He trailed off.

"Dash!"

"Only fooling. No, it's perfectly cool."

"And, us going to LA together, are you sure that's not a problem?"

"Hardly."

I smiled, tilting over the steel container of my black and white—not even a sip left, the fountain glass just a dollop of tawny brown.

"Want some of mine?" he asked, holding up his newly filled shake in the air.

Nah-ah, he was just trying to be uncharacteristically accommodating. Besides, I didn't really want it—still shocked with the month's worth of calories that I inhaled all from just one breakfast. I shook my head saying that I was fine, happy with what I had.

39

The weathered shed behind the pool became a substitute for the French Shack after it had been so insensitively demolished. Getting naked with boys, sneaking bong hits before family functions so they'd be interesting—doing all the things that separated me from my parents' world.

I opened up the shed. It was a life-size version of my hatbox, a maelstrom of the past invading my present. There was a rickety pogo stick, clamming nets with strands of seaweed dried at the end, boogie boards decaled with Hawaiian hibiscuses—from a tricycle to mountain bike—a virtual timeline represented through cycles akin to a height chart. Along with all the potting accessories my mother never used, since she gardened under the guise of her landscape designer. Last summer a skylight had been added to encourage my turning this into a studio, inspiring me to paint. A very sweet gesture by Mom even if it was more to make her feel better considering the grief I'd put her through ever since she'd so insensitively torn down the tree house. Have I mentioned that she insensitively tore down my tree house? I wondered if I should remind Mom that?

I put a pair of flower print gardening gloves on, feeling very Greenwich, and began to clear out the debris. Suitably exposing the walls, their cheerful clapboard and antique window frames in dramatic contrast to the floor's concrete surface, like daisies in an austere stainless vase. Almost industrial, the hardened surface paired with natural light—it was the ideal place to paint.

The door was similar to a stable's, the top and bottom detached. Daphne, connecting them, puttered in, a welcome diversion from laborious work.

"Hello," she said softly, so as not to startle me. "I have someone with me."

Emily peered from behind her mother's legs. She was dressed in riding clothes but hers were vastly different from Joanna's, soiled and rumpled—the child was actually on the horse, not just wearing the clothes as an accessory to be paraded, boasting the whole SUV packaged life.

"Hey, you! How was Jupiter today?" Jupiter is the horse she rides at Toppings.

She gurgled with excitement, her face stretched into a million happy places. "She went really, really fast. And when Laura told me to go slower, I went faster. But she didn't get mad. And then I gave Jupiter an apple and she burped."

I love that kids can speak in as many different directions as I have expressions yet I could still understand this special language.

"And next week I can jump!" Emily's eyes locked to her mother's the entire time.

"We'll see about that, Miss Emily. After we watch the scene in *Gone with the Wind* with little Bonnie Blue jumping for about a dozen times."

"Daphne! You should encourage this."

"I can't help but worry about this one," she said, tugging on a lock of Emily's hair that was parted to the side and pulled with a clip. How my mom used to style my hair.

"She's a bit wild."

Emily giggled. The sound of the Good Humor bell, "you can stay up late," and popping bubble wrap, all mixed into one.

Daphne continued, "We came from the Candy Kitchen and saw Joanna. She said we just missed you."

"Missed me eating about five thousand calories worth of junk."

"Don't fret. They don't count on hangover days." Daphne always said the right thing.

"Sooo, everything resolved with you and Dash?"

"Back to the way things were."

"Well, that's a relief."

Daphne then slid back against a cleared wall, knees bent allowing Emily to collapse in between her legs. I just loved how the two of them fit into one another.

"I had fun last night. There was a time when we acted out like that every other summer night."

"It's all different now," I said. "Speaking of which—remember this?" I held up a tennis ball attached to a long rubber band on an oval plank, one of the sporting good trends of yore.

Daphne laughed, then looked about the cluttered shed.

"It's a summer/sporting goods memorial in here."

"Speaking of which." I wheeled my old banana-seat purple bicycle with streamers sprouting from its handlebars. Probably had it the same year that Donny Osmond wore purple socks and I thought he was kind of cute. "How would a Miss Emily Trefry like this?"

Her eyes gleamed like spun sugar. Mouth gaped open like an O.

"That about answers it."

"Emily," said Daphne to me in motherly concern. "But it's so retro, special. Surely you don't want to give that up."

"Actually, you will be doing me a tremendous favor. Saving me from another addition to the inevitable dump run."

I looked at my first three-speed, a Raleigh Super Record. I remembered going to the bike shop like it was just last summer—the line of English-styled bicycles, inspired from a time when they were the mode of transportation, not just an afternoon ride to the beach. This one I would save for my daughter.

"Aside from a few attachments and some things I need to check in with my mother about, I am clearing this place out for a studio and you're welcome to rummage along with me."

"How splendid. What a great idea."

Daphne craned her body upward, pulling Emily along with her. She had her dad's hair, so dark you could get lost in it, but her features were more all-American, taking after her mother.

Emily took a fishing rod and looked ready to do a pole vault.

"Emily, you can poke an eye out!" wailed Daphne.

"Has anyone ever poked an eye out?" I asked Daphne.

She glossed over my question to attend to her daughter, placing the rod back in its place.

"Mommy," whimpered Emily, head propped back, looking at Daphne who towered over her like a monument. "Can I go look at the cabana?"

"Yes, sweetheart." A last stroke to her hair. I loved watching Daphne be a mom. She was so natural, beautiful—mature. Wearing tapered Bermuda khakis, a navy Lacoste T-shirt, so tiny and flattering to her figure it was probably one of Emily's. Her hair restrained in Chanel sunglasses—she really had the glasses-as-headband look down. Even the way she held her car keys had style, so delicate in her perfectly manicured hand, not one chip or blemish to a nail.

Daphne scanned the garden shed as if it were an ancient cathedral. "How exciting. I just love the idea of you getting into your inner glory—to paint again the way you'd get lost in your pictures when you were little—it's such a thrill to see you like this."

"I actually have a series of works in my head, the next part is putting them to canvas."

"Really, do you mind?"

"Not at all, just taking our beloved storybook characters and setting them in dark, more macabre scenarios. Little Red Riding Hood in fishnets, prostituting herself to the big bad wolf; Jack chopping the beanstalk, selling the beans to make a Wall Street killing. There really is a darker meaning to our little fables, we were just too young to get past the magic and happy endings."

Daphne looked a bit stunned.

"Not the lovely seascapes and Hampton cottages of the likes of Childe Hassam and William Merritt Chase, I gather."

"Sorry to disappoint. They covered that terrain magnificently. There are only so many ways to paint a windmill—from Chase to Lichtenstein. Windmills and beach dunes—that's not what inspires me."

"Well, I will most certainly be in the market for one of your wittier works. Something that represents us."

As girls we did share a fondness for *Alice in Wonderland*, not

Alice but the tea party that was virtually psychedelic. I'd have to buy a bag of weed for when I painted that one.

"Alice in Wonderland's tea party," I said with complete assurance.

She nodded knowingly.

"Speaking of which, Anne's shower—I have a favor to ask."

"Sure, anything."

"Promise to spike the muffins with sugar and butter but still pawn them off as fat free. Make them as fattening as your chocolate cherry cheesecake." I was silent for a moment. "Just be sure to save me a low-fat one."

"Emily!"

"It's just that this simple act will be the one pleasurable moment in this jail sentence of an afternoon."

"I'll see what I can do. But"—raising a finely plucked brow—"that Anne, I do think she has a nose as powerful as a dog sniffing out drugs in a bomb-proof case. I'll do my best to get past her fatdar."

Daphne and I then walked to the points of a triangle. Gathering Emily, taking the purple banana bicycle to their car. The purple streamers from the bike gleamed in the air as it was propped from the back of the convertible.

Dash was blanketed in *The Times* on the side porch, suitably knocked out. I removed a few sections to gently awaken him, and he twitched in shock and then regained his composure when he saw that it was me. I joined him in the lounge neighboring his, the air's breezes blowing through me.

"So you want the 'Styles'?" he asked, thoughtfully handing me the paper. I'm sure he finished it after the weekly scan to catch up on past acquaintances and who they settled on in the "Weddings" section.

"No, thanks. I'm actually a bit annoyed with the weekend *Times* today."

He gives me an oh-really-this-should-be-interesting look.

"A day as perfect as today for example, like I am really going to dawdle my afternoon over the paper. And then, come weekend's end, the pile will be sitting there reminding me of my current ignorance on what's going on."

Dash looked at me politely, not interested in contributing to this conversation. He probably didn't share my opinions on the weekend paper and was not up for a vacuous conversation.

An entire day later I awoke in the same spot. The smell from Dash heating up the grill induced me out of a sleep so powerful I could have drank half a bottle of Nyquil, which wasn't far off with the leftovers still contaminating my body.

40

I intended to spend the week at the beach, the idea being to get lost in my art, but the plan was as momentary as Joey Buttafuoco's stardom. Joanna put an end to it, insisting that I cooperated with *Elle* for a profile they wanted to do on me or, really, the damn bows in my hair. Officially putting an end to all ribbon wearing.

I dialed the number of an editor with a last name that sounded like an Austrian village. She answered the phone aggressively but, once I said who I was, she percolated obsequiously.

"Thank you for returning my request. Joanna mentioned that you're a bit shy."

Right, get to the point.

"Well," she continued in a more professional tone. "We just received these pictures from our party photographer and there's one of you wearing a ribbon. So we're going to slide in a story on this for our next issue."

If we weren't on the phone this editor would have seen an Emily smirk in record time. I said, not warmly, "Your readers want to know about my wearing ribbons?"

"Of course," she squealed. "It's really quite clever. I mean we've brought back ribbon belts, ribbon watchbands, ribbon trimmed accessories but, it's almost so chic by how easy it is, using ribbons for exactly what they're intended for. Hair accessories!"

She appeared to be quite pleased with herself, probably

wanted to earn extra points with her editor before she'd choose
the wrong bracelet for an editor's pick page—a decision that
would cost her another week of returning clothes from the fashion closet before she redeemed herself. To work at a glossy!

"And where did you get these ribbons? The picture I am looking at is a black grosgrain."

"That one is wrapping from a box of bath oil."

"Oh," she huffed haughtily. "Well, where do you get your ribbons?"

"From a hatbox of memorabilia, all bought from a former notions store that went out of business decades ago."

"I see." She sounded troubled. I was being terribly uncooperative.

Feeling more cooperative. "Why don't you just write whatever
you'd like?"

"Splendid idea!"

"One question, however, is this for your beauty or fashion section?"

"Uh—fashion?" she answered, back in her state of confusion.
"Why, should it be in beauty?"

"No, fashion makes sense. It seems to be more of a hair accessory story than hair-trend story."

"But that would be beauty!" she cried. I thought I was hearing
a girl on the brink of a tantrum.

"Shhh," I soothed. "It's really of no concern to me, just do
whatever you have to and I'll go along with it."

"Really!" she instantly cheered up, a sobbing baby handed a
new toy. "We were also considering you for the 'What I'm
Wearing Now' column. You know, the clothes that best represent
your style—and what are you wearing now may I ask?"

"A pair of aqua plaid pajama bottoms and a mud flap girl tee
that I designed. And this is pretty much what I'm always wearing."

"Uh, maybe we'll wait on this one, then."

"Sounds like a sensible decision."

"Well, then, I have arranged for a shoot at Milk Pail studios for
tomorrow—first thing."

Photo shoot? They have to shoot me after I just had finished
polishing off a few Ben and Jerry's for rewarding myself on
being so skinny? Feeling puffy with fat all over, I thought if only

there were some ointment I could have slabbed all over to de-crease the swelling.

"Set for tomorrow at nine A.M," she added.

Why was I being sentenced?

"Nine A.M.?" I questioned, shuddering at the complete absur-dity of this unhealthy waking time

"You are so cute—so cute! I bet you're one of those fabulous types, out from nine P.M. to five A.M."

"No, in bed at nine P.M. and getting up at ten A.M. is more like it."

"Not to worry!" I couldn't get past the squeaky voice. "I'll have a car sent for you. There will be a stylist, a makeup artist and I'll be there as well, to do the interview."

Interview? It was a bow in a hair, for God's sake. Yes, this was the kind of hard news reporting that I was sure worth her daddy's dollars in attending the finest schools.

Waking up late and making the car wait, I dressed in my pa-jama uniform and rolled out my door. I liked this driver. He didn't find the need to chitchat, taking me right to my destination.

Not seeming to notice that I was late, the stylist handed me a pair of orange leather pants that looked like they'd be too small for me when I was in the sixth grade.

"Didn't Liesl give you my sizes?" I asked, annoyed. She shrugged like this was my problem and I'd have to melt off ten pounds in five minutes.

Trying to fit a condom on an eggplant. After this I might have to have children in a Petri dish.

I was on the floor in a bicycle position, convulsing my legs madly, when Liesl walked in.

Squealing. "Emily!"

"Hi," I puffed in more of a gasp than greeting. She had on dark denim pants with a fitted suede coat in a soft lavender color. Her haircut said, *Hello. I'm Julie McCoy, your cruise director.* What is it with these girls in looking to campy Aaron Spelling shows for hair inspiration?

We both looked uncertainly to the pants.

"I may have better luck by just slabbing pieces of Fruit Roll-Up around my legs."

"Don't be silly. You're should-be-hospitalized skinny." Was this meant as a compliment?

"Rodolfo!" she snapped. A dark, lanky assistant appeared magically. He was more interesting than handsome. It was his olive skin tone with unforgettable sapphire eyes. Wearing a basic black tee and slim khakis—so simple, but on him he was ready to strut the catwalk. His eyes revealed a soft gentleness that I feared would be lost to a jaded gruffness after a few months working with Liesl.

"Don't we have something else?" she scolded. He left us, moments later appearing with a rack of blinding clothes seemingly inspired by the backstage dressing room of Janice Joplin.

There was one peasant top, orange tie-dye with Peruvian embroidery around the neck. I tweaked it from the rack.

"This reminds me of what I wore to my last Dead show," I said, more to myself than my fashion-forward company.

"You've been to a Dead show?" questioned Liesl in complete amazement.

"Yeah," I mumbled.

"Wow. That is like—like so completely cool."

Why was going to a Dead show so completely cool? In fact, it was far from being cool since I was quite the pseudo—only going to those concerts where people danced like they were in a snow globe because of a former Dead Head boyfriend who was now a commodities trader at his father's firm.

"I was never old enough to be able to go to one of those. And then Ben died."

"Who's Ben?" I was afraid to ask considering it was possibly her father and then I'd have to feign concern.

"Ben!" she shrieked as if this were obvious. "You know, the lead singer."

"You mean Jerry?"

"Ben. Jerry. The singer who got his own flavor of ice cream—with the cherries who also started the ice cream."

Okay. I would not continue this discussion any further because 1) This child was a complete moron, and 2) I was too young to start feeling old.

Liesl then pulled from the rack the same leather jeans, in purple and a size larger. She and Rodolfo congratulated themselves with such histrionics I wondered what their reaction was when receiving legitimately good news.

"Can I ask you something?" I interrupted. "If this is a ribbon story why are we spending so much time on what I'm wearing from the waist down?" They both looked to one another, perplexed.

The part of the body that stored laughter began to cave in. I couldn't help myself; a thunderous clap poured from my mouth, accented with a few sparks of spit. That should really be a fashionable vision to the *Elle* team. Four hours and two pictures later all for a piece of string in my hair that would be another scrap of memory to tie up my loose ends.

41

I basically had to write off the next few weeks to superficial obligations—the *Elle* shoot, Anne's shower, and next week's trip to
LA. The reality of life trumped my desire for a fresh approach.

The shower was a reminder of the perks of eloping, an ideal
venue to showcase the little outfits bought from little boutiques
to fill the ladies' little days. Guests were dressed in Scalamadre-
print pants, needlepoint shoes—all clothes that seem to be inspired by the decor of their living room even though there was
no specified theme written on the invitations.

Navigating clusters of guests with the motions of a bee, I was
unable to settle on a patch. I moved from conversations that attacked mutual close friends to a mother who advertised her
daughter's eating disorder as if she just earned the lead in her
school play.

When Dorit suggested we move to the side deck to watch
Anne open the presents, there was a shared excitement between
the guests as if they were the exclusive few to first view the Jackie
O. exhibit.

The girls oh-ed and ah-ed over gifts of place-card holders,
napkin rings, sugar prongs, and other accessories that looked to
be more of an effort when arranging a table setting while wasting valuable kitchen storage space—all to keep a few stuffy
bridal registry shops in business until the revered store owners
kicked over and sealed the inevitable retirement of the gravy
boat.

We heard stories of Anne and Jason's honeymoon, how her suffering from seasickness would be rendered impossible on this "floating mansion" Jason had arranged. They were cruising the coast of France and Italy for a month, and my mother had agreed to meet them on one of their port stops—apparently a hasty, dreaded commitment gathered from the nervous look she shot to Dorit.

Caught in their beams of gaze, I tried on an Emily face that was sincere and warm. Her expression was faraway, somewhat doleful as the impending move to Prague was now very real.

The tables were draped in white silky linen that were given extra sheen by the afternoon's rays, topped with white hydrangeas that erupted from minty glasses like heads of cauliflower. (Anne made no mention of the fact that the hydrangeas were white and not blue, which I was sure she would use against me with her next little favor to ask.) It was all so quaint and ladylike. Daphne and I couldn't even share a secret laugh over the fattening fat-free food because, aside from my Aunt Sophie who was always breaking the diet that she's been on for the past six years, the guests didn't dare touch anything carbohydrate.

If I were to have hired a stripper or if a Hilton sister had appeared wearing a Lily dress and pastel cardigan wrapped around her neck, the screeches of shock couldn't have caused as much commotion as when Anne announced the seating arrangements.

"And who would like to be placed next to Jason's adorable younger brother who went to Buckley, Yale, works at Goldman Sachs and is very eligible," she asked.

Ehhhh! The yelping sounds and riot of French manicured hands bobbed in the air, having the effect of the Chuckling Patch from *A Secret Garden.*

Daphne left my side to check on the dessert—plates of cut pears and coffee (natural diuretics), a cue for Mother to slink toward me. A very excitable guest agreed to relieve her from the task of recording what presents were given by whom, folding up the wrapping paper into a neat little pile while Dorit attended to its disposal in timed spurts.

"I know, this is a bit brutal for you," she said as if with a wink, which she couldn't do, having particularly sensitive eyes, something I inherited from her.

I fell back to the wall, my body heavy with emotion. It was so much easier to be with my mother right now. Probably because (1) She was leaving for a foreign country soon, or (2) The pickings for interesting company considering the function, or (3) We were actually *getting* one another.

I decided it was a combination of the three; some differences were just differences and rather than lure someone to your way you should accept them for who they were. I should have worked for the government defusing hostile situations between warring countries.

I replied to my mother with a lazy tilt of my head nestled on her shoulder.

42

With swank martini glasses and cocktail shakers, retro chic, I felt like a Bond girl as I arrived at the Chateau Marmont. Felt, but definitely didn't look, as my messy plane hair, romantic floral dress with a decollate trim (wrinkled all over) and flip-flops weren't particularly Bond babe. The porter led us through a secret pathway, taking me to one of the bungalows removed from the hotel rooms.

Dash had arrived on Sunday, the day before me, and was currently at work. His presence marked by his toiletry bag, left on the bathroom sink and containing no condoms. Then again, gold sealed condoms were left on our pillows like chocolates.

I was also grateful to have the time to myself, otherwise I probably wouldn't have been jumping on the beds and beginning my trip by ordering a pitcher of Stoli gimlets.

With an entire afternoon free I changed into my first bikini of the season, wrapped myself in a big fluffy bathrobe, placed sunglasses atop my head—then tossed the sunglasses into my bag because they didn't stay put—and did the very LA thing and sat lounge side at the pool.

There was a woman lying face down, the tips of her red tipped toes poking through the straps of the chair. She may have needed a shake—so still, I feared a drug overdose. Two chairs from her a guy read through some work papers. Sort of cute. His short hair tight and curled like a crown of broccoli, which was a bit distracting, but I loved the Vilebrequin shorts and the per-

sonally trained body beneath. A boy who was not blessed geneti-
cally but could compensate with great style and a healthy physique
was certainly clever. Daphne would even argue that these were the
best kind.

Considering that I was here on business, I took my sketch pad
out from my bag to work on *Wall Flower.* I scribbled furiously, but
somehow my drawing skills had abandoned me. Perhaps it was
the new environment, or that my head was not into it, or that I
was finally coming to the realization that all these years trying to
follow my passion had been based on pure luck. But it was probably the jet lag, LA air and incoming buzz from my drink.

"Are you okay?" I was interrupted by the not-all-that-cute-but-
there-was-something-real-sexy-about-him guy. He was not in as
clear a view as before because of the shift in sunlight but seemed
taller now that he was standing.

"Yeah," I said quickly, indignantly. "Why? Does it look like
there is something wrong?"

"Well, yes, actually." He nodded to the mound of snowballs
next to my chair.

"Oh!" I shrugged, followed by some silent *he, he, hes.* "Just trying to get through the endeavor of the day."

"Aspiring, successful? Business or pleasure?"

"All of the above," I answered evenly.

Sexy geeky guy took the seat next to me without asking. His
forwardness impressed me.

"So I gather that this is an opportune moment for us to dawdle our afternoon, briefing one another why we're here in LA.
There is a story with you?"

Oh, yeah, but an afternoon spent poolside would just be the
miniseries version.

"I'm an artist/illustrator sharing a really cool bungalow with
my best friend who I recently slept with and now we're back to
being best friends while the guy I really love has been revisiting
his psychopathic ex-girlfriend who looks great in lip gloss and
was probably the captain of her cheerleading squad because of
her really big boobs and blonde hair.

"I am also having a mild insecurity crisis over some very important LA meeting my agent set up and I will return to New

York and have an unhealthy addiction to the Lifetime Movie of the Week and artificial frozen yogurt. And you?"

He coolly answered, "J3 Hopper."

"Oh, right," I fumbled. "Names—good place to start. I'm Emily Briggs."

"Nice to meet you, Emily Briggs." He put his sunglasses back on and gazed into the sun, probably perturbed that he ever took the seat next to mine.

"J3 Hopper?" I questioned. "Sounds like one of the programs on my laptop that I have yet to figure out."

J3 laughed. His four-day-a-week weight-lifting-regimen chest pumped into the air to the rhythm of his laughter. While his body would be considered good, it was a bit too proportioned for my taste.

"So you're not a Ludite?" he asked without looking at me, face still directed toward the sun.

"Ah. No!"

"Great, completely refreshing considering that's part of what I do."

"And what do you do, oh cryptic one?"

"Play video games all day."

Perfect, another boy child, we would get along wonderfully.

"Do you like video games, Emily?"

"I suppose so, but I haven't really played any since I had an Atari. I was particularly good at Space Invaders."

J3 again laughed. My eyes were entranced by the syncopations of his chest and he was now looking at me. "Do you mind?" he asked, pointing to my pile of discarded drawings, then smoothed a rippled paper before I could nod that it was okay.

I looked over to his side to see which one he selected, practically falling from my chair. It was of Lily gazing up at a Hollywood sign, possibilities boundless. Although I'd just met J3, his smile looked sincere.

"I like it. A lot! Who knows, maybe we'll be able to work together someday." He then asked if he could keep the scrapped drawing, which I allowed him to have but became curious as to why he wanted it. Then, searching his eyes of two dollops of dark chocolate topped with gypsy moth brows, I heard him speak.

"So it sounds as if you're at a certain point, juncture. It seems so perfect for us to meet, as I am kind of going through a few things myself."

"Really?" It was my turn to probe, not terribly successfully. He just gave that sly smile—he was harder to crack open than a baby clam.

"If someone close to you had to give you advice about your new juncture, what would they say?"

How philosophical for poolside chatter.

"Mother or best friend?"

"Best friend. Mothers are too one-dimensional."

"Probably that I should come back to reality, grow up a bit."

"Growing up is overrated." Coming from a guy who earned a living from annihilating his opponent to pieces.

I returned to my drawing, less furiously than before. J3 fell into a hazy sleep. He looked comfortable but not as knocked out as the other lady, who I knew was not dead because she was now positioned on her other side.

Dash's voice awakened me from an unexpected doze. "Emily?" his voice boomed. Dash's workday dress and disruptive diction were so out of place on the relaxed pool deck that even passed-out lady lifted her glasses, sending a gaze of death to this intruder.

"Hey, Dash. This is J3." Dash's and J3's eyes were locked in battle. J3 then took off his glasses and they shook hands. Dash's tough guy demeanor changed back into his obsequious boyish one. I couldn't quite read what J3 was thinking, especially considering my TMIed spew from before.

Dash dragged over a lounge chair that made the sound of screaming monkeys, again annoying everyone who had laid claims poolside before his presence. He slid off his Tod loafers.

"You have a message from Gil Stephens at FOX. Some party at Falcon they want you to go to tonight. Probably a meet and greet situation under a more sociable gathering. Very LA."

J3 laughed.

"Why is this so LA?" I asked, directed to J3. "Where are you from?"

"I wish I was from somewhere. Somewhere that didn't have

check-ins, sanitized towels and dinner presented from silver domes."

This was curious.

"But I grew up in Palo Alto," he said to appease my questioning expression.

"Okay." I answered to Dash, "Let's do this party thing."

"Well, then you better get ready, it begins at seven P.M."

Chill. What was the rush? I then reached for Dash's wrist, his Swiss Army watch, which read just after 6:30 P.M.

"God, I'm all screwy." I made an awkward jostle from my chair, assembling my things to race from the pool. Dash, still seated, called to me, "I'll be up in a minute."

Fine, I said with a wave, turning away from him.

Cloppity-clapping up a few steps, I stopped mid-clop and turned back toward the pool.

"Hey, J3," I called down. "Want to come with us?"

"Actually was intending on going to that very party. Thank you, Emily, finally some people to rally with. Would love to."

There was a story with that one.

Out of the shower I became a bundle of terry cloth—big bathrobe and hair wrapped up in a fluffy white towel. I dressed effortlessly—a purple lace sundress from Calypso with a snug cardigan and Siegerson and Morrison strappy kitten heels that I bought especially for this trip. Easy to throw together and I'd been told by boys that they liked this look.

I found Dash in the common room. We ordered a pitcher of margaritas and I suggested that J3 swing by for some pre-drinks before we all ventured out together.

"So you really have no idea who J3 is?" muttered Dash, bewildered.

"Wrong," I pounced. "He works with video games and grew up in California. What else is there to know?"

Dash mocked me with a cacophony of cackles and a nod of his head.

"What?" I barked, Emily smirk in full regalia.

"You really don't know who he is, do you?"

"What, is this a goddamn game of Trivial Pursuit? Fess up."

"Have you heard of Moon Chip?"

"Wasn't that Gidget's boyfriend?"

"No, you moron. Moon Chip! The company that's going to put Sega out of business? They're beginning that new film technology that all the sci-fi producers are so jazzed by. This J3 Hopper is the CEO. He's a goddamn Bill Gates of the twenty-first century and you're just hanging with him poolside."

"Sorry, I'm behind on my *PC Weekly*. And I think 'moron' is a little strong here."

"Not if you read the business section or watch the news. The guy is a rock star in new technology."

"Well, why don't you call Mr. Rock Star and see if he wants to have some margaritas before we go," I huffed.

43

It was especially enjoyable being lightheaded in a new environment. LA gets a bad rap for its valet, for the shots of wheat grass sold at newsstands and for the number of aspiring something or others. It was similar to tequila: in small doses it's outrageous but go a little over the tolerance level and you will have over-the-toilet reactions.

Once we arrived at Falcon, Dash immediately started on the networking thing while I was in my naughty flirty mode, having a boldness that could never happen if sober. It wasn't weird flirting with boys around Dash. The fact that he had at least five messages from Katrina helped expedite things back to the way they had been.

After meeting all the FOX contacts, I was genuinely curious by their lack of seriousness and overzealous approach, a refreshing change from hardnosed New York editors.

I was speaking with Gil Stephens, a very handsome producer who was as cute as one of those leading characters on one of the soaps whom I could only identify by muted viewings on the gym television or covers of supermarket tabloids. He probably tried his luck on the daytime television run and, unsuccessful, turned to the other side of the camera. My nostrils filled from the exhalation of his minty breath while he twirled his Pellegrino nervously.

"Never drink on a weekday night," he said, probably in defense of my hypnotic stare at his melting cubes of ice and sprig of mint.

Gil began to discuss a series of topics foreign to my comprehension—all related to *the industry*. I nodded along with a vague air of indifference until he searched my eyes for what I believed was a needed response. I casually interjected, "interesting," causing a momentary look of confusion before he continued.

Apparently he was rehashing a birthday party he'd attended for his friend who'd invented 4545-50, a caller alert number. My lack of familiarity with this number caused some unnecessary histrionics. The number had now set Gil's friend up with the "fattest, most multidimensional Brentwood pad that could be straight from a Tim Burton set."

Now mildly interested in what he was discussing purely for sociological investigative purposes, I actually began listening to him. We even moved to a secluded part of the lounge so that he was my sole focus.

We must have been alone for a bit of time. After having that suspicion that I was being stared it, I searched the clumps of guests, who started to adhere to the sides of the room. Front and center was Henry.

Gil shifted a bit but it was enough to obstruct my necessary view. Claustrophobia became a very real issue. I couldn't make sense of anything that Gil was saying. His mouth moved wildly but the only sound was the heartthrob pulsing between my ears. My head swelled, I lost all sensory functions. Speaking after an emotional outpouring, moving after a day of skiing bumps, my heart pounded so hard that I feared the surface of my chest would expose the beat of the pulse, similar to that of a tree frog's.

Henry's shoulders alternated among other shoulders in the movements of a dancer. He approached me. He approached me with grace, confidence and in clear pursuit. My attempt to escape Gil's enclosure was a little less graceful. The only place to go was into the wall. The wall that I kept pushing into like a windup doll butting its mechanical head again and again, only my head wasn't mechanical.

Gil, happily recognizing Henry, suddenly flurried off in response to whatever the mental message Henry telepathically transmitted.

I was now face to face with Henry. No contact with the wall. No access to escape to. My mouth a giant O. What would come out from it I had no idea.

Henry looked to me with that bad boy smile. "No words. No thoughts," he instructed me carefully, slowly.

I tried to make sense of this but was in need of some clarification.

"If I can't speak or think, then what is it I am supposed to do here?" I asked, my voice suddenly returning to working order.

"I am going to kiss you now." Henry started to lean in but was intercepted by my hands, up in protest.

"And by you kissing me all of our problems will just—poof—disappear?"

"Well? Yes!"

"Okay!"

And Henry kissed me. That strangely familiar kiss that can only lead to something unbridled. There was no one in front, behind, or anywhere near. It was just Henry and I. Together the way I'd always wanted it to be.

I felt a tear roll down my face. Another one followed, causing me some alarm. I needed to turn off this overflowing spill. I quickly filled my head with thoughts of the day, Lee Press-On nails, "real tomato ketchup there, Eddie"—anything to prevent this inevitable downpour.

Holding in laughter and air while kissing Henry, the result was the most perfect happiness, a moment that would be ranked among my all-time greatest memories, right up there when Dad said we just got cable television.

I pulled away only because I needed to see if this was real. Henry was real, smiling a familiar smile that did prove that words sometimes were not needed.

Henry was the first to speak.

"Sometimes I fear that when you start to think, your mind spins out of control like a moose on skates."

"A moose on skates?"

He nodded.

"And when have you seen a moose on skates?"

We were simultaneously distracted. Across the room, Dash made his presence known. His big head buoying up and down among the patches of people, a goggled kid testing out his new swim gear among a pool of fluorescent floats. He was looking at me protectively and with sincere worry.

"How very LA of you," chided Henry. "Bringing your bodyguard to a party."

We both laugh and escaped hand in hand.

44

My desire to forgive Henry could either mean that I was a complete idiot or actually growing up.

We went to the bar at the Beverly Wilshire, neutral ground as Henry had been subletting an apartment nearby and spent what seemed an entire week reviewing what had happened between us.

But all issues seemed irrelevant in comparison to learning that psycho Tina was out of Henry's picture. She'd lured him into her twisted plot to return to California, mainly to have him back in her life, suspiciously after she discovered that he was having a life with me. He even questioned whether she was ever pregnant, due to inconsistencies on the details when prodded.

His absence for nearly four months, not even a note or E-mail, was due to his escaping life for the tasty waves of Hawaii and then returning to LA to enact a plan that he came up with during his period of exile. Apparently I was always included in this plan.

My meeting at FOX (which was to happen in four hours and showing up in the same clothes I wore the night before was a little lax, even in LA standards) was also part of Henry's deliberate plot. It was Henry's idea to include Lily in his new series with Duncan. Since these two different yet similar characters, this combination of art forms, was so innovative it was certain to be as successful a collaboration as Minnie and Mickey, Fred and

Wilma, Homer and Marge. Met by FOX with an it's-so-easy-why-didn't-we-think-of-it deal.

I treated Henry's purge the way you attend a loose thread on the hem of your dress at a swank party. Do you pull it to temporarily relieve that pesky loose end that dominates the amount of brainpower necessary for a real crisis, or do you leave it be and have it professionally attended to at a more opportune time? I decided not to pull the thread at that moment.

Returning to the hotel for a quick shower, I found Dash passed out on the *Dick Van Dyke* Show couch in the common room.

I dressed in my Manolo Blahnik suede, calf-hugging boots, white Marc Jakobs fitted pea coat and little black skirt. Going for the whole New Yorker goes to big LA meeting effect.

In the FOX reception area, twenty minutes late, I met Henry, Gil, and a man who looked like a stumped-out cigarette. I was happy to show some leg to make up for my tardiness in this testosterone-ridden room.

Stumped-out cigarette man was named Brad. When Brad announced that it was his idea to combine the two characters, his declaration was met with a round of applauding nods from our table—including Henry—and I knew that this was the man who had secured the show's fate.

"We'll make it a Christmas special," announced Brad. He was getting suitably riled up by all of the fawning nods. "I know, I know! Duncan and Lily will meet at a Christmas party!" His voice was raised to a spit-spewing level, excitability that would be more deserved for securing Julia Roberts to play the Mati Hari—a film script that I happened to notice when I glanced at his big black desk.

Everyone, including Brad, agreed that he was brilliant and that we were making a deal. Lawyers, agents, numbers and intended phone calls were being uttered about the room like available sizes and colors at Fred Segal.

Lily was going to be bigger than Britney. Henry was potentially a possibility. My life was dramatically unfolding along a new chain of events and all because of coming to this make-believe land of LA.

I love LA, I screamed to myself.

"I love LA," I screamed to Henry as we jumped up and down outside the FOX offices. Or, really, I jumped while his head bounced to my movements. Fearing that I'd kill myself, considering my shoe choice, I then composed myself.

"You're in the honeymoon period," instructed Henry. "Sorry to put it to you this way but since I've been here I've been feeling like a proctologist, surrounded by all of these assholes."

"Eww," I squealed like a girl.

But Henry really did have the LA power meeting thing down, still a bit miffed by his acquiescing to the Brad-the-Brilliant pageantry.

"And this is coming from a guy who thought New York has no soul?"

"You miss what you have when you leave it."

"What? What am I missing?" I implored.

"You're just an LA virgin."

I didn't like the fact that Henry was trying to instruct me on this one—taking the upper hand. Or that he'd used the word virgin in my context.

"Well, maybe I'm the one who has it right here. Going to LA for the honeymoon and leaving before the reality sets in."

45

I was ready to go home. Called to change my ticket to an earlier flight from the phone that hung on the wall in the room's bar area. Dash, versed in the wearing fluffy terry cloth in Andre Balaz–styled heaven, poked his wet ear with a fluffy white towel.

Hanging up, I had a few hours to kill before taking the red-eye. I looked to Dash with a moan.

"So the meeting went poorly I gather?"

"No—quite the contrary. This thing is really going to happen." I wandered off, coiling the phone cord around my pinky finger. Completely absorbed by the way the rubber snugly enveloped my finger in the same shade of nude. I snapped myself out of this mind-numbing reverie, realizing that the fixation I had on this cord was more appropriate for heroin addicts or girls who spent their days going on auditions.

"Really going to happen," I said again, looking to Dash as I unraveled the cord.

"Then why all melancholy?" Dash took the seat next to me. I loved that I had my big cute friend back. "This is such great news," he said.

"Yeah. I suppose it is."

"I get it. Or really I started to get it last night when I saw you sneaking away from me. This has to do with Henry."

"Oh, yeah, about that. I'm sorry that I was being such a freak. Just one of those moments that I didn't want to end."

"Before I'd ruin it?"

Um. Yeah! But I had to stop being so mean to Dash.

"Just my whole unhealthy running away from reality thing I suppose."

"If you are running away from reality then why the sudden desire to run back to New York?" Dash looked to the wall phone. "I heard you changing your ticket."

He was perceptive on this one.

"Listen," he said, soothingly. "I'm done with my whole LA thing as well. What's your flight info?"

"The red-eye. Delta."

The next thing I knew, Dash was using the phone to change his ticket to the same flight. Why did he have to do that? Now I'd have to be all polite and charming, sit with him when all I wanted to do was shots of tequila from the minibar before I left and then pass out on that horrendously long flight home.

He did, however, do the responsible Dash thing and arranged for our transportation to the airport. This wasn't a town that had doormen dressed in livery hailing down yellow cabs for you outside the carpeted front entrance.

At the Delta counter, praise the Almighty, Dash wasn't able to get a seat next to mine. As we shuttled away, the ticket man who looked too cute to be working at an airport exclaimed, "But wait a minute!" Ah, the life of an actor. "If I just shuffle her seat to the same row you can ask the person in between you both to move."

"That's great!" said Dash, before I could protest.

A guy with a seventies fro was already firmly situated in the seat in question. This might not be so easy.

"Do you mind if my girlfriend sits in your seat so we can be next to each other?"

Girlfriend? I was so thrown off by this, I assumed, tactic. Fro guy was gathering his things, ready to move.

"Oh, really, please. You really don't have to go through the trouble," I rambled desperately.

"It's really no trouble," said fro guy. His face looked elastic; probably had the ability to change into a variety of looks. He must have also been an actor; comedies, I assumed.

"But we are being such an inconvenience."

With his magazines and CD player in hand, fro elastic man said, "You're not being an inconvenience."

"But we are. You don't have to get up . . ." I trailed off as fro guy got up.

"Um, Emily," interjected Dash, annoyed. "This very nice gentleman has agreed to change seats." He then said to fro man, "And thank you."

I had to sit next to Dash.

"So!" he began in his annoying sprightly morning person way. "Isn't LA just great!"

"I am starting to have my reservations. The people, a bit synthetic."

"So LA is even more synthetic than New York?"

"Precisely!" I shouted a spit-screaming shout. I then paused, embarrassed by my overt display of histrionics. We were silent. A 4:00 A.M. in the morning silence. "Precisely," I said again, real quiet this time.

"And this is coming from the girl who does the are-they-real-or-are-they-fake check on every New York blonde she meets?"

"But at least they have some style. New Yorkers. In LA it's a lot of girls in tube tops and boys who look like Eminem. If I want to see that crowd I could just hang at the Riverhead DMV—shorter trip."

The stewardess asked us what we'd like to drink. After swinging down my vial of tequila, I passed out.

46

Returning to New York, my mind was as out of control as that moose on skates. I indeed had to leave the fantasy behind. LA was a place where one day you're in syndication and the next you can't even get an appearance on *Hollywood Squares*. Maybe with Henry and me, everything that I always thought I wanted could happen. But I had to protect myself.

I was sitting in Gramercy Park. Holding the key that entitled me to a special patch of greenery amongst the urban chaos. The chaos of New York was shielded by a square of wrought iron; I was in a protected space of trimmed boxwoods and gravel paths, which I shared with pigeons and, today, a very white, extravagantly dressed pigeon. Perhaps it was a pigeon wedding day orchestrated by some bored senior-citizen Gramercy residents. On closer inspection this was not a pigeon at all. It was a cockatiel. In fact it was *the* cockatiel—Callie's pearl choker was the giveaway. I swiveled my head to see if this major discovery was exclusively mine. And an empty park on Tuesday morning at 10:30 A.M. appeared to confirm that it was.

I remembered the article in the *Standard* advising what to do to if you spotted the cockatiel—call on a cell phone. My dial pad yearned for punching from my desperately in-need-of-a-manicure fingers. My mind spun out of control, like that moose on skates. Callie seemed happy with the pigeons. Who was I to determine otherwise? Be the one to secure her fate? Before the very real issue of the reward money invaded my caffeinated hazelnut infused thoughts (the trip back from LA had been a long one), the congregation of birds fluttered their wings into a muffled chorus. Blurred primary colors of shattering steel.

"Did you see that? Did you see that!" I said to no one. Callie was now a vision that would be catalogued as a bizarre memory.

It was Henry whom I called to share the news with. The person I thought of before my mind got in the way of things.

Henry, too, returned to New York after the meeting and we agreed to meet outside my coffee place. He greeted me by delivering a container of what I knew to be my decaf hazelnut while he fumbled with the plastic lid of his cup, coffee seeping over his skin like tanning oil.

"You okay there, bud?"

"Yeah. Just one of the side effects from giving up smoking."

"Really?" Was this a lure? "I'm impressed. And now I suppose I can hear about all the other things you've given up—failure to communicate, not being honest with me and so forth."

He said out of nowhere, "Why did you tell me that you snooped?"

"Excuse me?" I was thrown off by this sudden change in conversation.

"In the restaurant, when we broke things off. I could never understand why you felt the need to tell me that."

I pictured him replaying our talk on the Hawaiian shores, momentarily transplanted to that cold wet New York evening. It was now possible to realize that I was with Henry all that time, the way he was with me.

"Because I wouldn't have snooped if I already knew what I was looking for."

Henry was quiet for a moment. Also to my benefit because, until I said it, I never knew why I snooped.

"You know," he said. "My being set up with you wasn't quite blind. In fact it was pretty deliberate."

My brows raised into a curious pose.

"I saw you a few times at Pierce and Wilkinson. I wanted to meet you but never had the courage to pursue you on my own, so I had Joanna deftly arrange it."

Interesting. Now I knew whose camp Joanna was really in.

"And why are you telling me this?"

"Because I want to use what we've learned to our benefit. I want to start again. I want to make things better. I want you."

"And I want you too, *but.*" Henry had no room for *but.*

"Why don't we live together!"

"And that came from where?"

He shrugged. Apparently it came from nowhere.

"I don't think so." I had defused his momentary buzz. Henry's whole body collapsed. "If you could only understand the kind of experiences I had while we were apart. If *I* could only understand the kind of experiences I had while we were apart." Deficient in mental energy, I mustered on. "It was bad and good but mostly essential. This idea of having the ultimate is exciting. Beyond exciting."

Henry's placid face broke from gravity to the thousand little laugh lines that made a man look distinguished (while viewed as a sign of imperfection for the ladies). As irresistible as he was, I couldn't restrain the hurt that I was feeling.

"I still don't really know if I can trust you. The intensity of your emotions for this Tina—what kind of assurance can I have that she really is not an issue?"

"Tina?" he scoffed. "She's like the LA air—sometimes fragrant, but lethal. If you spend years inhaling the fumes, it will potentially kill you. Completely toxic."

Kind of tired of his little analogies.

"Kind of tired of your little analogies."

"Come on, Emily. Why do you have to make this so difficult? We took the time apart to realize that we need to be together."

Difficult? Me? Coming from the guy who gave me the heave-ho. This one annoyed me.

Henry, apparently not registering my abhorred expression, continued with bravado. "I know you. That this time we had apart reinforced your certainty that we are meant to be."

Was he being cocky at my expense?

"What do you take me for? That I just holed myself up in my studio, got lost in my work, evaluated our relationship, and considered therapy?" Of course, this was not far off the mark.

"No, no, no," he sounded like Anne with her wedding planner. "Of course I know that you didn't pathetically pine for me. It's just that . . ." he drifted. "Em, I can't help but assume that you feel what I feel. You make me feel like a little kid!"

"Which is partly what concerns me."

Henry took my coffee from my hand, his cup in the other and then placed them on the sidewalk. He kissed me. Everything solved with a kiss. And it wasn't a bad tactic.

"I have something for you," he said, pulling out a suede satchel, fastened with a glossy rope string. He dropped the bag into my cupped hands. It felt like jewelry, but not a ring. Prodding it open, I found a set of keys clasped in silver beads like a baby's bracelet.

"Henry?" I coaxed. "I kind of said that living together wasn't a viable option."

"No, it's not that."

I looked at him curiously. The keys to his apartment were still stowed in my desk drawer. I allowed him to lead me to the curb, where he successfully hailed a cab.

"Eighteenth and Tenth. In Chelsea," he instructed the driver. We were silent. Communicating through our held hands.

The cab delivered us to a sandstone building, casement windows framed by elaborately carved Greek columns, the kind of details only found on apartments that were created when communal living was considered a utopian phenomenon.

Inside the elevator Henry pressed PH. I was still silent because questions flew about my head like dresses flying from a closet. It was impossible to settle on one.

He unlocked the door to a hat shop, chocolate factory, toy maker's studio—all things cool but slightly quirky. A domed glassed ceiling above, a staircase as curvy as a piece of fusili leading to a loft and windows as big as bed sheets.

We both just looked about the space, in awe. Two kids stumbling out of the wardrobe and into a magical place.

"Kind of cool. Isn't it?"

My wide-eyed expression suitably answered his query.

"It makes for a pretty sweet studio and, since we will now be working together on this Christmas special . . ."

I nodded spastically.

"So. I'm starting to worry. I don't think I've ever seen you this quiet. Didn't know it was possible for you to go so long without words, actually."

"A lot's happened," I said, exhausted.

"Yeah. So?"

"I just need to think about this—take it all in."

"What do you mean? The studio or us?"

"Both," I said. Amazed at how levelheaded I was becoming.

47

Daphne invited me to see her redone apartment. I assumed that moving into a new space would have been easier than overhauling the old space. Fresh colored walls, an added guest room, a pantry and kitchen that somehow appeared bigger. I stared about in wonderment.

"We added on by buying the neighboring apartment and we knocked down a few walls," she said, while sliding a bunch of especially large stemmed sunflowers into a tall slender vase, frosty in texture with a slight tint of blue. Daphne really had this domestic goddess thing down. "With this new cooking stint going, I really need a high-grade working space."

High-grade working space she had.

She set out various bowls of fruit compote and a basket of assorted mini muffins, fat free I presumed, and then began making us some decaf hazelnut from the same machine they used at Starbucks. I loved coming over to Daphne's.

"Okay, we need to discuss this Henry situation," she began.

I hated coming over to Daphne's.

"Wasn't I supposed to be here to check out your new place and test some recipes?" I asked while popping a munchkin-size muffin into my mouth. It was gingery with a touch of cinnamon, a taste that would be hard to forget.

"This is amazing!"

She completely disregarded me. "Emily, you know you are the ultimate catch. Ultimate."

I gave her an Emily look.

"Stop it with the weird faces," she scorned. "You can't make it too easy for Henry."

Just then the nanny came into the kitchen, little Henry balancing on her bony hipbone while she reached for a bottle from the fridge. Wearing a crocheted halter top and creamy suede skirt, she was a massive dose of blonde hair, boobs that couldn't possibly be real (not that I was staring too hard), and ribs as thin as Fifi's.

"Vello," she said in a thick (sexy) Eastern European accent. Henry, loving his perch, gurgled and smiled.

"Sorry, I voped I didn't vinterrupt," she said, waving while she and the baby made their exit.

"Where did you get her from? ELITE models?"

"Sort of."

"Sort of?"

"She was on a shoot that I catered," said Daphne evenly while she handed me my decaf and took a sip from her cup. "We struck it up and she said she needed to find a place to live while she was pursuing her modeling career. Considering the added guest room and child care needs with my new career, I proposed a room and board arrangement for some light in-house sitting."

"You're okay with looking at that every morning?"

"Undisturbed nights have wondrous effects—her room is adjacent to the nursery."

"Clever," I said with a nod, then added dreamily, "If I looked like that I bet I'd never have had all this drama with Henry."

She wasn't letting me get away with this one.

"Please, Emily. The girl has a head full of noodles. You are not only brilliant, you are gorgeous. Do we have to have the bone structure conversation again?"

"No," I groaned. We'd had the bone structure conversation maybe 1,800 times. Daphne assumed that my having a bit of proportion to my cheekbones made up for not being statuesque, blonde and boobed.

"Enough with this insecurity rant. We're here to discuss Henry. You're being too available for him. You've made it easy for him and I fear he's taken advantage of your generous good spirit. I won't have him taking advantage of my Emily."

She was serious.

"But this whole idea of having to act a way that I normally wouldn't, it's not truthful. I don't like the idea of it. That Henry will be devoted to me only because I entrapped him." I repeated with a huff, "Just don't like it."

"You're making this sound so manipulative."

"Well? Isn't it?"

"No. It's not. It's about handling boys. They're complete morons. And you, Emily," she said in that oh-Emily tone. "You are giving them far too much credit." Daphne was making *them,* the boys, sound like some opponent.

"The only game I play well is the one with a top hat and hotels."

She took a moment.

"Do you think Henry is going through—went through—the pain that you've experienced?"

I took a moment. That wasn't a fair question. I reviewed my steps after our breakup—grief, confusion and trying to block him out like that period when I wore cowboy boots with miniskirts. Even though I prided myself in not being psycho girl or manipulative call girl—the phone call kind not the one who sleeps with men for free food—I did have my moments of weirdness. The over-analysis, the self-doubt.

Could I assume that Henry's emotions paralleled or were at least on par with mine? It wasn't like I had a surveillance camera in his head.

"It's not like I have a surveillance camera in his head."

Daphne's pouted face told me this was a cop-out answer.

"What?" I replied with a shrug of my shoulders and indent to my brow.

"I don't know," she said. Meaning that she thought I was being a complete dupe.

"I love him. Being with him makes me happy."

"Great. This is all wonderful, Emily, but for whatever reason that's as irrational as my desire to shop for fall clothes in ninety-degree heat. Boys want the girl they can't have. They want the chase."

"Here we go, the old hunters and gatherers analogy."

"It's a tried analogy because it's true. Rather than duplicate natty animals it would be more useful if scientists found the genetic component that proves this theory correct."

"Well, then, what am I supposed to do aside from assume the duties of a den lion? I mean, it's not like I've committed to him yet. Left the whole work studio thing up in the air."

"But you called him."

I looked up in the air. Nice overhead lighting.

"You called him, didn't you?" barked Daphne.

I looked at her with a shrug and silly guilty face.

"First off, you cannot call him."

I looked at her with that yeah-okay-right look.

"Do not call him!"

"Fine. Okay. I won't call him," I mumbled.

"Do not call him!" she again commanded. Like I didn't get it the first time?

"I won't."

"You will."

"Won't."

"Will."

"Won't."

"Will."

"Can we please stop this," I said, abruptly. "My brain is getting dizzy."

"Each time you have that urge to call him, call me," she instructed, the way she probably went over meals and sleeping times for her model/baby-sitter. I supposed this was also a form of baby-sitting.

"What is it with this whole phone call thing. That if I call him he'll be like, 'oh, Emily just called me. I really have control now.' "

"Yes! That's exactly what he'll say!" She didn't have to be so forthright. I was truly feeling like an idiot.

"Calling him is that jail card. 'Go to Jail. Go Directly to Jail. Do Not Pass Go. Do Not Collect Two Hundred Dollars.' "

"I hate it when I can't collect that two hundred dollars." I sulked like a little girl. "This is all so stupid." Slamming my hands to my knees and looking to my feet, I stole a surreptitious peek at Daphne. She was staring at me. It was a pretty scary look so I turned my gaze to my newly pedicured cranberry toes poking through my two-tone D'Orsay pumps. The shoe's trim perfectly complemented the deep red polish.

I stole another glance. That scary gaze was still firmly plastered to her face. I was a prisoner under her supervision.

"Would you please quit it?"

"No."

"Give me your cell."

"This is preposterous. What are you getting at?"

"Emily," she reprimanded, her hand motioning a come hither wave. "Give me the cell."

"I don't have it."

Not buying it. "I want the cell. Give me the cell."

"My cell?" I said, like the dizzy blonde that I sometimes am, even though my hair color doesn't justify it.

"The cell—give it to me!" She tried to swipe my bag.

"What?" I said, clutching my bag to my breast. "If I give you my cell, there won't be any other way for me to call him?"

She took a moment.

"Do not call him!" was her final declaration.

Fine, I wouldn't call him.

48

I hated it when Daphne was being such a good friend. I didn't know what was worse, my not being able to call Henry or my head feeling like the tip of a Q-Tip, clouded over from not being able to call him.

I sat, staring at my kitchen phone, trying to summon a ring. It rang! The phone was ringing! Henry and I were telecommunicatedly connected!

"Hello!" I yelped with glee.

"Really, Emily. This is not polite phone etiquette—your shouting into the phone like that."

It was Mother.

"Mom, I'll have to call you back." Click.

This whole phone thing was stupid.

And then the buzzer buzzed.

"Hello?" I asked suspiciously into the intercom, since I wasn't expecting anyone.

"Hey, Em. It's me."

I was silent. Wow, this not calling thing really did work.

"It's me. Henry," said the muffled voice from the ugly plastic paraphernalia mounted on my wall. Like I didn't know it was Henry. "Can I come up?"

I buzzed him up.

Henry arrived at my doorstep with a plastic container of Tasti D-Lite the size of a paint can. I loved that the boys in my life knew the gifts that I truly valued.

"Wow," I said to the enormous container. I wanted to tear off the lid so I could eat it immediately, preferably with a teaspoon while watching really bad television. "I didn't know it came in that size."

"It doesn't," he announced, heading straight to the freezer. "I made an arrangement."

I looked at him, impressed.

Henry walked over to the freezer, moving around a few containers of Ben and Jerry's and bottles of vodka, his reconfiguring unsuccessful.

"Don't worry, just put it in the fridge."

He looked confused.

"I like to have it slightly melted anyway."

"But there's enough to last you a whole month in here."

I don't think so.

"Oh. Right. Forgot for a moment who I was dealing with," he said, suddenly remembering that the five-gallon container of frozen yogurt would be as gone as overflowing gift bags at a fund-raiser without celebrities.

"So you think that a huge container of Tasti D-Lite will just make me fall all over you again?"

He shrugged. Henry, not having the knowledge of my Daphne therapy, was probably expecting that the container of Tasti D-Lite would have the effect of a little velvet box.

"This is my life you are trifling with, Henry. And I am too strong to put up with your boy confusion thing."

I was weak.

I was weak.

I was weak.

Henry pulled me into him and wrapped his arms around me—real tight, sincere. He smoothed my hair back and then looked to me. We started to kiss. Kissing him was as easy and natural as eating that Tasti D-Lite that I couldn't stop thinking about.

"Forgive me," he said, softly. His eyes swelled but he suppressed tears.

Suppressing tears, I asked, pleaded, "How? Tell me how, why I should forgive you?"

"Because I was guilty of clearing up a past situation. You can't start driving your car until you've paid all your speeding tickets."

Hmm. I better pay all my speeding tickets.

"Emily, forgive me."

"Let's just take it slow," I said, walking over to the fridge and reaching for the bucket of Tasti D-Lite.

And even though we ate the Tasti D-Lite with teaspoons to prolong the happy eating factor, we finished the container in what seemed like under five minutes. Despite the speedy inhalation, the taste from my most favored food lingered on.

EPILOGUE

Parlaying the success of the Lily and Duncan Christmas special, J3 Hopper funded our first movie, *Different Art Forms,* for his new film company. It was the first animated comedy to be the number-one movie in America over Memorial Day weekend. Henry began working on the sequel with J3.

Dash was assigned a television documentary that followed five families living in a suburban Connecticut town. He proposed to Katrina two weeks later. Katrina quit her job to plan the wedding.

Satisfying America's appetite for a new Martha Stewart, Daphne converged the fame from her cookbook, *What a Dish,* to become The *Today Show*'s food and entertaining correspondent. Negotiations were underway for her own series.

After serving too many detentions for her pranks, little Emily was enrolled in an experimental art school where her teachers professed she would become the next Jean Michel-Basquiat.

After being featured on the cover of the *New York Times* "Styles" section for his cosmetic surgery on such celebrity pets as Kitty Combs and Arf Osbourne, Preston opened a plastic surgery practice exclusively for animals.

The Briggs became Prague-centric—Catherine reluctantly returning to the States so that Oliver could appear on the kid-genius week of *Jeopardy.* Oliver won a set of drums after correctly answering the bonus question, that Burl Ives was the narrator of *Rudolf the Red Nosed Reindeer.*

Anne and Jason were expecting twins. She was due in late summer.

And Henry and me? Why do you ask? Are you interested? Really interested? That's why we have sequels. :)